A New Day Dawning

Gwen,

Blessings as you
read!

Sara
Whitby

A New Day Dawning

SARA WHITLEY

TATE PUBLISHING
AND ENTERPRISES, LLC

Published by Tate Publishing & Enterprises, LLC
127 E. Trade Center Terrace | Mustang, Oklahoma 73064 USA
1.888.361.9473 | www.tatepublishing.com

Tate Publishing is committed to excellence in the publishing industry. The company reflects the philosophy established by the founders, based on Psalm 68:11,
"The Lord gave the word and great was the company of those who published it."

Book design copyright © 2015 by Tate Publishing, LLC. All rights reserved.
Cover design by Samson Lim
Interior design by Mary Jean Archival

Published in the United States of America

ISBN: 978-1-68118-945-1
Fiction / Christian / General
15.05.28

To Emily and Matthew, who have faced a cruel world with more tough determination and humor than I ever could have done. You are both an inspiration to me and I love you.

Acknowledgments

Jesus always deserves all the recognition with each new book that I publish. From the moment my first book was headed off to editing, my prayer was this: "Use this book to touch just one person, Lord. Let them see your glory." My purpose in life is to bring glory to his name, and I hope that I have done a good job showing him off throughout these pages.

I have my wonderful husband Ben to thank as always. He pushes me in all the right ways—asking me how my writing is going, holding me accountable to marketing my books, and sitting beside me at every single book signing event and speaking engagement. I can see God's work in our relationship, how he just knew that I needed your business mind to help me through all the confusing aspects of publishing books. Thank you for taking on my big dream as your own and for partnering with me in sharing the love of Jesus with those who need it most. I love you, Ben!

To my family: you guys are the best. Thank you for supporting my dream and helping me spread the word about my books. You have always been the best cheerleaders and sounding board throughout my life. I am blessed to belong to you.

Special thanks to Erin and Karen for looking over my manuscript and helping me catch my silly mistakes. You are both wonderful friends and sisters in Christ!

And finally to all the staff at Tate Publishing, who are always a joy to work with, thank you for helping make my dream a reality!

Prologue

I'm sitting in a sterile hospital room chair; all life seems to have drained out of me. My mind is spinning in a thousand different directions, mostly trying to come to grips with what has taken place over the last hour. I have no idea where Tanner and Elysa are, and right now, I honestly could care less. This moment is mine only.

I'm picturing a pure blue sky. No clouds dare blot out the sunshine, no way. Rain clouds do not exist in this place—the thought of thick, heavy gray clouds about to release their cold drops of rain onto the ground below is unbearable. The only clouds floating across this sky are wispy, the kind of clouds that never amount to anything. There is no need for those puffy summertime clouds that offer a bit of solace from the scorching heat, because in this place, there is no insufferable heat. A cooling breeze is always blowing—just enough to gently flutter the millions of daisies gracing the meadow.

I can't get enough of those daisies. If I concentrate hard enough, I'm no longer sitting in this cold, unforgiving hospital chair. Instead, I'm running through this field, straight into the arms of the one I just released to my savior. She can see me and her eyes light up in joy, just like they always did when we made eye contact. She lets out her contagious belly laugh, and her little legs begin to pump. She isn't fast and she's a bit clumsy, but I smile anyway at the picture she makes. As she runs to me, her arms are stuck out at her sides, her hands gliding over the pretty yellow daisies. A brightly colored butterfly catches her eye, and for a moment, she stops to admire it, pointing and giggling at the new friend she's made. After blinking a few times, she remembers why she was running in the first place, and she turns to face me once again.

"I'm right here, sweetheart," I call out to her. "I'm right here and I'm never letting you out of my sight again."

She rewards me with a toothy grin and continues running toward me. She's so close to me now that I can smell her sweet smell—a smell I'd give anything to enjoy right now. My arms reach out to grab her, and my heart is breaking as the intense desire to scoop her into my arms just one more time overwhelms my soul.

Sooner or later, I am going to have to accept the fact that she is in this beautiful place alone. For now, I am unable to join her. While her life is just beginning in this place, my life will continue down on earth, somehow moving on without her. In God's timing, I will join her, and although I wish more than anything to be with her in this moment, I know I'm needed here.

A sudden flurry of activity pulls me out of the world I am busy building. A family rushes through the doors, and I do my best to quickly piece together what is happening. There are four of them—a frantic mother who is sobbing as she clutches onto her teenage daughter; the girl is pale and clearly caught off guard as in this moment the parent-child role seems to have reversed as she tries to comfort and be there for her mother. The father is supporting his young adult son, doing his best to appear stoic and in charge when deep down inside, he is probably just as frantic as his wife is. The handsome young man holds his middle, but I see little pools of blood forming behind him as the four stagger to the front desk. He has clearly been in some kind of terrible accident, and his life is no doubt hanging by a thread. The staff immediately springs into action and rushes the young man away, and I glance around at the people who share the waiting room with me. The blood has drained from everyone's face, and people whisper little murmurs of concern. Some are shaking their heads in disbelief.

I wonder what those people think of me. I'm not sobbing like the woman, but my world is just as out of control as hers is. I'm frantic. Do I look it? Do these people know how broken I feel in this moment? Should I be sobbing like the woman? Are my dry eyes a sign that I didn't love my child like this mother does?

Overwhelmed and not sure what to think, I close my eyes again and try to picture the meadow. The image doesn't come. All I can see are her big blue eyes looking up at me, pleading for me to make the pain go away. The deep purple bruises that made their home under her precious eyes haunt me still, a constant reminder to me that I *couldn't* make the pain go away. All I could do was hold her, try to soothe her fears and convince her that it would all be over soon.

It's over now. Her body is no longer racked with pain; her eyes no longer look deep into mine and plead to make her well. Jesus has made her well, and now he's dancing with her in that big, happy daisy field.

But where does that leave me?

Empty. Confused. Hurting. Angry.

She may be well now, the disease no longer consuming her tiny body, but for me, a far worse disease has just taken root.

PART I

Rising Waters

When you go through deep waters, I will be with you.
When you go through rivers of difficulty, you will not
drown. When you walk through the fire of oppression, you
will not be burned up; the flames with not consume you.

—Isaiah 43:2

1

Molly

My eyes closed in disbelief, and I let all the air inside my lungs come rushing out all at once. I wasn't ready for this! Tanner and I had only been married for one month! Surely this was too soon. Why had I allowed him to convince me to start a family so quickly after the wedding? Initially I had agreed wholeheartedly, as I loved Tanner with all my heart and wanted to give him everything he wanted. After all, I'd hurt him deeply in the past—I felt like I had to make up for shattering his heart and destroying all the hopes and dreams he'd had for us. A baby had sounded so fun and romantic—the perfect way to make up for robbing him of the fatherhood he had so fondly looked forward to living out with my first baby, Eden. For running away and refusing to contact him for almost three years. For giving up on the deep love we both had known always existed between us. My debt to him felt too great to even begin to repay, and a baby seemed like one of the only ways to make it up to him. To lessen my debt ever so slightly.

Needless to say, this was not how I pictured finding out about my second pregnancy. Because of the trauma of my first pregnancy, I'd had high hopes for the second time around. Instead of shaking hands from nervous terror, I wanted shaking hands from excited disbelief. Instead of tears of anger and pain, I wanted tears of happiness and delight. Instead of a clenching heart and a spinning head, I wanted a pounding heart and dancing feet. But none of those happy things were happening to me. Instead, it was like a terrible flashback to that dreary day all those years ago, where I had sat and cried my eyes out for what had seemed like hours in my little bathroom, positive pregnancy test in hand and a heart full of shattered dreams. I hated the way my throat was closing up in fear right now, the way my hands were starting to sweat, and how the room seemed to slant and spin around me. Where was the joy my heart craved? Why weren't my feet dancing, my fingers itching to pick up the phone and demand Tanner come home from work so I could tell him the good news?

I didn't have to think hard about this one. I knew why the joy was absent. I was familiar with the one who was tormenting me right now, as he'd done an excellent job doing just that during my running away years. I knew that from wherever it was God had thrown him, the devil was laughing up at me, sneering at me and telling me I was sure to mess this up. He was throwing the abortion right in my face, asking me how in the world I thought I deserved this beautiful second chance God was blessing me with. My head was about to burst from it all—his taunting threats seemed to echo around, swirling and bouncing off my already-fragile soul, ready to take root and sprout into an ugly mess of weeds that would take all my strength to chop my way out of. I didn't want to do this anymore! Why was I being put through this again, when it seemed I had just barely climbed out of the weed patch I'd been wandering around in for so long?

My heart oozed in sadness, so deeply hurt that what I had once thought to be my only option—my only way of escaping from the terrifying memories of Jason and what he had done to me—had really just broken me down and left me riddled with grief and regret. Aborting my child had not been a relief, like so many people probably believed it would be to a young rape survivor. I felt my heart break even more at the fact that in the world I lived in, people truly believed that in situations involving rape, abortion was the best choice. As if the life inside had asked to be brought into the world through such cruel means. And that worse yet, the children conceived through rape weren't truly human beings who deserved to live. I was ashamed that for a brief time in my life, I had bought into those lies. And I was even more ashamed that *because* I had bought into the lies, my child had paid the ultimate price.

There were days that I wasn't sure I could go on anymore, which baffled me because I truly believed that God had brought me through his refining fire and turned my horrible situation into beauty. My poor choices and rebellion had definitely saddened him, but because he is full of grace and mercy, he had taken something so tragic and turned it into good. Because of what happened to me, because God called me to walk along a broken path, I had stepped through his refining fire, and now I was pure and holy. He had used evil for good by strengthening my love for him and by giving me a passion to help other young rape victims. After a confusing, not to mention exhausting journey through the wilderness, I had finally, *finally*, returned to my Savior and allowed him to once again clean out the filth inside my heart and transform me into a new being in Christ.

But right now, I didn't feel like a new being in Christ. Instead, I felt unworthy. I felt guilty for bringing a new life into the world when another little life dwelled up in heaven, having been robbed of the chance to dwell here on earth with me. It didn't seem fair that I had disposed of her precious life with barely a second thought, and now here I was, ready to welcome a new life into my arms. I felt sick to my stomach with remorse. Where was the hope I had found after rededicating my life to Christ? Why couldn't I feel his loving arms encircling around me in this moment of weakness?

In the stillness of my bedroom, my soul heard the quiet whisper of God, causing chills to rush up my arms. *I have called you to throw off everything that hinders you, child. To run with perseverance the race I've marked out for you. You feel this way because you are not following my command: fix your eyes upon my son.*

That's when the tears finally leaked out of my eyes, and I let out a ragged sob. Of course I was feeling abandoned by God! I was choosing to listen to the enemy's voice; I was allowing him to feed me lie after lie instead of crying out to my Lord and Savior.

God, I'm scared, I confessed. *I feel so unworthy of this precious child you've chosen to bless me with. I hate feeling like this! I want all the joy that everyone else seems to have when they discover new life. Help me overcome my disbelief, God! I need you right now.*

My soul didn't hear his whisper again, like I desperately wanted to. But that didn't mean I was alone. I knew God was with me in this very room. I knew he was crying right alongside me, mourning the life that never was. But I also knew that he was keeping my tiny baby safe with him until the day I too was by his side, and that I needed to release her to his loving arms until I got there. Yes, there was sorrow. I expected that grief would always be lurking in the shadows of my heart. But if I dug deep enough, I could find joy in the fact that Eden's journey was not over. She was in a better place, and I was sure that she would want me to love this child in all the ways I hadn't loved her.

Nevertheless, I knew this pregnancy would be a roller coaster of emotions. There would be more days like this, I was sure of it, days when I took my eyes off my savior and began to feel my feet begin to sink into the cold, angry waves. I clung to the hope that when those days came, all I had to do was look up, reach out my hand, and cry out just as Peter had, "Lord, save me!" I knew Christ would continue to pull me out of the dark waves.

He might even ask me the same thing he had asked Peter. "You of little faith, why did you doubt?" I knew from past experience that it's never fun to come to the realization that you've slipped into the water once again. But it's a necessary learning process, of that I was convinced. After realizing our mistakes, our souls burst with joy when we then realize that *once again* Christ, in his great mercy, has chosen to pull us out of the waves when he very well could have let us sink down into them. He never does let us sink, though. If we reach out, he pulls us up. And our souls' right response, just like Peter and the other disciples, is, "Truly you are the Son of God."

With that truth taking root in my heart, I wiped the drying tears from my cheeks and heaved myself off my bed. Then, as if God himself was guiding my every move, I found myself wandering down the hall, past my sleeping daughter Elysa, to the closet that contained our games, old knickknacks, and some crafting supplies. Earlier that week at the store, I had grabbed a pretty journal off the shelf, then stuck it in here when I realized I didn't have much time for journaling anymore. God's hand must have been in that impulsive purchase, however, because I had the perfect use for it now. I would write letters to my baby within these pages—one letter for each month of the pregnancy. Truthful letters revealing my intense struggle to accept his or her presence into my life. Letters to help me deal with my past regrets. Letters that might not ever make it into his or her hands, but that was okay. I needed this. So with shaky hands, I took the journal—with the delicate faded-blue flowers gracing its cover—to my kitchen table and began writing.

Month 1
Dear baby,

I'm not ready for you. Or maybe I just don't feel ready for you. Regardless, you're coming anyway, so I guess I better start getting ready! Even in these first few weeks, I know what a miracle you are—to think that your tiny, forming body is already full of the hopes and dreams that God has put inside your heart just amazes me. A few years ago, I couldn't recognize that truth. Because I was scared and selfish, I told myself that your older sister wasn't really a person at all. I convinced myself that she was nothing— and that I was doing her a favor by sparing her an entrance into this world. I want you to know something, little one. This world can be cruel. People might hurt you. Badly. They might use you and lie to you. They might leave you when you need them most. But your Heavenly Father *never* will, precious one. Never. So don't be afraid to live, baby!

I might even fail you. In fact, I know I will! I feel like I'm already failing you by being so nervous and unsure of your arrival. Please know that it's not because I don't want you. I want you with all my heart. The timing feels a bit off, but that's just my human nature failing to see the big plan God has for us. So even though this is hard for me now, I know that when you're born it will all make sense.

I can't wait to meet you!

—◦◦◦—

"Oh my goodness. I can't even see my feet anymore," I pouted, looking at my extended pregnant belly in our bathroom mirror. Tanner's laugh rang out from the bedroom, and I craned my neck out the door to make a face at him. "It's not funny. Look at how huge I am!" I motioned to my middle. "I'm going to need a wheelbarrow pretty soon to haul this kid around."

I was partly teasing, of course. I was ecstatic about this pregnancy, considering how my first pregnancy had ended. The first few months had been rough, to be sure. You only had to page through my "pregnancy journal," as I was calling it now, to know that. Inside those pages lay all my fears, concerns, and doubts I had about myself and the baby. But I knew what an absolute miracle this was; what an amazing second chance God was giving me. Still, Tanner came to my rescue, like always. With a very serious face, he simply said, "You're gorgeous, Molly. Absolutely gorgeous."

I felt my face flush immediately. Tanner and I had only been married for a few months, and we hadn't been romantically involved for much longer. Yes, we'd been friends since age five, but after my running away, things had changed between us. We were still friends after it all, but nothing was the same when I returned. He was married and living in Oak Ridge with Leah, and I was living in Green Lake and working on healing and figuring out where in the world God was leading me, what he had planned for my broken life. I was still getting used to hearing Tanner compliment me in those ways—still trying to wrap my mind around the fact that not too long ago, the idea of spending the rest of my life with Tanner had been nothing but a selfish daydream. A completely inappropriate daydream too—how terrible it had been for me to long for Tanner as he was married to Leah. But now here we were, married and expecting our first child. Crazy—almost too much for me to wrap my mind around.

We had Elysa, of course, so this was technically our second child. But this baby would be *our* first child together. Tanner still even considered my first baby to be his as well, so in reality, this would be our third child together, if you thought about it that way. My deceased baby wasn't biologically Tanner's, but in his heart, she was his. She would forever be his little girl, even though he had never fathered her.

I was in my last month of pregnancy, and my emotions were all over the place. There was excitement first, but fear and shame often pushed and shoved their way into my heart, crowding out that excitement and getting me all mixed up inside. Just as I had the day I first found out I was pregnant, a tiny, sneering voice inside my head whispered lies to my soul. It attacked me night and day, telling me that I wasn't a good mother and that I didn't deserve this baby.

21

How could a loving mother abort her baby? the voice asked me. *If you did it once, you could do it again. You'll never love this baby because of that.*

The voice never got tired. It never gave up. It got to the point where I would wake up terrified in the middle of the night with cold sweat pouring off my body, confused and disoriented. I would shoot up and gasp for breath, clutching my middle protectively. Tanner would react immediately, reaching out to pull me close to him, smoothing my sweat drenched hair away from my eyes and whispering that everything would be all right.

I wasn't fully convinced that everything would be all right though. What if the voice was right? I only had to think back to the beautiful March day that I'd walked into an abortion clinic and snuffed out the tiny life that had been safely growing inside me to affirm that suspicion. *How* had I done that? If I had been so willing to take the life of my child, maybe I really *didn't* have the capacity to love any more children. Maybe love just wasn't in my heart.

I then began to question my love for the other people in my life. Surely I loved Tanner, right? I'd loved him my entire life. And didn't I love Elysa? Sure, it was a struggle at times because she was a constant reminder that after I had left Tanner, he had been able to move on. That he had closed the drawer of my memory completely shut and opened a brand new one, one that contained his future with Leah. It didn't matter that the future he'd planned with Leah had been so short. And so rocky. For a time, he had loved another, and it still hurt. But I loved Elysa regardless of that, right?

It terrified me that I had to try and convince myself that I loved Tanner and Elysa. Shouldn't love be easy? It had always come so easily with Tanner before! In high school, even before I had realized that I loved Tanner at this deeper level, it had been the most natural thing in the world to love him. I didn't have to think about it. It just happened. So why was I having doubts now? Why wasn't I falling into my role as wife and mother as easily as I always thought I would?

Perhaps this was just another side effect of the abortion. Even now, years after the abortion had taken place, the deep regret and gut-wrenching sadness when thinking about what I'd done still hit me like a load of bricks, stealing my breath away in disbelief. That's why I tried my hardest never to think about it. After all, I'd brought it to God and laid it at his feet. I'd asked for and received his undeserved forgiveness. I'd begun the healing process and still made it a priority, knowing that healing would be a lifelong process that I'd always have to work on. So why did these thoughts still plague me?

Maybe Tanner and I should have waited a bit longer to have our own kids. Tanner had easily convinced me to start our own family, though, and I think it was because of Leah's death. No one ever considers that a woman as young as Leah could die of breast cancer. Or from anything, really. We have this idea of invincibility—when we think of death, we think of other people, never stopping to consider that one day it will come knocking on our own door. When it does, it often brings us to our knees in shock and disbelief. Perhaps that shock and disbelief had caused Tanner to think that the same thing could happen again to me, and that he shouldn't waste any more time.

It was a valid argument. No one should have to go through what Tanner went through. I had been there the day of Leah's death trying to comfort him—I'd seen the raw pain firsthand and felt my words stick in my throat in uncertainty. It had caused me physical pain to see Tanner suffering so much, so I could only imagine what it must have been for him. And especially when it was supposed to be such a happy day! The birth of Elysa would always be tainted by Leah's death. It was understandable that Tanner wanted to make the most out of every moment. Who could blame him?

It was quite a struggle for me to step into Leah's shoes, though. So while I understood Tanner's zest for life and his desire to make every minute count, it was difficult for me. I felt like it was my job to ease his pain by complying with his every request—perhaps that was why I had been so easily swayed to have a baby so soon after getting married. I wanted to soothe away the hurt and confusion of his last year, but it was an exhausting job. And I wasn't sure how long I would be able to keep it up, even though I wanted to so badly. Tanner deserved it, not only because he had lost his wife but also because I had let him down in big ways in the past.

I didn't think I would ever fully understand just how much I had hurt him by running away. The reason I'd left the night I did was because I thought Tanner had gone behind my back and told Jason, the boy who had raped me and gotten me pregnant, about the pregnancy. I had clearly expressed to Tanner that I did *not* want Jason to know about the baby, but when Jason dragged me into a closet one Friday afternoon after school and demanded I kill the baby, it was easy for me to believe the lie he fed me—that Tanner spilled the news. I found out later that Tanner truly *hadn't* told, but that Jason had simply overheard my friend Kristina talking about it with some other girls. In order to get me to comply with his wish to get rid of the baby, he had brilliantly manipulated me, easily getting me to believe that Tanner had told him so that we would get in a fight and I would finally run away and do the one thing he wanted me to do—to kill the baby.

Although our fight about how Jason had found out was the worst fight we'd ever been in, Tanner hadn't meant all of what he'd said to me that night. He honestly thought we would be fine in the morning, after we'd both had time to think about and process it. For him, to discover my empty room the next day and realize that I was gone had absolutely crushed him. And that was the day he had changed forever—even though he had done his best to move on and work through the pain, he was never the same after I ran away. He had always been a pretty serious guy, but after that day, he deepened even more, realizing that life can change in the blink of an eye and that we weren't promised all the tomorrows that we wanted.

My regret went deeper still, because not only had I run away but I had also destroyed the one hope that Tanner had clung to after I was gone. He had been the only one truly looking forward to the birth of my first child, so when I left, he'd comforted himself by thinking of the baby, convincing himself that the reason I'd left was to protect her. When he found out years later that she was gone, another chunk of his heart had dried up inside him. I still got chills when I thought back to the afternoon Tanner found out about the abortion. My own heart had broken inside of me when I saw just how much it pained Tanner to come to grips with what I had done. His sobs still haunted me to this day, and I knew her death affected him just as much as it affected me. She had been *our* child, not just mine.

So now, after three great tragedies—my running away, the abortion, and Leah's death—he took nothing for granted, and every single day held some sort of special meaning for him. That's why sometimes, I had to let Tanner hold me close for long periods of time, even when the demands of the day made me want to pull away. It was like he was trying desperately to hold onto me, and I knew that in those moments, he was thanking God for our second chance.

Tanner's pain didn't change the fact that it was wrong for me to bend over backward to make him happy, though. That's not what marriage is all about. Marriage is about each person sacrificing for the betterment of the other spouse—it had to be a two-direction flow. Our marriage would never be strong if I constantly poured myself into Tanner and never received anything from him in return. That had been the main reason I was hesitant to begin a relationship with Tanner in the past. When I finally admitted to Tanner all those years ago that I was pregnant, he surprised me by then admitting that he loved me—that he'd loved me for years. My immediate response had been gratitude that he wanted to stay by my side and support me, but as time went by, I began to think that it wasn't such a good idea. Back then, I had been so empty. So, so empty. The rape had scraped my former bubbly, carefree self completely out of my body, leaving a gaping hole so deep and dark that I didn't think anything could ever make it full again. Not even Tanner's love. I worried about starting a relationship with him because I knew my emptiness would drain Tanner. He'd give and give and nothing would ever be enough for me. Now, though, the situation was reversed—Tanner was the one with a hole that needed to be filled. And I wasn't so sure that I was up for the task.

Except that now, I knew something about Tanner's hole I wish I had known about my own hole back then. I knew that Tanner didn't need me to fill him up.

He needed Jesus. To expect that I fill up his emptiness was selfish and unrealistic of him. Really, though, I didn't think that Tanner was thinking along those lines; it was more of my own projection. Having been in his shoes before with the same hole he had in his heart now, I knew how tempting it was to desire others to fill you up. But Tanner was much wiser than I had been as a terrified eighteen-year-old. He knew who would fill the emptiness. So really, it was up to me to stop crippling his healing process by simply going along with his plans. He didn't need that.

I was already pregnant, of course. It was a little too late to raise concerns about how fast things were moving along for us. And I didn't want to make Tanner think that I wasn't beyond thrilled about the fact that in a few short weeks, we'd have a sweet baby in our arms—because I was so thankful and excited. Yes, I was scared, just like I'd been scared with my first baby. But this time around, I had Tanner by my side for the long run to help ease my fears and to keep pointing me back to Christ.

I shook myself out of my wanderings, noticing that Tanner hadn't called out from the bedroom in quite a while. Must be getting late. I pulled my long brown hair back and secured it with a hairband, then splashed water on my face to wash away the day's makeup. After I patted down my face with a towel, I gazed at my reflection in the mirror. *Time to come out, little one,* I urged the baby inside me. *Mama's getting tired! Look at the bags under her eyes!*

"She'll be here before you know it," my mom had said with a chuckle earlier that day as we talked on the phone. "I remember feeling the same way with each of you kids too. But once she gets here, it's bye-bye sleep, hello 3:00 AM feedings! Try and enjoy these last few weeks as best you can." I could hear her chuckles through the phone lines. How I had longed to be sitting right across from her during that conversation!

"I'd be able to enjoy them more if I could actually sleep at night!" I exclaimed as she laughed in the background. "I've enjoyed it for eight months. Now I'm ready to enjoy motherhood."

"Oh, honey. You'll enjoy it all right. It's tough. The toughest thing you'll ever do in your life. But nothing feels better than watching your kids succeed." She paused, and I knew tears were flooding her eyes. "I'm so proud of the woman you've become, Molly," she squeaked. I sent a silent prayer of thanks up to God for our renewed relationship—what a miracle it was!

My relationship with my mother had never been stronger than after I'd left Iowa the second time. In the past, things had been rocky, as my parents' marriage had been crumbling and she'd begun working more and more to escape the loneliness she found at home. Because she wasn't there for me as much as she probably should have been, our relationship used to be shallow and void of much meaning. It was only after I'd run away and my parents had made the commitment to strengthen their marriage had her focus changed completely. My leaving had caused my parents to see just how important it was to be there for their kids. To be available to come to even in the darkest of circumstances. And because of this change, things were finally different between us. We finally had the relationship I had always craved.

A huge yawn overtook me, and I decided to join Tanner, who was by now probably deep in sleep. I flipped the bathroom light off and tiptoed across the dark room to our bed. And even though I was right—Tanner was softly snoring on his side of the bed— when I settled into my side, his arms instinctively reached out to me and pulled me close to him. I closed my eyes and smiled deeply. Could there be anything better than this?

Tanner and I had shared a bed long before marriage. Not in any kind of sexual way, but as an innocent sharing of friendship. In fact, my very first night in Oak Ridge, Iowa, was spent in his bed. My parents had endured a long day of unpacking and didn't feel like putting up a fight to get me back into my own bed, so I spent the night in Tanner's instead—my feet in his face and his in mine. From that night on, it became our special thing. So now, as a married couple, I was already an expert on his breathing patterns; I knew exactly when he fell into deep sleep and when he was about to wake up in the morning. He was definitely in dreamland right now, and I smiled as I tried to imagine what images where dancing across his mind.

I absolutely loved the history that Tanner and I shared—the way we were so easily able to read each other and interact as one person. It made the tougher aspects of marriage that much easier. This time last year, I had fallen asleep every single night dreaming about being married. About my happily ever after. Being a princess fan my entire life, I had bought into the idea that marriage would be all laughter and sunny days. That's how it was in all the movies! And yet in the movies, the happily ever after always ends right as the wedding bells ring out. The prince and princess kiss and wave happily to a cheering crowd, and then the credits begin to roll. The only thing you're left with is happiness, and as kids, that's what we expect. We don't want to work at a relationship. We just want the happily ever after.

It didn't come that easily though. Sure, there were plenty of days that were full of laughter and sunshine. Most days *were* easy. But some days were very hard. Some days, I didn't want to serve Tanner, to admit I was wrong, or to simply be there for him when he needed me. I never thought Tanner could ask so much of me, and yet just when I thought he absolutely could not ask for more, he did just that. I never realized how hard this would be.

It was worth it, though. All the days I just wanted to be left alone, all the days I thought I couldn't give one more ounce of myself to Tanner—they were worth it. Because not too long ago, Tanner had been very far out of my reach. The one person my soul had always longed for had once been denied to me. To have him here with me now—it was one of the biggest blessings in my life, aside from God reaching down from heaven, snatching me off of my path of destruction, and giving me new life. I would forever esteem what Christ had done for me on the cross higher than Tanner, because all else paled in comparison to the salvation given to me.

Tanner definitely held second place, though. And soon I'd have our baby in my arms, and I knew that she'd fight for space in my heart as well. I just hoped that the sneering voice would give up and leave me alone. Surely my heart had room to love another, and I didn't need to convince myself that I loved Tanner, Elysa, and our coming baby. I would always love them. The abortion was in my past, and I intended to keep it there. I wouldn't let Satan continue to torment me with those thoughts!

The baby kicked inside me, and I giggled. *Okay, little one. Enough for tonight. Mama's going to bed—she needs all the sleep she can get before you arrive.*

2

Molly

January 2014

"She's beautiful, Molly. She really is."

"A true gift right from God."

"Think of it this way—she'll probably never grow up to hate you! You don't have to worry about her wanting you to drop her off a block away from the movie theater to avoid being seen with you."

That was just a handful of the things people said to me in the first few hours of my daughter Elliot Harper Walter's life. I know that the well-meaning family and friends who were saying these things were only doing so because they wanted to make me feel better and because they simply didn't know what else to say. But I could see it in their eyes—they were uncomfortable. They *wanted* to apologize, to ask me if I was okay, but this wasn't the time and place to do so. After all, we had just welcomed a new life into the world! That was cause for celebration, not questioning and sorrow.

I was never so grateful for the silent communication that Tanner and I shared. One panicked glance when I absolutely could not take it anymore triggered him into action. "Why don't we all give Molly some time? Maybe we can go down to the cafeteria, get some ice cream for the kids," he suggested.

Murmurs of agreement rang out from all four of our parents and Delilah. Tanner scooped up a chubby seventeen-month-old Elysa, who had been toddling around getting into everything she could while Delilah and Greg gathered up their kids, Mandy and Luke. Silently they all filed out the door, except for Elysa of course, who never stopped babbling. Tanner brought up the rear, and right before he left, he paused in the doorway and said simply, "I love you, Molly. And I love Elliot. She's perfect."

I nodded and he left, gently closing the door behind him. The tears that had been burning behind my eyes for the last hour finally escaped, and they forged a hot trail down my cheeks. A single tear plopped onto baby Elliot's face, and I quickly swiped it away.

She was nestled in my arms, and I stared down at her fresh face. In these few short hours, she had already experienced a lifetime more of living than her older sister Eden—the child I had aborted when I was eighteen years old—ever would. Of course, I didn't really know that the child I aborted was a girl, as I had never asked and the nurse wouldn't tell me after it was all over, but my gut feeling was that the baby had been a girl. Perhaps it was because Tanner had so desperately wanted the baby to be a girl. Who knows? In my heart, it was a girl, and that's all that mattered.

Eden had never done any of the amazing things Elliot had done today. She'd never taken her first breath, never came crying into this world with a loud wail. She'd never blinked up at me, never made direct eye contact. She'd never been snuggled into my arms, and she'd never been held by Tanner as pure and absolute joy radiated off his face.

She'd never been loved.

Not even in the moments I'd wanted to keep her. She hadn't been the one I'd wanted. *Tanner* had been the one I'd wanted.

More than I wanted to love my baby, I wanted to love Tanner. So when *he* decided he loved her, I thought I had loved her too. But I hadn't, not really. How could I have walked into an abortion clinic in Minnesota only weeks later and ended her life before it had even really begun? Love wouldn't have allowed me to do that. I knew deep down, no matter how much it pained me to admit it, that I had never, not once, loved the baby who had been growing and developing inside me.

I loved her *now*, but what good did that do? My love would never bring her back. All I had were the memories of those few weeks she had been inside me. But more than that, I had a thousand regrets—regrets that would forever taint the memory of the sweet, innocent life I had decided wasn't worth the struggle. I had cast her aside thinking I was doing both of us a favor, but I had never been more wrong in my entire life. I wished more than anything that she was with me here today, oohing and aahing over her new baby sister. She deserved to be here.

I tried my best to push those awful thoughts away. Yes, Eden should be here today. But she wasn't, and no amount of wishing would ever bring her back. Elliot deserved more than this! Her life deserved celebration; this was hardly the time and place to be mourning over Eden. But what bothered me more than the painful memories of my deceased baby girl tainting this joyous day were the doubts I felt when I gazed down into Elliot's face. No new mother expects to experience this on her child's first day of life. She wants to hold her baby close, dreaming of the years to come where she will run, laugh, and play. She might even allow herself to look far into the future when the child will grow up, leave home, and spread her wings to fly after her dreams.

Elliot might not ever get to do those things.

So even though she had already done far more in her short life than Eden had ever gotten the chance to do, she'd probably never do all the things I dreamed for her, and it broke my heart.

I closed my eyes and held my breath for a few moments, wishing more than anything that when I opened my eyes, the face of my baby girl would somehow be different. But it wasn't. The same flattened nose and face was cradled into the nook of my arm, and the same upward slanting eyes looked up at me, eyes that begged me to love and accept her as she was. The same small hands still rested in my larger one, and I traced my thumb across the single crease that ran across her palm, toyed with the small pinky finger that curved slightly toward her thumb. Every feature was exactly the same as it had been at the time of her birth, and nothing would ever change them—no matter how badly I wanted things to be different, they never would be.

Elliot would always have Down syndrome.

As I tried to accept that fact, I heard the door click open. Tanner quietly slipped inside, offering me a small smile. "How's it going in here?" he asked.

A sad, desperate sob escaped from the deepest part of my soul. "Did I love her when they put her on my chest, Tanner? Could you see love in my eyes? Or was it obvious from my first look that I knew she had it?"

He sat down on the edge of my bed and took one of my hands in his, kissing it softly. "I could see it, darling. There was shock, yes. But there was love first," he answered.

"Are you sure?" I asked with desperation. "Because I *do* love her. I do. It's just…"

"I know," he said, kissing my fingers over and over. "I feel it too. I loved her from the second I saw her face, but there's an aspect of uncertainty that's there. It's scary."

I sniffed and looked down. She was still awake, still gazing up at me. I squinted at what I saw there, and I had to draw her up closer to me to see if it was real, not just a figment of my imagination. "Look at her eyes, hun. Do you see it?"

"See what?"

"I don't know. A depth, I guess. Like she's looking straight into me. See it?"

He leaned closer, then moved back again, just as startled as I had been. "Yeah, I do," he grinned. "I don't remember Elysa making that deep of a connection so early on."

Love me. That's what her eyes were saying to me. *Please love me. I know I wasn't what you expected. But please love me anyway.*

Another small sob escaped between my lips. "Of course I'll love you, baby girl. I'll always love you. I promise," I whispered, drawing her up to me and smothering her tiny face with kisses. Tanner moved in closer, and it was then that my mother somehow snuck in and was able to snap the most perfect picture of the three of us, a picture I will forever cherish as I look back on this first day of my daughter's life: Elliot eye's closed in contentment as I drew her close to me and touched my nose to hers while Tanner looked adoringly at me. There was so much love in the picture that my fragile heart could barely contain itself. From simply looking at the picture, I knew that this was the beginning of a long, hard, but extremely rewarding journey. Ready or not, we were racing along its rocky path, and even though I was scared, this time I knew exactly what to do.

Stretch my arms out to Jesus and let him lead me.

Too often when life gets hard, I try to step in and take over his job, formulating plans and trying to seize control from him. All that has ever done for me in the past is frustrate me until I finally realize that my own plans will always fail, simply because I am a sinful being. Only God's perfect plan for my life will lead me to the goal, so to save myself from the same heartache, I relinquished control of my daughter's life back to him. He had seen fit to bless me with her in the first place, Down syndrome and all, so it was my joy to release her back to him. His plans for her far outshined mine anyway, I was sure of that.

It became easier when my family and friends stopped trying to tiptoe around me, afraid that I would break. "Yes, she has

Down syndrome," I announced to everyone later on. "But she is our daughter. And she is beautiful."

"Of course she is," my dad rang out with sincerity. "Nothing short of a miracle."

I knew that Elliot would never have to wonder if she was loved. Even though we were scared, even though we had no idea what God had in store for her life, it didn't change the fact that we loved her more than she would ever know.

The following day, however, when we were preparing to bring her home, my fears returned with a vengeance. I will never quite understand how even after I surrender myself to God's plan the fears, doubts, and questions remain. Where was the overwhelming sense of peace my soul so badly craved? If God had given me this special needs child, why wasn't he giving me direction? Why couldn't I feel his presence? Why couldn't I hear his voice telling me exactly how I was supposed to handle all of this?

I turned to Tanner with wild eyes. "How am I supposed to send her out into a world that doesn't understand her, Tanner? That will most likely reject her. They'll eat her up! The world is cruel even to normal people—whatever normal means anyway. How does God expect me to do that?"

Tanner remained silent for a few moments, thinking. "It's not going to be easy, hon," he began softly. "But how can we *not* send her into a world that she might impact for Christ? We don't know that the world will reject her, and to keep her locked away…I can't justify it. Look at her, Molly." His voice dripped with love. "Look at her eyes again."

I looked down, and my heartbeat picked up at what I saw. Every time we made eye contact, it was the same—it was like she was looking straight into me, communicating with me on a level so deep I couldn't even begin to understand it.

"There's something about her," Tanner continued. "Yes, she's different. She *might* be rejected. But she might not. She might be just what this world needs. Someone who sees people."

I stopped to consider that. *I'd* needed someone like that as a terrified young adult. After I had aborted my first child, my life seemed to lose all meaning. It was like I'd stopped living altogether. I had simply existed after that, going about each day only because God kept waking me up in the morning. I had no drive, no passion moving me forward and propelling me out of bed each day. For the longest time, I couldn't figure out why I'd kept going either. It wasn't until someone had *seen* me that I had started living again. When I met Mary Beth, Delilah, and Luke in Kansas, I wasn't able to hide anymore, and they wouldn't let me continue living the way I'd been living in Minnesota. It broke their hearts to see me functioning as a machine, and they had been an instrumental part of bringing life back into my heart. With their help, I had been able to reopen my heart to Jesus, and since then, my life had never been the same.

Could Tanner be right? Could Elliot be the kind of person I had needed all those years ago? Someone who *saw* people, who understood them and would influence them for Christ? I had no way of knowing, so I had to consider the possibility that maybe Tanner was right. We couldn't keep her sealed off from the rest of the world just because we thought she might get hurt. Even though it was scary, we had to send her out there—because who knew who she would impact?

So we bundled her up and nestled her into the car next to her beaming big sister Elysa and took her home. Our cozy little town of Green Lake was so small it didn't have a hospital, so we had a good forty-minute drive ahead of us. Elysa chattered happily to her little sister the entire way, babbling her name over and over again in excitement. Elliot was hard for her to pronounce so it sounded more like "Ey-ot," which Tanner and I thought was adorable. "Nice baby," she said, reaching over to lay her hand on her sister's tummy. "Nice Ey-ot."

Elysa of course didn't know her sister was different. She had no idea of the challenges that awaited her, all the mean names kids would no doubt whisper behind her back. Or worse yet, right to her very face. Meanwhile Elysa would proudly walk into her classroom each year on the first day of school, fully accepted by her peers because of her slender face, slim body, and normal brain functioning. Elliot, on the other hand, would walk into a different classroom just down the hallway facing much different circumstances—and I just didn't think it was fair.

Yet the more I listened to Elysa's babbling, it dawned on me that even as Elliot would face rejection by her peers, she would always have one surefire friend. Her big sister. Someone who didn't care that she looked and acted differently. Someone who would always want to play with her and laugh with her, to trust her little girl secrets to. The bond between sisters is strong, and with these two so close in age, I hoped that the bond would be even stronger. I hoped that Elysa would never be embarrassed or ashamed of Elliot's disability. I hoped she would always be an ally and a friend, someone Elliot could run to when no one else would listen to her.

A sigh escaped my lips, and Tanner turned to smile at me. Taking my hand in his and bringing it up to his lips, he said simply, "I love you, Molly."

Tanner and I had gotten married in March of 2013, when Elysa was seven months old. Now she was seventeen months old, we'd had our own baby, and our first wedding anniversary was still two months away. So many changes in such a short amount of time. And yet when Tanner did those sweet, simple things like kiss the top of my hand, it still caused my heart to melt. Even after all the whirlwind changes and adjustments, I still felt like a sixteen-year-old falling in love for the first time.

Of course, I'd loved Tanner for my whole life. Maybe not on the level that I loved him now, but I'd always loved him. We met when we were five years old—he'd rescued me from a group of boys who'd pushed me off my bike, and since that day, we were inseparable. When we were in high school, I knew Tanner loved me on that deeper level. I'd just chosen to ignore it out of fear that if we started dating, we'd break up and things would never be the same. That's why I'd fallen so easily for Jason, the boy who had eventually raped me and gotten me pregnant. Tanner had always showered me with affection, so I was used to it. But when *Jason* showered me with affection it was a whole new experience for me, and I'd quickly chosen to forget about any possibility of a romantic future with Tanner. It had taken running away from home and from God himself, aborting my child and messing around with my ex-boyfriend Tyler, and then finally reconnecting with God in Green Lake for me to realize how badly I needed Tanner. When I returned, I'd expected to find him waiting for me back in Iowa. But he hadn't been waiting for me. He'd moved on with Leah after deciding I wasn't ever coming back.

I remembered the pain vividly. Nothing had ever hurt as much as hearing Tanner say he'd married Leah. I'd returned to apologize to the people who had been more than willing to support me and my baby, to ask for their forgiveness and to start over. I had thought that starting over with Tanner would mean dating and eventually getting married, so to find him already married to Leah had further crushed my already-fragile heart. There was nothing I could do but return to Kansas and figure out a brand new beginning for myself, as clearly my plan of starting over with Tanner wasn't going to happen.

So I did. I moved back to Kansas, got my GED, and started taking classes at the community college close by. Tyler had reentered my life as well, and for a while, I thought that we'd get married and adopt the little girl he'd fallen in love with while working at the children's home that she lived in. That had never felt right either, and it was then that I'd really begun to question what God was up to, what his plan for my life really was. I never would have guessed it would include Leah getting cancer and passing away, leaving me to step into her shoes as Tanner's wife and Elysa's mother. It sounded crazy just thinking about it. I still struggled to wrap my mind around all the tragedy that Tanner and I had been through—all the gates we'd had to open and hoops we'd had to jump through to finally find our way together again.

Every step had been more than worth it, though. It's always difficult to hear God's voice in the middle of hardships, but once the storm clouds have dissipated and the sunshine begins drying up all the messy puddles, it's easier to look back and see his hand in all of it. Of course I had never dreamed of my life turning out this way as a child. I never imagined that at eighteen, I would become a victim of rape and find myself dealing with an unwanted pregnancy. I never thought myself capable of running away from home, of walking into an abortion clinic and ending my child's life. I certainly never imagined myself married to Tanner just months after his first wife had died, and I hadn't thought about the possibility of having a baby with special needs.

It seemed like too much for one person to handle. Looking back, though, I could see where God had been working. As a child, I had given my life to Christ and made the decision to follow him, but how committed of a follower had I been? I'd *thought* I'd been as strong of a Christian as you could be, but the minute God lead me into a hardship, I panicked and ran. And even though I still didn't have a concrete answer as to *why* I had been raped, I knew that part of the reason was to make me stronger. Perhaps I would have always been a lukewarm Christian—someone who went to church and played the part but was unwilling to really give myself to God. Maybe I'd had to go through those dark things to see just how weak I really was. To see how much I needed God and to realize that I couldn't do life on my own. I couldn't save myself—only God could. Maybe I never would have grasped that without enduring those hardships.

That reason didn't give me all the answers, though, and I still had questions. But it *did* give me peace, because I had grown so much after walking through God's holy flames. Initially I had felt that his flames were meant to destroy me, or maybe even to punish me for being stupid and allowing Jason to draw me into his little trap. I thought the fire was punishment. When I walked out of the flames, however, I realized that they were purifying flames. It had been a refining fire, not meant to harm me, but to burn out all the bad parts of me so that I would have the pure heart God had always wanted me to have.

He had been there every step of the way. He'd been there the night of the rape, crying right alongside of me as out of sin, Jason took everything from me. Yes, I know he could have stopped it, and I know it had pained him not to. Just as it pained him to turn his back on his precious son as he stretched his arms out and died for us, it pained him to watch Jason rape me. But just as God had a plan for Christ's death, he had a plan for what had happened to me. Even if I didn't understand it or like it, it was the plan he had for me.

He'd been there the day I found out I was pregnant. He had heard my desperate cries. He'd listened to me curse and reject him, accuse him of abandoning me, positive that he hated me. His arms had been open from the beginning, but I'd rejected them out of stubborn pride, refusing to accept the love he had always so readily given to me and choosing instead to listen to Satan's lies. Lies that told me God didn't know what he was doing, that his plans for me were of destruction, not of good like I had always been taught.

He'd been there in those desperate hours of driving in the dark, searching for a place to land after Tanner and I had had our big fight. He'd sent me all the people I'd needed at just the right time, but even then, I managed to misuse them. Melissa had offered me a job and a place to stay, and then I used her to drive me to the abortion clinic and assist me in taking Eden's life. Then I'd met Tyler, the smooth and attractive young man who had brought laughter and sunshine back into my life. I'd dragged our relationship into the dirt, though, by rejecting my lifelong belief that sex was sacred and meant only for marriage and allowing Tyler to sleep with me.

Even then, God hadn't given up on me. He drove me out of the hole I was falling deeper and deeper into while in Minneapolis and lead me up and out to a tiny little town in the middle of nowhere—Green Lake, Kansas. I don't remember ever consciously making the decision to come to Kansas; it's just where I'd ended up. Surely God had been behind that though, as I'd then met Mary Beth and Delilah. They had been just the right people I'd needed to finally understand that running away hadn't solved any of my problems and that God still loved me and wanted the best for me. Our plans might not match, but it finally dawned on me that my life belonged to him. His plan was better. Harder, yes. Much harder. But better.

I could only hope that he was up to something similar now. This was not the plan I would have chosen for myself. If I was in charge, Elliot would have been born without Down syndrome. What good would come from this? Right now, I just couldn't see any good.

All I could do was pray that God would keep proving me wrong; that this plan of his really was much better than any plan I could ever dream up. Because this time, it wasn't all about me—it was about my child. The desperation was much deeper, and my heart longed for understanding. Right now, I didn't have answers. But I looked forward to the day God decided to grant me those answers. All I could do was love my daughter and cling to God's hands as the waves roared around me.

One day those waves would subside. I was sure of it.

3

Molly

February

"**A**re you tired?" Delilah asked as she sat across from me with her hands wrapped around a steaming mug of apple cinnamon tea. Elliot was officially one month old today, and this morning as I'd gazed into the mirror, I had thought it was pretty obvious how tired I was from my pale face, my limp hair, and the dark circles shadowing my eyes.

"Exhausted," I replied, and she reached her hand across the table to take mine.

"It'll pass," she said as she squeezed my hand. "The first few months are rough. But you'll get her on a schedule, and eventually things will calm down. It will take a while for you to feel like you're ever getting enough sleep, but it does get better."

I smiled. "Good. I don't know how you did it with Luke. I'm only going to school part time, and I can barely keep up anymore."

She nodded understandingly. "I got pretty far behind in my schoolwork in the months right after he was born. I'm actually very lucky that I was able to catch up and graduate with my class."

Her eyes took on a faraway look as she allowed herself to travel back to that hectic time in her life. "Looking back, I still wonder how I was able to pull that off. Lots of hard work, that's for sure. Late nights studying while at the same time feeding and taking care of Luke. Two summers of summer school." She shuddered. "I would never want to go back to that time. High school isn't all it's cracked up to be!"

I nodded in agreement. "I know. I wouldn't want to go back either. I mean, Tanner and I had fun the first three years of high school. But after everything happened…" I trailed off, not wanting to bring up any discussion of the rape, runaway, and abortion. That was never a fun subject to talk about over tea. "It just fell apart."

"But look what God has done for you two," she said with a grin. "He fixed what you once thought was broken beyond repair."

I shook my head in amazement. "I know. I still wonder sometimes if I'm just dreaming that this is happening. For so long, I'd rejected the idea of spending the rest of my life with Tanner, and then when I finally *did* consider it, he was out of my reach, already married to Leah. Do you know how hard it was to let him go after finally realizing how much I loved him?" I asked, not really looking for an answer, but just trying to allow her a glimpse into my journey.

"I can't even imagine it," she replied. "It was hard for me to watch David reject me, but when I finally realized that he would never love me or be there for me and Luke, it was pretty easy to let him go."

Delilah had gotten pregnant when she was just fifteen years old from the first boy she'd ever dated. She'd met David at youth group and had trusted him entirely way too much, which later had resulted in Luke. David wanted nothing to do with her after she told him about the pregnancy, even going out and getting a new girlfriend while Delilah was still pregnant. He'd at least paid child support up until she and Greg had gotten married, and he never put up a fuss when Greg adopted Luke. He had probably breathed a sigh of relief after he signed over all rights to Luke, never having to worry about supporting him financially anymore. I didn't even know the guy, and I didn't particularly care for him. What kind a man doesn't want to meet his own son? He had never, not once, met Luke. Never held him, never given him a chance.

She shrugged and sighed. "I mean, I never *really* loved him. I just really *wanted* to love him. I guess you could say I was in love with the idea of being in love. And I think it intensified after I got pregnant too, because then not only did I want David to love me but I also wanted him to love Luke. But he never did—he never loved either of us."

I loved these conversations with Delilah. Even though the darkness and desperation lay so far in the past for both of us, we still had to deal with the effects of the tragedies we'd experienced on an almost daily level. I assumed we'd always be striving toward healing, and these conversations were a key part in the healing process. Early on in the days after the rape and abortion, I'd tried to bury my hurts deep inside, hoping that someday I would eventually come out fine. That maybe the hurt would just melt away and I'd be happy again. But oh, how wrong I'd been. I only had to think back to my disastrous first attempt at a relationship with Tyler in Minneapolis to see just how badly burying my pain had been. Tyler had fallen fast and hard for me, wanting to move things quickly along and make a commitment. Things had ended just as fast, though, when he finally realized that there was something I wasn't letting him in on, something keeping me back from fully giving myself to him. Later when he came to find me in Kansas and I finally told him about the rape and abortion, it had clicked. I hadn't been able to really love Tyler because I didn't love myself and because I hadn't forgiven myself for what I'd done yet. And even after I'd come to forgive myself and made my way back to loving myself again, it still hadn't worked out between us. God had another plan for me, a plan that included Tanner, Elysa, and now, Elliot.

"Now that I'm married to Greg, it's easier for me to imagine the desperation you must have felt when you found Tanner married," she continued. "And we only dated for a few months before getting married—you and Tanner had loved each other for basically your entire lives! I don't think I would have been able to accept it as easily as you did, Molly. You were so at peace with it when you moved back here."

I laughed. "Really? Man, I must be one heck of an actress. I was pretty miserable."

She raised her eyebrows. "I never saw misery. When you came back, Molly, you came back a new person. Completely different than when you'd left. It was like in those few months back home, you were able to work through so much and come to this new place with God. It just radiated off your face."

"Really?" I asked again, slightly stunned. "I mean, yeah, I worked through a ton of stuff and was able to really reconnect with God. But I still had so many questions, and I wasn't too happy with my lot in life. Seemed like everyone else had moved on and I was still stuck in another ending, trying to figure out where in the world I was supposed to go from there. My parents had straightened out their marriage, Josh found Caitlin, and Savannah was just loving life." I sighed. "And Tanner was happily married to Leah. Everyone had their happy ending but me."

"Yes, but," Delilah said with a huge grin on her face, "God gave you a happy ending too! It just took a bit longer. And it's not even close to an ending. More like a happy beginning. See what good came from waiting for his plan for your life?"

"I know," I agreed happily. Just then, Elliot started hollering, and my face fell. "But why, after all I've already gone through, did God decide to give me yet another challenge?" I got up to retrieve my now screaming baby. Delilah sat patiently as I padded down the hallway to bring Elliot back with me. Poor thing was probably starving; it had been quite a while since I had fed her. I threw a blanket over my shoulder as I sat down. "Do you mind?"

Delilah waved her hand dismissively. "Go right ahead." For a while, we just sat in silence as Elliot nursed contentedly. "Do you really just think of her as a challenge?" Delilah finally whispered.

My heart tightened and I felt myself getting worked up—an instinctive need to protect and defend myself. "No," I said rather snappily, and Delilah recoiled slightly. "She's my daughter and I love her. But don't you agree that she's a bit more of a challenge than a normal baby would be?"

"Well, yes," she stammered. She swallowed, and I could see in her eyes the battle, the "should I say this or not?" look plain as day on her face. Inwardly I challenged her; I was ready with a thousand comebacks.

"Don't get offended, Molly," she finally offered. "I went through the same thing with Luke. He didn't exactly come at a convenient time. But he came anyway, and I had to deal with it. I know Elliot isn't convenient for you either. But she didn't ask to be born this way."

"I know," I croaked, trying to hold back the tears that always seemed to be hiding just behind my eyes, ready to slip out at any given moment. "I just…I don't understand why. I'm scared."

"Of what?" Delilah gently pressed.

I sniffed and uttered a sad laugh. "Everything. Of sending her to public school where the kids won't get her. Who will ask her why she doesn't understand anything. Who will make fun of her not only behind her back, but probably right to her face. And she won't understand how mean people are being to her! She won't be able to stand up for herself and fight them back."

Delilah shook her head. "You really want your children to fight back to the people who are mean to them? Doesn't Jesus instruct us to turn the other cheek when someone strikes us?" She waited for me to respond, but I sat in silence as I considered her words. "She'll probably handle bullying better than any other normal kid would just because she won't fully comprehend it. She'll love them, just like we're supposed to do to our enemies but so often fail at it because we let hate get in the way," she offered.

I stopped to consider this. It *did* make sense. Elliot would be able to love people in a way that most never would. Because she would never fully comprehend that some people are just plain mean, that some people get a sick kick out of watching other people suffer, she might not struggle with hate. She would just love them. What a wonderful example she could be to the kids her own age.

Still. I knew that even though Elliot would never fully comprehend the cruelty of the world, she would still have feelings. It would hurt her to get teased just the same as anybody else. And no mother wants that for her child. I never wanted to send her out into the world. I wanted to keep her safely inside with me where I could smother her with love and protect her from the harsh outside. I couldn't do that, though. It wouldn't be fair to her. Just because she was different didn't mean I could keep her cooped up with me forever. No matter how hard it would be for me, I'd have to let her out into the world someday.

Just like always, Delilah was able to see what I wasn't telling her. It was so easy to *say* I would be fine and that everything would work out, but she knew better. She knew I was still scared. She reached across the table and squeezed my arm, offering me a small smile. "God knows what he's doing, Moll. He does. He gave her to you for a reason. So even though you can't see the end result right now, you just have to trust that it's something amazing. When has he ever given you something that in the end didn't make you stronger or bring you closer to him?" she asked gently.

"Never," I quickly answered. She was right and I knew it. But we also both knew that even as I clung to his hand, this would always be difficult for me.

"And just remember," she added softly, "that I'd give anything to be in your shoes right now." I could see the tears welling up in her eyes as well, and a pang of regret sliced through my heart.

Delilah and Greg were having a hard time getting pregnant. They'd married in April of 2012, and as their two-year wedding anniversary quickly approached, they were still praying for a baby. Delilah was frustrated beyond belief because each of them had gotten pregnant so quickly with other partners. For some reason though, the two of them struggled. And here I was, asking God why in the world he had given me this child when Delilah and Greg longed for their arms to be as full as mine.

"I'm sorry," I whispered, shame coloring my cheeks.

"It's okay. I'll be fine," she assured me as she swiped a tear off her cheek. "Maybe it's just not God's will for Greg and me to have a baby together. And who am I to question his will?"

Now it was my turn to support Delilah, to remind her of God's good and faithful love. "Sometimes our crying out to God and asking why is better than just uttering an empty hallelujah, Lilah. That's one thing I learned while running away from God— questioning doesn't make us a bad Christian. A lot of the time those questions direct our faith and lead us straight to him in our search for answers. Don't feel bad about questioning."

"I know," she said with a broken laugh. "Deep down I know he has a bigger plan for our lives, so I try not to question it. I think sometimes I forget to be real with God, though. I mean, he cares about my concerns, right?"

"Absolutely," I agreed. "I know it's hard, though, when you're praying so specifically for something to happen and it seems like God is silent. It can feel like he isn't even responding. But maybe he's just saying, 'No, I have a different, better plan than what you have.' Just remember that, hon. He's there, he's listening. And he's answering. Maybe not in the way you'd like, but he's answering."

After spending these precious afternoons with Delilah, my heart was always so refreshed. How blessed I was to have her in my life. She was always a constant reminder that God truly had my best interest in mind at all times, because without her in my life, the hole in my heart would still be a giant, gaping wound.

Besides Tanner, she helped me heal more than anyone else in the world, and I would forever be grateful for her friendship.

She was right too about things getting better with Elliot over time. By her third month of life, she was already on a set schedule, much to my and Tanner's delight. She would go down by eight thirty every night right alongside Elysa, giving me and Tanner some much-needed alone time—something we desperately craved, as we'd never had much of that as a married couple. We had never gotten that special time alone as newlyweds, as we'd had Elysa to care for. Those hours after the girls were in bed were wonderful—just what I had always hoped for when daydreaming about married life with Tanner.

It was certainly not *everything* I expected, of course. Yes, it was nice to be able to cuddle with my husband after a long day of schoolwork and caring for the girls, but much of the time, I was too tired to do much of anything else with Tanner. He would often try to get me to play cards or some other game, but I almost always refused. He'd just sigh and flop on the couch, but I'd curl up beside him anyway, guilt pricking at my heart. Being the much too overly nice and understanding man he was, though, he'd always pull me closer to him and kiss my hair.

It did frustrate me a little bit that he was so quick to get frustrated at my lack of interest in game playing. And my lack of interest in being intimate. Not that I didn't enjoy that aspect of marriage, it was just that I was exhausted! I went to school two days a week while Delilah watched the girls, and those were long, incredibly tiring days. Class started at nine o'clock, which wasn't bad, but I had a half-hour commute, which meant I had to be up early enough to feed the girls, get them ready for the day, and drop them off at Delilah's. I was at school until two o'clock, then drove the half hour back home, picked up the girls, and started supper. When Tanner returned from work, we enjoyed supper together, cleaned up the kitchen, and played with the girls until it was time to start the bedtime routine—snacks and feeding, baths, pajamas, and a bedtime story. After that, we had those few hours to enjoy each other's company, and it bothered me that Tanner couldn't be a bit more understanding.

The three days I didn't have school weren't much better. Even though I didn't necessarily have to get up as early because I didn't have to drop the girls off, I didn't want to break routine. So every day, we were up at the crack of dawn, which over time begins to wear a person down considerably—especially since Elliot was still waking up for feedings at night. Lack of sleep was starting to get to me, and I had to work very hard at not snapping at Elysa during the day. She was in the beginning stages of the terrible twos, and she was into everything! I felt like I had to constantly watch her. For the minute I turned away, she was pulling lamps off tables or trying to pry the socket covers off so she could stick her toys into them. Between trying to watch her every move and care of Elliot, I didn't have much time on my hands. Any spare moment I got, be it from a rare afternoon that both the girls went down for a nap at the same time or Elysa would be willing to sit and watch a movie, it was easily filled with laundry, dishes, other random cleaning, or homework. Free time was no longer a concept in my life—it was only a distant memory. It was only a matter of time before I completely snapped—we could all feel the thick tension hanging in the air. A fight seemed inevitable.

Finally, it hit. Tanner's and my first fight as a married couple was probably the best thing that could have happened to us, though. We had never really fought much as kids, or even as teenagers. I had always been more willing to start a fight than him, but Tanner rarely took the bait. He hated conflict and was incredibly easygoing, which of course had always frustrated me *more* when I'd wanted to duke it out with him. The only real fight we'd ever had was the night I ran away. And because I'd run away after that fight and we'd missed out on the life we'd been planning together, we hardly ever had conflict anymore—why waste time on petty fights when tomorrow was not promised to us?

But one night, Tanner just could not handle it anymore. He asked me for the third straight night if I wanted to play cards with him, and when I refused, he threw the cards down at the table and kicked the chair in frustration. It scraped across the floor loudly, and I cringed as Elliot immediately hollered.

"Great," I oozed sarcastically. "Thanks a lot, Tanner. I finally get her down after an hour of screaming, and thanks to you, she starts up again." He sighed and started to walk down the hall to her, but I heaved myself off the couch and threw up my hand stop sign style. "Don't! I'll get her." He stopped in his tracks, and I saw fear in his eyes. He knew he'd messed up.

I forced myself to relax as I made my way to Elliot's room, not wanting to upset her more with my anger. She could feel anger and would never calm down if I wasn't calm myself. So I took a deep cleansing breath before entering her room and then flipped on her lamp so I could pick her up.

Almost instantly, she relaxed, but instead of putting her back into her crib, I allowed her to cuddle up into my neck. I smoothed my hand over her back and whispered calming murmurs, something only mothers know how to do. She melted into my arms, and I rocked her back to sleep in the corner rocker. Then I gently laid her back into her crib and kissed her soft head, not ready to return to Tanner's sour attitude.

Avoiding him would not solve anything, however, and I knew Tanner—he would want to talk about this issue and work through it before we went to sleep. In the few times that we had experienced conflict in the past, he never let me stew in anger. He always wanted to talk through things right away and work on solving them.

When I walked back into the living room, I found him sitting on the edge of the couch with his head in his hands. Even though I was mad at him, my heart still skipped a beat at the sight of him, especially since I knew he was praying. He must have known that he was out of line to react the way he did, and I loved that he was so willing to go to God with his shortcomings and work on combating the sin in his life.

I gently cleared my throat and he looked up. I offered him a weak smile, and just like I knew he would, he patted the open space beside him. When I joined him on the couch, he took my hand and kissed it, sending those wonderful shivers racing up my spine. There were no words to describe how much I loved him, even in the midst of trials—because I knew that I could still be living this life without him, and I knew how hard doing so was. So even though these conversations were tough, I thanked God for the opportunity to work though issues with Tanner.

I allowed Tanner to lead the discussion. As the spiritual leader of our family, I knew it was his God-given duty, and it was a duty he took very seriously. "I don't like the way things have been since Elliot was born, Molly. This tension…I hate it. But I also know it wasn't fair of me to explode the way I did, so before we talk about anything, I want to say I'm sorry."

I squeezed his hand. "Thanks," I whispered. "I forgive you." I knew this discussion was not over, however, because Tanner wanted to work though the tension. Which was good, but it was never easy listening to someone talk about the shortcomings and sin they saw in your life.

He sighed. "I don't want to sound accusatory or anything, babe, but if just feels like you've been pretty snappy with me since Elliot was born. And that you haven't been making any time for me. I mean, I like evenings chilling on the couch with you, but sometimes I want to do more. Don't you remember how we used to play games all the time as teenagers? It's our thing."

I smiled up at him. "It was our thing, wasn't it?" He nodded. "You always beat me though," I teased, trying to lighten the mood. It worked—Tanner couldn't help but crack a smile at me.

"Oh, so *that's* the reason you never want to play with me?" he teased right back.

I laughed, then returned to seriousness. "No," I admitted with a sigh. "I'm just so tired. This time when the girls are in bed is the only part of my day that I don't have to think or worry about anything." He nodded. "I guess lounging on the couch always sounds so much more appealing…but I know that's not fair to you."

He nodded. "I just don't want to lose the one thing we've always been able to do together—play. We've always played together. But now that we're married, we never make time to do it, and that scares me, Moll. We can't let the girls be our entire lives. We have to love each other first, then love the girls."

I nodded. "I don't want to lose it either, Tanner. I just…I don't know. I need help, I guess. I *want* to play with you…card games…*and* other games," I said with a wink, "but I feel like I don't have time to. I don't know." I was trying to find the right words to make him understand. "Maybe you can take over bath and bedtime on my school days so I have a little bit of time to just sit and unwind. I think if I just had a little quiet time, I would be much more willing to play a rousing game of Phase 10 with you. And an even more rousing game later."

He smiled. "Okay," he responded with a nod. "That makes sense, and I'm more than willing to do that for you. I need you to know that I'm on your side, hun."

"I know," I assured him.

"Good," he said with a grin. "So starting tomorrow, I take over bath and bedtime, then I whoop your butt in Phase 10, right?" he asked.

"You're on," I challenged.

And so our first fight saved my brain from frying. It was amazing how even a short amount of time to myself improved my mood. Tanner was an expert at giving baths and getting the girls into bed, but for a while, I still fussed and worried. I forced myself to leave him alone, though, after fretting the first couple of nights, wondering if he was doing everything right. He was a natural, and he didn't need me breathing down his back. Besides, I needed the time to myself. The girls would be fine under the gentle hands of their daddy.

Thank you, Lord, for the wonderful man in my life. I wrote one evening in my prayer journal. I'd recently discovered the joys of writing out my prayers—it helped me to focus, as I was so easily distracted in prayer. And it was wonderful to flip back through my prayers and see where God had answered—all the yeses, nos, not yets, and "Just you wait and sees!" *You have truly blessed me. Help me to always cherish Tanner, to make time for him even if it means sacrifice on my part. You've given us this amazing second chance—don't let me waste it!*

There would be more bumps in the road, no doubt. Especially with my continued worries about Elliot's future. There would always be more stresses, more rocks to climb over and holes to fight our way out of. But I knew that unless the Lord called Tanner home, he would always be by my side, helping me maneuver all the obstacles that came our way in this life. I constantly reminded myself that I could be walking this path by myself, and that made it easier. I'd much rather walk through a storm with Tanner than cruise through a calm sea without him. Yes, it would be hard. Yes, we'd have more fights and more difficult conversations. But he was worth it—after enduring all those years without him, I knew I wouldn't want it any other way. Hardships and all, I looked forward to as many years with Tanner as God decided to bless me with.

4

Delilah

April

Breath. *Just breath*, I commanded myself. *Don't get your hopes up. How many negative pregnancy tests have you cried over in the last two years?* I looked up into the bathroom mirror at my face, and my hopeful eyes stared back at me. If I dug deep enough into the trash can sitting next to the vanity, I'd find last month's negative test—and in a matter of minutes, another one would most likely be resting on top of it.

It wasn't fair. Why had it been so easy for me to get pregnant at the worst possible time before? I found it ironic that at fifteen years old, I had conceived the very first time I'd had unprotected sex, and now years later, as a married woman, it just wasn't happening for me. Why? I was a good mother to Luke and Mandy, wasn't I? In the seven years I'd raised Luke on my own, he'd done okay—and when Greg and I got married and I adopted Mandy, she had flourished immediately under my loving care. I had so much love to give a baby! So why was God withholding this from me?

With tears already forming in my eyes, I lifted the test up and choked in disbelief at what I saw staring back at me. Positive! It was positive! After two rocky, disappointing years, I finally had a positive pregnancy test.

My hands immediately flew to my middle, and I laughed in pure joy. "Hello, little one," I whispered. "It's mommy! I've waited so long for you, and now you're finally here!" With my head still spinning, I threw the bathroom door open and ran down the hallway to our bedroom, where Greg still slept peacefully. Feeling like a little kid on Christmas morning, I leapt onto the bed and woke Greg with a start.

"Whoa!" he exclaimed in shock. "Morning, my love." He pulled me close to him and nuzzled my neck. "Why don't you wake me up like this every morning?"

I giggled. "Because I don't have wonderful news to deliver every morning," I said mischievously. He cocked his head.

"I'm intrigued. Do tell."

"Well. Remember how right away when we got married we decided not to use any kind of birth control?" I asked, trying not to let the grin overtake my face.

"Yes," he replied, his own grin spreading slowly.

"And remember how for two years nothing happened?"

"I remember," he said, playing along nicely even though by now I was sure he knew what wonderful news I was delivering.

"Well, today breaks that disappointing spree. Because we're pregnant!"

The next hour of my life played out exactly how I had always dreamed it would. Greg pulled me out of bed and twirled me around, and we laughed in joy at the miracle God had finally granted to us. Then we lounged in bed discussing baby names and nursery plans, and talking to our newest family member. It was magical, absolutely magical—especially after what I had gone through with Luke all those years ago.

It had begun in much the same way. I'd nervously gone to the drugstore to pick out a pregnancy test, scared out of my mind. For different reasons, of course. At fifteen, it wasn't something I ever planned on having to do. Earlier this week as I once again perused the pregnancy test section in the store, I'd been scared simply because of all the negative tests I'd had to endure. Seems like I always got my hopes up too soon, but I couldn't help myself. This time, I was almost three weeks late, so it felt safer. Who knows why it had been late before? Stress, maybe. Still, I had hidden the test in our medicine cabinet, so Greg couldn't see it. Then I waited, beyond scared that I had jinxed myself by buying a pregnancy test so soon after my last negative one.

I'd done the same thing with Luke too. Buying the test was one thing, taking it had been another thing altogether. It had sat under my bed for another week before I finally took it. And just like I'd done an hour ago, I had paced my bathroom nervously, praying for a completely different answer. When I'd lifted the test almost ten years ago, my heart had sunk at what this morning it had jumped for joy at. Funny how the circumstances so affected my reaction.

I remembered the crushing disappointment of discovering my first pregnancy vividly. The one thing my mother had tried to instill into me as a child was that sex outside of marriage was not only wrong and out of God's plan for my life but that it was also dangerous. Dangerous because it could result in a teenage pregnancy and because it would be something I would have to drag along behind me for the rest of my life. She herself had abused sex as a teenager, and she'd gotten pregnant as a young adult too. And after living with a scumbag of a man for so long and getting pregnant with an even bigger scumbag after he left made her realize what a sacred, holy thing sex was. Not something to be taken lightly. After learning those lessons the hard way, she wanted more than anything for me to simply learn those same lessons by taking her advice—and not by personal experience.

Of course, it hadn't worked out that way, and immediately I'd known my mother would be disappointed in me. I knew that not only would I have to face her disappointment but I'd have to face David's too. He had talked all the time about the big plans he had for himself after graduation, and I'd known this would definitely put a kink in those plans. But I never thought he'd completely abandon me.

I still winced when I thought back to his reaction.

"I can't believe you let this happen," he accused. "You probably should have thought about getting on birth control." I couldn't believe that one! Neither one of us had thought about using any kind of protection, but he'd blamed that oversight completely on me. When I tried to stand up for myself and point out the very obvious fact that it takes two people to make a baby and that if he was worried about pregnancy, he should have suggested I find a way to get on birth control or that he pick up some condoms. He still wouldn't budge. "Don't pin this on me, okay? You're the one who's pregnant, not me. It's your body, your problem."

From that very first day, he wanted nothing to do with it. "I don't want to deal with this right now," he'd said in disgust. Not knowing what else to do, I'd given him some space, thinking that he'd come around and do the right thing. No such luck.

"I can't do this right now. I don't want to do this! I'm going to graduate and move away next year. You know I want to go to California. And I'm not going to let anything get in the way of that, okay?"

I could have made him stay. I could have dragged him to court and demand he take responsibility for Luke. But no judge could make David care. No law could make David stay with me and love me and Luke. I'd known from that first day that nothing would change his mind about the situation, and that it would be pointless to try and win him back. So we cut all ties to each other—aside from the little bit of money he sent me each month.

Besides that money, David had never made any effort to be there for us. To this day, that still cut me to the core.

So today, I cherished the vast differences in my two pregnancies. The first had been so rocky, and it had sent me spiraling so low that I'd even tried to take my own life. This time, however, there was so much joy my heart was about to burst.

"Let's go surprise my mom," I suggested with a grin. Telling my mother was something I'd looked forward to almost as much as telling Greg, and again it was simply from how hard it had been the first time. I knew that she'd be off the wall excited for me this time and just as supportive as she had been last time.

I never would have made it through my first pregnancy without her. It had been tough at first, as she'd found out in the worst possible way—at the doctor's office the day of my attempted suicide. Not the most ideal time to hear life-changing news, that was for sure. But after that initial few days of shock, she became my rock in that stormy time—the only one who had truly been there for me. I had friends, of course. But not many kids got pregnant in high school in my tiny Midwestern town. It was uncomfortable for them, unfamiliar. They had been there for me on surface level, by continuing to include me in get-togethers and thinking up baby names with me. But once Luke made his appearance, they slowly faded out of my life. Part of that had been my fault, as I'd devoted everything to Luke and stopped making the effort to maintain those friendships.

My mother, however, had been there every step of the way. Even though it was just as embarrassing for her to face everyone at church and in the community, she still held my hand and stayed by my side through it all. We couldn't change the situation, so why try to hide it?

"Who cares what anyone else thinks of you, Lilah honey? 'Let the one who has never sinned throw the first stone,' remember? That's straight out of John 8, sweet girl. Those people who accuse you of sinning, well, they themselves are sinners too. But God reaches out and forgives all of us just the same. So don't you worry, little girl. Everything's going to be all right," she had reassured one night. We were sitting in my bed, laughing at my huge pregnant belly when tears had unexpectedly sprung into my eyes, a product of the ever-lurking fear that followed me constantly during the pregnancy. With each passing month, I endured more judgmental stares and the whispers of my classmates and people in the community grew louder and louder. I knew it would only grow worse once Luke actually came, as I'd get judged for missing school to care for him, and that my every parenting move would be scrutinized; every mistake that even married couples made with their kids would be blown way out of proportion because I was a single teenage mother.

She never let go of my hand, though. She calmed each wave of fear as it hit and showered me with prayer and scripture when I was positive that I couldn't do it. And on the day Luke came, she cried in pure joy when the doctor placed tiny newborn Luke into her hands—I still remembered the first words she said to him.

"Welcome, precious one. We've been waiting anxiously for you! We're going to be best buddies. I can already tell." Then she'd gently kissed his head and began to sing softly to him. And she was right—from that first day, my mother and Luke were best friends. She was able to get him talking better than I was able to on most days, which was getting to be a miracle as he neared the magical world of adolescence. Scary to think that in a little over three short years, he'd be a teenager! Had nine years really gone by already?

We told the kids about the new baby over breakfast—nine-year-old Luke pumped his fists in excitement and five-year-old Mandy squealed in joy. After everyone calmed down, we joined hands while Greg led us in prayer, causing my heart to squeeze inside me in thankfulness for the kind of spiritual leader he was for this family.

He cleared his throat and began softly, "Lord Jesus, we thank you for this wonderful morning. We thank you that you have heard our prayer for a child to love. We know we don't deserve all that you do for us, but we are so grateful that you continue to bless us." He paused to sniff, and I squeezed his hand. "Please watch over Delilah as she carries our new baby. Bring him or her safely to our arms. Amen."

"Amen!" Mandy echoed in excitement. "When's she gonna be here, Mama? I want to play dress up with her and have tea parties in the backyard!"

I laughed. "It takes nine months for a baby to grow inside a mommy," I explained. "And then it takes a few years before the baby can actually play with you like that. And who knows? Maybe the baby will be a boy. He might not want to have tea parties in the backyard with you. You might have to learn some boy stuff."

"Yeah!" Luke agreed. "Like diggin' up worms and catching frogs in the backyard!"

"Ew," Mandy crinkled up her little button nose in disgust. "Boys can have tea parties, can't they, Daddy?" she asked Greg with giant, concerned eyes.

"Of course they can, angel," he reassured with a smirk. "Someone's got to teach him how to be a gentleman—sisters are perfect for that." He reached over and tweaked her nose, causing her contagious belly laugh to spill across our happy kitchen.

After a lengthy discussion on what was appropriate for boys and girls to do—or what the *kids* thought was appropriate, which resulted in Greg and I biting our lips to hold in our laughter quite a few times—we came to the conclusion that our baby, whatever gender it turned out to be, would be able to do both girl and boy activities because he or she would have both a brother and a sister to teach those things. That explanation satisfied them both, so with that important argument settled, we piled the dishes in the sink for later, changed out of our pajamas, and drove down to the diner to surprise my mom with the news.

My heart sank a little bit when we pulled into an overflowing parking lot at the diner. My mother's little restaurant had steadily grown in popularity each year after she opened, and it made sense. She made everything from scratch—even the delicious whipped cream she topped all her pies and milkshakes with. And aside from having good food, she gave out good service as well. Kind of amazing how she did it too, as she never had the place too overly staffed. In fact for a while, there it had just been her and Albert working, with me coming to help on the days she was absolutely desperate—working in the diner was never really my thing. As much as my mom wanted me to work with her, I wasn't good at it, so I became the backup help. Molly later joined the team, but now she only came to help when she was absolutely needed as well, as she was a full-time mother and part-time student—which didn't leave her time for much else. But Mom and Molly were carrying on Albert's legacy of love by ministering to the teenagers they'd hired on after his death. That was the only reason Molly stayed on staff—she wanted to be involved in the girls' lives and impact them for Christ.

Greg saw my face fall at the sight of all the cars. "She'll have time for important news, hon. Your mom's great about this stuff. We can wait if you want to, though," he offered.

"No, no. I want to today, while the emotions are still high." So we all piled out of the car and forged our way into the crowded building. I ushered the kids to the front counter and got them settled with Greg, and then began scanning the dining hall for my mom. I saw Molly zipping in and out of tables, and she flashed me a grin and waved at me when she finally saw me. Two of the teenagers, Jess and Alexa, were also scurrying around the floor, but Mom was nowhere to be seen.

"She's in the back with Chelsea," Molly came over and told me. "Something happened earlier today. They're duking it out in the backroom. I'm sure if you knocked, she'd come out, though."

"Any idea what happened?" I asked, wanting to prepare myself a little bit before bursting in on a potentially heated discussion.

Molly looked around to make sure no one was listening and then leaned in close to whisper, "Chelsea came in hammered this morning. Not hung over, but flat out *drunk*. Your mom wasn't thrilled about that, so she asked her to leave. She refused to, though, and she threw up in the kitchen a little bit ago. And that's when they started fighting. I haven't heard anything for quite a while now. Hope the poor thing's okay!" Molly said with a bit of a chuckle. "Your mom really knows how to chew people out."

I smirked. "Yeah, I know. But once she gets it out of her system, she's nothing but supportive. She just wants these girls to succeed," I explained.

"Oh, I know. Me too. It's frustrating, though, that they've all been with us for so long now and not much has changed."

"Yeah…man." I shook my head in disbelief. "Can't believe she came in drunk. Maybe I'll just wait for her to come out," I mused.

"You could always grab an apron and jump in to help."

"Very funny. You know how awful I am at waitressing," I said with a smirk.

She giggled. "I know. You are pretty terrible at it."

"Gee, thanks. I can always count on you to build my self-esteem," I called out to her as she walked away laughing. With nothing else to do but wait, I plopped down next to Greg and watched the chaotic diner with amusement. I was glad I was horrible at waitressing—it was an exhausting job that I never wished to do again.

Just when I was getting restless and about it give up completely, Mom finally emerged from the kitchen. She looked beaten down and defeated, but her sad eyes brightened when she saw all of us sitting at the counter smiling up at her.

"Well hello, everyone!" she chirped, instantly in a better mood from just the sight of us. "You have no idea how much I needed to see ya all this morning."

I rounded the corner and pulled my mom into a hug. "Can I have a minute with you?" I asked. "I know you're super busy and you just dealt with a nightmare, but I have big news for you!"

She glanced slyly over at Greg, but he just smiled and pretended to lock his lips with a key. "Of course I have a minute, hon. Molly's got it all under control out there—they didn't come to get me in the half hour I was gone, so I figure they can handle a few more minutes without me."

In the privacy of my mother's cozy little diner kitchen, I shared with her that I was pregnant in the way I'd always dreamed of doing so—as a married woman. This time, there was no shame, no embarrassment. This time, it was full of joy and excitement.

She couldn't stop the tears from spilling over onto her cheeks. "God is good," she said simply. "And I'm so happy for you two. For all of you—those kids are going to be the best older siblings anyone could ask for."

"I know," I said as my own tears began coursing down my cheeks. "We're all sort of in shock still. Well, Greg and I are at least. The kids don't know how frustrated we've been about it, so they're just plain excited."

"Well, me too, sweet girl. Been praying for this ever since you got pregnant with Lukey."

I cocked my head. "What do you mean?"

"Remember how crushed you were when you found out that first time? How hard it was for you to come to terms with the fact that you were going to be a mother at fifteen?" I nodded slowly, and she continued with a shaky voice. "I've never been so nervous in all my life, Lilah. I was so worried that you'd have a baby that you wouldn't love, simply because you were ashamed. It was the hardest thing to watch you beat yourself up—and I think I was partly to blame for that," she admitted shamefully.

"No, Mom—"

"No, I was," she said, cutting me off. "I put a high expectation on you to stay away from sex as a teenager. If my mom had done that to me, I would have felt the same way! Not that I think it was wrong for me to want you to not have sex…It's just…I don't know. I made it *such* a big deal. And it wasn't right of me to make you feel so awful about making a simple mistake, hon. I'm sorry about that."

I smiled and gave a small laugh. "Thanks, Mom," I whispered, never realizing how important it was to me that she apologize for that. "Means a lot."

"Should have done that a long time ago," she said with a sad sigh. "Guess I just didn't want to admit that I was wrong. Instead I watched you beat yourself up, and it broke my heart. And that's when I started praying for this day. I prayed that one day God would lead you to the right man—which he did—and that one day you'd experience getting pregnant again in a happy way. And now…well, it's a happy day."

I let out another joyous laugh. "It sure is, Mom. It sure is."

5

Molly

April

Chelsea slammed around the diner, violently yanking chairs off the floor to stack them on top of the tables, throwing down her rag to wipe down the counters, and almost breaking the white dishes as she pulled them out of the dishwasher. Even though I was years older than she was, I timidly steered clear of her, not wanting to cross her path for anything. As punishment for coming into work drunk the past weekend, Mary Beth had rearranged all the girls' schedules so that Chelsea had to close every single night—her least favorite job in all of the diner.

Well, technically Chelsea hated *every* job she had to do at the diner. It amazed me that Mary Beth kept her on staff with her bad attitude and saucy way of dealing with customers. So far, we hadn't received any major complaints about her, though, and she hadn't had any serious run-ins with customers—only with Mary Beth. So we had no grounds for firing her. Except for the recent incident, of course, but still Mary Beth refused to give up on the girl.

I understood that completely. There was just something about Chelsea that drew you in—she held us all at arm's length, but I had a feeling that deep down, she just needed to be loved. She was a gorgeous eighteen-year-old, with long dark hair and piercing green eyes, a shade so unusual I was convinced it couldn't be her real eye color. It was almost a death wish to bring up the idea of colored contacts, though—I'd learned that early on. You really had to tiptoe around her, as you never quite knew when she could snap at you.

I silently cursed Mary Beth for guilting me into closing with her every single night, forcing me to deal with her moodiness all by myself while we closed up. But Mary Beth didn't trust Chelsea alone in the restaurant, and besides herself, I was the only one old enough to be with her. I could have said no, of course, but things were so tense between the two of them right now and I knew that another argument would surely explode if Mary Beth was here instead of me. So regardless of how uncomfortable this was for me, it was the best plan. Plus, it was kind of nice to get out of the house for a few hours every night. I knew the girls were perfectly fine at home with Tanner.

A loud crash pulled me out of my little world, followed by a long string of profanities. With burning ears, I rushed to the kitchen to see what had broken. When I pushed open the swinging door, I found Chelsea kneeling in a pile of shattered glass.

"What happened?" I asked.

"Stupid glasses. Knocked them over when I was sweeping. And now Mary Beth's going to be even more mad at me—probably make me pay for these cheap glasses too," she muttered.

I gave her a small smile, but she just shook her head in disgust and continued picking up the big pieces of broken glass. I saw her swipe a single tear from her face, but I pretended not to notice, as she'd get even angrier if I brought it up.

"Here," I said, picking up the discarded broom. "Let me finish this."

"I've got it," she snapped.

"Chelsea," I commanded softly. "Let me finish this. I want you to go out there, brew a fresh pot of coffee, and sit."

She just stared up at me. "Why?"

I gave her another soft smile, hoping that tonight was the night she decided to trust me, to let me in just a little bit to her world. "Because I want to do it. Now go." She sighed dramatically but stood to leave anyway. "And I'll take care of this with Mary Beth. Accidents happen, Chels. She won't make you pay. About time we got new glasses anyway."

"Whatever," she muttered as she sauntered out of the room.

Oh, dear Lord. Give me the right words tonight! Keep my tongue in check.

As I swept up the shattered glass, I realized that in the two years Chelsea had worked at the diner, she was the only girl out of the three that I didn't know a single thing about. The other two had both opened up to me and allowed me a glimpse into their lives, but not her. I knew that Jess was dealing with an alcoholic father and possible child abuse and neglect at home, and Alexa had suffered a sexual attack under the hands of a foster child her father had taken in years ago. I had listened to both girls share their grief, fears, and anger, and I'd gotten the chance to share Christ's love with them. Chelsea, however, refused to open up even a little bit.

Mary Beth and I had learned early on that if we wanted to affect Chelsea, we had to take a different approach with her. Mentioning God, Christ, or anything spiritually related was a no-no; she was very unreceptive to that kind of talk, so instead we tried to live out our faith as best we could with her. We didn't want to come off as the "shove it down your throat" kind of Christians and scare her off for good. So we treated her with kindness. We listened to her grumblings and complaints with willingness, always making it very clear that we were there for her if she wanted to talk. And we tried to set a good example by loving each and every person that walked through the doors, regardless of how they treated us. That meant no complaining about angry, spiteful customers. You didn't hear any kind of negative talk about customers in our kitchen—well, at least not from Mary Beth and me. When the girls and busboys started talking badly about the customers, we'd gently remind them that our customers were valuable to us and didn't deserve to be talked negatively about. Most of them would nod begrudgingly at us, with the exception of Chelsea who'd just roll her eyes and curse us under her breath. Would we ever get through to her, crack through her very thick shell?

I tossed the swept-up glass into the garbage and surveyed the kitchen. It was absolutely spotless, much to my surprise. The counters shone brightly, all the dishes were stacked neatly in their places, and the stainless steel sink sparkled—Chelsea had done an excellent job. Usually she did as little as possible, never going above and beyond to be a good employee. Why now?

I shrugged, then pushed open the door to check out the rest of the diner. I was greeted with the same pleasant surprise—the whole place looked better than it had in ages. Albert had always done the little things that Mary Beth forgot about, and since his death, we noticed for the first time all that he'd done for the place. But as popularity had continued to rise after his death, Mary Beth simply didn't have the time to take care of those little details. All of a sudden, though, Chelsea had done just that. It looked amazing.

"Wow," I called out, clearly making it known that I was pleased with her work. "Impressive work. Hasn't looked this good in ages."

She remained silent from the booth she occupied in the farthermost corner from where I stood. I swallowed my frustrated sigh, however, and committed myself to trying once more in reaching out to her. So I grabbed a mug, poured myself some of the coffee Chelsea had just made, and went to join her in the corner booth.

"Chelsea," I began softly. "I've watched you drag around so much pain and anger for the last two years, and it breaks my heart. I just want to help you. Is there anything you need from me...from Mary Beth?"

She snorted. "Why do you guys even care?" she asked spitefully. "You both walk around like the stereotypical Goody Two-shoes trying to fix us. Well, let me tell you something, Molly." She leaned forward and narrowed her eyes at me. "You can't fix me." She stabbed a finger into her chest. "I'm too far gone for that, and honestly, I don't really want to be fixed. It's too much work."

I plopped into the seat across from her. "Been there, done that, honey. I've been in that same pair of shoes. In fact, when I first started working here, Mary Beth did the same thing for me that we're trying to do for you. Except she was a million times more in my face than she is in yours," I said with a chuckle. "That woman can spot a broken soul from miles away and won't give up on it until she feels God has done his work."

She rolled her eyes. "I'm sure whatever 'crisis' you went through," she said sarcastically, using her fingers to mimic quotation marks, "was mild. Nothing bad ever happens to you Christians."

I flat out laughed at her, and she squinted her eyes in disgust. "Please. You couldn't be more wrong."

She raised her eyebrows challengingly at me. "Oh yeah? What happened to you, then, huh? What sort of horrible thing did your God allow you to suffer through?" The way she said "your God" made it very clear that she wanted nothing to do with him.

Normally when I told people my story, I wasn't so forward about it, as it was such a touchy, uncomfortable thing to discuss. But Chelsea was being so pushy herself, and I figured this would be a good way to shock her into finally listening to me. "I was raped," I said. "And got pregnant from it—six months before I was supposed to graduate high school."

Silence.

She ran her tongue across her lips, then started slowly nodding. "All right," she finally said. "So something bad happened to you."

"Yeah, it did," I said with a sad laugh. "It was awful, and I was pretty mad about it too. Mad at God. I guess I used to think the same thing you do—that God doesn't let bad things happen to his followers. But bad things happen to us too, Chelsea. Bad things like rape. The worst thing about that whole ordeal, though, was that I ran away from God after it happened. And that's something I'm ashamed of to this day."

I couldn't believe that she rolled her eyes at that comment. Here I had just shared an intimate detail of my life with her, and she still wouldn't soften. "What happened to your kid?" she asked casually, causing my heart to squeeze within me. "When I started working here, you were single. Never saw a kid before you married Tanner."

"I got an abortion," I said flatly.

"No way!" she snorted. "You? Miss Goody Two-shoes?"

"Yes!" I admitted in frustration, trying to control my anger at her very different reaction to this news—everyone I had told in the past had to fight back tears, or at least swallow the large uncomfortable marble that became lodged in their throat. Her casual response made me angry.

Once again I swallowed my anger. "You know," I continued, "being a Christian doesn't make me a Goody Two-shoes. I'm still a sinful human who makes the wrong decision sometimes. But the great thing about being a child of God is that he's forgiven my every sin—past and present. I know I'll keep making mistakes. I'll still sin. But my God is bigger than my sin."

"Hey," she challenged, throwing up a hand. "Not everyone thinks abortion is a sin. Works out pretty good for some people."

"Maybe," I replied with a shrug. "I feel differently about it, though. It didn't work out so well for me, and I regret it every single day. Having gone through it myself, I know how it can make someone feel. I have a hard time imagining someone not feeling even a little bit sad after having an abortion. But I can't speak for everyone." Chelsea fell silent again, like she was shutting down right in front of my eyes. "Enough about me, though." I hoped to coax her into finally talking to me. "What about you? It's harder for you to hide from me, because I've tried to pull the same stunt you're pulling. But hiding from people who care about you won't help. I can tell you that from personal experience too."

She gave a sad laugh. "I don't need my pathetic story leaking all over town. I know people talk about me enough as it is—everyone seems to have their own idea of what I've been through—drugs, prostitution…I've heard all the whispers at school. But they don't have a clue," she said sharply. "I don't trust anyone here."

I cocked my head at her. "How long have you lived here?"

"Couple years. Moved here when I was twelve."

I nodded. "I've only lived here for a few years too. And I thought the same thing when I first got here. I didn't want anyone to know anything about me, because I thought that if they knew my story, they'd all reject me. But the funny thing about this town is how people care. No one rejected me when they found out about what I went through. And I don't think anyone would reject you either. I think they'd be a big help to you, if you'd let them."

She shook her head slowly. "I told you. I'm too far gone."

I smiled warmly at her. "You're wrong, Chelsea. No one is ever too far gone for grace. That's the beauty of it. None of us deserves grace, but God gives it to us anyway."

"He doesn't give grace to kids who make their moms commit suicide," she choked. I sat back in surprise, and my eyes widened. Tears sprung into her eyes, and she gave another sad laugh. "See? That's why I don't tell people! Because the few people I *have* told always react like that." She shot up out of her seat in rage, but I grabbed her arm.

"Chelsea, wait!" I cried.

"What?" she screamed, and I flinched, trying to hold my ground. "What do you want, Molly? Why can't you and Mary Beth just leave me alone? Everyone else does! Why can't you just talk behind my back like them and stay out of my life?"

"Because I've lived in shame, just like you! I've had people whisper behind my back too. It's not fun." She just stood there, fuming. "Look, I'm sorry for how I reacted. It was more of surprise from you actually opening up to me. Believe me, I'm not that easily shock-able. I've heard my fair share of tough stories."

"Yeah, well, mine probably takes the cake," she said dully.

"Try me," I challenged.

To my complete and utter surprise, she yanked her arm free and plopped back into her seat. "Want the short and sweet version? Or the long, sad one?"

"I've got all night. Tanner put the girls down hours ago. He'll be fine without me for a bit longer."

She closed her eyes and sighed. "All right. But you have to promise me that this stays between me and you. I don't want Mary Beth knowing right now."

"Fair enough," I agreed.

She took a deep breath and settled back into the faux leather booth. "I was born in Dallas, lived there up until I was twelve. Never knew my dad, and from what my mom told me about him, I'm glad I don't. My mom had me when she was pretty young—she was nineteen and still had two more years of school left. But when I came, I ruined all her plans and she dropped out."

"Not enough money?" I asked, hoping that if I asked questions, she'd realize I truly wanted to hear this story and help her out.

"Yeah. And she never let me forget about it either. Every time something went wrong or we were tight on money, she blamed it on me. 'If I didn't have you, my life would be a whole lot easier,' she used to say. So I grew up ashamed of myself, because she was right. If I hadn't come along, she'd have finished school...probably would have gotten married. But I messed it all up for her."

"You don't know what could have been," I soothed.

"Yeah, well. It's not hard to guess how it could have gone. My mom was beautiful…smart. She could have been anything she wanted to be. Instead she had me and did a crappy job being a mother." She swirled the coffee around in her mug, focused intently on watching it slosh around—was she trying to hold back tears or was I imagining it?

I remained silent, though, because I couldn't really relate. Sure, my mom hadn't been there for me as much as I would have liked when I was younger, but she was still a good mom. She loved all her kids, and even in my melodramatic teenage years, I'd know deep down that if I ever needed anything from my mom—including time—she would have given it to me. I just hadn't asked for it. So I kept my mouth shut, because I knew how unasked advice from those who had no idea of the pain I'd gone through simply annoyed me. No doubt Chelsea felt the same way.

She sighed and forged on. "It got really bad around the time I turned ten. We lived in the dumpiest part of town, in a disgusting apartment. I dodged school social workers constantly. They were always hounding me about my mom and wanting to know if she was taking care of me. She wasn't, of course, but she tried. She worked *all* the time—but it didn't matter. We were always behind on rent, never had enough food in the fridge, and we never got new clothes unless the stuff we had was completely unwearable— you know, toes poking through our shoes, jeans with more holes than fabric, shirts so thin you could practically see through them." She paused in sadness. "You have no idea how humiliating it was for me to come to school day after day wearing the same smelly old clothes. I got picked on constantly."

I felt my face burning in shame. Thinking back on my own childhood, I remembered crying when my mom wouldn't buy me the expensive clothes that the popular girls in my school wore. I had a deep obsession with them liking me—or at least with keeping them from laughing at me behind my back. But at least

I'd had nice clothes. Nice clothes that were always clean and fresh. I'd had a closet stuffed with more clothes than I knew what to do with as a kid, and yet I'd still found room to complain! Chelsea had had next to nothing.

Her eyes took on a faraway look as she went on. "I remember the landlady coming in one day and chewing my mom out for being late on rent while I cowered in the corner. She yelled so long that my mom started crying. When the lady left, she just sank to the floor and cried her eyes out—and the only thing I wanted to do was curl up next to her," Chelsea admitted with so much sorrow I felt my throat start closing up in pain. "But I knew she'd just push me away and blame everything on me again. Eventually she got up and locked herself in her room for a few days. I had to forge for food on my own while she tried to pull herself together—but I'd done that so many times before that I didn't think anything of it. She only came out because my school kept calling about my unexcused absences.

"I think something snapped inside her after that, though, and she got so desperate she turned to the only option she had left. At the time, I didn't know what she was doing, and when things started to turn around for us, I didn't even consider that she could be doing something illegal."

"What was she doing?" I asked.

"Selling drugs. And herself. I remember thinking it was strange when she started bringing men over, because I'd heard her complain so much about my loser father. And the men never seemed to make her happy—I knew they weren't boyfriends, and at ten years old, living in the neighborhood I lived in, I knew what she was doing. Still, she was ashamed of it and tried to keep it from me. She'd put me to bed and command me not to come out until she came for me in the morning, and when she did, she always had this dead look in her eyes. I didn't question it, though, because we suddenly had money and her happiness didn't matter that much to me. Whatever it took to put food on the table and buy new clothes for both of us."

I knew this story was about to take a drastic turn for the worse, and my heart was breaking inside me. Suddenly the deep pain and anger in Chelsea's eyes was starting to make a whole lot more sense.

"When the whole prostitution thing started, sometimes she wouldn't come back at all on the weekends—she didn't always have the men come to her," she explained. "Sometimes she went to them. So I didn't think much of it when she was gone from Friday until Monday one week. She always came back, and for some reason, I trusted that she always would. Because no matter how much she said she hated me, she always at least tried to take care of me as best she could. And she did come back—completely beaten up from the jerk she'd been with that weekend."

I winced, but Chelsea didn't even notice my reaction. She was completely engrossed in the story now, no doubt being transported back to that awful day. "She came in all bruised up, even had a black eye. And she didn't stop cursing from the moment she walked in. For a while, she just slammed around the kitchen. She must not have known I was sitting on the couch. But when she did see me—she laid into me big time."

"She hit you?" I asked in complete horror.

"No," she said, and I relaxed. "She *pummeled* me." Her tears now coursed down her cheeks, and I tensed. "I just wanted to die, because not only did she beat me up but she also kept screaming that she hated me, over and over again—which hurt almost worse. Just when I thought I was going to pass out though, she stopped. Looking back now, I know she must have been using— heck, she was probably so drugged up she had no idea what in the world she was doing. But somehow, she still realized what she'd done, and she hated herself for it. Next thing I knew, she'd locked herself in her room again, but after that, I didn't want her to come out...and she didn't."

I swallowed. "What…uh…what happened?" I asked, not really sure if I wanted all the gory details.

"Overdosed on whatever drug she was using. Eventually I went in to check on her, because usually I could hear her banging around in there when she holed herself away like that. This time though, I couldn't hear anything, and I got a bad feeling and went looking for her—when I opened the door, I saw her sprawled out on the bed, and I knew right away that she was gone."

Silence settled in around us as I sat in shock and Chelsea stared at the tabletop through dead eyes.

"I…uh…I don't know what to say, Chelsea," I finally whispered. "I'm so sorry."

She sniffed and wiped her eyes. "It's fine." I was grateful that she was being gracious with my answer, instead of rolling her eyes at me like she usually did. "Anyway," she continued, "I went and got my neighbor, and the cops eventually took me down to some women and children's shelter. And the next week, some lady shows up to take me away—my grandma. Never met the woman in my entire life. She hauled me up to Kansas, and here I am."

I tried to imagine what it must have felt like to walk in and find my mother dead in her bed, but it was absolutely impossible. And then moving up to an unfamiliar place with a woman I'd never met? Unthinkable. With no words to comfort Chelsea, I just sat there, stunned. But suddenly, Delilah's story came rushing back at me—Delilah had once tried to take her own life too! She might be the only one who could relate to Chelsea on some level. I knew Delilah wouldn't mind if I shared her story with Chelsea either, so I gave it a shot, hoping she'd be willing to talk with Delilah.

"I know saying I'm sorry doesn't mean much," I began. "And I can't relate in any way to what you went through. But I know someone who might."

Instead of reacting to my offer with some sarcastic remark like I was expecting, she simply asked, "Who?" Perhaps it was curiosity. Or perhaps she was finally tired of running, tired of dealing with the weight of her horrific past that now she was willing to reach out and take the help I was offering her.

"Delilah. When she was fifteen, she tried to commit suicide too. She hasn't lived through someone *else* committing suicide, but maybe she can help you process through some of the desperation and confusion since she was at that same low point. I know she had to go through some pretty intense therapy—maybe she can help."

"Maybe," Chelsea admitted. Perhaps my eyes were playing tricks on me, but I swore a slight glimmer of hope flamed up in her deep-green eyes.

"I can talk to her, if you want," I offered. "I won't give her any details—just that you guys might be good for each other. And I'll leave Mary Beth out of it."

Chelsea sucked in her bottom lip in deep thought. "Yeah, okay," she finally said, and I had to try my hardest not to jump out of my seat and dance around in victory. Finally, after two years, I'd gotten Chelsea to talk to me! And not only that, but I'd gotten her to agree to talk with someone who might actually help her. Someone who would point her to Christ, the ultimate healer.

Instead, I smiled and reached across the table to give hand a gentle squeeze. "It's all going to be okay," I assured her. "You're *not* too far gone."

She sniffed. "I hope you're right. Because things aren't looking so good for me. Haven't been for a long time."

"Trust me. You can find your way out of this."

When we walked out the front door later, Chelsea waited around for me to lock the place up instead of racing off to her car and zooming loudly out of the parking lot like she'd done all the previous nights. And even more amazing than that, she let me pull her into a hug and rub soft circles into her back, a small way to try and ease away the deep hurt she'd been experiencing for her entire life.

Tears ran down my cheeks the entire drive home. Everything was quiet and dark when I got back; Tanner must have called it a night when I didn't come home at my normal time. So I tiptoed into Elliot's room and gathered her sleeping form into my arms, breathing deep her baby smell. "I love you, sweetheart," I whispered, realizing after hearing Chelsea's story just how important it was to let my kids know I loved them. She gurgled happily in my arms, and I gave her one last kiss before nestling her back into her crib. Then I made my way down the hall to Elysa's room and peeked in. She was sprawled out in her new "big girl bed," and I quietly made my way across the room and perched on the edge. I smoothed her hair back and smiled— she was absolutely gorgeous, with the perfect balance of features from both Leah and Tanner. My heart squeezed in regret when I thought back to my struggle to love this little one. My current, continuous struggle, actually. It broke my heart.

"I love you, Elysa," I whispered, then leaned down to brush a kiss on her forehead.

She stirred underneath me, and suddenly her eyes fluttered open. "Mama," she babbled, and I melted.

"Hi, honey. Just wanted to say good night and that I love you."

"Love you too, Mama," she said through a yawn. Then she threw her arms around me and hugged me tightly.

Oh God, I prayed. *She deserves all my love. Help me always remember the story I heard tonight, and the importance of loving my girls. And bring healing into Chelsea's life, Lord. She needs you so badly.*

I knew he was the only one who could restore her brokenness. I just hoped that she'd let the story of Christ overcoming death and darkness infiltrate her life. I hoped she'd let him save her.

6

Molly

May

"Lilah, no," I said with a giggle. "I can't come with you and Greg to your ultrasound appointment. That's weird."

She made a pouty face at me. "No, it's not," she argued. "You're like a sister to me."

"Yeah, but still. Sisters don't go to ultrasound appointments. That's something for you and your husband to enjoy together." Four-month-old Elliot gurgled her agreement from my arms, and I smiled down at her. "You know Mama's right, don't you, Elliot?" I crooned. "Auntie Delilah is a little bit crazy. You better learn that early."

Delilah huffed and flopped back into the couch. "Fine. Be that way."

I let out a carefree laugh. "How 'bout we meet for lunch after? And go do the nursery shopping you've been hounding me to do since the very first day you found out you were pregnant."

She tried to hold her pouty face, but the very mention of going shopping for her baby's nursery was much too appealing, and a slow grin spread across her face. When she'd had Luke, space had been limited in her mom's little house, and the two had been crammed in Delilah's childhood bedroom, leaving little room for fun nursery decorating. This time around, she couldn't wait to decorate the small room she and Greg had kept empty for these last two years in hopes of God granting them a little one. "All right," she agreed. "Let's do it."

I'd never seen Delilah so happy. From the very first day I met her, I'd seen a deep sense of inner joy that radiated from her soul, and because of that, she was cheerful almost constantly, but ever since she and Greg finally conceived, she was flying even higher. Getting pregnant had been her heart's only desire since getting married, and for two years, it had been denied her. That meant that for the last two years, I'd seen Delilah try to hide behind disappointment and deep sadness, pretending she was at peace with the plan God seemed to have for her life. But knowing her as well as I did, however, I knew just how much she'd suffered. She'd clung to the hope that God would one day grant her this deep desire, though, and now she was swimming in an ocean of happiness.

An hour later, Delilah was headed to the clinic with Greg to meet her baby for the first time. When I shut the door behind her, though, the smile I'd pasted onto my lips all afternoon suddenly fell, and I sniffed back unexpected tears. What were the odds that Delilah would have a child with special needs? After Elliot was born, I'd done some research on Down syndrome and discovered that it affects one out of every eight hundred babies born in the United States, with as many as six thousand children born with it each year. Fairly common. I'd also learned that about fifty percent of those kids won't live past the age of fifty. What kind of hope did that give me? I couldn't make the same plans for my baby that Delilah was now making for her baby, who would most likely be born perfectly healthy. Normal.

I was beginning to hate that word. But I couldn't stop using it to compare the rest of the world to my daughter. Elliot lived in a world not made for her. In the years God would grant her, she'd live surrounded by people seeking the same things—to grow up, go to college, work their dream job, get married, have kids, grow old with their spouse—all things that I myself looked forward to doing. And I didn't think it was wrong to want those things; I just thought it was unfair that Elliot wouldn't be granted those things, simply because she wasn't "normal." She'd be left behind while all her peers went out in search of their American dream. How was I to plan for her? How was I to inspire her when my heart hurt so badly for all the things she'd never get to do?

But again, Elliot didn't need my sympathy. She needed my love. She needed my support. I had a feeling that as she grew older, her strange sense of perception would only intensify, so she'd probably be able to pick out my sympathy—something she'd no doubt resent. She'd want me to believe in her, and I so badly wanted to do so. Why was it so hard for me to commit to that? Why was it so hard for me to believe that even though she had Down syndrome, she could do great things? Granted, they'd probably look very different from the things I wanted for her, but who knew? Maybe she'd teach me more about life than I'd ever teach her. Maybe she'd prove me wrong.

While Delilah was at her appointment, I watched the kids for the afternoon. Luke was at school, so that left Mandy and Elysa running wild around the house as Elliot napped in her crib. It amazed me how much energy those girls had, and already I was looking forward to Delilah's return so we could go on our shopping trip. Tanner had promised to leave work a bit early so he could take over watching the kids. That way, Delilah and I could enjoy our outing free from kids hanging on our arms and begging us to make up our minds and get out of the store.

Later that afternoon, after Tanner had settled the kids in with a Disney movie, Delilah and I meandered through the aisles of the one and only home improvement store in Green Lake, breathing deep the delicious scent of hope that seemed to hang in the air. Delilah didn't just walk through the store, though—she danced, stopping to admire each and every possible paint color and trinket that would make her baby's nursery special. I would only smile and continue to follow her, murmuring my agreement at her good taste.

"How are things going with you and Chelsea?" I asked as she stood browsing through curtains. Chelsea hadn't offered up any more details of her life to me since that night we shared at the diner. In fact, she seemed to have shut me out again. Perhaps she was scared that I was judging her now, and she thought she had to be careful of what details she let me in on. Having been in her place, I knew how that felt—it had made me feel vulnerable just *thinking* about people knowing about my past. The easiest way to protect a broken spirit is to hide, to withdraw so far deep within yourself that even *you* begin to lose sense of whom you are. Or so it seems. Later on I had discovered that offering myself up—allowing myself to be vulnerable in a way that completely terrified me had been the best decision of my entire life. Just look where it had gotten me—the friend that my heart had always longed for in Delilah, a wonderful second mother figure in Mary Beth, and last but not least, Tanner. My heart was so overtaken with all their love now that it was full to bursting.

I wanted that so badly for Chelsea.

Delilah shook her head and let her hands fall from the pale-green curtain her fingers had been inspecting. "Are you sure she wants to talk with me? Every time I try and set up a time to meet with her, she cancels at the last minute."

I huffed, sending my bangs flying. "Darn. She sounded like she was really interested in meeting with you! What excuses has she been pulling on you?" I asked.

"Well, first it was that she had too much homework to do."

I laughed. I couldn't help it! The girl hated school, and we knew for a fact that she never committed any amount of time to doing homework—she'd told us herself. She did only what was completely necessary for her to pass her classes, and nothing more. "She needs to come up with a better excuse," I said with a chuckle, and Delilah joined in my laugher.

"I know. I let it slide the first time, but I didn't want to just give up on her, ya know?" I nodded. "So I kept asking, but it's hard to keep pursuing her without seeming pesky and driving her away," she mused.

"I know," I agreed. You really had to be careful around Chelsea—if she felt threatened in any way, she'd shut down, and trying to open her up again was only a fantasy. She had the strongest will of anybody I'd ever met before. How she was able to hold in so many emotions and never let a single soul in was beyond me. I'd tried to do that once too, but coming here had shattered that goal. Why wasn't the same thing happening with Chelsea? I'd *thought* that maybe her heart was softening and she was warming up to the idea of letting us share some of her burden, but now that dream seemed to be fading away as well. My heart just ached for her.

"Anyway," Delilah continued as she moved down the aisle to check out the cute baby wall decals, "she's gotten more creative with her excuses. Her grandma was sick. An uncle was in town. She was too tired." She shrugged. "I don't know what else to do, Molly. She really doesn't seem interested."

I nodded and trapped another sigh. "I'll see if maybe she'll open up to me again."

Suddenly my pocket was vibrating, and I pulled out my phone to see Mary Beth's name on my screen. "Two of the girls called in sick tonight, and I'm running a senior special tonight," she explained with panic dripping from her voice. "We're swamped and Chelsea and I can't keep up…She's not as good a waitress as you are, dear. Can you help this old woman out one more time?"

I smiled. "I doubt this will be the last time I come and give you a hand," I teased. "I love being there. Can't keep me out!"

"Oh, honey, you're just the greatest," Mary Beth gushed. "Whenever you can get here would be great. The sooner, the better, though!" She hung up quickly, and I laughed as I pictured her running around in her adorable white apron, a pencil no doubt stabbed into the graying bun she always had twisted on the top of her head. Even in the midst of craziness at the diner, I knew she had a smile on her face—not a forced smile either. She genuinely cared about each and every one of her customers; in fact, she had formed countless personal relationships with many of her regulars. After being somewhat of a community outcast in this small, close-knit community before she had come to know the Lord, Mary Beth cherished these friendships. It wasn't hard for her to be grinning and laughing as she bustled around the busy dining room floor.

I practically had to drag Delilah out of the store, promising that we'd come back soon to continue searching out the perfect elements for the baby's room. We hadn't made much progress today, as Delilah had been so delighted at each and every thing she'd seen. I sure didn't want to trade places with Greg right now— he'd have his hands full with this decorating project! I smiled as I thought of Delilah spreading out paint samples and paging through baby magazines in search of the perfect accessories, trying to get Greg to give his input. But Greg was a normal male, and it's not that he didn't care about the little details, it's just that they didn't mean quite as much to him as they did to her. I'd gone through the same thing with Tanner. While I hemmed and hawed over the perfect shade of purple to paint Elliot's room, he simply looked forward to meeting her and holding her for the first time. Greg would be patient with her though, just as Tanner had been with me, nodding and giving his input when asked and just going with the flow.

I walked into pure chaos later that afternoon. But I knew the drill. I flew into the kitchen, grabbed the faded black apron that had been mine since my very first day in the diner, and stuffed a notebook into the front pocket. When I pushed my way out onto the dining floor, Mary Beth shouted a greeting and waved me to the table that needed the most attention. I easily slipped into my waitressing role, relishing how nice it was to leave the stress of schoolwork, childcare, and housework at home with Tanner for a few hours. It was one of the only reasons I didn't leave this job completely. Tanner and I didn't really need the money, but for my own sanity, I stayed on, and I was grateful that Tanner was gracious in allowing me to escape for a few hours each week. Plus, it felt good to be needed, and Mary Beth's spunk seemed to always be just what I needed when I felt like the world was beginning to wear down on me.

Just when things were starting to slow down and I made the decision to leave within the half hour, a commotion at the front door stopped me. Four teenage boys tromped in, laughing loudly and pushing each other playfully. I recognized their faces, as they came here often to work on homework together or celebrate after another basketball game win. These were the stars of the Green Lake High School basketball team, and they acted the part very well. Basketball was the only sport the school excelled at, so to be the top players of that team meant instant popularity. Sometimes other teammates and wannabes would join them after their victories, but tonight they came alone. It didn't surprise me—no matter how many people tagged along behind these four, you could easily spot the difference in the insiders and outsiders. The four were the insiders—they were the ones that made all the decisions, the ones who decided if you were good enough to hang out with them, and if you were, they decided what your role in the group was and what you were and were not allowed to do. It amazed me any of the other kids wanted to be with such a group, but the need to be liked and accepted was so desperate during this age. Kids would do or be anything to be accepted into this group, but it didn't matter. In the end, it was always just the four. They used and abused the kids who wanted so badly to be liked and accepted by the stars. And they didn't care one bit how many people they hurt by maintaining their status.

When they had made their way into the building, they stopped and scanned the dining floor. One of the boys swatted the one next to him and grinned, then pointed to where Chelsea stood refilling a pot of coffee. Tonight she was wearing an awfully tight and extremely low-cut shirt—which her apron didn't do a single thing to cover up as she had it tied so loosely around her neck— which the boys seemed to appreciate very much. A particularly bold boy let out an insulting whistle Chelsea's way, and she shook her head in disgust. I rolled my eyes at their rowdiness but breathed a sigh of thankfulness when Mary Beth seated them in Chelsea's section—which meant I could still get out of here within the half hour and help Tanner put the girls to bed. About five minutes later though, I realized that Chelsea hadn't made an appearance at the boys' table. Soon the four were growing restless, craning their necks in search of their server.

"Where's Chelsea?" Mary Beth demanded after having to go over to the boys' table and take their drink orders. "I have too many tables already, and from the looks of it, I'll be losing you here pretty quick."

"Yeah," I agreed. "I'd like to get home in time to help with bedtime. And I feel like I haven't seen Tanner all day."

"Sure," Mary Beth said quickly. "I'm not asking you to stay. You've already helped me out so much today. We'll manage."

"You sure?"

"Yes. You get out of here. You work too hard for me. Those girls need you. No matter how good of a daddy that husband of yours is, every kid needs their mama."

I smiled. "All right. I'll get out of your hair just as soon as my last table leaves. Looks like they're about ready to go."

Just then, a little boy at one of Mary Beth's tables spilled his chocolate milk, and it was now flooding across the tabletop and onto the floor. She sprang into action, grabbing a dishcloth on her way over to help the embarrassed parents help clean up the mess. I glanced back over at my table, and noticing that they still weren't quite ready for their check just yet, I decided to go searching for Chelsea. The table of boys was getting pretty antsy by now, and I did not want to be roped into staying for another hour.

She wasn't hiding out in the kitchen like she sometimes did when she didn't feel like working, and she wasn't in the back parking lot smoking either. I decided to check the bathroom next, but when I pushed open the door, I stopped dead in my tracks from the sounds of someone crying.

"Chelsea?" I called out softly. "Is that you?"

The crying stopped immediately, and for a second, I battled with what I would do. Should I just leave and pretend I'd never heard anything in an attempt to not make her feel awkward? Or should I forge ahead and try to connect with her once again? Knowing that my window of opportunity was very small, I continued into the bathroom. It was there that I found the tearstained face of Chelsea; she was slumped in defeat on the bathroom floor.

"Honey, what's wrong?" I asked as I joined her on the floor.

She dragged her arm across her face to wipe away the tears and then took a huge shuddering breath in. "I can't go back out there, Molly. I hate those guys."

In that moment, I realized that being here with Chelsea was much more important than putting my girls to bed. I had countless nights ahead of me to do so, but I knew I didn't have many chances to really help Chelsea like I did tonight. So I settled fully on the floor next to her and asked, "Why?" I hoped that by not swooping in and simply commanding that she get over whatever issue she had with those boys and just do her job that she would open up to me again like she had a few weeks ago. I needed to be gentle and let her make the decisions; I needed to let her lead the conversation.

She surprised me by doing just that. "Those guys are such jerks," she began angrily. "I got drunk at a party a few weeks ago, and they all tried to have sex with me. They ganged up on me and had me halfway into a bedroom—and halfway undressed—before one of the only sober people there pulled me out. I don't even remember who saved me or how I got home that night, but I *do* remember them trying to take advantage of me. Now they won't leave me alone."

I sat in silence for a bit before responding, "That must have been very scary for you."

She nodded, and inwardly I was celebrating that this girl—a girl who tried so hard to act tough and put on an act that she didn't care about anything—was admitting that she was scared and overwhelmed. I hoped that she continued to let herself feel things, because then maybe she would agree to get some help—be it from Delilah or from a professional. She clearly needed it, but until *she* realized that she needed help, nothing would change. She had to want it.

"Can you just make them leave?" she asked, her green eyes big and pleading.

I sighed. "Until they've done something wrong here, I can't really do anything, Chels. Maybe I could take over the table for you." At this point, I had given up completely on getting home to help with bedtime. I expected her "tough girl" act to kick up again at this offering, but to my shock, she nodded her agreement. I was getting somewhere with her!

Just then my cell phone vibrated from within my apron pocket. A new text from Tanner read, "Elliot's been screaming for almost two hours. Nothing is working. I need you!"

If Elliot had been prone to screaming before bed, I would have told Tanner to just calm down and wait for me to get back. But screaming for this long was unlike her. Perhaps she was in pain and needed to be taken to the hospital. Tanner texted again a moment later and asked, "You coming home? I'm freaking out a little here."

"Sorry, Chelsea. My baby girl has been crying for almost two hours, and I have a panicked daddy who needs me. I'm afraid I can't help you out tonight."

The softness and vulnerability Chelsea had just exhibited dissipated quickly when I said this. Immediately she tensed up again and then heaved herself off the floor. "Fine," she said angrily. "Thanks for nothing, Molly." Then she stormed loudly out of the bathroom, leaving me sitting in bewilderment. I simply could not keep up with this girl! One minute she was letting her guard down, and the next she was right back at stacking bricks around her broken heart, trying desperately to keep everyone and everything out.

I made my way out of the bathroom and headed for the kitchen to hang my apron up and grab my purse. I felt awful for having offered to help Chelsea and then backing out, but what could I do? I had a commitment to my husband and children—they needed me just as much as Chelsea needed me. And being there for my family was much more satisfying than being there for Chelsea. My family *appreciated* my efforts; Chelsea just shut me out and resisted any attempts to help her. Why should I keep pouring so much time and energy into a girl who didn't really want me?

I knew the answer to that question when I stepped back out into the dining room floor and watched in amazement at what unfolded right before my eyes. I saw Chelsea standing reluctantly at the table of boys, scribbling down their orders while the boys teased and ridiculed her. I heard one of them say, "Oh, come on, Chelsea. We knew you wanted it. We were just gonna give you what you wanted!" My skin began to crawl as I thought back to what Jason had said to me after the rape.

You led me on the whole time. Don't pretend you didn't want to do it with me. I did not force that on you. I was simply taking control, giving you what I know you wanted. Stop acting like I attacked you, because I didn't. Now, I've been telling people we broke up, so work on getting over me. Got it?

It was all I could do not to fly across the room and lay into the boys. What a sight that would be! Doing that would be impossible of course, and even though I wanted to run over and defend Chelsea, fear was paralyzing me to the ground. The boy's words had hurled me straight back to the time right after my rape, and nausea welled inside me just thinking about my attack. It was eerie how similar what the boy had just said to Chelsea was to what Jason had said to me. No wonder she had been crying inside the bathroom! A phrase like that was terrifying.

So I just stood and watched. As Chelsea turned to fill their orders, I saw a hand reach out and smack her backside, causing me to gasp in horror and Chelsea to whirl around in anger.

"Don't you *dare* touch me, you little creep!" she screamed, throwing down her order notebook and storming across the floor to the kitchen. The diner fell silent, and Mary Beth looked at me in horror. I sprang into action then, finally able to shake the memories of my own attack.

I met Mary Beth in the middle of the floor and filled her in on what had happened, and her eyes closed in anger. Like a mother hen ruffles her feathers to defend her little chicks, Mary Beth took a deep breath, squared her shoulders, and walked swiftly to the table of giggling, sneering boys.

"Gentlemen, I'm going to have to ask you to leave," Mary Beth declared matter-of-factly.

The leader of the group let out a sarcastic laugh. "You serious?"

"Dead serious," Mary Beth said, her voice steady and strong. "Don't worry about paying for your drinks. Just leave." She leaned in and whispered, "*Now.*" The smiles slowly fell off the faces of the boys, and when they realized that the whole crowd in the diner was silently celebrating what Mary Beth has just done, they quickly left. In silence, this time. No more snickering.

When the boys were gone, Mary Beth continued serving her customers, acting completely normal so the crowd wouldn't focus so much on the boys and further elevate the situation. She knew they weren't worth gossiping about, because that would only increase their popularity. The best thing to do was put it behind us and carry on.

Feeling awful that I hadn't been able to step in as easily as Mary Beth had been able to, I turned back to the kitchen to apologize to Chelsea. I walked in to find her softly crying over the large pile of dishes in the sink. I froze again, wondering why it had to be so incredibly awkward to comfort a crying person. Chelsea made the first move, though.

"I can't believe she did that for me." Turing around to face me, she added, "I thought she hated me."

"Of course she doesn't hate you," I assured. "The reason she's so hard on you is because she *cares* so much. If this doesn't prove how much she cares about you, I don't know what will."

She swallowed. "I guess I'm just not used to that. No one has ever *really* cared about me before."

It was then that I realized how important it was that Mary Beth had been the one to step in and rescue Chelsea, not me. I'd been showing Chelsea just how much I cared for a good few weeks now. I'd gotten farther with her in these last few weeks than both Mary Beth and I had been able to for all the time she'd been at the diner. Now that Chelsea could see the depth of how much both of us cared for her, I knew we had reached a breakthrough. Maybe now she would soften up to Mary Beth, and we could finally reach her.

I pulled Chelsea into a hug before I left, and the next day, Mary Beth called to let me know that Chelsea had thanked her for asking the boys to leave. She cried as she told me this, and I had to shake my head. A simple apology had brought her to tears! It was such a small thing and yet so huge at the same time. Chelsea was finally able to see that she had value and worth, and that people cared about her. With this realization taking root in her heart, who knew what was next for her?

7

Delilah

July

"All right," the ultrasound technician said excitedly. "Time to make the big decision! Would you guys like to find out the gender?"

I looked at Greg and swallowed a giggle. He rolled his eyes. "Well, *I* don't want to find out. But *she* does, and she makes a good argument. I don't have to push this baby out in five months. So I guess I should humor her just this once, right?" he teased, and the technician laughed.

"Yes, your wife has a big job ahead of her. It's nice to have such an understanding daddy in the picture. You wouldn't believe some of the arguments guys will make when it comes to finding out the gender. You make a good point, though, and I like that."

I laughed. "Please, don't give him too much credit. We've battled about this for the entire pregnancy. I basically had to get down on my hands and knees and *beg* him to let me find out."

Greg jumped in. "Hey now, that's not true. I stopped her before she got all the way down," he joked, and Shirley, the technician, just shook her head in amusement.

"So we're gonna find out, then, right?" she asked, just to be sure of what we really wanted.

"Yes," I answered quickly. "Do it fast before he tries again to convince me not to."

Shirley grinned and positioned her wand over my belly, and I felt my heartbeat quicken in excitement. Finding out the gender would make all of this much more real, and I couldn't wait to go back to the home improvement store and pick out gender specific decorations and buy up all of the baby clothes in town to get my baby's wardrobe all stocked up.

"Looks like we have a little mister!" she sang out.

Greg squeezed my hand in excitement, and I grinned up at him. A boy! We were having a little boy!

I know Greg would have been just as ecstatic about a little girl, but I also knew how excited he was about having a son of his own. It had been easy for him to adopt Luke as his own son, but this was different. This boy was *his*, and he couldn't be any happier. We left the clinic that day hand in hand, smiling from ear to ear as we celebrated our son's life.

That weekend we went out and picked up a cheerful shade of green paint to begin spreading on the nursery walls. We decided to decorate using a safari theme, and I had plans to paint a big tree on the wall behind his crib. I planned to paint a monkey hanging from one of the branches, a toucan lounging in another, and a few other safari animals hanging out below. My mother had volunteered to come lend a hand, as she was incredibly gifted at painting. We already had the bedding picked out, and we'd also purchased a changing table and a dresser for our little man. Once the painting and mural was finished, we'd move in all the furniture, hang up the curtains, and add in all the last-minute details. I couldn't wait to see the finished product.

When I felt the first faint fluttering of movement inside me, I knew we had to pick out a name. Greg and I had spent quite a few late nights up discussing names and so far hadn't agreed on anything. I lay in bed one night with a smile playing on my lips, focusing on the teeny tiny movements of my son. It was just barely noticeable, like a little goldfish was swimming around inside of me. And even though my first pregnancy had been almost a decade ago, I knew it was him. Greg's breathing was beginning to slow, and I knew he was probably almost asleep, but then it hit me.

"Babe!" I said, reaching over to push him awake. "Wake up!"

He took a sharp deep breath in and sat up, disoriented. "What? What's happening? You okay?" he asked all at once, and I laughed.

"Yeah, I'm fine. Guess what?" I asked excitedly.

"What?" he replied as he settled back down into bed, rolling over—in his sleepy state, he didn't realize how important this moment was to me, so I reached out and gave him another little push.

"Wake up, Greg! This is important."

He rolled over and apologized. "You've got my full attention, love. What's up?"

"Jonas," I said.

"I don't know what that means," Greg replied through a yawn.

I laughed. "It's a name. I stumbled across it the other day in our baby name book. It's Hebrew. It means 'gift from God.'"

Greg didn't say anything, and I couldn't really see his face in the darkness.

"You hate it, don't you?" I asked in disappointment. He didn't seem to like any of my names.

"No, no!" Greg said quickly. "I was just trying it out in my mind."

"And?" I asked expectantly.

"And I love it," Greg said. I threw my arms around him and he drew me in close. "I think it's absolutely perfect. We've waited so long for him. He is certainly a gift from God."

In the next few weeks, Jonas's nursery came alive. The green paint was the perfect shade, and Mom had done a beautiful job painting the tree and safari animals. We moved the crib and changing table in, as well as the brand-new glider rocker that Molly and Tanner had given to us shortly after we told them we were pregnant. Molly had one just like it in Elliot's room, and she absolutely adored it. "When you sit up at night rocking your baby to sleep, you can imagine me doing the same to Elliot," she'd said with a smile.

In our excitement, perhaps we had gotten ahead of ourselves, and now all we could do was wait for our son to arrive. With each passing day, I grew more and more anxious to meet him. His movements were getting stronger, and the bond between us was growing deeper.

I panicked when I stopped feeling him move. Perhaps my mind was just playing tricks on me. I tried to ignore it for a few days, but I was nearing twenty weeks. I knew that his movements should be picking up, not slowing down. I had a doctor's appointment scheduled for the next week, so if I continued not feeling anything, I would definitely mention it. For the time being, I chose to ignore it, sure that I was just overreacting. I had waited so long to be pregnant, and I knew I was being a bit paranoid. It was probably best to simply calm down and wait to see what the doctor said.

I awoke two nights later with a start, my abdomen tightening in pain. I threw the covers back to get out of bed for a glass of water, hoping that walking would help with the pain. I flipped my bedside lamp on, and when I stood up, I saw the deep-red stain spreading out on our bed sheets. I gasped in horror, and Greg shot up out of bed.

"What?" he shouted, but then he saw the blood himself. "Oh my gosh. We need to get you to the hospital. Now."

He jumped out of bed and grabbed his phone as I just stood by the bed in shock, my breath coming out in short, raggedy gasps. "What are you doing?" I asked as his fingers flew furiously over the keys.

"Calling Tanner to come watch the kids."

I nodded, grateful that Greg was taking charge of this situation. Fear was paralyzing me, and my legs felt a hundred pounds apiece. The room was beginning to spin around me, and a ringing was overtaking my senses. I could faintly hear Greg's conversation with Tanner, but my mind was choosing to block everything out right now. I knew what was happening, and I was desperately trying to remove myself from the situation and run as far away as I could—somewhere safe and warm, a place I could fully protect and shelter my son.

It was a place I had gone to many times before—back when I was pregnant with Luke. Back then, I used to have horrible flashbacks of the night I told David I was pregnant. The night he cut me out of his life and left me all alone. I used to wake up in the middle of the night with cold sweat pouring out all over my body, strange images still swirling around in my mind from whatever nightmare had chosen to invade. Instead of running to my mom's room and jumping into bed with her like I wanted to, I had chosen to deal with it on my own, still feeling guilty from embarrassing my mom by getting pregnant so young. I didn't want to be any more of a burden on her than I already was. So I would strip out of my soaking wet pajamas, change into a new pair, and resettle into bed. I'd close my eyes, take a few deep breaths, and fall into my safe place. I'd pretend I was at a lake all alone, with heavy woods framing the crystal-clear waters. Birds would be singing softly in the background as my long tanned legs dangled off the dock. I'd stick my toes into the warm water, then get up and dive in. There I would float, for hours on end, staring up into the deep-blue sky and watching the puffy white clouds scurry overhead.

That's where I was right now. The only safe place I could go.

Greg gently took ahold of my shoulders and softly spoke my name, yanking me out of the warm water and bringing me back into my worst nightmare. "Tanner's on his way. He'll be here soon. Why don't you get changed and ready to go? I'll get a bag packed."

I nodded and swallowed, then slowly began to follow Greg's orders. I grabbed a pair of sweatpants from my dresser and wandered my way down the hallway to the bathroom, where I peeled off my bloodstained pajama shorts. I threw them in the trashcan, never again wanting to lay eyes on or wear those horrid, filthy shorts.

Ten minutes later, Tanner was sitting on our couch with his Bible in hand, promising to stay up all night in prayer as we began the long drive to the hospital, which was a good half hour drive away. "Call me if you need anything. I'll have Molly come over if this keeps you all night. Don't worry about the kids. We'll take good care of them."

We settled into the car and sped off into the darkness, fear suffocating us. Greg popped in a praise and worship CD, but I reached out and turned it off. I remembered Molly sharing with me how during the time after her rape and abortion she had cut music out of her life entirely, knowing full well the power music has in our lives. She hadn't wanted to listen to anything that when she heard years later would transport her back to that awful time in her life, and for the first time in my own life, I could relate to her. Listening to this CD would ruin the music for me, as I knew that when I heard those songs later, all it would remind me of was the night my son began slipping away from me.

I didn't have to explain myself to Greg. He understood completely, so we drove in silence. Tears began coursing down my cheeks, and Greg looked over to me with immense pain in his eyes. He reached over and took my hand in his, giving it a gentle squeeze. He continued driving with urgency, pushing the car further and further over the speed limit.

We pulled into the hospital right around three o'clock in the morning, disturbing the peace of the sleepy little waiting room of this tiny hospital. The nurses on duty sprang into action when Greg explained that he thought I was losing our baby, rushing to get me a wheelchair and racing me down the hall to an examination room.

A doctor was with us shortly after. I held onto Greg's hand as tightly as possible as the doctor worked to determine if our worst fears were coming true. He performed a series of tests, all of which I blocked out, hoping more than anything that if I just pretended that this wasn't happening to us, that it was all just a horrible nightmare, that it would go away. But in the end, I just couldn't escape from the truth.

"I'm so sorry, you two," the doctor said softly, taking his glasses off and pinching the bridge of his nose. "You've lost your baby."

Those words brought my world crashing down around me, and I began looking around frantically, finally taking in my surroundings. The doctor was looking at us compassionately, truly sorry to have to deliver such news to us. Greg still held tightly onto my hands, and his chin was quivering uncontrollably and tears were filling his eyes. My own tears were dripping off my chin, and I was having trouble breathing.

"No," I whispered. "No! No, please, there has to be some mistake! Please!"

The doctor swallowed and shook his head slowly. "I'm so sorry," he repeated. "Let me give you two some time alone. I'll be back in a bit to explain what to expect next." Then he left us alone to grieve.

All we could do was hold each other—and wonder why in the world God would finally bless us with a baby if he was planning on taking him away from us anyway. It just didn't make sense. I'd rather have never gotten pregnant in the first place than to have gotten so excited and attached to my baby, making his loss that much more painful.

The doctor reappeared a few minutes later and gave us a small smile. "I'm glad you two came in when you did. Some couples ignore bleeding, thinking it's something they can just address at their next appointment. However, in your case, Delilah, we need to deliver immediately in order to avoid infection. We're going to induce you to begin delivery, okay?" he instructed. My eyes darted between Greg and the doctor, and I swallowed, unable to argue or agree. The decision seemed to have been made without me anyway, so I nodded.

Greg called Tanner as I was being prepped for labor. Even though it was still only four in the morning, we knew that they'd want to be here for us. We would do the same for them if it was Molly lying in my hospital bed. Greg walked into my room and said softly, "They're on their way. They're gonna drop the kids off at Joey and Ruth's first and then pick up your mom."

Joey and Ruth were a young couple that attended church with us all. They had little kids as well and were a part of a small group with Greg, Molly, Tanner, and I. We met every two weeks to study the Bible and just enjoy each other's company. We'd only been meeting for a few months, and we still didn't know them that well, but I trusted them completely. I nodded but remained silent. No words would come. Only tears.

From that point on, the pregnancy began to feel real again. The labor progressed just like it had when I'd delivered Luke—and it hurt just the same. For a while, I was able to pretend that this was a normal birth, and that in a few hours, we'd have a screaming Jonas nestled into our arms. Reality is a cruel intruder, however, and I knew that my fantasy wasn't coming true. I was delivering a deceased baby.

Molly, Tanner, and my mother arrived just after five o'clock in the morning. Molly rushed in and ran to my bed, tears running down her face.

"I'm so sorry, Lilah. We'll be here for you the whole time. You just say the word, whatever it is, and we'll take care of anything and everything, okay?" she gushed.

"Thanks," I managed to croak. They made good on their promise, staying by my side as the hours rolled on. Finally, at around noon on that sticky July day, our tiny, perfect little Jonas entered the world. There were no cries, however, no joyous welcoming. The doctors placed my tiny son on my chest, just as they'd done with Luke all those years ago, and my heart clenched in pain. This wasn't right. And it wasn't fair.

I wanted this baby more than anything else in the world. I still carried around so much guilt in my heart from getting pregnant out of wedlock as a teenager, and from then on, I had been doing everything possible to make up for it. I'd skipped every party, school event, and dance so I could stay home and take care of Luke. In fact, I could count on one hand the number of times I had ever left Luke at home with my mom or Albert while I went out. I had sacrificed everything for Luke—my friends, my dreams of going to school—I'd worked long hours at a job I didn't like just to make sure he always had food, clothes, and a roof over his head. Why hadn't that been enough? Why was God punishing me for making one mistake?

I pondered these questions for the next few hours as my family, friends, and I said our hellos and good-byes to Jonas. We snapped as many pictures as we could and cried freely, mourning the little life that never was. We also planned what we would do next, as we wanted to honor the brief life of Jonas. To us, even though he hadn't been born alive, we still considered the time he'd spent inside me to be his life. And we wanted to give him a service, just as we would do for anyone in our lives that died. Since Jonas hadn't made it to twenty-four weeks, there was no need to register him. However, we still wanted a birth certificate, and we wanted to take his body with us to bury.

The next few weeks of my life were a cold, sad blur. I somehow glided through life, but I felt detached, like I wasn't really in my body at all but floating somewhere above watching my sad form stumble through each day. Even on the day we buried my sweet little son, I felt like I wasn't really present. Perhaps it was because I desperately *didn't* want to be living my life right now. I wanted to rewind to a week ago and warn myself to take it easy, to do everything in my power to protect and shelter Jonas from his inevitable death.

Of course, there wasn't anything that I could have done. Lying flat on my back wouldn't have helped. The miscarriage hadn't happened because I'd done something wrong. It had just happened.

After we buried Jonas, my friends and family tried their best to return to normal. No one really knew how to act around me, and even though they tried to hide that from me, I felt it. I felt their pity. I felt their uncertainty. They did the only thing they could do—they carried on as normally as possible, hoping that after a time, I'd do the same.

But I didn't.

I couldn't. For days, I laid in bed, sending Luke and Mandy off to Molly's house while Greg was at work all day. I cried. I slept. And I yelled at God.

How dare you do this to me!

I don't deserve this God, not after all I've been through.

Why me? Don't you think I've suffered enough already?

What kind of God are you anyway?

Day and night, these questions and angry statements rolled through my mind, consuming my every waking moment. Greg watched me through concerned eyes, and after a few days like this, he called in Molly's help, hoping she'd be able to offer encouragement and advice.

She came creeping in one afternoon, calling out softly, "Hi, Lilah. Can I come in?"

"I guess," I mumbled through tears.

She padded over to where I lay in my bed and then gently climbed in beside me, pulling me to her side. For a while, she lay beside me in silence, simply holding me and stroking my hair.

Then, she spoke up, breaking the heavy silence that had reigned in this room since I returned after delivering Jonas.

"I know the pain you must be feeling, sweetie. There's an emptiness, and it can feel like nothing will ever fill that hole. But you know that's not true, right?"

I swallowed the lump lodged in my heart and squeezed my eyes shut. "This is different, Molly," I spat, angry at her for trying to compare the pain she felt after her abortion to my miscarriage.

She sat up beside me. "How is this different?" she asked with confusion in her voice.

I sighed and sat up as well. "Because. I *wanted* my baby, Molly. I was fighting for him. I *knew* the worth of his life."

She sat in silence for a while, and I could see her cheeks heating up in anger. "So the fact that you wanted your baby makes his loss more painful than mine? Since when did this become a competition?" she challenged.

"It's not a competition," I retorted. "And if it was, I'd win. You took the life of your baby. God took mine away. It wasn't my fault, and it's way more unfair."

She gave a sad laugh. "Wow. I can't believe the words that are coming out of your mouth right now. I'm the only one in your life who can relate to you on losing a baby, and you throw my abortion in my face, as if my loss is any less painful than yours. As if I don't care at all about that life. Well guess what, Lilah? I *do* care. I loved my baby just as much as you loved Jonas."

Now it was my turn to throw out a sad laugh. "Then why'd you abort her, huh? If you loved her as much as I loved Jonas, why didn't you fight for her?"

Molly's face crumbled, but my heart had hardened just enough over the last week that I didn't care one bit. There was *no way* the pain from Molly's abortion compared to a miscarriage. Because just as I'd said, I *wanted* Jonas. I wanted him more than anything. Clearly Molly hadn't loved her baby, and what she had been feeling after her abortion was just guilt, not the deep sadness I was experiencing after losing someone I loved desperately. And because Molly hadn't really loved her baby, her pain would never compare to mine. Ever. It was wrong of her to come rushing in here, thinking she could save me or relate to me in some way. She'd never be able to relate to me.

"I don't need to explain myself to you," she finally said. "And frankly, I shouldn't have to put up with this crap." With that, she heaved herself out of my bed, stomped out of my room, and slammed the door loudly as she left.

I didn't see her for weeks.

I replayed our conversation over and over again in my head, each time coming to the same conclusion: I was right and she was wrong. My pain was worse than hers, and she had no right waltzing in and comparing our situations. I didn't need her in my life if she thought our situations were comparable, and that it was appropriate to bring up her abortion while I was still grieving the loss of my baby. I'd heard enough of her stupid abortion in the last few years! She should be over it by now.

The concern in Greg's eyes grew bigger and bigger, but he didn't push me to get over the pain. After a full week of moping around in my bed, I knew I at least had to get up and take care of my family as best I could. Besides, I didn't want my kids over at Molly's house anymore. As far as I was concerned, our friendship was over. So even though pain and sadness reigned in our home, I thought it was better for my kids to be with me than with Molly.

Last summer, screaming and laughter had bounced off the walls as Luke and Mandy played together. This summer, an eerie silence echoed through the house. Luke holed himself away in his room with books, and Mandy would sit and color on the coffee table for hours. I didn't know what to do with myself—I'd sit on the couch, numb, and watch Mandy churn out picture after picture. It was as if the kids didn't want to break me or cause me any further pain. It was amazing how perceptive they were. Guilt began to prick at my conscience, but I brushed it away. If the kids really had decided to lay low in an attempt to protect me, I'd take it. I'd rather be sitting in silence than trying to chase around two rambunctious kids, pretending my life wasn't falling to pieces around me.

Greg continued to watch me with concern; I could see the battle in his eyes clear as day. I knew he was wrestling with approaching me about my behavior. Still, he continued to tiptoe around me, handling me like a little china doll who could break at any moment. July melted into August, and soon the kids were heading back to school. Luke would be going into fifth grade this year—his last year in elementary school—and Mandy would be starting kindergarten, which she was bouncing off the walls in excitement for. As the summer had gone on things had loosened up with the kids—Luke started spending more time outside his room, and he'd take Mandy out back to run around, which I appreciated. The kids truly did deserve better. I just wasn't willing to give them that. The guilt continued to grow, though, as Luke had to step up and become more of an adult than he should at his age. But because he'd done so, things with Mandy had gotten better. She quickly turned back into the bubbly little girl she was with Luke's help.

"Mandy needs a backpack, Mom," Luke said one afternoon, about a week before school started. "She hasn't stopped talking about it for weeks. You need to take her to get one."

"Oh," I replied, completely unaware that Mandy had been talking about school. Had I really not been listening to a word my children had been saying since Jonas had died?

So I took the kids out the next day and got them all stocked up for school. New clothes, new shoes, all the essential supplies, and a brand-new pink, sparkly backpack for Mandy. She clutched it tightly to her chest the entire drive home, than promptly wrote her name in thick permanent marker across the front pocket as soon as we came through the door. For the first time in months, I had spent a normal afternoon with my children. I had talked to my children. Listened to them. Smiled. I had even laughed.

Life was moving on without my permission. My kids were growing and learning, excited about the coming school year while just across town at the cemetery their baby brother lay lifeless in the ground. For Luke's and Mandy's sakes, I had to pull myself together just a little bit to give them a normal start to their school year. On the first day, I cheerfully woke them up, made them pancakes, and walked them to their classroom doors. Luke ran off when he spotted his friends, waving a happy good-bye and wishing his little sister good luck on her first day. Mandy held tightly to my hand, suddenly silent after weeks of excited chatter.

I glanced down at her serious face. She'd always been so serious, a bit shy and reserved too. Worry creased her tiny face, and I squeezed her hand.

"Are you nervous?" I asked.

She nodded. "Yes, a little bit," she said, sounding much older than her five years.

"Don't you worry, sweet pea," I answered, giving her hand another squeeze. "You remember meeting your teacher last week at the open house, right?" She nodded again. "And you loved her! Remember how nice she is?"

"Oh yes," she said with a smile. "She's very nice."

"Then what's wrong?"

She stopped and looked up at me, tears filling her blue eyes. "I'm worried about you. Who will take care of you while me and Luke are here? Who will make sure you're all right? Who will hug you when you start crying 'cause you miss Jonas so much?"

I swallowed, guilt hitting me so hard it about knocked me over. Is this what my five-year-old had been thinking for the past few months? Had she really spent her days worrying about if I was all right, when she should have been running through the sprinklers and making memories?

I crouched down so that we were eye to eye, screaming kids running all around us. I wiped the tears from her face and blinked back my own. All those days I had spent watching her, thinking she hadn't seen me crying—she'd seen every single tear. No more. It ended today. I cleared my throat and said, "Honey, it's not your job to take care of me. I appreciate that you love me enough to want to take care of me, but it's my job to take care of you, right?"

She nodded. "Right," I continued. "I'm sorry I haven't been doing a very good job of that. You're right about me being sad about Jonas. I loved him very much, and I wasn't ready to let him go. But he's not coming back. You know that, and I know that, but I've been having a hard time accepting that. Does that make sense?"

"Yes," she whispered.

"I wish you didn't have to see me so sad, sweetheart. It might take a while for me to not seem sad. But you're helping me get better, just by being you. So I want you to go into school today and not worry about me one bit, okay? I'm gonna try a lot harder to get better, I promise."

She smiled up at me. "Okay."

With that, I stood up, took my daughter's hand, and walked her up to her teacher. Miss Macintosh reached out her hand for Mandy to shake, and Mandy did so enthusiastically. I stepped back to let her make her own way, a bit worried that she'd let her shyness get the best of her and come running back to me. She didn't. She got in line behind a few other kids and smiled at me, giving me the go-ahead to leave. I waved at her and smiled back, and then the bell rang. Tears again filled my eyes as I watched Mandy march into her first day of school.

My first tears that weren't about Jonas.

I then drove home with dry eyes. Those brief moments with my daughter had opened my eyes to just how selfish I'd been for the past few months. Yes, I was grieving. But I'd taken it to an unhealthy level, and my kids had paid the price—no five-year-old should be worrying about leaving her mom at home on her first day of kindergarten. I only hoped that her little mind would forget about this morning entirely—that she wouldn't grow up thinking she had to protect me.

I wandered into my silent house, unsure what to do with myself for the seven hours until I had to pick up the kids. This was my first school year without a kid home with me running under my feet. Of course, I'd expected to have a newborn to care for. I hadn't prepared myself for an empty house.

For the first time in months, I felt a pang of loneliness for Molly. I'd been angry at her for so long, and the anger had prevented me from missing her. After my morning of clarification, however, I desired her company more than anything. How stupid of me to react to her kindness the way I'd done. She truly had been the only one who could have related to me, and yet I'd pushed her away and treated her terribly. Flashbacks of our last encounter bombarded me, and I winced at how harsh I'd been.

I wanted my baby, Molly. I was fighting for him. I knew the worth of his life.

You took the life of your baby. God took mine away. It wasn't my fault, and it's way more unfair.

If you loved her as much as I loved Jonas, why didn't you fight for her?

Had those words really come out of my mouth? Had I really been so cruel to my best friend, who had taken the time to comfort me with her own busy life waiting for her at home? The friend who'd been by my side for the last four years, listening to me pour out my sad story time and time again, who'd prayed with me and held my hands and understood deeper than anyone else ever had? I knew I had to make things right. Not today, not when I was still trying to put the first pieces of my life back together. I needed to make things right with my own family, and with God, before I went to Molly.

In the meantime, I needed some busy work to occupy myself. The house was in disarray because I hadn't cared enough to clean or even tidy up since Jonas died. Greg had done the best he could, but a man's standard of clean hardly comes close to a woman's. I started in the kids' rooms, scooping clothes off the floor and stripping their bedding off to throw in the washer—I couldn't recall the last time I'd washed their sheets. As I worked in Mandy's room, I came across the large stack of drawings she'd been working on all summer, and my breath caught in my throat as I paged through them.

She was truly gifted at drawing. She'd carefully drawn pictures of our house, our backyard, of her stuffed animals—of so many things in our home. Page after page of true beauty, and then I came across pictures of our family. First she'd drawn each of us individually—there was a picture of Greg, myself, Luke, and Mandy. Then she'd drawn the four of us together. Her next set of pictures caught me off guard—so many pictures of Jonas. Some of him alone, some of him in my arms, and some with him lined up with the rest of us.

This must have been her way of coping with the loss. I hadn't realized that his death had affected her in any way; I had just assumed that since she was so little she didn't understand what had happened. These drawings proved that she *did* understand, and that she missed her brother. Tears pricked at my eyes once again as guilt washed over me. I'd spent the whole summer feeling sorry for myself and making myself emotionally unaware when questions had swirled around in my daughter's head. She had needed me, and I hadn't been there for her.

I selected my favorite family picture that she'd drawn and hung it on the fridge. When I picked the kids up from school later that afternoon and Mandy saw in hanging there, she simply smiled and looked up at me. She didn't have to say a word—her smile said it all. In that moment, she knew everything was going to be all right. We were going to make it through this.

8

Molly

September

Ruth sat across from me on this sunny September morning, sipping coffee and munching on the cookies I'd made the day before with Elysa and Tanner while Elliot had happily babbled from her playpen in the living room. Elliot was surprisingly good at entertaining herself, much more than Elysa had been at her age. She absolutely loved being in her playpen—Tanner and I would dump a bunch of toys and books in there and she'd be content to play by herself for much longer than even two-year-old Elysa was. The three of us had enjoyed a carefree afternoon of cookie baking, then settled into the couch for an evening of Disney princesses and laughter.

The day hadn't been *totally* carefree. No days were anymore, not since that sticky summer day that Delilah had spat out ugly, hurtful words while I was simply doing my best to support her. While she had been curled up in bed for days, crying over her baby, *I'd* been the one taking care of Luke and Mandy, on top of taking care of my own girls. Greg would drop them off with a sheepish look in his eyes and an apology on his lips, which I would always brush away. I reassured him that it would only be a matter of time before Delilah would realize that her family needed her. She'd realize that this type of grieving was hurting her family, and she'd work on coping in a healthier way. After all, I'd seen her make great attempts to heal from her teenage pregnancy throughout all the days of our friendship. Delilah was always adamant about dealing with issues head on and walking toward healing. She lived her life with the mind-set that healing is a lifelong process, something we had to work on doing every single day of our lives. Surely she would return to this way of thinking after the initial shock and anger wore off. Right?

But the days continued to pass without a single change. Delilah didn't seem to realize how dangerous this type of grief was. I could see the fear in Greg's eyes, the uncertainty about how to deal with his wife's behavior. I thought about his first wife often, about how she'd run off and abandoned him and Mandy. Her memory was on Greg's mind too, and he admitted to me that he was having nightmares about Delilah doing the same thing. I doubted that Delilah would ever do that, but the fear that she might kept Greg from speaking up and encouraging her to get some help.

That's when he came to me.

"Please, Molly. I need your help. I don't know why it's so hard for me to speak up about this to her. I don't agree with what she's doing, but I'm scared she'll go off the deep end if I say something. I thought maybe you could, since, ya know…" he trailed off, not wanting to say out loud that maybe I could relate to Delilah because of the abortion.

I nodded. "Sure, I can give it a try."

I really did understand what Delilah was going through. There is no pain like the pain of losing a child. While our situations differed slightly—she had lost her baby naturally while I'd made the choice to end my baby's life—I could still relate. No doubt she was experiencing guilt, just as I had after the abortion. She probably obsessed night and day over what she could have done differently—resting more, eating differently, taking more vitamins. Dreams most likely intruded as well, vivid dreams that took her right back to the night she'd lost Jonas, just like I'd dreamed about the horror of the abortion room over and over again. Maybe she was also hearing phantom crying—that had been the worst part of my entire ordeal. Back when I'd been living in Minneapolis with Melissa and her friends, I used to hear phantom cries all the time. I'd even go wandering around the little apartment, flipping on lights and stumbling on furniture, searching for my baby.

I knew firsthand the guilt, pain, confusion, and heartbreak that comes from the loss of a child. Greg was right to come to me. I'd driven over to her house confident that with my help, Delilah could finally start off on the road to healing. While she'd never be the same as she was before this happened, things would get so much better once she realized how much precious time she was wasting. I didn't want her stumbling around in the wilderness for as long as I had, running away from the truth of what had happened and refusing to let healing enter her soul.

Delilah simply hadn't been ready to begin that journey, however, and in her deep sadness and pain, she had hurled the most piercing, horrible words that she'd ever spoken to me. In the moment, I hadn't been able to separate my emotions from logic, and I'd taken her words personally and left, slamming the door as hard as I could. Tears had run down my face as I jogged out to my car, and for the entire drive home. When I pulled into the driveway, I realized I wasn't in good enough condition to walk in and take care of my family—I was hurt, deeply hurt, and I needed to work through it a bit before coming back. I could see Tanner playing with the girls in the living room through the big picture window, so I sent him a quick text letting him know I'd be back in time to help with dinner. Then I drove off, not even sure where I was headed—driving is so therapeutic for me, though, that it doesn't even matter. I headed out of town on the highway and just cruised, letting the simple beauty of the cornfields soothe my heart. When I returned an hour later, I was much more in control. While I was still deeply hurt from the things Delilah had said to me, deep down I knew that she hadn't really meant them. She was blinded by pain and confusion, and sooner or later, she would come to grips with the reality of her situation and finally begin the long journey toward healing.

Tanner and I agreed that it was best to let Greg and Delilah deal with what was going on in their home. Tanner called Greg and let him know that we were here for him if things got out of control, but for the time being, we were taking a step back to let them figure it out as a family. While we didn't necessarily agree with how Greg was handling it, we felt that it wasn't really our place to say anything.

It reminded me of my senior year of high school, when I'd foolishly followed Jason into a trap that had taken me years to find my way out of. While Tanner's love had been right in front of my face, I'd chosen to walk past it for Jason. Tanner and my friend Kristina hadn't agreed with my decision to date Jason due to his bad boy reputation, but after a while, they realized that nagging wasn't doing anything to change my mind. They were too emotionally involved to give good advice, so they'd chosen to take a step back and let me figure it all out on my own.

Tanner and I knew the merit of confronting a fellow believer about their sin. Jesus said in Matthew 18 that,

> If another believer sins against you, go privately and point out the offense. If the other person listens and confesses it, you have won that person back. But if you are unsuccessful, take one or two others with you and go back again, so that everything you say may be confirmed by two or three witnesses. If the person still refuses to listen, take your case to the church. Then if he or she won't accept the church's decision, treat that person as a pagan or a corrupt tax collector.

We had studied this verse intently the first few days after Delilah's outburst, trying to figure out what to do. We came to the conclusion that perhaps Greg's hesitance to confront Delilah about the way she was handling her grief didn't fit into the same classification. Yes, Delilah was hurting her family by choosing to stay in bed all day and not taking care of them as she should be, and, yes, as the spiritual leader of the family, Greg should be stepping up and confronting his wife. But I had already gone to Delilah to try and get her to see the damage she was doing, and it hadn't done any good. We didn't think bombarding them with more people would help either, not when Delilah was so fragile.

It was messy. We fretted about our decision for weeks. We missed our friends, and we were scared that we were making the wrong decision. Still, we had offered to Greg that he come to us if things got worse, and he never called. We would be there for them in the blink of an eye if Greg thought it necessary, but in the meantime, we stepped back, prayed for them all the time, and waited to see what God would do.

This was easier for Tanner, because he wasn't as close to Delilah, or even Greg, as I was. When Tanner and I had gotten married and moved here permanently, he'd fit in with the three of us right away; he and Greg were getting to be very close. But he was still in the newness stage of the friendship, and he was able to more logically look at the situation than I was. I worried about Delilah constantly because I knew how confusing and lonely it can be after pregnancy loss happens. But I was still angry at her for so callously throwing the abortion in my face and claiming that the pain I'd felt from that—the pain I *still* felt from that—couldn't compare to the pain of losing a child from miscarriage. Even as we prayed for healing, I struggled with my anger, and a part of me felt that she deserved to suffer for being so heartless. At the same time that I was missing her, I was breathing a sigh of relief that Greg hadn't called us in to help him.

The miscarriage had made things awkward for our small group Bible study, which is why Ruth was here this morning. She had been texting me throughout the summer asking when the next small group meeting was, and I kept telling her that I'd get back to her, that things between Delilah and I were tense, and that Greg and Delilah were still trying to regroup after the miscarriage. As the weeks rolled by, she got concerned, so I finally invited her over to explain the situation to her. After a cup of coffee and polite small talk, I figured it was time to be honest with my new friend.

I explained to her that Delilah and Greg had been waiting and waiting to have a baby, which is why Jonas was so special to them and why the miscarriage was affecting them the way it was. She nodded politely as I went on to describe the afternoon that I'd approached Delilah about her behavior, being careful not to go into deep detail about how cruel she'd been to me. My goal with this meeting wasn't to badmouth Delilah but to simply fill Ruth in on the situation.

"I'm so sorry I didn't call you and invite you over earlier. It's just been a really confusing, sad few months. I guess Tanner and I didn't even realize how beneficial it would have been to share this with you two and be praying together," I admitted.

She waved her hand dismissively. "Don't worry about it. It can be hard at the beginning of a friendship to know how to deal with heavy stuff like this. I kinda pieced together that Delilah wasn't doing well because she stopped coming to church. How's she doing now? I saw her at the school this morning dropping off Mandy and Luke—she looked okay to me."

Today was the first day of public school—Mandy's first day of kindergarten. I was a bit sad that Delilah and I hadn't reconciled yet, because we'd planned back in May to drop Mandy off together. She was special to me, because for a while, I had thought that I would be her mother one day, back when Greg and I had briefly dated. I was glad that she'd been able to pull herself together enough to drop Mandy off for her first day, and from Ruth's description, Delilah hadn't looked like a wreck and drawn attention to herself.

Ruth had dropped off her two boys—Derrick, who was going into second grade, and Carson, who was also going into kindergarten—off at school and then had come over here with her youngest, Anna. Anna was two years old and the perfect playmate for Elysa, and the two of them were happily playing with the play kitchen set in the living room as Ruth and I sat and talked.

"I haven't heard from her since that day, actually," I admitted sadly. "We've been in contact with Greg, letting him know that we're here if he needs us, but he hasn't called us either. It's been a lonely summer," I said, my throat closing up and tears threatening to spill onto my cheeks. Ruth reached across the table and squeezed my arm supportively.

"She'll come around," Ruth assured. "Honestly, when I saw her this morning, I didn't see a woman on the verge of losing it. She looks like she's handling it. Wouldn't surprise me if she reached out to you soon."

I nodded and sniffed. "Do you think we did the right thing? By stepping back and letting Greg handle it?" I asked.

She raised her shoulders. "I don't know. Stuff like this isn't easy. I'm not sure what I would have done. Greg hasn't called you, so I guess we shouldn't be too worried. Not much of a help, am I?" she said with a laugh.

I shrugged. "It's tough," I admitted, sniffing again and trying to keep the tears from falling. "I just really miss her."

"I'm here if you need to vent, Molly. Back in Wisconsin, I had a really complicated group of friends, and sometimes the best therapy is to just get it all off your chest. I won't judge you, I promise," she teased, although behind the laughter, there was seriousness—as a Christian, it felt so wrong to talk about a friend behind her back. At the same time, bottling it all up wasn't helping me either, and perhaps by letting Ruth into my situation, she'd be able to offer up godly advice and wisdom. After all, she wasn't involved emotionally like Tanner and I were. I'd just have to be extra careful to not let this turn into gossip and slander—but sharing my honest hurts and questions would probably be healthy.

In that moment, I felt the relationship between Ruth and I change. We went from being casual, polite "just barely know each other" friends to "I can be totally honest and open with you" friends, and I loved it. For five years, Delilah had been my one and only friend; it felt wonderful to have gained another soul with which to share life's joys and hardships with.

I hung my head and whispered, "You have no idea how much it hurt to have your best friend hurl something so painful right in your face." I had shared my testimony with our Bible study so Ruth knew all about the abortion. "I mean, Delilah and I have been talking about our pasts together for so long, and she's never, not once, told me I had no right to be sad about what I'd done. She's always been so supportive and understanding…I don't know why she did that."

Ruth nodded. "Like I said, I had a really complicated friend group back in Wisconsin." She and Joey had moved down to Kansas earlier this year when Joey got a new job. "It was a poisonous group, really—if one girl ever did something to offend another, and believe me, this group was dramatic enough to find offense in literally everything—it was a bloodbath. The girl who committed the act would be shunned while the rest of us rallied around the attacked, and I honestly didn't think anything was wrong with that. Until it happened to me. I don't even remember what I did—probably said something about someone's kid and didn't realize it. Anyway, I found myself shunned and was heartbroken. I got nasty messages from the other girls, telling me how heartless and mean I was and that I needed to work on the sin in my life if I wanted to ever be a part of the group again. I was desperate for their friendship, though, as they were my only friends and we'd been together for years, so I apologized for whatever it was I did and they let me in again. It went on and on like this, every girl got her turn as the outcast. But after it happened to me, I just didn't feel okay with it anymore, and I left. I get it, Molly. I do. I probably wasn't hurt as deeply as you were, but I still get it."

I shook my head and said with a laugh, "Why are girls so mean?"

Ruth laughed as well. "No clue. One of life's greatest mysteries, I suppose."

"It just bums me out because our relationship hasn't ever been like what you just described, you know?" I said sadly. "From the very beginning, Delilah and I clicked because we had gone through so much of the same stuff. We've had only a handful of fights, and even during those times, it never lasted more than a few days. I don't know what to do!"

Ruth fell quiet, fiddling with the handle of her coffee mug. "Have you tried reaching out to her? Maybe apologizing?" she asked boldly.

I licked my lips, suddenly nervous. One thing that comes from a close friendship is the ability to push and challenge each other, sometimes confronting them even if it hurts the other's feelings. I knew she was right. I had hurt Delilah too, by being too quick to take offense to her words and not being sensitive to the fact that she was hurting deeply—so much—that she hadn't been able to control what had come out of her mouth, which she no doubt later regretted. I'd then walked out and slammed the door, not once thinking that those actions could have hurt her just as badly as she'd hurt me. It had never crossed my mind that I might have to be the first one to reach out, to swallow my pride and offer up an apology.

"No," I admitted sheepishly. "Hadn't even crossed my mind, actually." Shame was making my face red and hot.

"I know it's not what you want to do. I think you have every right to be mad at her, Molly. But you're also her best friend, and she probably misses you and needs you."

I hadn't thought of that either. All summer I'd been convinced that since she hadn't come to me with an apology, she truly didn't need me. But maybe, just like me, she was letting stubborn pride get in the way of the special relationship that we shared. Maybe the best thing I could do for her was to put the anger and bitterness aside and go to her, try again to comfort her and ask for her forgiveness. If she rejected me again, I'd continue praying for her and give her space, but I wouldn't sit around feeling sorry for myself.

Later that night, after dinner, baths, and bedtime stories, Tanner and I sat snuggled together on the couch, a cheesy sitcom playing softly in the background. Out of nowhere, he looked over to me and said, "Ya know, I've been thinking that maybe it's time for us to reach out to Greg and Delilah. It's been weeks! I'm getting worried."

I laughed softly. "I was thinking the same thing this morning. Actually, Ruth got me thinking about it. She suggested that maybe I'm the one who is supposed to apologize to Delilah. I've been sitting here feeling sorry for myself, waiting for her apology, but I've hurt her too. She might still be too consumed by grief to be able to see her wrongdoing, but I'm not."

Tanner nodded. "Good point. I agree with her. Been thinking the same, just didn't know how you'd respond if I suggested that you apologize first. You think you're gonna do it?"

I nodded. "Yeah, I do. It's definitely not gonna be easy. But I think it will really help Delilah. We've always been able to help each other work through everything—I think if we find a way to get past what happened back in July, we could do the same again."

Tanner gave my hand a gentle squeeze, then dropped a light kiss on my forehead. "I think you're right. Proud of you, Molly girl," he said, making my tummy squeeze in happiness at the use of my old nickname. I was so grateful for Tanner, for his quiet strength and wisdom in the middle of chaos. I imagined trying to deal with this without him, and I winced. If things hadn't turned out the way they did, Tanner would still be living back in Iowa with his wife Leah, happily raising Elysa with her, probably another baby by now too. I wouldn't want to face the messiness of life with any other person.

I planned on calling Delilah the next morning and went to bed excited. I woke up, however, with panic and dread churning in my stomach. This could potentially go very, very wrong. Maybe she'd screen my call and not even answer. Or maybe she'd pick up and scream at me to leave her alone forever. Scenario after awful scenario ran through my mind, and I almost chickened out. Tanner took the time before leaving for his office to hold my hands while he prayed over me, however, and that gave me the courage I needed to pick up the phone, dial Delilah's familiar number, and hold my breath while the phone rang and rang and rang. My heart pounded and my palms were clammy with sweat. Finally though, she picked up.

"Oh, Molly, I'm so, so, *so* sorry!"

Healing balm to my aching, cracked soul.

9

Molly

September

All I could do was cry. I had waited and waited for Delilah to call me and apologize, when all along I could have simply picked up the phone and this could have happened weeks ago. How had I ever thought that things might be over for us forever?

Elysa came running over to me when she heard me crying, and she clung to my leg in fear. I could hear Delilah crying as well, and I let out a sad laugh. "Elysa's freaking out," I explained to her. "This girl can smell sadness, I swear. You wanna come over?" I asked, the once familiar question now sounded so foreign on my lips, but I was never happier to have asked her this.

"Of course I do," she said through a hard sniff. "Don't have any kids to wrestle into the car now that Mandy is in school. Be over in five minutes."

She made good on her word, and in five minutes, she was bursting through my front door and flying into my arms. We held each other and rocked back and forth for the longest time, crying and mumbling apologies and soaking each other's shoulders with tears. This time apart had been one of the most difficult periods in my life, and considering all that I'd been through, it meant that Delilah was more than just a friend to me. She was a sister, and not just a sister, but a sister in Christ—one who had seen me through darkness and despair and who had been fiercely loyal for so long. Even though for a time we had let stubborn pride wreak havoc on our relationship, we were able to reunite joyously and with forgiveness in our hearts, ready to pick up where we left off and get back to what we were best at—helping each other heal.

When we finally pulled back, Delilah smiled and admitted, "I was literally going to call you just minutes after you did—I was finishing up loading the dishwasher, that's why it took me so long to pick up. I had some nasty gunk on my hands."

I laughed, savoring how good it felt to laugh once again with my dearest friend. "Coffee's brewing as we speak," I said, leading her to the kitchen. She picked up nine-month-old Elliot on her way, who was just now learning to sit up on her own. Babies with Down syndrome reach developmental milestones later than other babies do, so even though most babies were crawling and getting into everything by now, we were celebrating this milestone with just as much enthusiasm as if she'd done it months before. I was a bit shocked to see Delilah pick up my baby and snuggle her close after struggling with her son's death for the last two months. After my abortion, I had avoided babies like they held some kind of transferable disease, too afraid that the guilt and sorrow of aborting my child would overwhelm me. I figured Delilah would feel the same and steer clear of my little ones, but Elliot didn't seem to faze Delilah even the slightest. They were pretty good buds, I supposed, as Delilah had watched Elliot for me while I went to school last year. For a while, I worried about where to send the girls when classes started up next week, but I decided to wait to ask Delilah if she'd be up for that again until I knew for sure that she was doing okay.

We settled into the bar stools at my long kitchen counter, enjoying the rich aroma of the coffee and content in being in each other's presence once again. Delilah closed her eyes and breathed in deeply the scent of Elliot's sweet baby smell, sending her smile wobbling. This morning's conversation was going to be difficult, no doubt about it. I would be careful in how I related to Delilah, not wanting her to think that by bringing up the abortion I was trying to steal her attention or play down her sadness in any way. Although I knew exactly what she was feeling because I had experienced it myself, I wanted Delilah to feel comfortable just spilling everything to me. So I waited, even though it broke my heart to see her in so much pain. I so badly wanted to jump in and comfort her, let her know I knew just how she felt, but I bit my tongue.

For a while, silent tears coursed down her cheeks, and she struggled to catch her breath. I sucked my lower lip into my mouth and bit down hard—seeing Delilah like this was killing me. I had never seen her so broken. I closed my eyes and imagined what it must have been like the day Delilah had almost taken her own life; she had struggled so much while she was pregnant with Luke, and I wondered if she had cried like this back then. It didn't seem fair that someone could suffer so much in one lifetime.

She finally let out a long, shaky breath. "I don't get it, Molly. Greg and I waited and waited. For years, the only thing we asked God for was a baby. So why, when he finally decides to give us one, does he take it away?" she sobbed. At this point, Elliot was looking up at Delilah with fear in her eyes, and I reached over to take her from Delilah. She gave her to me willingly, putting her head into her now free hands and letting the sobs escape. I soothed Elliot while Delilah composed herself, the sobs eventually melting into hiccups. When she looked up at me, her eyes were red and puffy, and her face was about the same. She looked awful.

"I'm so sorry, hun," I offered softly. "I don't have any answers for you."

She swallowed and nodded. "I don't know what to do...how to move on. I haven't prayed since the day he died. I'm so mad at God that the thought of praying makes me want to be sick," she admitted, shame coloring her cheeks. "I hate that! I didn't even feel this way when I got pregnant with Luke! I mean, the situations are so different because I had been foolish with David all those years ago, but I know God could have prevented my pregnancy. My life could be so different right now, but this is the path he's led me down. Why?" She was not really expecting me to answer. "Why does it feel like God is punishing me for the mistakes I made over a decade ago?"

I took a moment before answering, knowing how fragile Delilah was right now. "Honey, we've talked about this a lot. You know Luke wasn't a punishment. God isn't like that. You know what our true punishment is, and how Jesus took that punishment with his death and resurrection. I know you know that."

She heaved a sigh. "Of course I know that. But it *feels* like God is punishing me! He seems like such a distant being right now. I don't feel any comfort or peace. Like I said, the thought of praying to him makes me sick. And it makes me feel guilty, as if I don't feel guilty enough already from miscarrying. I know it wasn't my fault, that I was doing everything right. But you know how I am! Always thinking of the what ifs. I can't help but think I'm somehow responsible for his death—that I could have saved him by doing things differently," she said with desperation, her words coming out in a fast, confusing jumble. "I'm scared, Molly. What must God think of me? Blaming him for taking my child from me, being so angry at him I can barely utter his name? I just...I feel so unworthy."

Even though my arms were full of Elliot, I leaned over and pulled Delilah into a hug, and she threw her arms around my neck. "How do I fix this?" she asked, leaning back into her chair. I got up to put Elliot back into her playpen and checked on Elysa, then returned when both seemed to be playing happily. I wanted to focus all my attention on my sweet friend.

"You can't," I said matter-of-factly. Delilah let out a puff of breath, sending her bangs flying.

She let her head fall back. "I knew you would say that. And I know you're right. I just…" She stared out the sliding glass door into my backyard. She turned back at me with a sad smile tugging at the corner of her lips. "I don't know if I can trust God anymore. Not after all he's led me through. What if he keeps leading me into these awful storms?" she asked with wide, scared eyes. "I don't know how much more of this I can take."

"I've been there," I offered, hoping that she wouldn't stiffen up and shut me out. "Trust me, I've been there. And as much as I hate to say it, Lilah, he just *might* keep leading you into storms. He did it to me. His plans are not always what we expect or want. But I have to believe that he has the ending all written out—that he has a plan that's shaping us into exactly the kind of people he wants us to be. The key to dealing with this, honey, isn't to overcome it all at once. That's impossible. Just take one step at a time. Celebrate the small successes. And right now, even though you feel like you can't go to God with this, know that for weeks, I've been lifting you up to God's throne," I said with a smile and a reassuring squeeze to her arm. "Tanner and I haven't stopped praying. Neither has Greg, I'm sure, and I know your mom has been too. You're not alone, sweetie. We want to help you."

She nodded and fiddled with her wedding ring, trying to keep herself composed. She looked up at me with gratitude and whispered, "I don't deserve you."

I melted, but guilt pricked at my heart. I wasn't a saint in this situation—for while I had lifted Delilah up in prayer with Tanner for all these weeks, I had also wrestled with bitterness and hate. I realized that I hadn't even apologized to Delilah for not being more understanding and for simply giving up on her and slamming the door, not bothering to check up on her and help her deal with the ever rising waters of her life. I took her hands in mine and looked her straight in the eyes. "I'm sorry, Delilah. I should have been able to see that your outburst was coming from a place of deep sorrow. I of all people know firsthand the bitterness that can take root in your heart after something like this happens. I should have never left that day. I shouldn't have slammed the door and never looked back. I should have called you and checked up on you. Instead, I let myself feel like a victim and expected you to come crawling back to me. That wasn't right, and I'm sorry. Do you forgive me?"

She looked slightly taken aback, but then she smiled—a true, deep, genuine Delilah smile. "Of course I do, silly goose," she said, poking the ticklish spot on my middle that she was so good at finding, sending me giggling.

Funny how a cup of coffee can change things so quickly.

Delilah's journey to healing was only beginning, however. This morning of coffee and conversation had been a good start, but the demons would continue to bombard Delilah day and night. This time, though, I was there for her—like I should have been there for her back in July. She was still in a very dark place, and I didn't feel that it was right to ask her to watch the girls for me while I went to school, but Ruth graciously stepped in and took them into her full, happy house. Life fell back into its normal chaotic rhythm, with school, the girls, my marriage, household duties, and caring for Delilah demanding all my attention. After five years of working in the diner with Mary Beth, I finally had to leave, as much as it killed me to do so. I had grown so attached to the cozy little restaurant, with all its craziness. It's where I had been found, where I had stopped running away from God. It's where I had found a second mother in Mary Beth as we rolled out pie crusts and chopped up vegetables for her killer homemade chicken noodle soup. It's where I had gleaned so many priceless lessons from our dearly missed friend, Albert, over cups of coffee during breaks. The diner was truly a second home for me, and quitting my job was much more difficult than I had ever expected.

Mary Beth pulled me into a tight hug the day I went in to tell her to take me off the schedule. "I'm gonna miss you so much, sweet girl. But don't think I'm taking your name off payroll just yet. You ever want to come back here, you just walk in and grab an apron. I won't stop ya," she said, tweaking my nose. Mary Beth was so good at making me feel like a twelve-year-old, but I just laughed.

"All right, you silly thing," I teased. "You sure you can spare me?"

"Psh," she spat, flapping her dish towel at me. "Thanks to your constant nagging, I have more staff now than I know what to do with! Although no one will be able to replace you, I think we'll be able to manage."

"Good," I replied. "How is Chelsea doing?"

"She's doing all right. Still as sassy as ever, but since that night with those horrid boys, she hasn't been as sassy to me. Think she finally realized just how much I care," Mary Beth answered with a quaver in her voice. It was evident that Mary Beth cared deeply for all three teenage girls we'd hired on after Albert's death, but she cared especially for Chelsea. Believe it or not, the sweet, honest, Jesus-loving Mary Beth used to be a wild, rebellious, angry teenager just like Chelsea was, and she could relate to her more than Chelsea would ever know. The three girls were making my decision to leave extra hard.

"Ya know," I said thoughtfully, "maybe it's a good idea to keep me on payroll. I want to keep up with the girls. Think you could squeeze me in for a few Saturday shifts every now and then?"

She wrinkled her nose and pretended to be deep in thought. "Gosh, that might be tough," she answered, trying hard to keep the smile from overtaking her face. "I'll see what I can do, honey. Don't get your hopes up." I gave her a playful swat. She pulled me into another hug before I was allowed to leave, and I promised to bring the girls and Tanner in soon to visit her.

I left with a pit forming in the bottom of my stomach. Who would have thought that leaving such a low-paying, physically exhaustive job would be so difficult? I had a beautiful family waiting for me at home, needing me, but a part of my heart would always remain back in the cozy walls of Mary Beth's diner. I would cherish the lessons I'd learned there and keep the warm memories of falling in love with my life here close at hand. The fact that Mary Beth was willing to let me come back anytime I wanted gave me peace.

I thought that cutting at least one slice of craziness out of my life would calm things down a bit, but suddenly I found myself trying to stay afloat in the rising floodwaters. This semester of school was proving to be much more difficult than I imagined it to be, and I was weighed down by my heavy course load—I was still only going to school part time, but the classes I was currently enrolled in were the heart of my psychology major. Large projects and hefty papers overtook my life, and deep circles grew under my eyes from late nights up perfecting my assignments. Last year, my full days with the girls had been just as busy as school days, and I had no idea things could get worse. I felt like I was always stumbling around like a zombie from lack of sleep—some days, I literally could not remember a single detail about what had gone on. The days all blurred together, but somewhere within all this madness, I made time to minister to Delilah, who was battling her demons harder now than ever. Every other week, we took Elliot and Elysa out in the stroller for a walk around town to chat about her healing, but as the weeks went on, I felt myself growing weaker and weaker.

Meeting the newest member of our little community was the last thing I had needed on a chilly October day out with Delilah and the girls. Delilah had offered to push the stroller, finally noticing for the first time how exhausted I was. She even offered to turn around and let me take a nap, but I waved her off. Looking back, I wish I had taken her up on that offer, because then we might have avoided meeting Cassidy, at least for a few weeks. She ended up making our church her home church and grating on my nerves every chance she got, and this first encounter had foreshadowed our rocky relationship almost perfectly.

Delilah and I didn't notice her until she was right in front of us. All of a sudden, there she was—all six feet two inches of her, with insanely long, smooth brown hair flowing out of the knit cap protecting her ears. She looked modern and stylish; she was dressed in dark wash jeans with fashionable purple walking shoes peeping out from the slight flare, a tight pink exercise shirt and matching jacket. Her blue eyes were large and crystal clear, and her cheeks were flushed from the cold. She made Delilah and me, who were both dressed in baggy sweatpants, T-shirts, and old sweaters look frumpy and much older than we actually were.

"Well hello there!" she boomed. "My name's Cassidy Wilson, just moved here with my husband and little girl a few weeks ago." A tiny little girl emerged from behind her mother; we hadn't even noticed her because of her mother's flashy outfit and large, equally as flashy personality. She had a distinctive southern twang; they had clearly moved up here from somewhere down south. She stuck out both hands at once for us to shake, and Delilah and I shot stunned glances at each other while we awkwardly shook her hands at the same time. "This here is my little girl, Addison Claire. Say hello to the nice ladies, Addie!" Literally every word that came out of this woman's mouth was loud.

Addison timidly moved forward and very politely mumbled, "How do you do?" as she shook our hands.

Cassidy clucked her tongue and shook her head, scrunching her mouth into a scowl. "Sorry about that. She's usually not so rude to strangers. She's still a little upset about the move up here. Our whole family's back down in Texas. Had to leave behind her grandmamma, and she ain't too happy 'bout it, are ya darlin'?"

Delilah and I again exchanged flabbergasted looks. If shaking two complete strangers' hands and asking, "How do you do?" was considered rude to this lady, I wondered how *actual* rudeness would cause her to respond.

"Oh!" she exclaimed, seeming to notice my own children for the first time since our sudden encounter. "Just look at these two cuties!" She leaned forward for a closer look. I pushed back the sun visor protecting Elliot's face, and when Cassidy got a good look at her, she jerked back. "Oh my." The first normal-volume words she'd spoken yet. "Oh my. Something's wrong with your little girl."

"Excuse me?" I asked, shocked. No one had ever said anything about Elliot's appearance before. Kids at the supermarket would sometimes pull at their mother's sleeves and ask why she looked different than other kids, but I never let that bother me too much. As kids, they were just curious and didn't know any better. I expected adults to have a little more tact than this woman was demonstrating.

She shrugged. "Oh, well you know what I mean. She's retarded. A Down's baby, right? I can tell by her eyes, her chubby face."

Delilah and I froze in shock. There are a few things you never *ever* say to a parent of a child with Down syndrome, and this woman, whom we had just met, had said pretty much all of them. My baby wasn't *retarded*; that was such a foul, insulting term to use. She was developmentally delayed, yes, but she wasn't retarded. And Elliot wasn't a Down's baby—she was a baby *with* Down syndrome—her diagnoses didn't define who she was. It was a condition she lived with, but it wasn't her identity.

For a few awkward moments, the woman just stared at us with huge, expectant eyes. "Am I right?" she finally asked.

"Yes, Elliot has Down syndrome," was all I could reply.

She clucked again, violently shaking her head. "You poor thing. No one deserves that. I'm so sorry, honey."

I could no longer disguise how much this woman disgusted me. I openly looked over to Delilah who had horror written all over her face. Before I could return to face the woman and spit something nasty at her that I would later regret, Delilah jumped in. "Excuse us, we really must be on our way home. Time for the kids to go down for a nap. Bye." With that, she whipped the stroller around and quickly started walking away, leaving me standing in shock with my mouth hanging wide open. I snapped out of my shock and turned around without saying a word, leaving Cassidy and Addison standing alone in their ignorant confusion.

"Wait!" Cassidy called out. "Was it something I said?" Neither of us said anything. "It was nice to meet you!" I peeked behind my shoulder to see Cassidy jumping up and down and waving both of her arms good-bye. Did she always use both hands out of place like that, I wondered?

Once we were back in the safety of my own house, I sat down on the couch, numb. Delilah unloaded the girls and checked their diapers, letting Elysa run off to pull out her toys and spreading Elliot's changing mat down on the floor to take care of her dirty diaper. I looked at her with wondering eyes. "I had no idea those kinds of people existed in the world," I finally said. "How could someone be so incredibly heartless and cruel?"

Delilah shook her head. "No idea. I mean, look at this little cutie," she cooed, picking a freshly changed Elliot up and snuggling her close. "How can you look into this sweet little face and see anything other than beauty?"

I smiled at my best friend, beyond grateful that she had been with me during this strange encounter. Who knows what I would have said if Delilah hadn't stepped in and removed us from the situation? When it comes to my kids—especially Elliot—I was extremely protective. No one says the harsh, cruel words that Cassidy had and got away with it!

"The weirdest part was," Delilah went on, "she didn't even seem to realize how rude she was being. Did you notice that?"

"Yes!" I exclaimed, growing angrier and angrier by the second. "I'd like to meet her mother and shake some sense into that woman!"

"Tell me about it," Delilah said with a firm nod. "If I ever said anything like that as a kid or even now, my mother would *pummel* me!"

I laughed, knowing that without a doubt Mary Beth would do just that. She was full of fire, that one was. When we told her about the encounter later on, the flames ignited in her eyes, and she shook her head in rage.

"The nerve!" she seethed through clenched teeth. "You poor, sweet girl." She pulled me into a famous Mary Beth hug. "You know that every single word she said wasn't true, right?"

"Of course," I reassured her. While each and every day raising a special needs child was a struggle, I knew the worth of Elliot's life. I knew she was more than her diagnosis. I was having a hard time coming to grips with the fact that not everyone in the world knew those same truths, though.

And while I tried to put the whole encounter behind and forget about loud-mouthed Cassidy and her "rude" daughter altogether, the woman was making that extremely difficult. Suddenly, she was everywhere—walking past my house every day, eating at Mary Beth's just a table across from me, and even showing up at my church and joining my Sunday school class! I couldn't escape her, and I had no idea just how much of a run for my money she was about to give me.

10

Molly

October

"There she is again!" I screeched like some paranoid stalker. "I'm telling you, Tanner, she walks past our house every single day—sometimes *twice* a day!" I let the curtain fall back into place and began to turn away but then leaned back in and craned my neck to see Cassidy scurrying on her way. "And she always looks so perfect!" Was she doing this just to make me angry?

Tanner came waltzing into the room, swaying to some oldies tune. He was slightly obsessed with music from the 1960s and 1970s; we had stacks of CDs from artists like the Temptations, the Manhattans, the Commodores, and many others that I couldn't name. Tanner always had them playing softly in the background of our home, and he'd waltz around the house singing to me and the girls, and he'd really put on a show when any of us was upset.

"Honey, you are my shining star, don't you go away, oh baby," he crooned. This was one of his favorites—"Shining Star," by the Manhattans. He took me in his arms and pulled me close, nuzzling my neck. "I wanna be, right here where you are, 'til my dying day, yeah baby." I smiled and let my head fall back in carefree laughter, savoring how it felt to be safe and secure in Tanner's arms. Elysa and Elliot smiled from where they sat on the floor with their toys.

"Mama and Dada dancing!" Elysa yelled, clapping her chubby hands together in delight.

We continued swirling around our makeshift dance floor, stepping over toys and books as we swayed to the smooth voices of the Manhattans. When the song ended, Tanner pulled me into a kiss that sent a zing of energy up my spine and caused my breath to catch in my throat. "Don't let this lady get to you, my love," he whispered. "Nothing she can say will change the fact that we love Elliot just as she is. Let this one roll off your shoulders."

For a split second, I wanted to accuse Tanner of not caring enough about Elliot. A part of me wanted him to be just as fuming mad as I was at this bold woman. When I had told Tanner what she'd said, I saw a flash of anger in his eyes and he tensed up. But as a man, he was able to look at the situation differently than me—I viewed the situation through an emotional lens, Tanner viewed it through a more logical lens, and he was able to better see that it wasn't worth it to get so worked up over it. Yes, it upset him that ignorant people would make rude, insensitive comments about his daughter, but he was choosing not to let anger get the best of him. Tanner was confident about the love we gave Elliot, knowing that with our full support she would be able to come home to the safety of our arms when this happened to her in the future—which it no doubt would. I was working on doing the same.

The weeks rolled on, and other than the daily speed walk by my house in her sporty little outfits and perfect hair and makeup, I didn't see much of Cassidy or her daughter. In order to regain a bit of my sanity, I kept the curtains closed on the big picture window; I didn't need to work through a panic attack every day from seeing her walk by. That worked well, and I felt myself regaining more control. Slowly I was able to forget about the incident and refocus on my busy life.

After an incredibly busy October—I had tons of major papers and projects due that month—I breathed a sigh of relief. A night out trick-or-treating with my little goblins was just what I needed. Tanner and I met up with Delilah, Greg, Ruth, and Joey and lined up all the kiddos for a group photo, and then headed out for a night of fun. Elysa was dressed up as kitten, and Elliot was dressed up in a fluffy turtle costume. It was hilarious to watch her try and make sense of the costume—she spent most of the night pulling on the little green head covering and glancing over her shoulder trying to figure out what was on her back. Elysa and the rest of the older kids ran ahead of us, their laughter echoing back to their watchful parents. Halloween in Green Lake is an absolute blast—the town is small enough that you can hit almost every neighborhood and say hello to just about everyone. There was also a Halloween event going on at the church, which is where I'd met Delilah five years ago.

Delilah had been twenty-one at the time, and Luke had been a tiny five-year-old dressed up as a pirate. Mary Beth had been hounding me for weeks to go to church with her, and when I kept refusing, she got creative and invited me to the Halloween party at the church. With no good excuse not to go, I went, and I would forever cherish the first time I met Delilah and Luke. We made a point to stop back there every year and reminisce, grateful at how far we had come and praising God for all the good things he had done for us in the last five years.

I was too busy trying to get Elliot situated in her stroller when we first walked into the church, so I didn't notice that everyone in our group had grown silent. When I finally got Elliot all snuggled in and stood up, I realized everyone was staring at me. "What?" I asked. And then I saw her—Cassidy, dressed up as a 1920s Flapper girl, running the cake walk in the center of the game booths.

"What's she doing here?" I asked. "Who let her in here?"

"Molly!" Tanner scolded, grabbing my arm. "She's not a criminal. Anyone can volunteer to run a game station."

"I know that," I snapped, yanking my arm free and adjusting my sweater. "I just...It surprised me, is all."

"You gonna be okay?" Delilah asked.

I nodded, embarrassed by the scene Tanner and I had just made. "What booth is your mom running?" I asked, trying to change the subject and redirect the focus off of me. "We can say a quick hello, send the kids through a few games, and get outta here. It's getting late anyway." I pretended bedtime was the reason I wanted to hightail it out of here. Everyone played along nicely and murmured their agreement that bedtime was drawing closer and closer and that we probably shouldn't stay long. We managed to maneuver past Cassidy and found Mary Beth running the ring toss both. She gushed over the kids' cute costumes and let them all play the game until they won a prize. After that, we wandered around for a bit, greeting friends from church, and when I thought the coast was clear, I motioned for the door. We were five feet from the door when she ambushed us.

"Well hello, everyone! Don't we all just look too cute for words tonight? I could just about eat you all up!" Cassidy declared loudly, and Ruth's two boys, Derrick and Carson, looked at their mom with wide, horrified eyes. The woman's personality was absolutely overwhelming—even kids could sense that her boldness was a little out of place.

I forced a smile and said, "Hi, Cassidy. We're just on our way home. Time for bed, right, everyone?" I asked, to which the group nodded and agreed.

She waved her hands dismissively. "Oh, of course. I'm letting Addison stay up tonight. Don't wanna ruin her fun by making her go home to bed. She's over at the Pin the Smile on the Jack-O-Lantern booth with my husband, whom I don't think you've met yet, have you?" she asked with a bit of sass, and I had to work very hard at not rolling my eyes. "But of course you have little ones. I think Addison is old enough to stay up late tonight—she's three, did I tell you that?" She kept jabbering on and on. "Look at me, holding all of you up. Go ahead, I'll see you soon!"

I turned around and breathed a sigh of relief that she hadn't made any comments about Elliot, but Cassidy wasn't quite through yet. She came closer to get a good look at all the kids and to tell them how cute they looked. When she got to Elliot, she did her annoying tongue cluck and shook her head. "So sorry, honey. It's just too bad, really. Poor thing."

I sucked in my lower lip, and Tanner moved in to pull me away. "We really should be going now," he said before I could let my anger speak for me. "Nice to meet you, Cassidy." He then ushered me out the front door.

The blast of cool air that hit my cheeks when I stepped outside was just what I needed to simmer down from my most recent encounter with Cassidy. "Breathe, just breathe," Tanner whispered into my ear. "She's not worth getting worked up about, okay? Forgive and forget. You have enough on your plate already to let this eat you up inside."

I let the tears fall. "You don't understand, Tanner. I'm her *mom*. Protecting her is my job. I hate that this woman thinks she can say such horrible things about my baby right in front of my face! She needs to be stopped!"

He grasped my shoulders in his hands and gently shook me so that I was looking into his eyes. "Hey," he answered gently. "I *do* understand. While I might not show it like you do, what Cassidy says about Elliot drives me just as crazy as it drives you. You have to realize, though, that people like her have been taught to think this way for their whole lives—I doubt that confronting her would do anything, expect make you even angrier. Like I said, she's not worth it, okay?"

I didn't agree. I still thought that somebody needed to tell her to knock it off, but I wasn't about to argue with Tanner in public. So I simply wiped the tears from my eyes, took the stroller from Delilah, hugged her and Ruth good-bye, and settled my kids into their car seats. I didn't say much on the way home, and the quiet drive through the sleepy streets of Green Lake was actually helping to calm me down. By the time we pulled into the driveway a few minutes later, I could tell that my heart rate had returned to normal and my hands were no longer clenched into angry fists.

Was Tanner right? Were people like Cassidy taught to be this ignorant? The idea made sense—when little kids made remarks about Elliot, their parents would always pull them aside and explain to them why it was wrong to say such things. As kids, they honestly didn't know any better, and they needed to be taught what was and was not socially acceptable to say. What had happened to Cassidy? Had no one ever taught her that God creates some of us differently than what the world sees as normal? Did anyone ever tell her, "If you don't have anything nice to say, don't say anything at all?" Perhaps she'd grown up around parents who talked about people like Elliot the way she was doing now.

Still. That didn't excuse her bad behavior. What she was doing was wrong and hurtful, and even *if* she had grown up thinking it was okay to make such remarks, she could still be taught otherwise. She could learn to better keep people's feelings in mind; learn how to sensor her thoughts. Maybe because I was so emotionally involved I shouldn't be the one to teach her those lessons, but surely *someone* could, right?

I tried my hardest to keep following Tanner's advice—to let her insensitivity roll off my shoulders, to forgive and forget. But gosh, she was making it hard. The Sunday after Halloween, not only did she attend the church service but she was also in our Sunday school class! I selfishly crossed my fingers and hoped she would move on and decide not to make our church her home church, but she continued showing up week after week. She was invading every area of my life, and there wasn't a thing I could do about it but bite my tongue and keep Elliot as far away from her as I could. When she started volunteering in the nursery, I pulled Elliot out and made the best of her squirming and loud babbling. Most Sundays, I would end up leaving the service to walk around with her, and Tanner would raise his eyebrows and shake his head when we got up to leave. He still thought I was overreacting, but it really was for the best.

"If I let her be in the nursery with that woman, I'll just get worked up. I'm trying *not* to let her get to me—keeping her away from Elliot is helping me do that," I explained, trying to get him to see that I wasn't being unreasonable but that I was working to follow his advice.

"You can't hide Elliot away from the world forever, Molly. The world is full of insensitive people like Cassidy, and Elliot has to learn how to face those people," he countered.

"She's still a baby," I argued. "She doesn't have to face people yet. When she's old enough to do so, I'll try my hardest to let go. But right now, I'm going to protect her—and myself—from Cassidy, okay? I get that you don't agree with me, but pressuring me like this isn't helping."

He sighed and rubbed his neck, struggling with what to say. "All right. I see your point. Right now, it probably isn't doing any harm to keep her away from Cassidy. But I'm serious about Elliot learning to face people. When she gets older, she'll need us to help her learn what to say and how to react when people say mean things to her, not hide her away."

"I know that," I said, trying to keep my voice under control. I just needed Tanner to be understanding right now, to put aside the logic and realize that I was hurting. I didn't need a parenting lesson right now—I needed for my best friend to stand by my side and whisper that everything was going to be okay.

Even with all the drama brewing, the weeks passed quickly, and soon we were celebrating Thanksgiving. We headed up to Oak Ridge to split the holiday between our parents—we spent

Thanksgiving Day with my family and the day after with his. Because Tanner had a full-time job to get back to, and because so many painful memories lingered for both of us in our hometown, we only spent those two days in Iowa before heading back. Before leaving, we stopped by Leah's parents' house so they could visit with their granddaughter—it was so easy for me to forget that Elysa had three sets of grandparents. That visit was a little awkward for me, to say the least, but it was important to Tanner that Elysa knew her biological grandparents. They made plans to travel down during the summer to spend more time with Elysa, which I knew would be a little hard for me. I tried my best not to think about Tanner's first marriage, as it brought me back to the painful day when I'd seen Tanner for the first time in over three years. I'd come back thinking we could pick up where we left off, and finding him married had been crushing. I would try my hardest not to let my feelings get in the way of Elysa's relationship with them, however. The three of them deserved to know each other, no matter how awkward it was for me.

Life seemed to get even more chaotic after Thanksgiving, as if it wasn't chaotic enough to begin with. I had two more weeks of classes before the winter break, so I spent much of my free time studying and pounding out papers. I looked forward to Christmas break with as much eagerness as a little kid anticipating a coveted gift under the tree.

Because all three couples in our small group Bible study had little kids who all had busy schedules, we decided to have a Christmas party get-together at the beginning of the month and not meet again until after the New Year. On the first Friday of December, we all gathered together at my house for all the Christmas goodies a person could dream of, laugher, and a white elephant gift exchange. In the middle of the craziness, we heard a knock at the door, and I jogged over to answer it, still laughing at the funny story Ruth had just told. The laugh caught in my throat and caused me to choke when I opened the door to see Cassidy standing outside with a plate of Christmas cookies.

"Oh!" she exclaimed. "Ya'll havin' a party?"

I swallowed my shock and plastered on a smile. "Yes. Just having a little Christmas party."

"Well, it's a bit early for that, don't ya think?" she asked, which was probably supposed to be a joke, but it didn't come off that way. Did she have an opinion on *everything*?

Too early for a Christmas party, but not too early to start delivering Christmas cookies? I wondered.

The room had grown quiet, as if everyone was leaning forward in their seats to listen to how I would react to seeing Cassidy here. "Well, you know how busy the Christmas season can be," I explained in my most cheerful voice. "Just wanted to get the party out of the way before our next meeting."

She raised her eyebrows. "Oh. So is this a Bible study then?" she asked, and inwardly I smacked my head. *Please, please don't ask to join!*

I nodded. "Yes. Yes, it is."

"Oh," she said again. "How nice. I was just thinking how wonderful it would be to join a Bible study. If ya'll are looking for a few new members, Johnny and I would be willing to join. That's my husband's name," she explained. "Whom I still don't think ya'll have properly met yet."

"Of course," I said sweetly. "We will definitely keep you in mind."

Her eyes narrowed ever so slightly. Then she sniffed and stuck her nose up into the air. "I look forward to hearing from you." She turned to walk away, cookies still in hand, before she realized what she was doing. "These are for you," she said, and then she walked away again.

"Thanks!" I called out into the dark, but she didn't turn around. I shut the door and turned to face the group with a sheepish look on my face.

"Yikes," Ruth said, breaking the awkward tension that had rushed in when I'd opened the door to see Cassidy standing there.

I let my head fall back and I groaned. "I'm sorry, guys. I know this sounds horrible and rude, but I *don't* want Cassidy to be a part of this group!" I whined.

No one spoke. Everyone suddenly found something interesting to stare at or to fiddle with—anything to avoid eye contact with me. Finally, Tanner spoke up.

"Look. This is a church appointed small group. Anyone can join. If we refuse to let her and John in, they'll take it to the pastors. Do we really want to have to explain to them why we don't want them in our group?" he asked.

Again, silence. More staring, more fiddling.

Tanner took the lead once again. "We don't have to decide tonight. Let's try to enjoy the rest of the night, and we can wait to make a decision until the next time we meet. Sound okay to everyone?"

Murmurs of agreement rang out, and my heart sank. This group was too nice to say no to Cassidy and John, and I knew that whether or not I liked it, they would soon be sitting on my couch, eating my snacks, and participating in our Bible study. I would let Tanner know how I felt about it later of course, and things heated up in our house in a hurry when I did.

Tanner and I had never fought this much—it seemed that every other day, we were duking it out. I was frustrated at his lack of understanding for my feelings; he was frustrated that I was unwilling to give Cassidy a try. But the woman had not given me one good reason to give a relationship with her a try! I *knew* that if I ever said anything about her "perfect" daughter, she would have my head—so why was she allowed to pick on mine?

In the end, all the arguing and tears got me nowhere, and in January, Cassidy was sitting happily on my couch—with her perfect hair and makeup and flawless outfit—munching primly on fudge and scanning the room over and over again with her judgmental eyes, no doubt criticizing my every decorating choice. I was already dreading meeting at her house, as I knew she lived in one of the biggest, nicest houses in Green Lake and probably had her home professionally decorated. Her "perfect" family probably always cleaned up after themselves. I bet there were never toys and books lying around like there was at my place, no play kitchen set shoved into the corner of the living room because there was literally no room for it anywhere else. We were quickly outgrowing this house but needed to pay down some debts before upgrading, so I had to make the best of what I had.

I hated that something I had once so eagerly looked forward to had turned sour. I hated that the very sight of this woman caused my blood to boil. She didn't have to utter a single word to get me riled up; she held so much power over me and I couldn't stand it.

One night, she took things a bit too far. It was nearing the end of January and we were discussing the sermon that Pastor Dennis had just preached on—Matthew 8, where Jesus heals a centurion's son because of his deep faith. It had been an excellent sermon, and Greg suggested that we all go around and describe a time in our lives when Jesus healed us, be it a health or a spiritual issue. I smiled politely as Cassidy described healing after giving birth to her daughter, and my throat tightened up as I listened to Delilah describe the healing that God was still doing in her life after the tragic miscarriage from the year before. When it was my turn, I knew exactly what I was going to talk about, and for a moment, I forgot about the haughty woman sitting just across the room from me.

"I have to say that the work God did in my life after the rape and abortion are the biggest moments of healing in my life," I said. Cassidy's eyes got as big as saucers, but I ignored her and continued. "I was a wreck back then—I've done my best to explain to all of you how bad it really was, but I doubt you'll ever be able to understand. I *hated* God. Didn't want to have anything

143

to do with him. It's thanks to many of you in this room that I'm a much-different person now," I said through a smile.

Cassidy gasped in horror and covered her mouth with her hands. "You had an abortion? Well, that explains so much," she said, shaking her head in disgust.

I let my mouth hang open and glanced around to see if anyone else was reacting the same way I was. I was a bit relieved to find that the group was just as shocked as I was, and it gave me enough courage to ask, "What's that supposed to mean?"

Cassidy threw her hands up in the air and huffed, as if it was the most obvious thing in the whole world. "What kind of a Christian gets an abortion?" she asked. "It makes sense that your daughter was born the way she is. A Down's baby."

Silence.

This was the final straw. Not only had this woman attacked my baby but now she was attacking me! I was not about to let her get away with this.

"Who do you think you are?" I spat, my blood absolutely boiling. "What gives you the right to come in here—"

Tanner cut me off and stood up. "Okay. That's enough," he boomed, and I cringed, preparing for him to pull me into the next room and ask me what in the world I was thinking by letting this awful woman get the best of me.

To my complete and utter surprise, Tanner did just the opposite. "I'm sorry, Cassidy, but I'm going to have to ask that you and John and Addison leave. Now."

She blinked up at him and asked, "Excuse me?"

"You heard me. It's time for you to leave."

"Well!" she huffed, standing up quickly. "Of all the nerve. Come on, John." He followed without a word. She screamed for her daughter to come upstairs from where the children were playing in the basement, and Addison came bounding up without a word as well, obeying her mother and putting her coat on. They left, slamming the door behind them.

We all sat in silence for a few moments, trying to figure out if that had actually just happened. Finally, when I couldn't hold it in anymore, I burst into tears. The group moved in to comfort me, and we agreed to cut our meeting short and figure out what to do next time, when our emotions weren't so supercharged and we'd had some time to really think about what had happened. We ended the meeting with prayer, and I clutched Tanner's hand as he prayed, "God, we need your healing here tonight. Give us clear minds. Help us to know how to deal with this. Calm our hearts and give us peace. And be with Cassidy and John so that they might see the part that they played in what happened tonight and perhaps change their hearts. Remind us that it isn't our place to change them—only you can do that. We ask for your guidance as we figure out what to do next. Amen."

I spent the next day simply trying to calm down and put the whole incident behind me. The phone rang the next evening, however, forcing us to revisit the situation sooner than we had planned. Tanner answered it, and after a few moments, he mouthed to me, "It's Pastor Dennis." I rolled my eyes and sat back into the couch, letting my head fall back in frustration. It figured that Cassidy would go straight to the pastor and blame the whole thing on us.

"Hold on, Pastor," Tanner said. "Can I put you on speaker phone so Molly can be a part of this? Great."

"Hello!" Pastor Dennis called out cheerfully, and I breathed a sigh of relief that he didn't sound upset. We'd known each other for a long time, though, and I knew he trusted me.

"Hi, Pastor," I said. "How are you?"

"I'm good," he replied. "Got a strange phone call from one of our newest churchgoers this morning that I just wanted to clarify with you two before I made any judgments. Can you tell me what happened?"

Tanner and I did our best to fill him in on the details of the past few months without making Cassidy sound like a monster.

"Basically, Pastor Dennis, Cassidy doesn't seem to understand how her blunt comments about Elliot having Down syndrome are affecting our family. She said last night that Elliot was born the way she was because of things Molly had done in her past," Tanner explained.

"Ah," Pastor Dennis replied. He didn't need any more details, as I had gone in several times to talk with him and his wife about the rape and abortion. He knew everything. "Well, that's not quite the story I got this morning from Cassidy, but I want you both to know that I trust you. And between the three of us—I mean this, don't tell anyone—this isn't the first time I've received a complaint about the Wilson family."

"Really," Tanner said, trying not to sound surprised. I choked on a giggle, and he smiled and swatted me.

"Unfortunately, yes. Now I understand that you asked them to leave your group?" he asked.

"Well, not exactly," I said. "We asked them to leave the meeting because things were getting out of hand. We haven't made any final decisions, but honestly we're not sure if it would be a good idea to let them come back."

Pastor Dennis paused for a moment and then cleared his throat. "It's definitely not an easy decision to make. Someone is hurt in every situation. I'm not about to tell you what to do, but I think you might be right. I'm glad that the group has been contemplating letting the Wilson's stay, but in all honesty, some people just don't mesh well with certain groups. If you'd like, I can give the Wilsons that same opinion and then help them find a more suitable group," he offered.

"If you think that would be best…" Tanner trailed off.

"I do. I really do," he said. "Normally I'd try to get the group together with me to work it out, but I'm not sure if that would be a good idea. Cassidy was pretty upset this morning and said she wasn't too keen on a meeting with me. I'm not happy with the situation, but I know how much you've been through, Molly, and

I don't agree with what Cassidy said to you. I think it would be in everyone's best interest if the Wilsons simply found a new group."

When the conversation was over and we hung up the phone, Tanner and I sat on the couch in silence. While it was a relief to have the situation taken care of, we felt a little weird about it. Guilty, like we should have tried harder to make the best of the situation. We trusted Pastor Dennis's judgment, though, so we dropped it and didn't question it.

After walking around for a few days with guilt heavy on my shoulders, I decided to throw the guilt out. I even allowed myself to celebrate a bit—while I would still see Cassidy at church and around town, I wouldn't have to interact with her so closely.

And I would be able to protect my daughter for a few more years.

PART II

Raging Seas

I hear the tumult of the raging seas as your waves and
surging tides sweep over me. But each day the Lord
pours his unfailing love upon me, and through each night
I sing his songs, praying to God who gives me life.

—Psalm 42:7–8

11

Delilah

April 2016

I sat in between Molly and Ruth during the women's Bible study that we all were a part of with my heart pounding and my palms sweating. We had been reading through the gospel of Matthew for a few months, taking our time to slowly wind our way through the passages and really soak in all of Jesus's teachings. Today we were in Matthew 21.

The leader, an older lady named Barb, asked Molly to read the next passage, verses 18–21, and with a clear voice, she began,

> In the morning, as Jesus was returning to Jerusalem, he was hungry, and he noticed a fig tree beside the road. He went over to see if there were any figs, but there were only leaves. Then he said to it, "May you never bear fruit again!" And immediately the fig tree withered up. The disciples were amazed when they saw this and asked, "How did the fig tree wither so quickly?" Then Jesus told them, "I tell you the truth, if you have faith and don't doubt, you can do things like this and much more. You can even say to this

mountain, 'May you be lifted up and thrown into the sea,' and it will happen. You can pray for anything, and if you have faith, you will receive it."

Guilt churned in my stomach, and I wanted to squirm out of my chair and curl up into a ball right there on the floor. I was desperately struggling to believe my Savior's words—doubt was crowding out the faith that had once come naturally; there seemed to be no room for anything else anymore. I felt that I couldn't come to Jesus in prayer and ask for anything, because I no longer believed that my prayers would be answered—at least, not answered in the way I'd hoped. It simply seemed that my desperate prayers for a baby had fallen on deaf ears for years, and now I was being forced to accept a reality that for so long I was convinced would never be real.

The reality that I was never going to have another baby. Ever.

After the third miscarriage, I knew it was true.

Three miscarriages.

Three positive pregnancy tests that left me reeling, my heart so full of joy and plans beginning to churn in my head. Three babies that I had fallen hopelessly in love with, whose sweet faces I had only seen on an ultrasound machine. I had the ultrasound pictures of all three miscarried babies tucked away in a baby book that would never be filled with pictures of their first wobbly steps, their first birthday parties, or their sweet elementary school photos. I would never get to write in their dates of birth, their length and weight on their first days of life, or any of those other cherished first memories.

Three babies that never made it past the second trimester. Three precious little lives that would never know the warmth of their mother's arms, the love of two amazing older siblings, or the tickle of their father's beard on their cheeks.

I tuned out the discussion, trying hard to act natural and look as though I was politely listening to the women around me sharing their thoughts about the passage. I pasted on a smile and nodded every once in a while, but in reality, my mind was a million miles away.

Was God even listening to me? And if he was, why was he saying no? I had prayed with great faith, just like this passage said to do, and still nothing. With every miscarriage, another piece of my heart cracked off and slipped away, and a bitterness was creeping in. Didn't the Bible also say in Psalm 37 to "Take delight in the Lord, and he will give you your hearts desires?" What was I doing wrong? Was my faith not good enough for God? Had I not prayed hard or long enough? Did I not sing enthusiastically enough during Sunday morning worship? Was I not reading enough Bible stories to my kids before bedtime? What else could I do to prove to God that I was a good mother—a good mother who just wanted a little baby to pour even more of the love in my heart into?

I squeezed my eyes shut and shook my head, then sucked in a cleansing breath. I needed the devil to get out of my head! No matter how much I wanted to blame God for my three miscarriages, I refused to do so. I also refused to blame myself—I had been a devout follower of God for too long to fall into this trap. I knew there was nothing I could do to earn God's favor. I didn't deserve to be saved from my sins, but I chose to accept his free gift of salvation anyway, knowing that I would never be good enough for him. The beauty of grace is, though, that none of us will ever be good enough for God, and it doesn't matter—Christ stands in our place and declares us to be worthy, then welcomes us into the family of God as pure, forgiven children.

I still struggled to understand why God gives us some things, denies us others, and takes some things away—especially things I considered to be good things. What bad could come out of having another baby? Molly was proving to me that even the things the world labels as broken, such as her daughter Elliot's life, were the most beautiful things you could find. Even if I had a child with a disability or some kind of illness, I would graciously accept such a child and pour out all the love I had to give into that little life.

I also struggled to understand why God would allow me to get pregnant, only to miscarry before I got far enough along into the second trimester, when the babies had no chance of surviving outside of me. Discovering I was pregnant, getting excited and beginning to prepare for a new life, and then losing that hope before it even had a chance to take root was a heartbreaking, exhausting process. I almost wished that I hadn't gotten pregnant with those three babies, because losing them was killing me. Although I would have been left with an aching emptiness from never conceiving, surely it would be better than the throbbing sorrow of losing three children, right?

Keeping this bottled up inside of me was killing me. Besides my closest family and friends, no one knew about the other two babies I had lost. News of the first miscarried baby and my dramatic response to it had been town gossip far into the following year that it happened until another town scandal took its place. Not wanting to be the center of attention again, especially because I had *already* been in that position with my teenage pregnancy, I had kept the news quiet. Now, though, the desire to share with these kind, compassionate women overtook me—I didn't want their sympathy or to shift the attention onto myself, but I wanted the group to be praying for me. The devil was trying his best to worm his way into my heart and mind, working as hard as he could to beat down my faith until all that remained was a cold and bitter disbelief.

I refocused my attention back to the group's conversation. A middle-aged woman was sharing about her struggles to share the gospel with her aging father. Sue was a kind woman, with deep chocolate-brown eyes that glowed with the love of Jesus. According to her story, she had only become a Christian when she met her husband after graduating from college. She had been raised in a faithless home, and her mother had died in a car accident before Sue realized how important it was to tell her about Jesus. Tears shone in her eyes as she talked about her mother—she clearly held onto a lot of regrets and agonized over where her mother was now spending eternity.

"I visited with my grandma a bit after my mom passed away, and I got to ask her about my mom's spiritual life. She did say that for a time in high school and college, my mother had attended church with a boyfriend, but after breaking up with him, she just sort of stopped going. I hope that she accepted Christ during those years, but who knows? I know my dad's not gonna make it much longer, and I don't know if I could handle the stress of worrying about his eternity too." She sniffed and dabbed at her eyes. "I've been praying as hard as I can and bringing Christ into every conversation possible, but he's resisting so hard. Feels like he's never gonna soften up," she ended quietly.

The group murmured around her, and I sat back a little deeper into my chair. Now was clearly not the time to jump in and share my own struggles, as it would be insensitive to shift the attention onto me when Sue so clearly needed the group's love and support. I waited as a few women offered words of encouragement and advice from their own personal experiences with loved ones resisting the gospel. Barb then stopped the group and prayed for Sue, encouraging those closest to her to lay their hands upon her shoulder. I peeked over to Sue as Barb prayed—tears were streaming down her cheeks and silent sobs wracked her body. When the prayer ended, Sue wiped her eyes and expressed her deep gratitude for the support, and silence then settled in the room.

"Anyone else have anything they wish to share?" asked Barb. Our time together was quickly coming to an end, and I wanted to have a bit of time for the group to do the same thing for me that they'd just done for Sue. There is something so unique and powerful about a large group lifting you up to the Almighty God, pleading to him on your behalf.

"I have something," I timidly ventured, encouraged by Molly's smile and nod. I took another deep breath in. "Most of you know that a few years ago I lost a baby boy. And I didn't react in the best way." I gave a small laugh. "But most of you *don't* know that I lost two more babies after that one. And my doctor doesn't think I will ever have another baby."

"Oh, sweetie," Barb crooned, similar to the way a grandmother might do upon hearing such news. "I'm so sorry."

"Me too," I responded, deciding right then and there to be completely transparent and real with the group. No doubt a handful of the women in this group had experienced at least one miscarriage in their life and could relate to what I was going through. No need to sugarcoat it. "It's killing me. And the devil is trying his best to beat down my faith—it's so tempting to just run outside and scream up at the sky. Ask God why he would do something like this three times, ya know?" I was not really looking for an answer, just expressing my deep anguish and struggle to trust the Lord through this.

Cassidy, the bold young woman who had moved to Green Lake just a few years ago, must have thought that I *was* looking for an answer because she jumped in in her usual shocking manner. Normally Cassidy simply ignored me, sending me forced smiles and fake friendly waves to play the part of the good Christian woman she was trying so hard to pretend she was. Molly was normally her target, something I resented about Cassidy because Molly was doing a terrific job raising her two beautiful girls— Cassidy couldn't seem to look past Elliot's Down syndrome to see the charming, bubbly two-year-old that she was. She took every opportunity to cluck her tongue at Elliot, to shake her head and express just how sad it was the Elliot wasn't a normal little girl.

"Well, isn't it obvious?" she asked, popping the gum she had been chomping through the entire meeting.

No one moved a muscle; no one said anything. After a few moments of shocked silence, I could see eyes shifting around the room; women silently asking each other if they should challenge Cassidy. Barb finally cleared her throat, shifted uncomfortably in her seat, and asked, "Now, Cassidy, what do you mean by that?"

She settled into her seat. "Well, like I said, it's pretty obvious. I mean, you've shared with us before about your teenage pregnancy. Why would God give you another baby after defiling the marriage bed in that way?" she asked.

My jaw fell and heat rushed into my cheeks. The way she said "defiling the marriage bed" made it sound like I had committed some kind of horrible, unforgiveable sin.

"That's quite enough, Cassidy," Barb insisted. "Let's remember to keep each other's feelings in mind before we speak, okay, ladies?" I heard a hint of anger creeping into her voice.

This wasn't the first time Cassidy had said something so insensitive. In fact, Barb had had to take Cassidy aside a few times after the meeting ended to remind her to think before she spoke—I'd walked in on one of those meetings on my way to grab a jacket that Luke had left in one of the Sunday school rooms the previous Sunday. Still, the woman seemed to possess no filter! I wondered how she slept at night.

"Look," Cassidy countered, not one to give up easily. Barb raised her eyebrows and sat up straight, squaring her shoulders in a challenge. "This isn't hard to figure out. God punished people all the time in the Bible for sinning. Just think about the flood. Or Sodom and Gomorrah? Turning Lot's wife into a pillar of salt? Really, this isn't so shocking. Delilah sinned, and God just might be punishing her for it."

I could sense Molly tensing up beside me, could feel her desire to stand up and give Cassidy a piece of her mind. She resisted, thankfully—we didn't need this turning into any more of a mess than it already was. I should have known that sharing this would result in Cassidy attacking me and calling me a dirty sinner. If only I had kept my mouth shut!

"That's enough, Cassidy," Barb declared loudly. "I'm not sure how you were raised or what you were taught in your home church, but here in this church, we believe that all sins are equal in God's eyes, and all sins are dealt with in the same manner—we are forgiven through the blood of Jesus. Our punishment for all sin is death and eternal separation from God, which he has so graciously chosen to rescue us from by offering up his son. I think that God allows things to happen to us and that because of sin, we suffer earthly consequences, but I disagree with you, Cassidy. I don't think Delilah is being punished."

Cassidy smiled and gave a forced laugh and then threw up her hands in mock defeat. We all knew she could have gone on and on, causing a big theological debate on whether or not God punishes us for sinning. We all breathed a sigh of relief that she was letting it go this time.

"Okay, okay. We all have a right to our opinion. I didn't know that we had to censor everything we said in this group. I thought it was a safe place to be honest. I guess not."

Barb swallowed the snarky comment on her lip like the gracious woman she was. "This *is* a safe place to be honest," she insisted. "But like I said, we need to be aware that our words have a direct impact on those around us. We build each other up here, not accuse each other. If someone is struggling with sin in their life, we gently steer them in the right direction. But we do so in *private*. If you can't seem to do that, then perhaps this group is not for you."

Again, silence settled over the room as we waited to see how Cassidy would respond. "I'm fine," she squeaked. Was her voice cracking? Did what Barb said and her threat to have Cassidy removed from the group finally get through to her? "I'll work at it."

"All right then. Let's close in prayer, shall we?"

I clenched my jaw as the group bowed for prayer. It wasn't fair that Cassidy had ruined the chance for the group to offer support and encouragement to me! I was trying my hardest to combat these feelings of unworthiness, trying to convince myself of the very opposite of what Cassidy was accusing me of. She'd never know that I had already so roughly wrestled the idea of God punishing me for getting pregnant out of wedlock. With all the doubt and fear already crowding my heart and mind, Cassidy's words had been the last thing I needed.

When the meeting ended, Cassidy made a quick exit. The rest of the group stalled while they pulled on their jackets, waiting for her to leave so they could offer their apologies and kind words. Knowing that the group didn't agree with Cassidy made it a little better, but I still walked out with a stinging heart.

"Hey," Molly said softly as she gently steered her two girls to her car. "Wanna go for a picnic down at Anderson Park? I'll go pick up some food at the store and meet you two down there, if you're up for it."

Anderson Park was a beautiful park, especially this time of year when the trees were beginning to bud and the air smelled fresh and clean—the promise of a new beginning after a long Kansas winter. I looked over to Ruth, who was already nodding her head. "Sure, that sounds great," I answered. Neither Ruth nor I had any kids to worry about since all of ours were in school, so an afternoon lounging on a blanket in the park would actually be relaxing with no kids to chase after or keep occupied.

Twenty minutes later, the three of us, plus Elysa and Elliot, were laughing and munching on sandwiches and carrot sticks. I closed my eyes and silently sent a prayer heavenward, thanking God for blessing me with such wonderful friends to help me through such a difficult season.

After a while, the girls got antsy, and Molly sent them ahead to play in the sandbox so she could still sit and chat with us. Elysa was four now and could handle that little bit of freedom, but we still kept a watchful eye on them—Elliot was a little over two years old still, and the fact that she had Down syndrome made her a bit more of a handful. Still, both girls were well-behaved, and Anderson Park was safe. The girls would be fine.

When conversation between us lulled, I sighed. Molly gave me a small smile, squeezed my arm, and said, "All right. Go ahead."

I giggled. "Even after all she's done to us, would you believe me if I said I can't believe she did that?" I asked. "I mean, come on. We were in Bible study! You don't say stuff like that at a Bible study! Who does she think she is, trying to tell me that I'm being punished for what happened over a decade ago? She just...She just drives me crazy!"

Molly and Ruth listened as I continued to vent. They didn't chastise me or lecture me about how as Christians we should love our enemies. They just listened.

After my rant, Molly squeezed my arm again. "You know I can relate," she said. "After Cassidy and John left the small group, she constantly shot me death looks whenever I saw her. Like it was all my fault that things didn't work out. And she *still* makes comments about Elliot every chance she gets. I can't believe she is so ignorant and insensitive!"

Ruth didn't really have any stories dealing with Cassidy—she was pretty soft-spoken and tended to keep to herself, which left her relatively drama free. Still, she couldn't deny the fact that Cassidy's behavior was unsettling, and she admitted to us that it bothered her as much as it bothered us. Molly and I had grown fairly close to Ruth, and we could see her motherly, protective love when it came to how Cassidy treated us—she just choose not to verbalize her feelings as much as we did, and again, that was because Cassidy hadn't targeted her in any way.

Molly went over to check on the girls and make sure Elliot wasn't shoveling sand into her mouth, which she was known to do, and then settled back onto the cheery-red checkered picnic blanket. My mom had given the blanket to me when I finally moved out of her house, back when I still worked as a receptionist at the law firm and Luke was only four years old. The blanket held so many memories for me—countless hours lounging at this very park with my mom, soaking in the sun and laughing up at the shapes we saw in the clouds. Family picnics when my sisters and their families came to town in the summer, back when Albert was still alive and acting as a stand-in grandpa for us. Luke and I had made good use out of this blanket too; as a little boy, he'd loved fixing up peanut butter and jelly sandwiches and chocolate milk to eat on this blanket. Now he was twelve years old, a young man, really, who was keeping busy with sports and friends and didn't have time to laugh with his mom while eating a sandwich and drinking chocolate milk. I was glad that Molly, Ruth, and I were able to make a few more happy memories with this old blanket.

"Look." Ruth pointed across the park. "Is that Cassidy?"

Molly and I squinted through the bright sun and nodded. "Looks like it," Molly said.

For a few moments, we just watched her as she and Addison, now five years old, marched properly across the green grass to a picnic table not far from us. Cassidy took a kitchen sanitizing wipe and wiped down the metal table before spreading a plastic tablecloth over it, then began pulling out a boxed salad from the grocery store for herself and what looked to be some kind of wrap for her little girl. We continued watching her in silence, shaking our heads as she ate her salad without any kind of dressing. Both of them drank bottled water, and when Addison spilled hers, we cringed as Cassidy began lecturing her about being responsible. "Ladies, don't spill things," she said. "Now help me clean this up."

With burning ears, we tried to return to our own conversation, but Cassidy didn't make it easy. The woman was just so loud! Within the first ten minutes of the two of them arriving in the park, we were more than ready for them to leave—mostly just because we felt bad for Addison. Mandy was seven years old and still spilled at least once a week at the dinner table. It's just part of being a kid. Kids are messy. When they spill and make mistakes, the last thing you want to do is lecture them. Instead, you gently correct them and help them to make better choices in the future. Greg and I would help Mandy clean up whatever she spilled, then remind her that she needed to watch her hand gestures while at the dinner table. Her mouth moved a mile a minute during dinner as she went on and on about her day and all that had happened to her. Instead of getting frustrated that she was taking her sweet time to learn the lesson we were trying to reach her, Greg and I were happy that Mandy wanted to share her day with us. We hoped she was always this open with us, especially as she slipped into her teenage years.

When the two of them were finished eating, Addison ran off to play by herself on the playground equipment. And then we watched Cassidy sit by herself at the picnic table, and we saw something we had overlooked for the two years she had lived in Green Lake. Loneliness. For the first time, it occurred to us that Cassidy was alone in this town. At church, Cassidy, John, and Addison sat by themselves. At Bible study, Cassidy arrived and left alone. On her many walks around town, we never once saw one other person accompanying her. And now, as her daughter found other children to laugh, chase, and play with on the equipment, Cassidy sat alone.

Without having to say a word to each other, I knew we were all thinking the same thing. What had we done to reach out and be a friend to this woman? All we had done was take her actions personally and use our anger to fuel our dislike of her. We hadn't taken the time to really get to know her, to find out how she had turned out the way she had and if the friendship of even just a few women could help changer her attitude. After all, the Bible commanded us in Ephesians 4 to "be kind to one another, tenderhearted, forgiving one another, as God in Christ forgave you." Guilt again pricked at my heart as I thought of the grudge

I was holding against Cassidy, which began the day we had first met her and she had been so insensitive about Elliot.

Surprisingly, Molly was the one to voice her opinion on Cassidy being alone. "Guys, I know she's hard to love. Even hard to tolerate. But no one deserves to be alone."

"I agree," Ruth said. "I think we should at least try and go sit with her. She may not want us to, but I think we should try."

They looked to me, knowing that because I had been the most recently affected by her, it would be the biggest struggle for me. I jumped in right away. "Definitely," I agreed.

So we packed up our leftovers and folded up the blanket, and then made our way over to Cassidy, knowing full well that she could turn up her nose to us and wave us away. If she did that, though, we could at least say we tried. And then we could continue trying.

To our amazement, Cassidy looked up at us with a smile. "Hello, ladies," she said with a wave. "Beautiful day, isn't it?" She acted as if nothing had happened this morning, but I let it roll off my shoulders. If we wanted to cultivate a friendship with this woman, we needed to simply let go of the resentment and forget about all the times she had hurt us with her words. And by doing so, we were able to have a decent conversation with Cassidy, who was quite funny once you got past the snooty personality that she seemed to hide behind. I got the feeling that Cassidy was simply trying to impress us—that she had been from the beginning, as if by moving to Kansas from Texas, she needed to seem better than us, more refined.

Everyone has a story, a history that has shaped them into the person they grew up to be. I knew that was the case for Cassidy, and I wondered what that story was. Did she grow up under a string of successful older siblings, always trying to live up to their reputations? Was her father strict with high expectations, expectations that were impossible to fulfill? Why was she the way she was today?

We wouldn't find out in one afternoon of surprisingly pleasant small talk. But maybe, just maybe, we would slowly crack open the shell that Cassidy had carefully constructed around herself with the simple act of being a friend to her.

12

Molly

May

"Are you sure?" I asked Chelsea as she sat trembling across from me in a booth at Mary Beth's diner, her hands so tightly wrapped around a ceramic mug of coffee that her knuckles were white.

"I'm sure," she said with disappointment dripping from her voice. "Took three tests this morning. I'm definitely pregnant." She hung her head and sighed.

I nodded. "Okay. Well, it's not the end of the world. I can help you. I've lived through an unplanned pregnancy before, remember?" I gently reminded.

Chelsea was twenty years old now, and remarkably she was still working at the diner. Things had been rocky between her and Mary Beth until that night over two years ago that Mary Beth had stepped in and stopped a rowdy group of boys from harassing her. Ever since that night, things had been better, as Chelsea had gradually learned to trust Mary Beth and let her guard down ever so slightly, to let her in and help bring healing to her wounded heart, just like I had all those years ago. Still, Chelsea remained relatively guarded around Mary Beth—around everyone, really—and the young woman was a constant source of stress for her. The flippant attitude, snarky comments, and general lack of respect constantly grated on Mary Beth's nerves, but I simply reminded her that Chelsea behaved that way to prohibit anyone from getting close to her. Thanks to my degree in psychology, which I had finally earned just a few weeks ago, I knew that Chelsea was probably trying her hardest to keep everyone away from her because in her past, the one she had been closest to—her mother—had let her down in a tremendous way by taking her own life. Why risk getting close to anyone if the same thing could eventually happen? In her mind, it was better to keep everyone shut out to avoid the pain of losing them altogether.

Although I no longer worked at the diner and hadn't for quite some time, I kept in contact with each of the girls Mary Beth and I had initially hired on after Albert's death. Jess, the fiery redhead, had graduated from high school and gone on to nursing school, which she was able to pay for almost completely on her own thanks to the long hours she had logged at the diner. Her mother was no longer with her alcoholic father and therefore wasn't supporting his drinking problem and was able to help Jess out with tuition and spending money. Back when Jess first started, she had doubted that her dream of going off to college would ever be a reality, and I was ecstatic at the way things had turned out for her. I chatted with her on Facebook every once in a while and enjoyed reading her posts about classes and looking through the fun pictures she took with her new college friends.

Alexa had graduated as well and was studying to be an elementary school teacher, which I thought suited her quieter personality well. She had always been good with kids while working; she seemed able to put any child at ease and make them feel special. I also enjoyed her Facebook posts and pictures—both girls seemed to be doing remarkably well, which brought both

Mary Beth and I so much joy. All those tough days with the girls seemed to be paying off, not that their success was entirely our doing. Still, having a solid support system cheering you on didn't hurt, and I knew that the support we gave the girls had given them a confidence boost and raised their self-esteem. Both Mary Beth and I looked forward to watching them continue to grow and develop into confident women.

Chelsea had finished high school but opted out of college. "School just isn't my thing," she'd said with a shrug when I'd asked her about her future plans before her high school graduation. So instead of packing her bags and enrolling in classes, Chelsea moved into the apartment building that I had lived in before getting married with a few friends from high school and took a second job at a daycare center, which she seemed to be enjoying. I never pictured Chelsea as much of a kid person, but she spoke highly of the children she worked with and never had a bad thing to say about that job.

She continued to surprise me, because she had also started dating. Chelsea was so good at keeping people away, at never giving anyone a chance to earn her trust or get close to her, so allowing someone in was a big step for her. Especially a boy. In high school, her gorgeous looks had gotten her into trouble with the boys, even though she never really put herself out there—she just seemed to attract their attention. She had despised their attention, though, and I assumed the reason for that was connected back to her mother, who in desperation had turned to prostitution to support her and Chelsea. She didn't think very highly of men because of that.

Her boyfriend Chase was quite a bit older than Chelsea was—he looked to be nearing thirty. I never asked her about his age, though, because I never quite knew how Chelsea would respond. She was extremely high-strung and got upset very easily, and I assumed her guard would fly up if I questioned the age of the only person she had ever decided was worthy enough to date. He

167

seemed nice enough, though, so I didn't push my luck. I was also thankful that she seemed to be taking the first steps out of the prison of loneliness she had locked herself into for so many years; I didn't want to risk sending her back in.

After only a few months of dating, she moved out of her apartment and in with Chase, and I guess the two hadn't been careful enough when it came to preventing pregnancy. I knew from Chelsea's sad eyes that the pregnancy hadn't been planned, and she wasn't thrilled about it either.

"Thanks, Molly. You're the first one I've told, and I figured you'd have good advice for me."

I tried to hide my shock that she hadn't even told Chase at this point. But, thinking back to my own unplanned pregnancy, I knew how confusing and terrifying the experience was. In the initial shock, it was difficult to formulate any sort of a plan, and keeping the news bottled up safely in order to put together some semblance of a plan felt better than inviting other people in to give advice that wasn't appreciated or asked for. I gave her a soft smile, quietly urging her to trust me. "Well, there are really only three options. Have you given any thought about what you're gonna do?" I asked.

She shook her head no. "It's still so fresh, ya know?" I nodded, allowing myself to travel back in time eight years, back to the winter I'd gotten pregnant. I couldn't believe that much time had passed, and that even though almost a decade stood between the choices I had made back then and my life now, the regret was still as fresh as ever. I wanted to take Chelsea into my arms and rock away the fear and confusion, to convince her to not even consider the idea of aborting her child, but I knew I couldn't do that. This wasn't my choice to make, and Chelsea didn't need me pushing her into something too quickly. What she needed was an honest opinion, a shoulder to cry on, and a sounding board to bounce ideas off of. I hoped and prayed that after she wrestled with all three options—abortion, adoption, or keeping the baby—that she would choose an option that resulted in life.

Although I tried my hardest to avoid labeling myself either pro-life or pro-choice because I disagreed with the ways both movements handled the fiery issue, the one thing I hated the most about the pro-choice movement was the hesitancy to keep women fully educated about their choice. To many on this side of the debate, the woman should be allowed to make a life-changing decision without fully understanding the ramifications of her choice. Any law that attempts to legislate how a woman can obtain an abortion is struck down almost immediately, and it bothered me that even if the law is written to protect the life of the mother, the pro-choice movement still resists. I thought back to 2012, where Texas attempted to pass a law that required doctors who performed abortions to have hospital admitting privileges within thirty miles of where the abortion was performed. It also restricted how doctors administered abortion-inducing drugs. The argument against the law was that the provisions placed an unconstitutional burden on women's access to abortion. People were outraged that women might have to drive a longer distance to get abortions, but no one considered that women have died from complications from abortions and that the new restrictions would potentially save lives. Many clinics closed down after this law was written, proving that they could care less about the health of their patients. If they truly wanted to provide the best care possible, those clinics would have done everything in their power to comply with the new regulations and keep their doors opened.

In reality, the abortion industry is only about one thing: money. They don't want the government to require that women be fully educated about their other two choices because if they walked out of the abortion clinic doors and decided never to come back, they lost out on the profit. When women see their babies and hear their heartbeats, they are less likely to abort. When given information about adoption and support and encouragement to give their baby life, the scary situation becomes much easier. So why, if the other two choices are good for women, does the pro-choice movement want to keep women in the dark?

It baffled me. Pro-choice really means pro-abortion. In their minds, the only choice should be abortion, and we shouldn't require that women fully understand their other options.

This is why I didn't want to push Chelsea in the direction *I* really wanted her to go. I didn't want her to begin feeling the same way about my philosophy that I felt about the pro-choice philosophy. Everything within me was screaming to demand that Chelsea keep her baby. I desperately wanted to transfer the regret and sorrow I still felt from my abortion onto her shoulders just so she could get a taste of what she might feel if she made the same choice. But I couldn't do that. I wanted to handle it differently than the pro-choice and pro-life movements. I wanted to stand by Chelsea's side, hold her hand, and declare that no matter what she chose, I would still love her. I wouldn't look down at her or judge her, as so many in the pro-life movement unfortunately do. I wanted to sit down and show her all the options she had—*all* of her choices, not just the one I wanted her to choose. Instead of keeping her in the dark and pushing her into a choice that she wasn't sure she wanted or understood, like the pro-choice movement was apt to do, I would lay it all out for her and let her be the judge.

But not right now. Now was not the time to lay out all the options and map a direction to follow. Now was the time for getting a handle on the wide range of emotions I knew she was feeling, for taking deep cleansing breaths and realizing that an unplanned pregnancy wouldn't ruin her life.

"How are you feeling at this point?" I asked, encouraging her to make some sense of her emotions so that she wouldn't make any decisions based off of how she was feeling right at this moment.

"I'm doing okay. I mean, I definitely didn't plan on this happening. I never imagined myself having any kids, so it kind of feels surreal at this point. But it's not like I have any big plans that this baby would be getting in the way of. I'm not in school. I'm living on my own and supporting myself. Maybe it's *not* the end of the world," she admitted.

I nodded, once again allowing myself to think about my unplanned pregnancy and the differences between our situations. At the time I had gotten pregnant, I had been surrounded by family and friends who would have supported me and helped me through it, and I still managed to think I was all alone, forcing me to take drastic measures that ultimately cost me my daughter's life. Chelsea had Chase to help her through it, but other than him, she didn't have many others in her life that she could turn to during this difficult time. She had no mother, no father, no siblings, no real close friends—I suppose she had the few girls she had lived with right after high school, but she hardly spoke about those friends so I assumed they weren't the type of friends she could go to with news this big. She had me and Mary Beth of course, and her elderly grandmother, but still. Who knew how Chase would respond? How much support would she get from an aging grandma already worn-out from raising her grandchild? Was Chase ready to be a dad?

Even though her support system was shaky, Chelsea was able to look past that and see that keeping her baby *was* possible. It would be tough, to be sure, but she was a confident young woman and I knew she would be able to handle it.

"Of course it's not the end of the world. A baby will certainly *change* your world, but it won't bring it to an end," I assured her.

Over the next few weeks, I visited the diner frequently, bringing four-year-old Elysa and two-year-old Elliot in to brighten Chelsea's day. I wanted to show Chelsea the joy and happiness my two girls gave me, even though it was tough to keep up with them at times. Elysa was the master at spilling, which would send her into tears when she realized that she'd made a mess that somebody else had to clean up—Elysa was extremely tenderhearted and hated to make anyone sad or upset, which caused her to overreact at times, thinking she was hurting people when she actually wasn't. Elliot was my busybody, always reaching and grabbing at things she shouldn't be. Keeping track of two busy, independent bodies while still trying to manage your own life is exhausting, but at the end of the day, when I tucked in my two sleeping beauties and kissed their little button noses, the stress of the day melted away. I knew that in eight hours, I would be up and at it again, running around and trying to keep tabs on my active kids while somehow getting all that needed to be done taken care of—but I couldn't, and wouldn't, imagine my life any other way.

With her first trimester quickly coming to an end, I knew that Chelsea soon would only have two options left—having and keeping her baby or pursuing adoption. The longer you wait with an abortion, the more complicated it becomes, and Chelsea had told me in the beginning that if she chose abortion, she'd do it in the first trimester to keep things as simple as possible. She hadn't brought abortion up again, and I breathed a sigh of relief. Perhaps the lies the world fed expectant mothers like Chelsea wouldn't get through to her.

Then, out of the blue, Chelsea shocked me with her decision. "Chase isn't ready, Molly," she said to me one afternoon as she brought me a check for the lunch the girls and I had just shared. "He said he wants kids someday, when he has a better job and more money. And he doesn't feel like he'd be a good dad yet. Says he wants to be carefree and enjoy life for a while before he gets tied down to a family."

Inwardly I cringed. Why did women have to shoulder all the responsibility? Why couldn't more men step up and realize there was more to life than hanging out with friends and sitting around playing video games? Chase was old enough by now to have a stable job. How many years had he wasted if he was still stuck in a job that wouldn't provide for one more mouth? My heart ached for Chelsea, who for these last few weeks had watched my girls through hopeful eyes and who had allowed herself to soften up and stop pretending to be the tough, unreachable girl she had been playing for too many years. I had seen genuine happiness in the last few weeks, but here today, I saw a glint of sadness. It seemed that Chase had made the choice for her, and that wasn't fair.

Jason had done the same thing for me. He'd made me feel like the bad guy by somehow turning the rape back on me, for standing in the way of his dreams of playing college basketball and living a normal life. His threats to go after Tanner and my family scared me enough to stop considering keeping the baby, or even giving her up for adoption. Jason had said that he didn't want there to be any chance of a lost, confused teenager chasing after him in hopes to build a relationship with him. He didn't want to own up to what he had done, and he didn't want to take responsibility for it—so he made me take care of it for him.

I didn't want that for Chelsea, and for a while, it seemed that she didn't want that either. I had gone through all her options with her and shown her where the closest abortion clinics were and what to expect both physically and emotionally after an abortion. I'd explained how her pregnancy would progress if she chose to keep her baby and how my own labor and delivery had gone. I was honest about the fear and the pain, but I was also honest about the immediate love that flowed out of my heart the minute I laid eyes on my gorgeous little Elliot, Down syndrome and all. I gave her information about adoptions and helped her research potential adoption agencies. She knew all her options, and I had hoped and prayed that she would choose life.

But after it was all said and done, she had made up her mind, and I tried to hide my sadness as best I could. Perhaps Chelsea's experience would be different. Perhaps in a few years, if she and Chase were still together, they'd plan for a baby and be ready to raise it. Although my own experience had been traumatic, I had to come to terms that it might not be for everyone—for someone who lived without Christ and didn't know that he doesn't make mistakes and that he plans for every life, it made sense. Because Chelsea didn't know her own worth in the eyes of Christ, she was unable to see the worth of her unborn child.

I had tried my best to sneak those truths into our conversations, being mindful that Chelsea was still very much closed to any talk of Christ and faith. "Your baby's life isn't an accident, Chelsea," I explained. "*You* might not have planned for this baby to come, but have you ever thought that God planned for your baby to come?"

She shrugged. "I don't know. I'm not a Christian, Molly. You know that. I'm still not even sure I believe that God exists after all I've been through. I mean, I've come a long way and things are definitely going better now, so I'm working on the idea of God. I'm just trying to make the best decision here, for everyone involved. I'm still not sure what that looks like or if God belongs in the equation. It might take a little more time," she explained.

Having known Chelsea as long as I did, I knew not to push it much further. Her beliefs didn't line up with mine, but that didn't make her a bad person. She was wrestling with what she believed in, and I knew that God was in the midst of all this. After all, I had once been lost, wandering around in a wasteland of hatred and bitterness, all of which I directed at God. But after I stepped through the fire and looked back, I was able to see where God had clearly been through my experience. He had been there every step of the way, just as he was here now with Chelsea. Perhaps he was using this rocky time to lead her to his arms.

Before leaving the diner, I took Chelsea aside and asked, "Do you have a plan for the abortion? Have you done all your research and really thought about it?" I asked.

She rolled her eyes and nodded.

"Hey," I gently chided. "I've been through this before, remember? I *didn't* do my research, and I regret it every single day. I *should* have an eight-year-old waiting for me to pick her up after school today, but I don't. I know you might not feel the same way I do about abortion, but if this is the decision you're going with, I want to make sure you've thought it through."

"I *have*," she responded. "Don't worry about me. I'll be fine."

I gave her a small smile. "Moms always worry. I may not be your mom, but I still worry. I just want the best for you."

She softened ever so slightly. "Thank you. I do appreciate all you've done for me. You're one of the only people in the world who actually cares about me. So thank you."

"Of course, honey. So...who's taking you? Make sure you have a ride to and from. And call me if you need anything after it's over."

"Chase is taking me. The appointment is next Thursday in Wichita."

I leaned in to give her a hug. I didn't know what to say. "Good luck" and "best wishes" felt inappropriate. Next week, a life would be lost. What do you say in that kind of situation? I opted to say nothing, because Chelsea's strong-willed personality wouldn't appreciate any of the things I really wanted to say to her, like, *Run away. Fast. Run away and don't ever look back.* But I didn't. If she got the abortion and regretted it, I would be here to help her through it. If she got it and *didn't* regret it, well, then I guess her life would continue on without a hitch.

I walked around with a heavy heart the entire next week. On Thursday, I had Delilah take the girls so I could spend the day in prayer. Her appointment was at two o'clock, so although I was praying for her all day as I cleaned my house and researched potential jobs, at two o'clock, I went to my bedroom, got down on my knees, and pleaded before God to change Chelsea's mind.

I didn't feel an overwhelming sense of peace after my hour of desperate prayer. My heart was just as heavy as ever, and dread was weighing me down. Maybe I was wrong to have presented all that information about abortion to her. Maybe I should have spouted off all the negative side effects I had, and still did, suffer from. Maybe I should have tried harder to steer her away from abortion at all costs.

But really, that might not have made any difference. Chelsea was only twenty years old—her brain, specifically her frontal lobe, was still developing. The frontal lobe is the part of the brain that involves the ability to recognize future consequences resulting from current actions and to choose between good and bad actions. Because this part of her brain was still developing, she might have rejected any steering because she wasn't able to see the future consequences that could result from an abortion, much like I hadn't as an eighteen-year-old. In her desperation to prove her point—that I was wrong—she might have just ignored me anyway.

On Friday afternoon, our doorbell rang and Elysa flung the door open wide, and to my shock, I saw Chelsea standing on the other side. She was beaming. My heart twisted up inside me. Had she come to gloat? Prove to me how easy the abortion had been for her? I was impressed that she was up and walking around so soon. I remembered being in pretty bad pain, but part of that might have been emotional pain. Guilt for doing something I knew had been wrong, even though I had tried my hardest to convince myself otherwise.

"Hello, Miss Elysa. May I please come in?" Chelsea politely asked my smiling daughter, who was proud of the fact she had opened the door and was seemingly in charge of whether or not our guest was to come inside. She peeked over to me and I nodded.

"Yes," she declared matter-of-factly. "Please come in."

Chelsea ruffled Elysa's curls as she stepped past her. "Hi," she said simply.

"Hey," I said back, trying my hardest to not make this an awkward situation. Although I had told Chelsea that I would support and love her through whatever decision she made, she knew how I felt about abortion. "Um, do you want to sit and have some coffee? Or tea?"

"Some tea would be great, thanks," she said as she settled down at my kitchen table. She fidgeted as I got the water boiling, and I ordered myself to keep it together during our conversation. I popped a VeggieTales movie in for the girls in the living room and then poured two steaming mugs of water and set them down on the table.

"How are you feeling?" I asked to start things off.

"I feel great," she responded with a grin, and I gave her a forced smile.

"I, uh," I stuttered, commanding myself to get a grip. I cleared my throat. "I'm glad. It was much harder for me."

She gave a soft laugh and hung her head. For a few moments, she gazed into her mug. Then she looked up and said, "I didn't do it, Molly. I couldn't."

My heart jumped inside me. Had my day of prayer actually helped save the life of Chelsea's baby?

"You didn't?" I asked in complete shock. "Why not?"

She sighed. "Well, I went through the mandatory counseling that Kansas law requires before an abortion and just shrugged it off. The doctor had nothing new to say that you hadn't already told me. But when I walked in there...I don't know. It didn't feel right.

"I told Chase I was having doubts, but he told me it wasn't the time to have doubts. We had already driven all the way there. So I tried to ignore it, but then I had an ultrasound," she explained, and I smiled. Women who see their babies before an abortion are less likely to actually go through with it.

"When the lady asked me if I wanted to see the image, I almost said no. I think she assumed I would—I mean, I don't exactly look like the motherly type, ya know? Dark hair, heavy makeup, young. But before I knew what was happening, I was saying yes and seeing my baby. After that, it was all over. I started crying and freaking out, and I ran out."

"What did Chase do?"

Her eyes fell, and I knew the rest of the story wouldn't be as happy. "He was upset. But at least he didn't leave me in Wichita. He hardly spoke a word on the drive home. Right now, he still doesn't want to be a dad. Told me he needs a break to figure it all out."

I nodded. "I see."

"So I moved out yesterday. Don't really know what I'm gonna do at this point. I crashed with my old roommates last night, but I don't think moving back with them is an option, because there's just not enough room for a baby."

"What about your grandma's house?" I asked.

She shrugged. "My grandma is pushing eighty. She's not in the best condition to take in two extra house guests."

I knew I would have to talk it over with Tanner before I could really offer to let Chelsea stay here, but right now, we had plenty of room. Tanner and I had bought a house that we could grow into—three bedrooms upstairs, which we currently occupied, and two unoccupied bedrooms downstairs. Chelsea was also stubborn and proud. She wouldn't want to accept what she thought was charity, even if it meant a stable place to stay while she got on her feet.

"I know you probably want to do this on your own. But if you need a place to stay, just until you get everything all figured out, you're welcome here. I'd have to ask Tanner first of course, but I know he'd say yes."

I expected an eye roll and a hair flip, but instead I got a grateful smile and two furiously blinking eyes. Eyes that were trying as hard as they could not to betray the strong, independent young woman possessing them.

"Thank you," she whispered. "I would appreciate it until I have a better plan in place."

"No problem, sweetheart. And I'm still here to help you through it, if you want my help."

For the rest of the afternoon, we talked and laughed, something we had never done before. Although we'd gotten fairly close during the time that I had been helping her put together a basic plan for handling her pregnancy, she had still held me at a safe distance, never really letting me in. Now, though, I was an invaluable source of support to her, and I was thankful that she was willing to let me do so.

After dinner that night, when Tanner had wholeheartedly agreed to taking Chelsea in for a time, I watched Elysa curled up on the couch with a book. At four years old, Elysa was already a decent reader; it's something we had been working on when we noticed Elysa's love for stories. She would sit for hours and pour over picture books, eating up the simple stories and delighting over the drawings. I knew how engrossed she got in her stories, so I took the risk of discussing a touchy subject while she was so close to us.

Tanner was clearing dishes from the table when I asked, "Did people really advise you and Leah to abort Elysa after Leah was diagnosed?"

He stopped in his tracks, slowly turned around, and said, "Why do you ask?" I could see the pain in his eyes, the pain that always showed up when we talked about her. He would always hold a special place in his heart for Leah, which still caused a twinge of jealousy to rise up inside me.

"This whole thing with Chelsea has got me thinking about it. It's weird to think that our whole lives could be so different now if you'd listened to people's advice," I explained.

He wandered to the sink and nodded. "Yeah, that is weird," he admitted. "I try not to think about it, but, yes, a few people gave us that advice. People I never thought would—people in our church."

I looked back to Elysa, still gobbling up the storybook propped up by her little legs as she lay on the couch. If Tanner and Leah had listened to that advice, there would be no Elysa. There would be no Elliot. The two of them would still be married and living together in Oak Ridge, and I'd be who knows where doing who knows what—maybe up in Minneapolis with Tyler and Jenny, and maybe a few kids of our own. Crazy.

The next day as I was buzzing around the house washing sheets and pulling together supplies to make Chelsea feel at home in our guest room downstairs, Elysa tugged on my shirt and quietly asked, "Mama?"

I looked down into her innocent blue eyes and smiled at the picture she made—cookie crumbs still stuck to her face from our lunch over an hour ago, an apple-flavored juice box in her little hands, the straw clamped between her lips.

"What is it, sweetheart?" I asked.

"What does 'abort' mean?"

I swallowed hard and tried to conceal my horror. I guess Elysa hadn't been as engrossed in her storybook as I thought she had been last night as Tanner and I discussed the issue.

I crouched down to her level and took her little shoulders in my hands. "Why do you ask?"

"I heard you and Daddy talking about it last night," she explained. "You asked him if people told Daddy and my other mommy to abort me. What does that mean?"

How do you answer a question like this and try to make sense of it to a four-year-old? I'd read many stories on the internet of grown men and women discovering they had survived an attempted abortion, and the information was too much for even an adult to handle! How was I supposed to explain something this serious to my four-year-old?

I took a deep breath and began—I wasn't about to brush this off and allow Elysa to walk around with unanswered questions. I wanted her to always feel comfortable to come to me with any question, and if I told her she was too young or that she wouldn't understand, she might not trust me in the future.

"Well, honey, it's complicated. First, you know about your other mommy and about how much she loved you?"

Elysa nodded seriously. "She died so that I could keep living, right?"

"Right," I said. Tanner and I decided right from the beginning that Elysa deserved to know about her mom, the woman who had sacrificed everything so that she could live. She would never have to feel unloved if she could remember that once upon a time, her biological mother had sacrificed her very life to grant that same gift to her daughter.

"Well, your other mommy found out that she was very sick after she was already carrying you around inside her—in her tummy," I explained. "It was the type of sickness that doctors couldn't give her medicine for because the medicine would hurt you, and your other mommy, and Daddy, didn't want to hurt you."

She scrunched her face up. "So what did they do?"

"They decided not to take any medicine. They didn't want to take any chances because even though you weren't born yet, they loved you very much. But some people don't understand that, and that's where the word *abort* comes in." I paused to search for the right words. Abortion is so graphic; it was hard to come up with an appropriate description. "Sometimes mommies don't understand that the babies inside them are really people like you and me. They don't love their baby, so they take the baby out of their tummy before the baby can live outside the mommy on their own," I explained, hating the confusion and horror playing out on Elysa's face.

"They kill the babies?" she asked bluntly.

"They do," I confirmed.

"So..." She looked up at me with deep sadness. "People told Daddy and my other mommy to kill me?"

I wanted to backtrack to last night and never bring up the subject of abortion within Elysa's earshot, because now she had the idea that her daddy had once thought about killing her! I pulled her close to me and stroked her hair.

"Daddy and your other mommy never once thought about listening to those people. Those people were only thinking about your other mommy and helping her to get better. But trust me, honey," I soothed, bringing her back out so I could look into her tear-filled eyes. "They never thought about it. They loved you way too much."

A single tear dripped down Elysa's sweet face. "Did I kill my mommy?"

"No, of course not, Elysa. Your mommy knew that God loved you and wanted you to be born. God had a special plan for you even while you were in your mommy's tummy. And he also had a plan for your mommy—a plan to take her home with him to heaven. Does that make sense?" I asked, and she nodded. "You didn't do anything to your mommy, sweetheart. It was all a part of God's plan. Sometimes we don't understand his plan because it's hard and it hurts, but we have to trust that he knows what's best for us."

I pulled her in for another hug. I hoped that Chelsea would never have to have this conversation with her future child, because it was torture. I sent a silent prayer up to God, thanking him for sparing Chelsea's child. I praised him for helping her see the worth of her child, and I prayed that he would use me these next few weeks or months—however long Chelsea was with us—to shine his light and bring her home to Jesus.

13

Chelsea

May

What am I doing here? I don't belong here. And I certainly don't deserve to be here.

My fingers were curled around the shifter, and my foot was ready to stomp on the breaks; my arms were itching to throw the car into drive and go screeching off into the distance. From there, I wasn't sure where I would go or what I would do. It had to be better than accepting this charity from Mr. and Mrs. Walters, though, right?

My mind wandered back to the days and weeks right after my mom had taken her life. While child protective services searched for any trace of family, I was moved in with a well-meaning foster family trying to do the same thing Molly Walters was doing now. That family, whose name I had long forgotten, wanted to take me in, to offer me food and a warm bed of my own. To hope that they could somehow convince me that there was still good in the world, that I was worth something, and that there was some big plan for my life that I couldn't see at the time but that

I needed to hold out for and just keep walking toward. How was I supposed to believe that back then after all my mom had put me through? After she died, I was half-starved, dirty, and didn't have a cent to my name. In fact, I had walked into that foster home possessing only the clothes on my back. My case worker had taken me to my old apartment to help me gather my things, but as I wandered through the musty rooms, I couldn't find a single item that I wanted to take with me. I had no childhood treasures tucked away anywhere, nothing that held special value to me, as my mom and I had bounced around from building to building escaping eviction after eviction—each time we ran, we took nothing with us, simply the clothes on our backs. It was fitting that I do the same thing the final time I left that world.

Although the circumstances were much different in this situation—it definitely wasn't as bleak—I was still having a tough time believing that there was any sort of plan for my life. Up until a few months ago, my mind-set had been slowly changing. Things were moving along nicely between me and Chase, I was working two tolerable jobs, and I had no real worries. Chase took good care of me; he made me smile and forget about the dark world that seemed to always be lurking in the distance. He was the only person I'd really let get close to me in all the years I'd lived in Kansas, and much to my surprise, it felt good. I always figured that if I let people get close to me, they'd end up disappointing me somehow. Or hurting me. Leaving me, just like my mom did. Giving up and forcing me to fend for myself.

I guess I had been right all along. Just when I thought things were going along smoothly and that my life was finally turning out how I had pictured it might all those lonely nights my mom entertained men just to make enough money to feed us for the weekend, it all came crashing down around me. By letting Chase in, by trusting him and allowing myself to love him—or allowing myself to *think* I loved him—I had made myself vulnerable. With my walls and my guard down, he had destroyed the picture in my head, and just like that, my dream life was gone. Now I was alone again, left to pick up the pieces that someone else had helped to smash but refused to help me collect and put them back together. All because I had chosen my baby—*our* baby—over him.

With nowhere else to go, I had little choice but to heave myself out of my car, grab my one small bag of clothes and toiletries, and trudge up the walkway leading up to Molly and Tanner's house. I had only been here one other time—the afternoon I shared with Molly that I hadn't been able to go through with the abortion. All the planning sessions we'd had had taken place at the diner, where I could be in charge of how long the meetings went and could escape any time I wanted. Her house had looked almost exactly as I imagined it would—cheerful paint splashed up on every wall with tasteful decorations hanging perfectly as they should, shiny wood floors with homey rugs hugging them, and everything in its place. Neat as a pin. It figured, as Molly fit the perfectionist role quite well. I rolled my eyes as I knocked on the door, already pasting on a fake smile to hide my disgust at Molly's perfect, orderly world. A world I had been denied my whole life and clearly would never be invited into to enjoy.

When Tanner swung the door open, I was greeted by a much-different scene than I had on our previous encounter—what seemed like hundreds of toys littered the floor, Elysa was running wild, and Elliot sat screaming in a corner while Molly strained to hear what the person on the other end of her telephone was saying. She had a finger jammed into her ear to try and block out the noise, and she looked like a mess. Her hair was pulled back into a ponytail, but little tendrils had escaped and were flying freely around her head, making her look even more frazzled than I'm sure she felt. Instead of the dark wash jeans, modest blouse, and sweater ensemble that she usually wore, she was dressed in cutoff sweatpants and a baggy Iowa State T-shirt. Tanner didn't look to be in any better shape, and it was only a little past noon on a Saturday—must have been a rough morning.

I took a step back and prepared for the "Sorry, we're not ready for you, and we already have enough chaos in our lives" speech that I was sure was just on the tip of Tanner's tongue. Instead, he greeted me with a hearty "Hey, Chelsea! Come right on in. We've been waiting for you."

I tried to hide my shock—this family didn't look like they had done any waiting today; it looked more like damage control to me. I gave Tanner a weak smile, stepped in and tried to avoid the toys on the floor. Didn't want to break one and become the bad guy on my very first day.

For a while, I just stood there feeling extremely awkward and out of place, watching the family's daily life playing out in front of me. Molly wrapped up her phone call, picked up her screaming toddler and settled her on her hip, and snapped her fingers at Elysa, which stopped her dead in her tracks. "You know you're not supposed to be running in here, especially with all your toys on the floor. We don't want you to get hurt. Now, if you want Daddy to take you outside, then you need to work on picking this all up. Go."

Elysa sighed and began scooping toys off the floor. Tanner dropped to help her, and together they cleared the floor, turning the boring chore into a fun game by seeing who could pick up more toys than the other. Molly still hadn't said hi or even acknowledged me at this point, so I continued to simply stand and observe. It would take a while to feel at home here—to feel comfortable enough to move around and claim my own space. For now, I had to follow Molly's lead.

Finally she turned to me. "Hey. Sorry for the mess. And noise. Better get used to it though, 'cause it's like this more often than not."

"But it was so..."—I searched for a word—"controlled last time."

She laughed. "Yeah. That happens once in a blue moon. The girls had both taken naps that day, and I had gotten lots of cleaning done while they were down. Most days, it's a struggle to get them both down. Maybe you're a good luck charm," she teased. "I can only hope."

Molly left Tanner to care for the girls while she took me downstairs to show me where I would be staying. The guest bedroom was bigger than the room I had shared with Chase, and it was much homier as well. A fluffy green comforter was pulled up over the bed, a nightstand stood next to it, and a basket overflowing with extra blankets sat at the foot. There was a big closet that would make my tiny wardrobe look even more pathetic and a striped brown rug that pulled the whole room together. I turned to Molly. "This is nice."

She smiled. "Thank you. I love decorating, but this room hasn't been used that much. I'm glad someone can enjoy it for a while."

She showed me the guest bathroom—the first bathroom that would be completely mine in my entire life. I shook my head at the little touches Molly had put into this room as well. There was a small jar that housed little travel-sized shampoo and lotion bottles, the kind you find in hotel rooms. She also had a few candles stashed around the room, and she showed me where the matches and bubble bath was. "Just in case you ever need an escape. This tub is huge—look," she said, pulling back the curtain to reveal a large jet bathtub. "Elysa loves using this tub, but I convinced her to share with you. Consider yourself lucky. She isn't always this generous."

I gave a small laugh and tried to blink back the tears that were burning behind my eyes. "Thank you," I croaked, trying to sound as normal as possible. "This is wonderful." Never in my life had I lived in such a nice place. My grandmother's house was dated and tacky, the apartment I'd shared with the girls was cheap and poorly built, and Chase's place had been a total bachelor's pad. It was refreshing to live in an updated, clean, well-decorated space. No matter how much it was killing me to accept charity from these people, I had to admit that this was a nice change of pace.

Molly left me to unpack and get acclimated. Unpacking took less than ten minutes, and after I had all my clothes tucked away and hung up, I flopped on the comfy bed, not wanting to journey upstairs and endure polite small talk just yet. I stared idly up at the ceiling with my hands unconsciously resting on my belly. On my baby. When I realized the protective way my hands were situated, I moved them behind my head. Up until a few days ago, I hadn't allowed myself to really think about what being pregnant meant—that I was carrying around another life inside me. It had only recently moved from being something I could control and get rid of without a second thought to a permanent, life-changing event.

Was I ready for this? Kids had never been a part of my plan. When picturing how my life would play out as a child, I imagined moving far, far away from Kansas and traveling the world. I wanted to see the Eiffel Tower, Big Ben, and the Great Wall of China. I wanted to fall in love—over and over again. To make big mistakes and learn from them and become the wise, beautiful woman I so desperately wanted to be. For too long I had been controlled by other people—my mother, my grandmother, Chase—I just wanted to be free. A pregnancy put a damper on those plans, though, because now my baby would have control over my life. Now I couldn't travel the world, because I would be stuck at home with a baby.

I sighed and squeezed my eyes shut. *One day at a time*, I told myself. There was still a way out of this. I could go back to that abortion clinic if I wanted to. I knew that if I called Chase up and told him I'd changed my mind, he'd take me back in a heartbeat and together we'd take care of the pregnancy and start over. Or I could give the baby up for adoption, like I knew Molly thought was best for me. Regardless of what path I chose, I had *options*, and I wasn't about to get hung up on all this sadness and frustration. Enough with the pity party. Even though life wasn't turning out how I dreamed it would, it was still my life, and I was in control.

When I wandered upstairs later that afternoon, I had to smile at the picture the Walters family made. Molly was stretched out on the couch with Elysa snuggled up close to her, snoring softly. Tanner was sprawled out on the love seat with his legs hanging off the end; Elliot was sleeping peacefully on his chest. A movie played softly from the TV, and I drank in the moment of peace. Maybe being a parent wasn't *all* bad. It had to feel good to fall asleep with your child safe and secure in your arms, waking up to a sticky sweet kiss from their sleepy lips. I swallowed the lump forming in my throat, pushed thoughts of motherhood out of my mind, and plopped on the recliner to wait for the family to wake up.

Dinner was a rushed affair. Molly had prepared a surprisingly delicious chicken dish—she'd arranged chicken breasts down the middle of a dish and added in red potatoes and green beans on either side, topped it with melted butter and a packet of Italian seasoning mix, and then popped it in the oven to bake. I then watched Molly and Tanner love their girls, bathe them, and safely tuck them into their little pink beds. Then they again collapsed onto the couch, looked lovingly into each other's eyes, and sighed in contentment. It was clear to me that they adored their girls and enjoyed every second of their chaotic life.

We spent a quiet evening watching their current favorite television series on Netflix, and when Molly and Tanner began to yawn around nine thirty, I swallowed a giggle. "Well, I'm going to escort my beautiful bride to bed," Tanner said, dropping a kiss on a beaming Molly's forehead. "Feel free to use the TV—you can watch anything on Netflix, and we've got a couple old DVDs and Blu-rays in the drawers under the TV. Help yourself to anything in the fridge. Door is already locked, so if you could just make sure all the lights are off up here when you head to bed, you should be good to go."

And with that, I was once again left alone. Being so hesitant to accept charity, I didn't make myself quite as at home as Tanner and Molly clearly wanted me to. I absently channel surfed but couldn't find anything decent at that time of night. I wasn't about to pull a soda out of their fridge and rummage for a movie from their collection, so I figured turning in early wasn't such a bad idea. If I did decide to keep the baby, I'd need to make the most of a good night's sleep while I still had time.

As I lay in bed, staring up at the ceiling once again, I marveled at how different living here was from what I pictured it to be. Maybe Molly *wasn't* the little Goody Two-shoes I always imagined her to be. She didn't always have her house in order, her kids weren't always well-behaved and clean like they were most of the time in public, and her marriage wasn't perfect. Although she and Tanner were a good team, I'd seen the tension and frustrations leak between them as they worked to get dinner on the table and food into two small kids' mouths and to wrestle the two sticky, squirming girls out of their clothes and get them bathed without completely drenching the bathroom floor with water. I watched Molly roll her eyes when Tanner let Elysa jump out of bed four times to get "just one more drink of water," and I saw Tanner hold back biting comments as Molly brushed off his suggestions and pushed ahead to do things her own way. For the first time, I was seeing them as real human beings—human beings who were just as broken and dysfunctional as I was. I knew their backstory. I knew the things Molly had done and how Tanner had waited to make Molly his wife. I knew about Leah, about Molly's struggle to accept that Tanner had loved another woman. But their struggle seemed to be somehow different than mine—at the end of the day, they had still ended up snuggled up on the couch, holding hands and quoting lines from the show, as if their past had never happened or that they hadn't endured such a long chaotic day. Why was that?

Why was their mess so different than mine? I thought back to my first year in the diner, when Molly had been walking through some of her loneliest, most trying days. I overheard her discussing with Mary Beth how much she missed Tanner and how unsure she had been to move forward with her old boyfriend Tyler and the little girl he wanted to adopt. I saw her tired eyes as she bustled around the diner, eyes that had spent all night studying for her GED as she struggled with her feelings of unworthiness. Still, even as Molly had been dealing with all of that, she never once sat down and complained. I could see that life was draining her, but she never gave up fighting for what she wanted, never let her circumstances get in the way of reaching out to me and the other girls at the diner.

When people interacted with Molly, they could see the same things I saw, the same brokenness and heartache—but they didn't look at her through pity-filled eyes like they did to me. No one shook their head at Molly when they thought she wasn't looking, no one clucked their tongue at her and told her to "keep your chin up," or fed her some other cheesy inspirational line. Those were the things *I* got from people, but Molly was met with something quite different—it was like the people who encouraged her had some strange connection to her, some special understanding that I just didn't share. It could be that I was more closed than Molly was. My dark hair, piercing green eyes, and cold way of keeping people out made it harder for people to connect with me, to genuinely encourage me like they did with Molly. But why was Molly able to keep herself open? Why hadn't the harshness of life affected her like it had me? How was she able to keep her head up, eyes looking forward, and heart open to wherever it was that she would end up?

Was her faith in God really that powerful? I was still having a hard time believing that a simple faith in a God who may or may not exist could affect someone so powerfully, but how else could I explain the way Molly acted? Suddenly I wanted to hear much more of Molly's story and about her life in Minneapolis— how she had acted during the time she had abandoned her faith. Perhaps she had been different while living there—more like me.

I asked her a few days later, when things fell into a nice rhythm and I felt a bit more comfortable moving around in the Walters's house. Elliot was down for a nap, Elysa was pretending to run a bakery in the living room, and I had two hours before I needed to be at the diner. Molly expected brashness from me, so I didn't hesitate to come right out and ask.

"Can you tell me a little bit more about your days in Minneapolis?" I asked.

Her eyes opened a little bit wider in surprise, but then she shrugged. "Sure," she agreed easily, and for the first time, I really started to appreciate Molly's openness. "What brought this on?"

"Just curious," I said, breezing over the real reason I wanted to know. "Going through some of what you went through has got me thinking, that's all."

She nodded. "Well. Where to begin? I moved up, well, I ran away, actually, back in March of 2008 after Tanner and I had a fight. After my rapist found out I was pregnant, he somehow tricked me into thinking Tanner had been the one to tip him off. I went to a small Christian school and there was no way to avoid seeing that guy, so I was trying my best to steer clear of him— part of that plan was never letting him find out that the baby was his, which Tanner had a hard time with. At the time, he didn't know I had been raped, and he thought it wasn't fair to keep the pregnancy a secret from him," she explained. "Anyway, my rapist ended up finding out, and to scare me away, he threatened to go after Tanner and my family, and I was furious that Tanner had caused all of this to happen. I accused him of a lot of bad things, packed, and left." She had sadness dripping from her voice.

"I didn't plan on ending up in Minneapolis. I just sort of started driving. I think my brain must have taken over as I was trying to process all that had happened, though, because my family and I had driven the route to Minneapolis many times on family vacations. When I got there, I had no plans to stay, but things just started falling into place. I met a girl in need of a roommate. She had connections to a job in a diner, and all of a sudden, I had solid plans. I got the abortion within my first week of living there and tried to forget about it from that first day."

She paused and swallowed. I felt my heart tighten up inside me when she mentioned the abortion. As I watched the pain and regret transform her face, I felt a wave of gratitude wash over me. It had been almost ten years ago that Molly had gotten her abortion—ten years—and she was still shaken up about it. I couldn't imagine carrying around that kind of sadness for so long.

"What did…I mean…how did you cope?" I asked, probing for more details.

She gave a sad laugh. "Not in a way I'm proud of. I moped around in bed for days right after the abortion. I remember being in excruciating pain, but after all these years, it's hard for me to remember if I was actually in physical pain from the abortion or just in emotional pain, ya know?" she asked, and I nodded. "The girl I was living with wasn't the most supportive person—definitely not what I had needed at the time. Since we worked together and she had pulled some strings to get me a job, she was pretty obnoxious about getting me back to work at the diner. When I finally did pull myself out of bed and got back into the world, it became a little easier to simply function."

"What do you mean exactly?"

"Well…I guess the best way I can explain it is this: After the abortion, I knew immediately that what I'd done was wrong. I'd made the wrong choice. My heart realized it, but my brain wouldn't let me dwell on it. It was like my brain was trying everything in its power to protect me, and it did that by refusing to think about it. I buried my regret, my guilt. I stopped looking myself in the eye when I looked in the mirror, and my body somehow kept moving on without my permission. I walked around like a robot basically."

I nodded. Molly still wasn't giving me the details I wanted. I thought back to the night in the diner long ago, back to the week

Mary Beth punished me for coming to work drunk by closing up for a five straight days—my least favorite shift. Mary Beth arranged for Molly to close with me on those nights to keep an eye on me, and one night, I broke a stack of glasses. I remembered swearing like a sailor and Molly kicking me out of the kitchen so she could clean up my mess. Then she'd sat me down and shared her story with me, and I vaguely remembered her sharing that the worst part of her experience in Minneapolis was that she'd abandoned God and her faith. It wasn't until she'd hooked up with Mary Beth and Delilah that'd she come back.

"Where was your God in all of this?" I asked, hoping to disguise my genuine interest in the doubt I always whipped out around Molly. She would expect this type of question and wouldn't mistake it for a personal interest in her faith; she'd think I was simply expressing my skepticism.

"Oh, he was there the whole time," she said enthusiastically. "I just wasn't walking with him at the time." She smiled. "I know you didn't grow up in Sunday school, but have you ever heard of Jonah and the whale?" There was a twinkle in her eye.

I nodded. "I don't know the details, just that a whale swallowed up a Bible guy."

She laughed. "Yes. That 'Bible guy' was given instructions from God to go to a city called Nineveh to warn the people about God's impending judgment on their city. He didn't want to go, so he ran away. He ended up on a boat headed for another city, and in his anger, God sent a nasty storm that threatened the lives of all the people on the boat. Jonah knew that he was the cause of the storm and had the crew throw him into the sea. Then the storm stopped."

I rolled my eyes and Molly just chuckled. "Hear me out, okay?" she asked, and I nodded for her to continue. "After Jonah was thrown out of the big fish—the Bible actually says big fish, not whale, but who knows what it was? Anyway, the fish eventually spat Jonah out when he realized what he had done and how foolish he had been to think he could hide from God. Then Jonah followed God's original instructions, went to Nineveh, and the city repented and was spared."

I squinted. "Not quite catching the connection here," I admitted.

"If you had grown up going to Sunday school and I mentioned the name Jonah, the moral of the story would pop into your mind immediately—that it's impossible to hide from God. That's the point the Sunday school teachers always want to make. We can try to ignore God, to walk along without him or even hide from him like Jonah did, but God isn't easily fooled. He knows where we are at all times. He walks beside us even as we refuse to come to him and ignore him. It's impossible to hide from him. So even though I was convinced that I had left God behind for good while living in Minneapolis, he was still there."

I shook my head in confusion. "But how can you say that?" I asked. "You talk about that time in your life with such disgust—I know you wish those years had never happened. How can you say God was there the whole time? If he *was*, why didn't he stop all those bad things from happening? Why didn't you change your mind in the abortion clinic?"

Molly took a deep breath in. "Good questions. Believe me, I struggled with those exact same thoughts. It's hard for me to accept that for my entire life, I had believed abortion was wrong, but that I was able to abandon that belief so quickly. It's hard for me to think about having sex with someone I'm not married to, but I did that without a second thought, like it was no big deal." I almost interrupted, but Molly wouldn't let me. "I know you don't share that belief, and that's fine. But I truly believed that sleeping with someone you're not married to was wrong—I still believe that. It makes me sick thinking I was able to abandon my morals. But God didn't make me sin, Chelsea. I chose to do that myself. I knew that abortion was wrong. I chose to listen to the world, to the devil, over God, though, and my child paid the price. Could

God have stopped me? You bet. But being a Christian doesn't mean you're a robot—God doesn't control your every move and keep you from sinning. Christians still fail miserably, and they don't deserve the grace God has given them. I think that God lets us make choices he knows aren't good for us because in the end, we can learn from them. We can come back to him and ask for his forgiveness—and we will receive forgiveness each time we come to him. Does that make sense?" she asked with kind eyes, eyes willing me to believe her story of faith.

"Kind of," I responded. "I can see where you're coming from. You're saying that just because God has the power to do something, doesn't mean he will—that he allows people to make mistakes so that they can learn and become better people, right?"

"Exactly," she said.

I nodded and then glanced over to the clock. "I better get ready for work. Thanks though, Molly. For everything."

She smiled. "Anytime, kiddo," she said, making me feel young again. Even though I was only twenty years old—still just a kid, really—my difficult life and current circumstances were making me feel quite a bit older than my twenty years. Being here with the Walters family—it was changing me, as difficult as that was for me to admit. I didn't want to become just a charity project for these people. I wanted to get out of here as soon as possible, to avoid falling into their religion and somehow believing that their faith would save me. Religion was just a crutch for weak people anyway. Not something a strong, independent woman like me needed.

Just because Molly struggled without faith didn't mean that I was doing the same. I didn't need some distant God to come galloping in on a white horse to save the day. I didn't need to be saved. I would save myself.

14

Chelsea

September

"You're very good at coloring," little Elysa said to me as we sat at the kitchen table with a *Sesame Street* coloring book and crayons. She was working on a picture of Bert and Ernie talking on the phone, and I was coloring a picture of Cookie Monster whipping up a batch of cookies.

"Thank you," I answered. "You're not so bad yourself. That looks good."

She put her red crayon down, picked up her coloring sheet, and scrutinized her work. "Yeah, well, it's not as good as yours."

I smiled. "I've had lots of years of practice. When you're old like me, yours will look like this. It just takes time."

That satisfied her, and she returned to her work, slowing down and peeking over at me to watch how I outlined the picture and colored inside the lines. Molly shot me a grateful smile from her perch over in the kitchen where she was busily chopping vegetables for the homemade chicken noodle soup she was making for dinner that night. The Turners were joining us for dinner, and Molly wanted everything to be perfect. Having spent so many years learning from Mary Beth, she had nothing to worry about—everything she made tasted wonderful.

My phone started vibrating, and it clattered on the table, startling Elysa and causing her to jerk the green crayon across her page. "Sorry, sweetie," I apologized. She shrugged.

"I'll just give this one to Ellie," she said. "She won't mind that it's not perfect."

"That's a good idea." I glanced down at my still-ringing phone, and my stomach tightened when I saw the name on the screen. "It's Chase," I said to Molly. "Wonder what he wants."

"Guess you'll have to answer to find out," she said, sending me a wink. I didn't really feel like talking to Chase, who hadn't bothered to contact me since the day I'd walked out of the abortion clinic. Now I was already six months pregnant! He'd missed out on so many doctors' appointments by now and hadn't helped me formulate any sort of plan. Curiosity was getting the best of me, though, so I trotted downstairs and answered.

"Hey," I said once I was safely inside my bedroom door. I wanted to ask "What do you want?" but bit my tongue. Maybe he had called to apologize or to offer to help pay some of my medical bills, and starting the conversation off on a sour note might send him running back in the other direction.

"Hey, Chels," he responded. "How are you?"

How am I? Let's see—my belly is now bursting with life. My feet are swollen and puffy, not to mention achy. And a good night's sleep is fast becoming a fantasy for me. I'm living out of a spare bedroom with people I hardly know, and my boyfriend abandoned me because I wouldn't abort his baby. I feel alone and scared, and I still don't have a clue what I'm going to do once I deliver. How do you think I am?

"I'm okay," I said, swallowing all the words I wanted to say, ignoring the deep desire to make him feel awful for abandoning me.

He sighed. "Look, Chels, I miss you."

I rolled my eyes. I didn't really miss him. I missed what we *used* to have before getting pregnant, but I didn't miss how he had treated me after I changed my mind about getting an abortion. I didn't respond.

He sighed again. "I know you're mad at me, and I don't blame you. But come on—how was I supposed to respond after you bailed on our plan?"

"How were *you* supposed to respond?" I asked in shock. "I get that it was kind of a surprise, but let's get something straight here, Chase. *I'm* the one who's pregnant. *I'm* the one who would have been sitting in an operating room aborting our baby. *I'm* the one who would have walked around for days and weeks after it was over wondering if it was a mistake. I know a baby is a game changer—but I never asked you to stay."

"It was kind of implied," he challenged.

"But I never specifically asked you to," I clarified. "Like I said, a baby is a game changer, and I understand that you feel you're not ready to be a dad. Why would I ask someone like that to stay with me and be a parent?"

"So you're not gonna drag me to court?"

"Look, you have legal obligations," I reminded him. "This baby is biologically yours—if I decide to keep the baby and you decide not to be involved, you still have to pay child support. You know I don't have the money to do this on my own. I can be a single parent—I don't need your help raising this kid. I *will* need your financial support, though, and, yes—I *will* drag you to court if you don't cooperate."

"But you said *if* you keep the baby. Still thinking of getting an abortion?"

I laughed. "No. I'm six months along, Chase. I've felt the baby move. There's no way I'm getting an abortion. I'm looking into adoption, though."

"Oh," he said simply. "Well, if that's the case…I mean, if there's not gonna be a baby in the picture anymore, maybe we could start over. You could move back after giving it up."

"Seriously?" I asked, horrified. "Wow, how generous of you, Chase. Really. Offering to let me move back in with you and start dating again only if I give the baby up? Why would I want to live with a person like that?"

"Would you please stop making me seem like such a horrible person?" he asked with real sadness dripping from his voice. "I realize that I'm not the one having the baby. But that doesn't mean it's not affecting me or that I shouldn't have any say. I didn't have a dad growing up, and because I had four other siblings, my mom worked a lot—I didn't see many examples of what a good parent looks like. Can you blame me for being a little hesitant to jump into fatherhood?"

I closed my eyes, counted to ten to calm down, and began again. "I understand. I can relate completely—I didn't have a dad, and my mom died when I was twelve. After that, I lived with my grandma, who was too old to take me in in the first place. I didn't have a good example either, but that doesn't mean I can't learn. I'm watching my friend Molly and her husband Tanner raise their girls, and it scares me. They are great parents, and their kids are still little terrors sometimes. They look exhausted all the time, and I know Molly worries about messing her kids up constantly. Parenting isn't easy regardless of how you were raised or your current situation—but if I decide to keep the baby, I'm gonna do the very best I can—that's really all I can do."

For a while, he remained silent, and I brought my phone away from my face to see if he had hung up on me. He hadn't, so I waited. Then he said quietly, "I think you'll be a great mom."

I smiled. "Thank you. I think you'd be a good dad too."

He laughed. "I'm not so sure about that."

I thought back to something Molly had mentioned a few days ago, something about parenting classes being offered through a local church. "They're not trying to brainwash you into raising your kids in the church," she had assured me. "My friend Ruth is helping teach the class, and she showed me the curriculum. It's not a faith-based class at all. You should consider it."

"But you could learn," I reminded him. "I'm thinking about taking a parenting class. Starts in two weeks. You should think about coming—even if we don't end up raising this baby together, I think it would be good for you. Who knows, you might have a family someday, right?"

"I might. I'll think about it. Let you know by next week?"

"Sounds good."

"All right. Well, I'll let you go," he said. "Take care of yourself."

"I will."

"Bye, Chels." I was about to hang up when he added, "I love you."

I held back a sad laugh, unsure how to respond. "Bye, Chase."

And with that, I hung up. I hadn't been sleeping well at night because of how uncomfortable I was getting, and somehow that short conversation had drained me even further of what little energy I had left. I couldn't believe he had offered to let me back into his life if only I gave the baby up! Why couldn't he have called to apologize and beg for my forgiveness? To tell me he wanted to be a father and to marry me and build a life together as a family of three?

I was surprised at how open he was to enrolling in the parenting class, though. I had expected him to dismiss the idea immediately. If he came to the classes and learned how to be a good dad, maybe he would change his mind. Maybe we could get back together again and make it work this time. Maybe there was still hope for us after all.

I didn't hear from Chase again in the next two weeks, so I enrolled in the parenting class by myself. When I walked through the doors to the class, my heart fell—the whole room was full of beaming, happy couples. The church was offering a few different classes—one was a first time parenting class, one a class for those with toddlers and preschoolers, and another was for those with older children. This was of course the first time parenting class, so I knew that all of these bright-eyed couples were happily and anxiously awaiting their first baby's arrival. I wanted to sink quietly back out the door without drawing any attention to myself, but something made me stay, and suddenly I was walking in, head held high, vowing to not let myself feel inferior to these people simply because I was a single mom.

I recognized Molly's friend Ruth from how she had described her to me; she had curly shoulder-length brown hair and a kind smile. She walked quietly, with graceful movements—she seemed like the kind of person who was able to sit down and have a conversation with just about anyone. I noticed that she was pregnant herself, probably in her fifth or sixth month. Molly hadn't mentioned that to me. Ruth was helping two other people lead the class, a married couple whose names were Seth and Kayla. Kayla, who was a bit more outgoing and talkative than her partner, took the lead in opening discussion.

"Welcome! We are so glad you're here for our first time parenting class. We thought we'd start off my introducing ourselves and our spouses and telling the group what you know about your baby—the gender if you know, any names you're considering—and what you're most excited or nervous about."

Inwardly I groaned. I would be the odd one out from the first meeting! The leaders assumed that everyone here was married. That's what living in a small conservative town got you. Because I was sitting in the back, I knew I'd have time to bail if I wanted, and as my turn to speak got closer and closer, the more tempted I was to do so. Finally, I couldn't stand it any longer, and I stood to leave, only to bump into Chase on my way up.

"What are you doing here?" I hissed as he took my arm and brought me back to my seat.

"I'm here for a parenting class, what else?" he said with a grin.

I shook my head and resettled into my seat, my heart now pounding. I'd spent two weeks letting the fact that Chase had once again abandoned me fester inside me, and his showing up unexpectedly was making it hard to keep hating him—which I really, really wanted to do. Chase didn't deserve forgiveness or understanding for abandoning me! Why couldn't he just stay away and let me keep hating him?

When it came time for us to introduce ourselves, everyone just assumed we were a couple and that Chase had simply been running a bit late. He took the lead.

"Hello, my name is Chase MaHooney. This is Chelsea. Chelsea is six months along, and we don't know the gender yet. Don't have any names picked out either. Guess we better get thinking!" he joked, and the group laughed politely. With the introductions now over, I relaxed, content to just sit and listen. To disappear into the group. Luckily for me, the introductions were the only interactive part of the class—at least, the only mandatory interactive part. The teachers asked questions and expected the group to answer, but thankfully they didn't call on the quieter ones, like me and Chase.

This session focused more on the last few months and weeks of pregnancy, how to tell if labor had begun, what to bring to the hospital, and what to expect in labor and delivery. Ruth explained that as the class progressed, we'd move into other topics, such as the first few days of parenthood, getting your baby on a schedule, and dealing with postpartum depression. Later on, we'd discuss parenting techniques and touch on discipline and other issues that came with raising kids. So far, I was pretty overwhelmed, as I tried to avoid thinking about my eventual delivery as best I could. I had a pretty low pain tolerance and wasn't exactly looking forward to it. It also overwhelmed me to think about postpartum depression, as I had already dealt with so much in my life. Could I handle any more emotions swirling around in my head?

One day at a time, I reminded myself. *You don't have to deal with it all at once. Just keep an open mind.*

Keeping an open mind was something I was working on. All my life, I had worked to become self-sufficient, determined not to rely on anyone for anything because I knew I couldn't trust people. I had been abandoned before by my mom, what was stopping others from doing the same? To me, it was much safer to shut everyone out and focus solely on myself. To trust no one and reject all forms of advice or encouragement. As a teenager, it had been easy. I'd really had no worries or cares in the world. Convincing myself I was invincible and all-knowing hadn't been difficult, as there had been no real threats and no decisions to make that I couldn't make on my own. Now, though, I was in foreign territory—I knew absolutely nothing about having a baby or being a parent! I knew next to nothing about pregnancy, labor, and delivery, and because I hadn't been raised by a good parent, I didn't know the first thing about discipline or raising a decent kid. So even though I felt my blood pressure rising with each piece of advice and tip Ruth, Seth, and Kayla gave to us, I instructed myself to take deep, cleansing breaths to relax and to remember that I wasn't alone. I had Molly and Tanner helping me.

When class ended, I wanted to quickly stand up and make a swift exit, but before I could make my getaway, Chase asked, "Do you want to get ice cream?"

No. I don't want to get anything with you, my mind screamed. However, my body was screaming something else. This summer had been unseasonably dry and hot—more so than usual. The dry heat had carried through the fall, and needless to say, it had been a miserable last four months. There wasn't a moment that I wasn't dripping with sweat, even inside air-conditioned buildings, and ice cream had become my escape. I was almost ashamed at how much ice cream I had consumed over the summer and how much weight I was putting on because of it. After delivering, I was worried about how different my body was going to be, as I had always been thin and toned. Hopefully I would be able to get my prebaby figure back.

Still, the worries about my weight and drive to get away from Chase at all costs lost out to my desire to alleviate my constant state of misery, and I found myself agreeing. Chase rewarded me with a smile, and we walked out together. He put his hand on the small of my back, as if to lead me, and I stiffened. His hand dropped. We were *not* a couple anymore—this simple, natural thing that a normal couple would do without a second thought was completely unacceptable, and if Chase wanted to keep a relationship with me, he needed to play by my rules.

Once outside and a good distance away from the church, I turned to him with a scowl. "None of this boyfriend-girlfriend stuff, Chase. We're done. You don't touch me unless specifically asked, and I make the rules. I agreed to ice cream. That's it. Don't try to get me back. Not happening."

Chase threw his hands up in surrender. "Okay, okay. Sorry. I was just trying to be nice."

"Well, don't," I spat.

"Fine," he retorted, and for a while, we walked in silence. Green Lake was small enough that there wasn't a year-round ice cream shop, but a local family operated a small shop in the tiny downtown area that was open from May until October. The little building was big enough to house only the necessities, meaning there was no indoor seating and you couldn't even go inside to order—you had to either use the drive thru or order from a window and take your ice cream to go. And since Green Lake is such a small town, everything is in walking distance, so we continued walking in silence the entire way over.

When we got there, Chase offered to pay for me, and I let him—not because this was a date but because I was saving every cent I earned to support the baby, should I decide to keep it. Buying ice cream wouldn't put a dent in my savings of course, but every penny mattered.

Once we both had our ice cream—we'd both gotten vanilla and chocolate twist cones—we crossed the street to a park and settled onto a wooden bench. As Chase sat, enjoying his ice cream, I caught him looking at me with appreciation, and my cheeks turned pink. Pregnancy had been kind to me; my already-thick black hair had somehow gotten thicker and shinier. It had never looked healthier. My skin was glowing, still sun-kissed from the afternoons I had spent with Molly and her kids in their backyard, splashing in their kiddy pool and watching the girls run through the sprinklers with glee. And aside from my ankles swelling, my long legs were still thin and tanned. I had to admit that being admired felt good, especially when I didn't always like what I saw when I looked into the full-length mirror in my bedroom. I was my worst critic.

"I want to apologize for how I've been behaving through this whole thing," Chase finally said after our long period of silence. "I think I'm just overwhelmed by the thought of being a dad—for being responsible for another life. Kinda freaky, isn't it?"

I nodded. "I feel the same way. I still don't know if I'm gonna keep the baby, though."

He pulled his lower lip between his teeth. "But doesn't the thought of adoption make you...a little sad?"

I raised my eyebrows. "Does it make *you* sad?"

"Little bit," he admitted then laughed. "Weird how I can feel so scared and inadequate when it comes to the idea of parenthood and yet the idea of not knowing my kid freaks me out almost as much."

I had no idea Chase felt that way, especially since he had been so upset when I walked away from the abortion. I felt my heart tighten up inside me—it wasn't really fair that Chase didn't want to be a parent, but that the thought of adoption made him sad. If he wanted to be a part of our child's life, the only option was to help me parent. I wasn't about to let him manipulate me into keeping the baby and then once again abandoning me! If he wanted to be a parent, he needed to make up his mind. And quick.

Keep your cool, I reminded myself. Chase wouldn't respond if I shut him out, and I didn't want to drive him away with a bad attitude. If he was softening up to the idea of parenthood, I couldn't push it. It might not be a quick decision like I wanted. I just had to be patient. After all, it had taken me a while to warm up to the idea of being a mom. It was only fair that I give Chase the time to do the same.

"It's taken me a while to warm up to the idea of being a mom. I just want to make the best decision for the baby, ya know?" I asked. "Maybe I *could* be a good mom—I could learn. But would I be able to give the baby everything it needs? Stability? Love? Could I even provide for all their needs? I get freaked out pretty fast when I stop and consider what it means to raise a kid."

Chase turned to me. "Look, Chels. Maybe we should give us another shot. Maybe you wouldn't be a good mom alone. Not saying that you couldn't, 'cause I think you could, but we both want what's best for our kid. Maybe that means raising it together. What do you think?" he asked with hopeful eyes.

I swallowed and look him straight in the eye. "I don't know, Chase…"

"We don't have to decide today," he said, covering my hand with his as I sat gripping the edge of the bench. I commanded my heart to not respond, but I couldn't deny how good it felt that Chase was offering to come back and be a family with me and the baby. "Let's take it slow this time, okay? I'm not asking you to move back in or to marry me. But can we at least start hanging out together again?"

I tried to think of one good reason to say no. But hadn't my one wish for the last few months been for Chase to walk back in and offer exactly what he was? Even as I had been holding everything that he'd done wrong against him and using that to justify my hatred, I had *still* wanted this more than anything else.

"Yeah, I think that's a good idea. I mean, even if we don't end up back together, it's probably good to build some kind of a relationship, for the baby's sake. The baby deserves for us to get along," I agreed.

Chase burst into a smile, but I saw him holding back all the happiness that was surging through his body—Chase is a very passionate person, and he has a hard time holding in emotions. I knew that he wanted to jump in the air and celebrate by swinging me around, but instead he remained on the bench and was content to simply smile.

"Thank you," he whispered. "I'll let you be in charge of how much contact we have. You decide when and where."

I was glad he finally realized my need for control and that he wasn't going to be pushy and demanding about how much time we spent together.

And for the first time in months—years, really—I felt at peace.

"I didn't really know Chase before you got pregnant, but even so...he seems different," Molly commented one evening. Chase had come over for supper and was now sprawled out on the floor building a block tower with Elysa and Elliot. He and Elysa would stack the blocks as fast as they could, then Elliot would knock it down, laughing loudly and clapping her hands each time the blocks came tumbling down.

I nodded. "He does. We're trying to get it all figured out—it's all still so unclear and we're scared, but I think it's gonna be okay."

"Good!" Molly said with a smile, and then she stood up to begin clearing dishes. I stood up to help her, but she shooed me away. "You do enough around here. Women who are seven months pregnant no longer have to help. Take advantage of it while you can." She winked. Right now I had no plans to move out so after the baby came I was expected to help out again. I had a sizeable amount of money saved up because Molly and Tanner didn't charge rent, plus they opened their kitchen to me and told me not to worry about buying my own groceries. Moving out was a possibility still, but there was no certainty as to when that would happen.

"I remember being single and tight on cash," Molly had said when I first moved in. "We're at a point in our lives now where we can afford to help you out—and we want to. You just worry about saving up and making a plan for that baby of yours."

Molly and Tanner had done more than enough for me, and yet they were always striving to do more. Because I *still* hadn't decided if I wanted to keep the baby or go with adoption, they told me I could continue living with them for as long as I needed—even after the baby was born.

"That room's plenty big enough for a crib," Tanner said. "And since we're up in the third story, we won't be able to hear a thing at night. We're used to crying babies during the day too."

I didn't want to overstay my welcome, but it seemed that the Walters genuinely wanted to help out in any way possible, even if that meant I occupied their spare bedroom for a little longer than expected. Soon I'd have enough money to afford a rental house, but it would be a bit longer for me to gather household necessities. It was frustrating to be so tight on money.

When Molly and Tanner began gathering up the girls for their bedtime routine, Chase and I headed out for a walk. Now that October had come the weather was a bit kinder, and I welcomed the cool fresh air on my skin as we walked down the road. We walked in a comfortable silence, and after a few blocks, Chase reached over and wove his fingers into mine. I let him, and warmth spread through me. Was a future with Chase really possible?

As the weeks went on, I allowed myself to consider the idea more and more. Chase was logging away as many hours as possible at his job, and any spare time he got was spent with me. He had never been as tender and as thoughtful as he had been in the last month, and as my belly kept expanding and the baby kicked and moved with more strength, I let myself dream of our future as a family of three. No matter how inadequate we felt and no matter how scary the idea of parenthood still was, I knew that we could learn to be good parents. No one is really prepared to be a first time parent anyway, right?

But if you watched closely, Chase wasn't as convincing as he was trying to be. To the casual observer, like the hopeful Molly, Chase's changed behavior seemed like a dream come true. But she didn't spend as much time with him as I did—she didn't see the empty, faraway look in his eyes and didn't see him constantly texting his roommates about what video game they were playing, what the score of the game was, or about how epic last night's beer pong session had been. I gave Chase credit for trying, but deep down, I knew that the life I wanted for us—the American dream life—wasn't what he wanted right now. Although Chase was about to become a father, it didn't mean that he was ready or willing to stay and be a parent.

So when Chase asked me to marry him one month before I was to give birth, I hesitated. Was I ready to thrust Chase into a life I *knew* he wasn't ready for, no matter how hard he tried to convince me he *was*? Was I ready to constantly compete for his attention, to show him that a marriage and a family was truly better than hours of video games and beer pong? Was I ready to try and draw him back from wherever he went when his eyes glazed over like they did with more and more frequency?

Why *was* Chase proposing when he clearly didn't want this life? Was it guilt? Shame? The desire to please me? Were those feelings enough to keep him, or would he get bored after the baby and wedding were over and real life settled in? Would he dare abandon me again?

He hadn't proposed in any sweet way—there was no ring, and he hadn't even gotten down on one knee. If he had gone through the trouble of picking out a ring and planning a sweet proposal, I might have gotten caught up in the excitement and let that get in the way of reality: that Chase wasn't ready, that he didn't want this life, and that if we got married, I would spend our whole lifetime together vying for his attention and trying to get him to see that the baby and I were worth it.

"I'm so sorry, Chase," I said as his face fell. "But I just don't think getting married is a good idea."

"Why not?" he asked. "Don't you want me to take care of you? Isn't that why you've been spending so much time with me?"

Right there, the truth was ringing out loud and clear—Chase thought I was only after the security he could offer me, and he felt guilty about not giving that to me. "Being taken care of would be nice," I said gently. "But be honest, Chase. When you think about your life—right now—do you see marriage and family in your future? Do you think of sleeping with me and only me for the rest of your days, for trading the video games and beer pong for bath time and bedtime stories?"

He hesitated and swallowed. His silence answered for him. I shrugged. "See? I know this isn't what you want."

He threw his hands up. "I'm just trying to do the right thing, Chelsea. Part of being an adult is doing things you don't really want to do."

"Yeah, like paying bills and doing your own dishes," I argued. "Not getting married. No girl wants to be proposed to and then get told that it's just something adults do. Something you don't really *want* to do but *have* to do."

"I...that's...I didn't mean it like that," he stammered.

I commanded myself to be a little gentler. Chase's intentions were good; he was buying into the idea that marriage would fix us, that just because we had gotten pregnant meant we should get married to "legitimize" our child. I agreed that it was best to raise a baby in a family, with a mom and a dad, but I wasn't convinced that we were the right mom and dad for the job.

"I know. I'm sorry, but I don't think we should get married. I'm not going to commit myself to a lifetime of fighting for your attention. I think one day you'll be a good dad. But you're not ready yet, and I know you don't want it right now."

He fell silent and then let his face fall into his hands. After a few moments, he looked up and asked, "What do we do now? I mean, with the baby."

"I don't think I'm ready either, Chase," I admitted.

"So what? You're gonna give the baby up?"

I nodded. "I think so."

He sighed. "I think that's a good idea," he finally said. "I mean, it's not easy. I was actually getting a little excited. That kid's gonna be cute."

I smiled. "Yeah. But I think it's what's best. We can agree to an open adoption, if we find the right couple. We don't have to just hand the baby over and never see him or her again. What do you think of that idea?" I asked.

He bit his lip and thought for a moment. "I think I could live with that."

And just like that, we had a plan. A real honest-to-goodness plan. One we both felt good about, even though it would be hard. I had never felt more grown up than now, because for once in my life, I had made a big decision, one that required me to sacrifice my own desires for someone else. Although I would carry around an emptiness after giving up my baby, I knew I couldn't give my child the life I wanted him or her to have—the life I never had. A life I didn't think Chase and I could provide together and certainly not a life I could provide on my own. I truly felt that the only way was through adoption.

Chase and I agreed to remain friends, and he wanted to be there when I delivered, wanted to hold and say his hellos and good-byes to the baby. Not a permanent good-bye, if we secured an open adoption, but a good-bye to the life we had started imagining in the last few weeks: a life as a family of three.

As I lay in bed that night, I allowed the hot tears that had been building all evening after I rejected Chase's proposal to roll down my cheeks and soak my pillow. Getting ahold of my out-of-control emotions was proving to be much more difficult than I imagined! So much had changed over the last eight months. First I had gotten pregnant after never even considering the idea of motherhood. Then I had been dead set on getting an abortion and moving on as if nothing happened. That plan had of course deteriorated when I saw my baby through an ultrasound machine, but deciding to keep the baby had brought on a whole new slew of emotions. I constantly agonized over what to do: Should I keep the baby and raise it myself? Should I allow Chase back into my life, allow him to "save" me by marrying me and then endure a marriage that I knew wasn't meant to be and that Chase didn't really want? Was adoption truly the way to go? It seemed that whatever I considered, I had doubts about. Why couldn't there be some sort of a sign? Or a sense of peace to let me know I'd done the right thing?

Perhaps I would never know. Maybe I would wonder my whole life if I had done the right thing. Agonizing over my choice wasn't helping, though. And in my despair, I found myself doing the one thing I never thought I'd do.

I prayed.

15

Chelsea

November

When I felt the first pangs of labor on the quiet Friday after Thanksgiving, I commanded myself to stay calm. The minute I showed any panic, I knew Molly would spring into the overprotective mother bird that she'd become the closer we became throughout my pregnancy. I knew she had my best interest in mind, but it was also a tad overwhelming. So overwhelming, in fact, that I would rather suffer through the beginning stages of labor on my own than have to endure her fretting, worrying mother hen tendencies.

Molly still had no idea that I was going to give my baby up for adoption—which was causing her to freak out even more than she already was about this whole ordeal. Normally Molly didn't step foot into the room I was occupying in the basement, but curiosity got the best of her and she snooped. When she discovered that I didn't have one shred of baby supplies, she gently asked me if she could throw a small baby shower for me at her church to gather some things for me.

I almost told her. But something held me back. I needed this decision to be mine and mine alone. Even from the beginning, I had known that Molly thought that adoption was the right decision for me to make. Having lived through both an abortion and raising children, she knew more than anyone how ill-equipped I was to deal with both of those decisions. I wasn't emotionally stable to deal with the feelings of sadness and regret that sometimes follow after an abortion, and I didn't have the means to raise a child either. Still. Even with these sound truths ringing in my mind, I didn't need Molly's reassurance that I was making the right choice. I didn't need her telling me how responsible and loving I was being to give my child a better shot at life. I needed to come to those conclusions on my own.

I'd needed the time to consider keeping and raising the baby. Some of the most magical nights in the past nine months were the ones dreaming about holding my baby for the first time, of smelling that sweet baby smell as I rocked him or her to sleep, and of soothing away the tears in a way that only mothers know how to do.

I'd needed the time to work on my relationship with Chase to consider the possibility of a future with him as a family of three. And even though none of those dreams were going to become a reality—at least for now—it had been worth it. I wasn't the same cold, guarded person I had been before getting pregnant. I'd learned the value of coming to others for advice and help, swallowing my pride and accepting that help, and letting people in and giving them a chance to prove themselves trustworthy. And even though I was about to lose the fragile dreams I'd been building over the last few months, I also knew that I had gained so much from this experience. I'd grown and changed into someone I could hardly recognize, someone I knew my mother would be proud of.

I humored Molly, though, and sat through a remarkably pleasant baby shower. I had expected suspicious glances and shaking heads and women leaning over to whisper into each other's ears of what a shame it was that someone like me had gotten pregnant—someone so unprepared and confused, with no future or hopes of assembling the type of life these ladies were living. But I didn't get any of those things. The women who gathered in my honor were eager to hand their gifts to me and to ask me questions about my pregnancy and encourage me with advice from their own. The room was full of smiles and laughter, and I left with all the essential baby supplies—a large stack of diapers, a pile of soft, cuddly blankets, a closet full worth of adorable baby clothes, and even a crib. The women had all pitched in to purchase the crib, and my heart melted in gratitude.

I almost walked out on the adoption after the baby shower. Even though Chase and I wouldn't be getting married, if I kept the baby, he would at least pay child support. I had more than enough money by now to make a deposit on a rental house and pay the first few months of rent while on maternity leave from both my jobs. And I had all the essential baby supplies. Maybe I could make this work!

But then I would have flashbacks to my childhood. Memories of a struggling mother who never seemed able to provide enough food or decent clothes and of empty, meaningless Father's Days that caused anger and confusion to build with each passing year assaulted me with a vengeance. How long would Chase want to stay in the picture? Would he eventually grow tired of supporting a child and leave one day, causing the same emptiness and confusion to grow within our child? Would I hit hard times just like my mother and find myself unable to put food on the table? Would I be forced to send my child to school in dirty, worn clothes from a secondhand store because that's all I could afford?

My heart broke inside me when I realized that I truly wasn't ready. I may have the money and supplies to take care of my baby for now, but I had to face the reality that down the road, things might change. As a single mother, I couldn't offer my child all the things I wanted for him or her, no matter how much love was growing in my heart. Love didn't pay the bills or put food on the table. The good intentions of a single mom don't make up for the missing stability that two parents can provide. I knew I could do it. And that the loving support of a mother can still provide a good home. But it wasn't the life I wanted—for me or for my baby.

So I made the most loving decision I could. I chose to give life and then hand my child over to someone who could love, support, and raise him or her in a way I couldn't, no matter how much I wanted to.

Molly and Tanner watched me with quiet suspicion as I stretched out on the couch trying to mask my growing uncomfortable state. Normally I would try to be as helpful as I could after supper by clearing the table and then entertaining the girls for a bit, but tonight I was content to cuddle with Elliot as Winnie-the-Pooh played softly from the TV. When the first powerful contraction squeezed my midsection, taking my breath away in shock, I knew I couldn't keep quiet any longer. I sent Molly a look of fear, and she quietly explained to Tanner that he needed to take over bed and bath time while she took me to the hospital.

Tanner gathered the girls up and herded them down the hallway while Molly gently helped guide my arms into a coat that I hadn't been able to fully zip up for three months. She opened the door of my car, complete with a car seat nestled into the backseat, still under the impression that her house would be expanding by one tiny member sometime during the next day. I allowed myself another brief moment of sorrow, but the physical pain of labor was increasing by the minute, making it impossible to focus on anything else. We endured a surprisingly quiet, calm trip to the hospital the next town over, free from Molly's nervous worrying. It never ceased to amaze me how easy it was to misjudge the people closest to me.

In the following hours, I did my best to detach myself from reality. Fully aware that in the end, no matter how much I hemmed and hawed about my decision, I would hand my baby off after hours of labor. I would do all the work and only enjoy a few moments of the result—I'd decided to meet and hold the baby before my social worker came and took him or her from me. Chase decided at the last minute that he too wanted to meet and hold the baby, knowing he would probably regret it for his entire life if he didn't. So as Molly and Chase held my hand and coached me through contractions, as the doctor came and announced it was time to push, I only allowed myself to listen to physical commands. I ignored the comforting murmurs of support Molly and Chase offered. I didn't take in any of my surroundings. When it was all done and over, I wanted to remember none of it. None. Moving on would be so much easier without the sad, heavy baggage of memories.

An eight-pound six-ounce, twenty-two-inch-long healthy baby boy entered the world at 5:02 AM on Saturday, November 26, 2016. Instead of placing him on my chest, as Molly was clearly expecting them to do, the nurses first took him away to be cleaned up and wrapped in a blanket.

"Did you ask them to do that?" she asked after making the mandatory congratulations that follow after a baby is born.

"I did," I wearily replied.

"Oh," she responded, trying to mask her confusion. "Do you want me to give you and Chase some time alone when they bring him back?"

"That would be nice," I said, and with a nod, she left.

For the next hour, Chase and I held our nameless baby boy in silence. Tears pricked at my eyes and my heart swirled in confusion. How would I hand this beautiful child over to Jamie, my caseworker? How would I go to bed tonight empty, after spending the last nine months getting to know this little boy?

How could I make a life for myself knowing that wherever I went, a piece of me would always be in a little town in Kansas?

Jamie came in after our hour was wrapping up to see if we were ready or if we needed more time. I knew more time would just make it even more difficult, so I gave her a brave smile, wiped my eyes dry, and told her we were ready.

"Your friend Molly wants to know if she can come back in," Jamie said. "What should I tell her?"

"She can come in," I assured her.

Molly came in with an even more perplexed look than when she left. "I just ran into Greg and Delilah in the waiting room," she said. "They were talking with the woman who was just in here. Am I missing something?"

I swallowed the lump in my throat. "I'm giving the baby up, Molly."

Her eyes registered the news with shock, but she remained calm and composed. "Why didn't you tell me?"

"Because I needed to arrive at this decision on my own. In your mind, adoption was always the road you thought was best for me. I wanted to come to that conclusion on my own—without the constant reassurance from you. It's hard to explain, but..." I trailed off.

"No, I understand completely," she said with a small smile.

"I got to choose the family with the agency I went with," I explained. "I flipped through page after page of Kansas families when I found the Turners. I knew the minute I saw their profile that I wanted them to raise my baby."

Molly broke out into a grin and shook her head. "How long have you guys been keeping this from me? Delilah never even told me they were trying to adopt."

"I waited 'til the very last minute. Chase and I broke up in September," I said, glancing his way with a sad smile, "and once I knew we couldn't be a family of three, I decided to go with adoption. It's killing me. But I know I can't give this little guy the life I want for him." I looked up at Molly to see tears filling her eyes. "The life I never had. I want so much more for him. I know Greg, Delilah, and their kids can give him a good life."

"You *do* realize who the grandma of this little boy is, don't you?" she teased, knowing the rocky history Mary Beth and I shared.

I laughed. "I know she's going to play a big part in giving him the life I want for him. She helped save me, Molly," I said with a cracking voice. "I can't think of a better grandma than her."

"Well, she'll be honored to know that, I'm sure," Molly said. She rubbed her hands together and began backing toward the door. "I'm sure I'll have the chance to formally meet him soon. Let me know if you need anything." She slipped out into the hallway, trying to give Chase and me a bit of privacy before one of the hardest moments in both our lives.

Jamie came back after Molly left, and I handed the baby over to Chase so he could say his last good-byes. Although this would be an open adoption, I didn't plan to stick around Green Lake for much longer, and I didn't know when I would see him again. Chase planned to move away as well—after such an exhausting chapter in both our lives, a change of scenery would do us good. He didn't have much of a plan in place, but for now, he was set to move to Montana in three months to meet up with an old college buddy who owned a ranch. This good-bye was heartbreaking for both of us. The uncertainty of our next meeting and thoughts of all that we would miss in our time apart were making this a whole lot harder than I ever imagined.

Chase snuggled his son close and kissed his nose, and then handed him back to me. I closed my eyes and allowed myself to make one concrete memory of the day—I breathed in his sweet baby smell, wishing I could bottle it up and carry it with me always. I ran my thumb across his smooth skin, memorizing the way it felt under my finger. And I brought his cheek next to mine and allowed my tears to brush onto his, promising to never forget the few moments of intimate connection we'd shared.

And then I handed my son over to Jamie and watched her leave with him, my arms already aching with emptiness just as Delilah's and Greg's were preparing to welcome him in to theirs.

—⏤꜓꜓⏤—

As I walked along the warm, sunshiny sidewalk in downtown Kansas City, I took the time to tilt my head back, close my eyes, and breathe in the fresh scent of spring. Today little Jude was six months old—and boy was he a cutie. Before moving to Kansas City, Delilah insisted I give her my new address, which was currently a small one-bedroom apartment, so she could send me pictures and updates of Jude. My dated fridge was full to bursting with pictures of his first six months of life, lists of what milestones he had reached, what his favorite foods were, and the things he enjoyed doing. The Turners were currently treasuring his deep belly laugh, which, according to Delilah, he rewarded them with for just about anything. Last week, she sent me a video clip of one of his laughing spells through e-mail, and I just about wore out the Replay button from how many times I clicked it. From the sounds of it, he was content, happy, and well-adjusted.

For once in my life, I could say the same thing. I was working part time at a grocery store, mostly stocking shelves on the weekends for extra cash as I worked at a youth program during the week. Though my job at the store was boring and monotonous, it allowed me some wonderful uninterrupted thinking time, something I had never really allowed myself to do for my entire life. Having lived through such turmoil, I was discovering that my coping mechanism had been to shut down completely. In order to protect myself from breakdowns and flashbacks later on, I had simply blocked out the more traumatic portions of my life and then never allowed myself the luxury of thinking back or retrieving memories. As a child, this had probably been for the best, but as an adult, I was working on allowing myself to live in the moment, to *feel*, to think.

I didn't get much of a chance to think during the week. From 9:00 AM until 5:00 PM, I worked with at-risk youth, kids who couldn't seem to function in the foster care system or who were about ready to age out of the program and find themselves completely alone. I knew exactly what these kids were going through—I knew what it felt like to be labeled as poor, lazy, and unmotivated. I'd sat through the same lectures these kids got at school from well-meaning teachers and guidance counselors that they just needed to "buck up, have a better attitude, and try harder." But after years of living in poverty, of never even having enough money to just get by, and of being told there is no future for you and that you'll just end up like your parents, the willpower to "buck up, have a better attitude, and try harder" quickly fades. Without the love and support of parents or grandparents or even a mentor of some kind, problematic kids in the foster care system face a bleak future. The program I worked at matched kids with long-term mentors to walk beside them, teach them basic life skills, and just be someone the kids could rely on. For some of the kids, their mentor was the only stable person in their life, the only one they could turn to for support.

I was currently working with two young ladies. One was living in a residential treatment home and finishing up her high school education in the program. The organization I was working for recognized that some students simply can't learn through public education—perhaps their home life was so much of a distraction to them that just like me, they shut themselves off from the world and no teacher, no matter how good, could seem to get through. Perhaps the constant worry about where their next meal would come from or where they would go for the night if dad started beating up mom again kept them from focusing, and they never learned how to properly sit and pay attention in class. So a small group of high school teachers were available to help those kids, with more of an individualized teaching approach.

Amira was bright, I could tell. She was a feisty fifteen-year-old who put up a false front, one that screamed, "I don't care, leave me alone, and stop wasting your time," but the delight that lit up her eyes when she made a connection with what she was learning was too powerful to hide. She was of mixed race, unable to identify all the unique backgrounds swirling around in her blood, and in her old neighborhood, this made her a target. She was raised in an all African American neighborhood, where knowing who you were meant knowing where you came from. Family was everything. Her nineteen-year-old brother, also unable to identify his exact ethnicity, had practically raised her, and together, the two of them fought to protect their honor. This is what had landed him in prison and Amira in the program. I imagine that if she had been raised in the right environment, with parents who had the good sense to buy milk instead of drugs and who encouraged her to do well in school, she would have flourished at a young age. While it pained me to think about what she *could have* been, I was delighted to see what she was turning into now.

I met with her every morning after breakfast. The girls in her home all ate breakfast together, each taking a morning to prepare food with the "home mother" Anita, the lady who devoted her life to these girls and was on-site 24-7. Anita had her own private apartment on the first floor of the building, which she shared with her husband Patrick and spunky dog Rico. Patrick and Anita had two grown kids and had fostered for over twenty years, mostly kids from the inner city of Kansas City. They were excellent at what they did.

After Amira helped clear dishes and clean up the community kitchen, we met for two hours. For the first hour, we just sat over a cup of coffee and discussed whatever was on her mind, and the second hour we worked on the service learning aspect of the program. Each of the girls was supposed to develop some kind of service project and carry it out. Amira was still in the planning stage, but she had some good ideas floating around in her head and it was great to see her get excited about something.

Amira's afternoons were filled with school, preparing, eating, and cleaning up from lunch, two hours of free time, and then dinner preparation. Dinner was the best part of the day, which I sometimes joined in on, because the girls were loud, fun, and relaxed. Never-ending stories flowed from every direction; I never quite knew where one ended and another began. Once in a while, a pang of jealously would surge through my body—I had needed this at their age. I had needed the support, the direction, and the community. This type of program simply couldn't exist in Green Lake, however, and I was just thankful Mary Beth and Molly had stepped in and filled that gap.

In the afternoons, I helped with the after-school program held in the next building over, where I spent most of my time with my second young lady, Faith. Faith was in the foster care system and was a lonely, lost little girl—she was an only child of a single mother who was in and out of jail so frequently that Faith had spent more of her life with a foster family than with her own mother. This isn't an easy thing for a nine-year-old to swallow. She was also shy and a bit awkward—her knobby knees and frizzy brown hair were often the target of bullies. There were a few kids in the program who picked on her, and my heart broke when she would just wilt under their cruelty. So I worked to develop a positive self-image in Faith while at the same time working with the teachers at the program to foster an antibullying environment at the program. Progress was slow, and on most nights, I dragged my heavy heart home in despair. I wished more than anything that I could see the good results that were sure to follow Faith with the support I was able to give her.

Sunday afternoons were my free time. I worked in the store from 7:00 AM until noon, and from there, I tried to fill the empty space with anything I could. I taught myself to knit. I allowed myself to get sucked into TV shows and watched them late into the night on Netflix. I bought a couple cookbooks and tried my hand at cooking and baking. Anything to keep my mind off the smiling baby boy plastered all over my fridge. Because no matter how full my life was in Kansas City, no matter how good it felt to have a place and a purpose, and no matter how many kids I came into contact with and poured out my love into, there would always be one kid on my mind. One kid who I wasn't able to love and support the way I so desperately wanted to.

My son, Jude.

16

Molly

December 2017

"Okay, this is what Chelsea wrote," I said, glancing up as Delilah juggled a chunky, giggly one-year-old Jude. I smiled and began reading the letter.

> Dear Molly,
>
> Now that a year has passed since Jude was born, I wanted to take the time to thank you for all that you did for me. I would call and tell you personally, but giving birth made me a much more emotional person and I would probably end up crying my eyes out!
>
> It was hard for me to focus on anything else but myself when I was pregnant. I couldn't fully appreciate the sacrifices you made to be there for me until after Jude was born. I was so focused on feeling sorry for myself and trying to make up my mind about what I wanted to do that I couldn't see all that you were giving up to lend me a hand. I will forever be grateful for the time, energy, and, yes, even the prayers that you gave to me.

Thank you for not judging me as I jumped through all the hoops before finally deciding to give Jude up. My heart hurts just thinking about the day I walked into the abortion clinic. My first desire is to keep this part of my journey a secret from Jude. He should never have to struggle with the idea that his birth mom considered ending his life. But then I take a step back and remember what changed my mind—seeing his face. He was the one who convinced me that he was worth it! What a powerful little dude. I know the decision is ultimately up to Greg and Delilah, but I think he should know that just seeing his face changed everything for me.

Enough of the heavy stuff. I have some juicy news for you! I met a boy last month!

This isn't your ordinary boy. I'd heard about him for such a long time and simply written him off. I convinced myself that I didn't need saving, which is what he is all about. I thought I could do life all on my own. But living life here in Kansas City, away from Jude and at my crazy job, I realized that I can't. Now, before you start getting all concerned that I'm putting my faith in some guy with the hopes that his love will save me, wait until you hear who it is.

I met a boy named Jesus. And I said yes.

Love,

Chels

Tears streamed down my face, and my heart was pounding inside me. I looked up to see Delilah dabbing at the corners of her eyes as well. "I never thought it would happen," I finally said with a laugh. "She is the most stubborn person I have ever met!"

"We serve a big God," Delilah simply replied.

"We sure do," I breathed. "I'm gonna have to call her later and hear all about how it finally happened." I glanced over to the clock on the stove. "She's still at work. Maybe I can catch her tonight." I saw Delilah retreat into herself, something I realized a few years back was a coping mechanism for her. When she was faced with tough news or an overwhelming situation, she would clam up and retreat somewhere deep inside her mind—a safe place she told me she'd dreamed up while pregnant with Luke.

"What's on your mind?" I gently asked her, smiling as she was jolted out of her safe place.

"Oh," she said. "Her comment about telling Jude about the abortion kinda…freaked me out, I guess. My first instinct is to keep it from him too. But maybe she's right. Maybe it would help him make sense of the adoption later on. You know, if he ever starts asking questions about why his mom gave him up."

I nodded. "It's a tough call to make right now. I mean, if he grows up knowing Chelsea, which he will because of the open adoption, he might have a better idea of why. He might not ever ask. If he's fine with the way his life turned out, I don't see why you'd have to tell him. If you tell a happy child that kind of news, it might do more harm than good," I explained.

"True," she said wistfully. "It doesn't really matter to me that she considered getting an abortion. The important thing is that she *didn't* go through with it. And that our family finally found its missing piece in Jude."

I smiled, thinking back to the day Jude was born and what a shock it was to discover that Greg and Delilah were adopting him. Well after her third miscarriage, I'd gently suggested they think about adopting and Delilah was always very resistant to the idea. Deep down, I think she was under the impression that having a child "the right way" would somehow redeem her from her out-of-wedlock pregnancy. She never came out and said that, but I knew her well enough—she is one of the most spiritually mature people I'd ever met, but if you go down deep enough, you'll find the scared fifteen-year-old pregnant teenager that she'd once been, trying to figure out how to fix what she'd done. Although she knows she is forgiven through Christ's redeeming death on the cross, Satan still wormed his way into her heart every now and then—the journey to complete healing would stretch out in front of her forever; it was a battle she'd fight for her entire life.

One particular incident changed her mind about adoption. Back when Delilah and Greg successfully got pregnant for the first time with their son Jonas, the two had been beyond thrilled—they never expected that after waiting so long to get pregnant that they might miscarry, so they began planning for him with fervor. Losing him had been devastating, sending Delilah into a paralyzing tailspin that had once seemed like it was going to destroy our friendship. With the help of good Christian counseling, they had gotten through it, as well as the other two miscarriages, but losing Jonas had been the hardest for them because they had a name picked out, his nursery had been ready and waiting for him, and he seemed to be the answer to their long-unanswered prayer for a child. Greg, wanting to surprise Delilah, had designed and ordered a special decoration for their son's nursery—a few weeks after losing him, it arrived in the mail, and not wanting to upset Delilah, Greg had hidden it away. Delilah never knew it existed until she found Greg admiring it one Sunday afternoon. When she found him running his hands over the gift he'd gotten—a set of uniquely decorated letters spelling out the name "Jonas" to hang above the crib—Delilah knew it was time to accept the fact that having a child together might not be God's plan for them, and refusing to adopt was hurting Greg. She could see the deep longing he had for another child, and that afternoon, they decided to put their name on a waiting list for a child.

When Chelsea's caseworker called to ask Greg and Delilah if they wanted to consider adopting Chelsea's baby, they had been shocked at how quickly things seemed to fall into place. They had only been on the waiting list for a few weeks! Finding out that Chelsea had picked them out herself melted their hearts, and they knew God was up to something big. After the journey they had been on to have a baby together, they rejoiced at the way God was providing for them.

Changing the subject, Delilah said, "So Mandy tells me that Elliot is really enjoying singing in the choir for the Christmas program."

I smiled, glancing over to the living room where Elliot was building a wobbly tower of wooden blocks. I still marveled at her ability to play so nicely on her own—it had made Elysa's transition into school that much easier. "Yes, she's loving it. Ya know, when she was born, I worried that she'd never get to enjoy a hobby. As sad as it sounds, I didn't think she'd ever develop any skills or abilities. Shows how little I knew about Down syndrome back then," I shared with a sad smile.

"It's understandable," Delilah soothed. "Down syndrome is still so misunderstood."

"Yeah," I said sadly. "I mean, she's not the world's best singer, that's for sure! But she has fun doing it and she loves it. And no one seems to mind that she's completely tone-deaf and sings three times louder than the rest of the kids." I held back a giggle.

Delilah laughed along with me. "Of course no one cares. Elliot is the sweetest, most loving kid at our church. Everyone in the church would protect her at all costs—don't forget that, Molly. That kid is loved," she said, stabbing a finger in the air for extra emphasis.

As soon as the warm fuzzy feeling that talking about the effect that Elliot had on people spread throughout my body, a knock at the door from the one person who had always bristled around her echoed through the living room. Cassidy Wilson.

Our relationship had gotten considerably better over the last few years, but Elliot continued to be an issue for Cassidy. We silently agreed to be a part of different Bible studies and Sunday school classes in order to keep things civil between us, and we were able to have relatively decent conversations. She definitely wasn't the kind of friend I could call up for a cup of coffee and an afternoon of carefree conversation like I was able to do with Delilah and Ruth, but at least we could mingle together peacefully at church and around the community. The last major scene we'd had was when she'd made those outrageous comments about God punishing Delilah for "defiling the marriage bed." With things going so well between us for so long, I certainly wasn't expecting what was about to happen.

Before I could get to the door to let Cassidy in, Elliot was scrambling to her feet to do it herself. Had I known who would be on the other side, I wouldn't have let her, because Cassidy didn't even try to hide her disgust about Elliot. She wrinkled her nose at Elliot's smiling face and walked right past her without even a word.

"Yoo-hoo! Molly?" she called cheerfully as she made her way into the kitchen. When she saw Delilah sitting at the counter, she stopped. "Oh. Hi, Delilah. Wasn't expecting to see you here. I actually have something private I'd like to discuss with Molly, if that's not too much trouble."

I watched with slight amusement as the shock of Cassidy barging in on our quiet conversation time and asking her to leave registered on Delilah's face. The woman was absolutely ridiculous, walking in uninvited and expecting my current guest to simply leave without a problem.

"Um, well," Delilah stammered, looking to me for help. "I mean, I guess I can, if that's what you think is best, Molly."

I shrugged. "I'm sure whatever you have to say, Cassidy, can be said in front of Delilah."

Cassidy forced a rigid smile. "Well. I'd really like to just keep this between you and me, if we could," she said sweetly. Too sweetly.

I let out a small sigh, knowing full well that whatever Cassidy had in store for me was not going to be pretty. The last thing I wanted was my biggest ally walking out on me and leaving me alone to fight with my emotions and keep my cool. "Fine," I reluctantly agreed. "I'll call you later, Delilah." She gathered up her coat. As she wound her scarf around her neck, she sent me a warm, encouraging look, a look that said, *You can do this! Be the better person.* Before she left, she gave my arm a squeeze, and I sent her a thankful smile. She bent down and dropped a kiss on Elliot's cheek before closing me in alone with Cassidy.

Cassidy promptly made herself at home by settling into the seat that Delilah had been warming up for the last hour and a half and by asking me for a cup of coffee. As if this woman needed caffeine in her system—she was enough trouble as it was! As I poured her a cup, I sent up a silent prayer upward, asking for patience and compassion.

Cassidy didn't waste time on small talk. She cut right to the chase as soon as the steaming mug was in her hand. "I sat in on the children's Christmas concert practice during Sunday school last week," she said innocently. "My, my, does that child of yours love to sing." The way she was talking reminded me of the twisted way the evil stepmother talked in *Cinderella.* All sweet and innocent but really meant to drive knives into my heart.

I nodded. "Yes, she's really enjoying her first year in the choir. Nancy said Elliot is doing great and even gets on other kids' cases when they are squirming and messing around," I said proudly.

"How nice," she said. "I really enjoyed last year's concert. I'm a little concerned about this year, though."

"Oh?" I asked, playing ignorant, as if I didn't know that Cassidy was alluding to the fact that because Elliot was singing this year the concert would be ruined. "How come?"

Cassidy took a big swig of coffee, set her mug down, and looked me square in the eyes. "I'm going to be honest with you, Molly, and please forgive my bluntness. But your daughter cannot sing. I mean, it's not her fault of course. But why should the rest of the choir pay the price for that?"

I lifted my chin in defense. "For the record, Cassidy, saying 'forgive my bluntness' doesn't give you the right to be mean. Talking about a person with Down syndrome as if they can't hear you or as if they can't understand—which she both *can*, by the way—is just as hurtful as saying it to someone not living with Down syndrome. She has feelings, you know. And so do I. Frankly, I don't appreciate you coming over here and insulting both me and my daughter, so if you don't have anything else to say, I'd like you to leave," I said, trembling with suppressed anger.

Cassidy remained firmly in her seat and brushed off my comment as if I was joking with her. She smiled and swallowed a laugh. "Now, now, calm down. I'm not attacking you. I'm just telling you like it is, because I don't think anyone else in your life is doing that. You can't keep pretending your daughter is normal and letting her do all these things that are ruining everyone else's experiences," she said with a laugh. "That's not fair to the rest of us."

I narrowed my eyes at her. "Your daughter is in dance class, right?"

She puffed up with delight. "She is."

"Okay," I said. "Let's say that she's not good at dance. She just flat out stinks at it."

She bristled. "But she's doesn't. She's actually very good."

I commanded myself not to roll my eyes. No six-year-old is really any good at dancing. "Let's just pretend, okay?" She nodded. "So Addison is terrible at dance. At all the recitals, she sticks out like a sore thumb, and it's obvious that the performance would go smoother if she wasn't dancing. But Addison doesn't care. She loves dancing and it brings her so much joy. Would you pull her out?"

"Well, that's not really a fair comparison," she retorted.

"What do you mean?"

"Addison can practice and get better. Your daughter can't do that."

I stared at her in shock. Cassidy couldn't even say Elliot's name. She was so disgusted with her! Clearly this woman knew nothing about people living with Down syndrome if she could make such a bold statement about their ability to practice and master a skill. Sure, it might take them a bit longer to do so, but they can! I saw Elliot do it all the time.

I cleared my throat. "Perhaps you should go home and do some research about Down syndrome," I sweetly advised. "You'll be shocked to discover that Elliot can practice and improve at just about anything she does. And for that reason, I will not be pulling her from the program, which I'm sure that's what you came to ask me to do."

Cassidy gave me a polite nod. "I see." She stood up and began putting her coat on. "I guess I will be on my way then, since you've answered all my questions. Thanks for the coffee," she said as she left, conveniently avoiding Elliot on her way out the front door. When she was gone, I let my body melt in defeat and the tears well up in my eyes. It wasn't fair that Cassidy could come in my own home and be so rude while I had to smile and be polite. It wasn't fair that she could attack my daughter and I was expected to just swallow it like it wasn't absolutely killing me.

I took Delilah's advice, though. I choose to be the better person. I didn't run to Pastor Dennis or the choir director. I didn't call my mom crying like I had done so many other times about something Cassidy had said or done. I prayed for her. I prayed that she could see Elliot as a *person*, not a nuisance that needed to be taken care of and hidden away so that everyone else could lead a comfortable life. The difficult thing for me to grasp, though, was the fact that Cassidy seemed to think that everyone in the town was being forced to step out of their comfort zones when interacting with Elliot—she was the only one who ever vocalized that she had an issue being around her. Everyone else in the town seemed to love and genuinely care for Elliot and didn't have a problem with her at all. How could she not see this?

The night of the concert, Tanner and I sat as close to the front as we could possibly get in order to record Elliot's first performance on stage. She stood up proudly in her red sparkly Christmas dress and grinned in delight when she saw us waving at her. She waved back and shouted, "Hi, Mommy! Hi, Daddy!" before remembering that she was supposed to be quiet. She clamped her hand over her mouth, and the audience gently laughed. She wasn't the only squirmy, excited one in the group, of course, and the audience expected that kind of behavior. I couldn't resist twisting around in my seat to see how Cassidy was responding to Elliot's outburst, but I couldn't see her in the dim lighting. I shrugged and refocused my attention to Elliot and Elysa, who was a row up from Elliot, keeping a watchful eye on her little sister.

The program was divided into two sections—the younger kids, ranging from three to five years old sang first, followed up the elementary school kids. The younger ones sang with gusto and swayed along to the music, and the crowd chuckled in delight as only half the group actually did the actions that went along with the words. I sat with tears streaming down my face as Elliot sang every word and performed every action. I wanted to stand up and shout to Cassidy, *See! She* can *practice and master new things! Just look at her go!*

I clapped louder than anyone else, and I even jumped to my feet as the kids bowed with pride bursting off their faces. Tanner joined me and pulled me close to him, savoring the first of what I knew to be many triumphs to come in Elliot's life. When the kids shuffled off the stage and found their way back to their smiling parents, the older kids took their place on the risers. I scanned the faces to find Mandy, now eight years old, and Ruth's two boys Derrick and Carson. Derrick was ten so this would be his last year in the children's choir, and Carson was Mandy's age. It took me until about halfway into the older kids' performance before I noticed that Addison was missing from the group. Had Cassidy pulled her out after I refused to pull out Elliot? Was perfection really that important to her? Elliot wasn't even in the same choir as Addison!

I tried to convince myself that Addison must have come down with the flu, but the thought that Cassidy might have pulled her out just because of Elliot continued to nag at me. I couldn't go home without knowing, so after the performance, when the crowd moved on to enjoy the traditional feast of cookies and lemonade, I sought out Nancy, the director.

She nodded and said sadly after I confided my suspicion with her, "Yes, she came to me and asked if I would talk to you about taking Elliot out of the choir. I didn't even entertain the thought, Molly. I straight up told her no." A hint of anger was in her voice. Nancy was in her sixties and just the sweetest little thing ever, so I had to smile at her feisty answer.

"Well, it's too bad that Addison has to suffer because of her mom's stubbornness," I said, my face burning at the snarky little comment that I hadn't been able to keep in.

Nancy pulled me into a hug. "Don't you worry about them. We'll just keep praying that Elliot works her magic on them. It's darn near impossible not to love that little girl. They'll come around," she insisted. "Now go enjoy those babies—they won't be babies forever, you know."

I smiled and nodded as Nancy turned and bustled away, trying to dodge the dozens of mothers who wanted the chance to talk with her about how much talent their child had and what kind of discount they could get on voice lessons. Her words rang in my ears, and I found myself in a strange sort of déjà vu as I walked back to the fellowship hall in search of my family. Hadn't I said something similar to Delilah years ago, back when Luke had been a tiny seven-year-old and it had just been the two of them scraping out a living together? The scene had been much the same—Luke was standing on the stage in a bright-red bow tie, his chin thrust out in pride as he sung the words to each and every song. It had been my first official Christmas living in Green Lake—the first Christmas I had voluntarily spent after heading home and tying up all the loose ends that I'd left behind in Oak Ridge. I remember feeling Delilah shaking slightly beside me, tears running down her face as she realized that her baby-faced son was growing up much too fast and that a much-crueler world, one that she couldn't fully protect him from, waited for him outside the warm church. *He's got a couple more innocent years ahead of him. Just enjoy this time. It goes by in the blink of an eye.*

How easy it had been for me to say that to her back then. Back when I was single and had absolutely no clue how hard it was to raise children. Before I had Tanner or Elysa or Elliot to remind me just how cruel the world truly is—after all, it was one thing to go through an extreme trial yourself but another thing altogether to watch someone else endure the same. Back then, it had just been me. I knew how harsh the world was, but it hadn't crushed me. I'd come through stronger than before, but I only had to go home and sit across my mother for a cup of tea and conversation to remember how difficult it had been for her to come to grips with what had happened to me. It broke her heart just thinking about all that I had gone through, and no amount of reassuring would ever truly ease her heart. In her mind, she knew that I was fine, that I was healing and moving forward with life. But the thought of me being raped, of being locked in a prison of silence for far too long and trying to drag a heavy load behind me all on my own, could reduce her to tears in an instant.

Nancy could breezily tell me to enjoy my children and walk away and immediately forget that she'd even said the words. She could browse the tables overflowing with goodies and load up her napkin with cookies and lemon bars and sip watery lemonade from a white Styrofoam cup without a second thought about what Elliot was going through. She could go home and tuck herself into bed next to her husband and breathe a prayer of thanks to God for her three happy, grown, "normal" children while I prayed that Elliot could have just a taste of a world that was being denied to her because she was living with Down syndrome.

I knew that the adults in Green Lake loved Elliot and accepted her without resignation. All except Cassidy, of course. And I was glad for that, I truly was. But no matter how many adults swung my daughter up into the air just to get her to share her contagious belly laugh, it didn't stop their children from wrinkling their noses at her when she picked her nose and stuck whatever she had found into her mouth. It didn't excuse the fact that their kids flinched a little when Elliot toddled over to join them, laughing too loudly and unable to contribute to their conversation. Her peers would always struggle to accept her, and that hurt.

I loved my daughter. It didn't matter to me that she had Down syndrome. We don't love our children based on a condition they have or don't have. We love them because of the sheer gift it is to call ourselves their parent. We love them because they are ours.

But watching Elliot suffer at the hands of children and adults like Cassidy made enjoying her a little more difficult for me. No mother wants to see her child get hurt. I would always love Elliot. But enjoying her would always be a bit of a struggle for me.

17

Molly

January 2018

Mom guilt was washing over me with full force after the thoughts I had at the Christmas concert. I tried to convince myself that those thoughts weren't really true—that just because my daughter had Down syndrome and struggled to find a place beside kids her own age didn't faze me in the least. That her unique personality simply caused me joy, not frustration. That enjoying her was as easy as taking my next breath, not something I had to remind myself to do each day as I struggled through raising a child with a disability.

It was supposed to be easy, right? I *wanted* it to be easy. But comparison was slowly stealing my joy, and I couldn't help but compare Elliot's development to Elysa's and cry at night when the picture of Elliot struggling to do tasks that Elysa had mastered much earlier in her life kept me tossing and turning. A simple outing to the park with her, which was supposed to be an easy, enjoyable thing, always caused my heart to sink a little when Elliot tried to keep up with the other kids her age but just couldn't. She tried to join in on their fun, but because she was different, she was left out. She would often end up sitting down in the sandbox on her own, shrugging her small shoulders and digging in, seemingly accepting the fact that she wasn't quite the same as the other kids and working to keep herself occupied while her mommy sniffed up tears on the sidelines.

It wasn't like every minute was hard. Elliot brought immense joy into my life—at times I was grateful for her unique personality, that she wouldn't grow up to be just like everybody else. I loved watching her conquer something that she had been struggling with for a long time. When she pulled her socks on by herself for the first time last week, Tanner and I had clapped and cheered for her, savoring her toothy grin and hilarious belly laugh. On those days, I would fall asleep dreaming of sitting in the stands of a basketball game, proudly wearing a Special Olympics T-shirt and screaming my lungs out cheering her on. I knew that life with Elliot wouldn't be easy. Or normal. Or what I expected at all when I dreamed of having kids. But I knew it would be worth it.

On a particularly cold January night, I sat on the bathroom floor pouring warm water over Elliot's head as she sat in the tub and laughed and laughed in pure joy. I'd stick some bubbles on the top of her head, tell her how silly she looked, and then dump a cup of water over her hair and savor the sound of her laughter filling up our home. It was then that I saw the bruises decorating her tiny back.

"What happened to your back, sweetie?" I asked her.

"Dunno," she answered, not concerned in the least bit.

"Does your back hurt?"

She shook her head.

I called for Tanner to come in and check it out, and he shrugged. "She and Elysa were rolling around on the floor the other night, pretending to be fighting bears or something. I bet that's what the bruises are from," he said.

I breathed a sigh of relief. On my first day at home with Elliot after she was born, I had started researching information about what raising a child with Down syndrome was really like. The one fact that always stood out to me, causing the hair on the back of my neck to stand straight up, was that kids with Down syndrome have a much-greater risk of developing leukemia—like a twentyfold increased risk. As if watching my child struggle to make sense of the world and to fit in wasn't enough, I had to worry about cancer. Seeing those bruises on her back caused me to jump straight to the worst conclusion possible, but if the girls had been wrestling the night before, I had nothing to worry about.

Right?

Once the word *cancer* skirted across my mind, though, it was like it was all I could focus on. Every time Elliot seemed more tired than usual or felt even the tiniest bit more warm than normal, I could feel my blood pressure rising. Surely after all that I had already been through, God wouldn't lead me through yet another storm. He couldn't. I wouldn't make it through this one if it cost me my child. I was willing to walk through any fire if it meant God was refining me into the person he wanted me to be. But asking me to walk *beside* my child through her own storm—a bad storm like cancer? There's no way he would do that.

I was really tired of being wrong.

"No, God. Absolutely not. You've asked me to do some hard things before, but this is too much," I hissed while sitting all alone at the abandoned city park—right now, the wind was whipping my hair all around and the bitter winter chill was seeping through my clothes and making me shiver; it was understandable that no one was here right now. Usually the carefree chatter of children rang out across the park, but today all was silent. Except for the wind, of course. But this lonely park bench was the perfect battle ground for me and God—and boy, did I have a bone to pick with him!

His argument was pretty convincing. *My child,* he whispered to me, *I have said, "If any of you wants to be my follower, you must turn from your selfish ways and take up your cross daily, and follow me."*

How is this being selfish? I questioned angrily. *It's my child we're talking about, God! Isn't it my duty to love and protect my child?*

Remember, dear daughter, that, "Since you have been raised to new life with Christ, set your sights on the realities of heaven, where Christ sits in the place of honor at my right hand. Think about the things of heaven, not the things of earth. For you died to this life, and your real life is hidden with Christ in me."

I have been! I argued. *Haven't I been faithful to you for my whole life? Yes, I made mistakes. I ran away. But I came back to you! I trusted that you would take care of me!*

I could almost hear his soft chuckle. *Beloved, "My thoughts are not your thoughts. And my ways are far beyond anything you could imagine. For just as the heavens are higher than the earth, so my ways are higher than your ways and my thoughts higher than your thoughts."*

What does that even mean? I wondered cynically. *My thoughts are not your thoughts?* And yet as I sat there and thought about it for a while, I knew I couldn't accuse God of not taking care of me. He had been with me every step of my life—even the years I despised him and didn't trust him one bit. Even then, he had provided for my every need and made sure I came safely through his refining fire. Could these quiet whisperings be trying to tell me that once again, God had a plan for my life? A plan to take care of me that I just couldn't see right now?

Suddenly the wind ceased, and all was silent. I lifted my head and scanned the playground, fully convinced that at any second, Christ himself would round the corner and join me on the damp wooden bench. He didn't, of course, but as I closed my eyes, Christ's words to his disciples rang in my mind. *"Peace I leave with you; my peace I give you. I do not give to you as the world gives. Do not let your heart be troubled and do not be afraid."*

I let out a sad laugh. *I don't feel at peace, God! My heart is breaking,* I admitted as a lone tear trickled down my raw and chapped cheeks.

My child, he whispered straight to my soul. *What do you think I was feeling as my only son was flogged, forced to carry a heavy cross, and then was put to death by the very people I sent him to save? I feel your every hurt, dear one. For I have felt the very same way.*

Tears then began coursing down my cheeks as that truth sunk in. As a child, I had memorized a passage in Hebrews about God understanding our pain because he himself had experienced every sort of emotion that we on earth will. Somehow my brain was able to remember it all these years later, and I rolled the words over and over again in my head.

> Because God's children are human beings—made of flesh and blood—the Son also became flesh and blood. For only as a human being could he die, and only by dying could he break the power of the devil, who had the power of death. Only in this way could he set free all who have lived their lives as slaves to the fear of dying. We also know that the Son did not come to help angels; he came to help the descendants of Abraham. Therefore, it was necessary for him to be made in every respect like us, his brothers and sisters, so that he could be our merciful and faithful High Priest before God. Then he could offer a sacrifice that would take away the sins of the people. Since he himself has gone through suffering and testing, he is able to help us when we are being tested.
>
> Hebrews 2:14–18

The peace my heart had so desperately been craving for the last few chaotic weeks flooded my heart, and I looked up to heaven in thanks. *God, I know your ways are good. I've seen you work in powerful ways in my life. I feel you, and I thank you for your presence here with me today. But even so...this time...I just don't see how you'll use this for good.*

I understand, dear one, he reassured me. *When my son was hanged from that cross, all hope seemed lost as well. You have read about him calling out to me, "My God, my God, why have you forsaken me?" But even as Satan laughed, even as he thought he had won, it wasn't over yet. And it's not over for you, my child.*

I desperately wanted it to be over. When would the struggle ever end? Why did I have to make my way through one trial and come to peace with my place in life only to walk straight into another one? What was the point?

Deep down, I knew. The point was that even in my lack of faith, God remained, refusing to let me wallow in self-pity. His unquestionable voice continued to flood my ears. *Remember, my beloved, that "suffering produces perseverance; perseverance, character; and character, hope. And hope does not put you to shame, because my love has been poured out into your heart through the Holy Spirit, who I have given you." Trust me, my child.*

I let out a shaky sob. *I'm trying. I really am. But I'm scared, Lord. So scared.*

I know. But think on the words of David, dear one. "Even though I walk through the darkest valley, I will fear no evil, for you are with me; your rod and your staff, they comfort me." I am here. And I am not going anywhere. Trust in me.

Did I have any other option? Of course I could resist these whisperings and refuse to trust in the plan that God surely had for my life. But looking back, doing so had never turned out in my best interest. The first time I had seized control from God, I later walked into an abortion clinic and aborted my first child—something that still caused pain to slice through my heart when I allowed myself to think back on that event. The abortion was living proof that taking control—that trying to do God's job—did *not* work out. So really I was only left with one option.

To trust God, just like he had gently been urging me to do for the last half hour.

Even though I didn't like it and even though I just didn't understand how it would work out for my good, I decided to trust him anyway. Time to slide out of the driver's seat and into the passenger seat and to buckle in and wait to see where God would lead me.

And as the long journey began, I clung to his sweet promise: "The lord himself goes before you and will be with you; he will never leave you nor forsake you."

At eighteen, I never thought I would get raped. But I did. I never thought I could ever be angry or desperate enough to run away. But I did. I never thought I would abandon my faith and walk away from God. But I did. I never thought that after losing Tanner and rejecting Tyler, I would end up married to Tanner in the end. But I did. I never thought I would have a child with any kind of disability. But I did. And I never thought, that after all that I had already been through, that I would be the mother of a child diagnosed with leukemia.

But I was.

When Tanner and I could no longer come up with explanations as to why Elliot had stopped running around after Elysa and instead spent most of her time napping on the couch, why she seemed to have a fever every other day, why more and more bruises appeared on her arms and legs, and why she winced every time we picked her up, we took her to a specialty hospital in Kansas City. We walked in expecting the doctors to wave their hands dismissively and advise us to discourage our girls from roughhousing so much.

We left with a child diagnosed with acute myelogenous leukemia.

The drive home from Kansas City was quiet. The girls slept peacefully in the backseat, unaware that the safe little world we had been constructing for them wasn't so safe anymore. An invader was smashing through the brick walls, trying his hardest to destroy all that Tanner and I had worked for to give our girls a good childhood. Our quiet little life—one that had always consisted of carefree laughter and lazy Saturday afternoons watching Disney movies on the couch together—would soon be transformed into a world of cold sterile hospital rooms and chemotherapy.

Tanner and I threw a plan together as quickly as possible. The doctors said we needed to start treatment immediately and referred us to a cancer center in Kansas City. The drive home was simply for us to collect our clothes and toiletries and turn right around. The Ronald McDonald house was expecting us the following day. Which just so happened to be Elliot's fourth birthday.

The mom guilt kicked into full blast as I tucked my four-year-old daughter into a hospital bed when she should be sleeping safely in her own bed after a day of cake and party games. Instead, the cake I had ordered from the grocery store was now growing stale in the bakery department, untouched and ready for the trash bin. Pink wrapping paper filled the bin in the corner of her little hospital room, the toys and stuffed animals she'd opened hours before keeping watch over her when I couldn't. With tears running down my face, I kissed her nose good night and slipped out of the room and into Tanner's arms.

Minute after minute passed as I silently sobbed into Tanner's strong, sturdy chest. I wasn't worried about Elysa, as my mom had arrived a few hours ago and agreed to take her back to the Ronald McDonald house to put her to bed. We were supposed to join them after putting Elliot to bed, but my feet wouldn't move. It didn't feel right to leave Elliot alone, not when she didn't have a good understanding of what she was doing here. What would she be feeling when she woke up in the middle of the night and couldn't remember where she was? Or when she realized I wasn't there to greet her first thing in the morning and a nurse was there instead?

I didn't have to speak one word; Tanner knew exactly what I was feeling. So he called a nurse and had her wheel in a rollaway bed for me, which I rolled right next to Elliot's bed. I took her chubby little hand in mine, pulled the blanket up under my chin, and prayed.

I didn't sleep one minute that night. I simply prayed, trying my hardest not to just scream at God and demand he tell me why he saw fit to allow Elliot to get cancer. Instead I just prayed that he would spare my daughter, that the treatment would do its job, and that he wouldn't ask me to give up a child when I had already discarded one. My heart could only take so much—he would understand that, he just *had* to.

Over the next few weeks, life took on a predictable rhythm. Elysa was meeting with a private tutor to ensure that she didn't fall behind in school while Tanner, my mom, and I helped Elliot deal with her chemotherapy treatments. She was doing what was called remission induction chemotherapy, the first stage of treatment meant to kill as many of the leukemia cells as possible to cause the cancer to go into remission.

After a month of tossing and turning at night, waking up from nightmares of burying my sweet daughter, things didn't seem to be getting any better. She moved on to what was called consolidation therapy in an attempt to kill the remaining cancer cells. With sad eyes, the doctors kept reporting that Elliot didn't seem to be responding to chemotherapy, and soon we were lost in a world of confusing medical terms and new treatments and surgeries and therapies that we could barely keep straight before a new one was thrown our way. Time after time, the doctors came in the room struggling to meet our gaze, reluctant to give us more bad news. But it kept coming anyway, no matter how difficult it was for them to say and how soul crushing it was for us to hear.

By March, the doctors were advising us to make plans to take Elliot back to Green Lake and arrange for in-home care. After a short but extremely intense three-month stretch of every treatment, surgery, and therapy available to us, we had exhausted all of our options. Our days with Elliot were numbered, we were told, and it would be best to take her home, make her comfortable and safe, and just wait.

I had held myself together for three months. I had been strong for Elliot, holding her hand and smoothing her disappearing hair back from her face and whispering that it was all going to be okay. That God was by her side and that he would make her better. That soon she would be out of her hospital bed and at home where she belonged.

She'd be going home, all right. But not as a healthy cancer-free little girl. No, she'd go home as a terminally ill little girl, confined to a bed while she watched her sister run and play without her.

This realization brought me to my knees outside Elliot's room. The cold hard floor hurt beneath me, a reminder that this was real—I wasn't dreaming, about to wake up and run down the hall to see my perfectly healthy child sleeping peacefully in her bed. The cancer was real. The terminal diagnosis was real. The child that I loved more than my own life was slipping away from me, and there was nothing I could do to stop that from happening.

Tanner sunk down beside me and pulled me close, wrapping me securely in his arms. He ran his hand down my tangled, unwashed hair over and over again. For what seemed like hours, we stayed like this in the middle of the hall as doctors tiptoed around us, lost in a world of unspeakable pain. It just wasn't fair.

In this moment, I felt like Job, the man in the Old Testament that God had allowed Satan to test. God had bragged up his servant Job to Satan, and Satan then retorted that the only reason Job was faithful to him was because God had always protected and blessed him. I always giggled a little reading this passage, as I imagined God turning up his chin, folding his arms and saying, "You're on, Satan. Go ahead and test my servant. Just don't hurt him physically in any way." With the ground rules firmly set in place, Satan went to town wreaking havoc on Job's life. He took away his animals, servants, and even all of his children. Everything he had toiled for and loved, gone in one fell swoop.

The only difference was that I had *already* been through trial after trial. Tanner and I both had lost so much. After coming through the flames of my rape and runaway, I thought that God was surely done bringing more trials into my life. I had come out stronger and more in love with him, more committed to following him. Why did he have to lead me back into chaos? What other lessons did he need to teach me?

Back at home, Tanner and I tried our best to make life as normal as possible for both the girls. A nurse was on duty 24-7, and although we appreciated having nurses around to help care for Elliot, especially one nurse whose name was Sonia, it served as a painful reminder that no matter how much we tried, normal was a thing of the past for our family. Elysa was old enough to know what was happening, and the sunshine that usually shone from her happy eyes was replaced with fear and worry as she sat beside her little sister, holding her hand and singing along to their favorite Disney movies. My heart just about broke each day as Elysa came home from school and was immediately at her sister's side. She could have been running around, playing with her Barbie dolls and leaving Elliot to entertain herself. But she didn't. She sat by her side, held her hand, made her smile, and gave Elliot a reason to keep living.

It didn't matter, though. The medicine we were pumping into her was just to ease the pain, and the hope that Elysa gave to Elliot would ultimately fail her. As the days crept by, we could see the fight leaving Elliot. She was in so much pain, and I could barely look into her blue eyes—eyes that pleaded to me to make her better, to give her a second shot—without my own filling up with tears.

On a quiet Friday evening after Elysa was in bed, Sonia sat Tanner and I down at the table. With a deep sadness emanating from her eyes, she said, "It's not looking good, you two. I think it's time you took her to the hospital, where a team of doctors can keep a closer eye on her. And when it happens..." She did not wanting to say the words "when she dies." She looked down. "When it happens, there will be more people around to help you deal with it and take care of all the details for you." She sniffed hard. "I'm so sorry. I've gotten so attached to her during my time caring for her. I can't imagine the pain you are going through." She reached across the table to take my hand. "Please let me know if there is anything else I can do for you."

Tanner cleared his throat. "Of course. Why don't you head home for the night," he suggested. "We'll take her in first thing in the morning."

She nodded and gave us a brave smile. "I've worked with a lot of families around the area, and I just wanted to let you know that I could feel the power of the Holy Spirit here. Many of the families around here are Christians or claim to be, but there was never a doubt in my mind that you two love God. He'll bless you for that, I'm sure of it. Don't give up on Him," she said, and all I could do was nod because my throat was closing up on me. Could she see the doubt dancing across my eyes? Was it *that* obvious that I was struggling to trust God with Elliot's future? It was easy for her to spout of those words. Living it out was much harder, and I knew I was falling short.

When she left and Tanner and I were standing alone in our cluttered living room, I fell to the ground, much like I had done the day we found out Elliot's cancer was terminal. "I can't do it anymore, Tanner," I sobbed, letting my head fall into my hands. "He's asking too much of me."

Just like he did before, Tanner scooped me up into his arms and held me close. "I know," he said soothingly.

Anger welled up in me. "Do you, Tanner?" I asked, pushing away from him. "God has asked me to walk through a heck of a lot more than he's asked of you."

A look of shock passed across his face. "Why are you comparing our hurts? You think this isn't absolutely tearing me apart, Molly, just because I haven't been through as much pain as you've been through? You know, when you left during senior year, I thought my life was ending, because you *were* my life! And then you came back after I had waited and given up hope on you, making me feel guilty for not holding out just a little bit longer...how do you think that made me feel, huh? I was married but guilty that I hadn't waited for you! And then when my wife gets pregnant, I lose her to cancer, just like I'm losing my daughter to cancer now!" he seethed, on the verge of yelling, which would surely wake up the girls. "Don't you dare say that this is harder for you than it is for me, Molly. She's my daughter too."

I knew I was just looking for somebody to blame, somebody to take my anger out on, but after hearing Tanner finally put into words just how painful seeing Elliot slip away from us really was for him, I immediately regretted what I'd said. I crawled across the floor to where he sat shaking and wrapped my arms around his heaving shoulders. "I'm sorry, babe," I whispered. "I shouldn't have taken my anger out on you. I'm sorry." I could feel the fight leaking from him with each word.

"I need you to know that I'm on your team, Molly. We have to do this together. God isn't just asking *you* to give Elliot up to him. He's asking *both* of us. This is *our* battle. We need each other," he said.

I kissed his shoulder. "I know."

—◄◅〰▻►—

Sonia was right. From the minute we saw Elliot's eyes flutter open the next morning, we could see a difference. The fight had been slowly leaking out of her for weeks, a deep pain stepping in and taking its place. That pain was magnified this time, and we looked at each other in fear. Sometime today, we'd lose her. We could just tell.

I called up Delilah, who had been my rock and biggest supporter beside Tanner throughout our three-month battle with cancer and asked if we could drop Elysa off with her for the day. "How's Ellie doing?" she asked with a thick voice. Delilah and Elliot were extremely close, and the terminal diagnosis was hard for her to come to grips with.

There was no sugarcoating my answer. "She's dying, Lilah. We can see it," I sobbed.

For a few moments, we just cried. No words would come. Then Delilah sniffed and said, "Bring Elysa over. I'll try my best to keep her busy. Let me know when you want me to bring her to the hospital."

From there, the rest of the day was hard for me to recall, as I felt that I was experiencing the day in choppy, confusing blocks of time. I can't recall driving to Delilah's house. I don't remember checking Elliot into the hospital, and I couldn't tell you any of what the doctors told us. At times the day dragged on, and I felt as though I had been sitting beside Elliot, watching her breathe for days, not hours. Other times I glanced up at the clock and cursed myself for not making better use of my last day with Elliot. And then suddenly, Delilah and Greg were walking in with Elysa, and I looked over to Tanner in a moment of panic.

"I called them," he explained. "I can tell you're not really here. Doctor said she could have just a few hours left."

I swallowed and nodded, and then scooped Elysa up into my lap so she could see her sister. Elliot was awake; although I'm not exactly sure you could call her state of mind truly "awake." Her eyes were open, but she had stopped responding to us. Communication on her part had been reduced to slow heart-wrenching blinks. As time continued passing, she opened her eyes less and less—time was surely not on our side. We crowded in as close as possible—

Tanner and I held tightly on to her chubby little hands while Elysa clung to me in fear. We almost sent her away with a nurse to have her join Greg and Delilah in the waiting room, but she refused to leave her sister's side. She told us with a brave voice, "I want to be here when Ellie meets Jesus."

Looking at it through the eyes of my daughter, the moment that Elliot's heart stopped beating could have been a miraculous moment. Her pain was gone, and she was finally whole. But I wasn't able to look at it that way. I could only look at it as a mother who wasn't ready to let her daughter go and who was so angry at God for taking her away anyway.

The only thing I wanted to do in the first quiet moments after Elliot slipped away was to scream. To take my daughter into my arms and demand that God bring her back to me—but not as a child with cancer. As a healthy child with a good future stretching out in front of her.

Of course, our reality was different than my fantasy. Much different. And instead of yelling at God and demanding him to return my child to me, I squeezed tight the daughter I *was* holding in my arms and kissed her head. I could feel her shaking under my arms, so I rocked and soothed her. She knew her real mommy had died of cancer so that she could live. How difficult it must be for her little brain to understand that she had lost yet another important person in her life to the same cruel disease.

As our team of doctors and nurses came in to offer their condolence and to let us know what to expect next, I handed Elysa over to Tanner and excused myself. I hurried out of the room and walked as fast as I could down the hall.

"Molly, wait!" Tanner yelled, putting Elysa down outside Elliot's room. "Where are you going?"

"I need some time, Tanner," I explained through tears. "I'll be back." I reached up to wrap my arms around his neck and kiss his cheek. "I won't be long." He nodded and then turned back to tend to Elysa.

With that, I resumed walking down the hallway and burst out the door. Sunshine assaulted my senses, and I silently cursed up at the sky. How *dare* the world continue on without taking time to acknowledge the fact that my life was crumbling down around me? Why couldn't the sky fill up with dark clouds and pummel the ground with angry raindrops like it did in all the movies? Why did life have to be like this?

Once outside, I didn't really know what to do next. So I started running. I wanted to run far enough away that I landed in a different life altogether—one free of cancer and rape and heartbreak and all the horrible things I had already dealt with. Of course I knew that wasn't possible, so when my lungs burned inside me, I slowed and stopped, and then dragged myself back to the hospital. Back inside, I still wasn't quite ready to face Elliot's lifeless body, so I dropped into a chair in the waiting room. It was then that I started dreaming what Elliot might be up to now. The image of the daisy-filled meadow came easily to me, as daisies had always fascinated her. The sky above the meadow was clear and sunny, and I could see her running alongside the flowers, running her hands over the yellow petals and laughing that deep, contagious laugh.

The family of four bursting through the door pulled me out of my daydream—the mother, father, daughter, and injured young man moved as one body, and when the staff saw the blood trailing behind them, everyone sprang into action. Having just been through a traumatic experience, my heart went out to the frantically sobbing mother and the scared-looking daughter. Watching your child suffer, watching their life hang on by a thread feels almost as if it's happening to *you*, not to them, because your child is your very life. My own deep anguish was forgotten for a moment as I panicked right alongside a family that I didn't even know.

When they disappeared through the emergency room doors, though, I remembered. Down the hall, my child's body lay lifeless and cold. Her pain might be gone, replaced with the holy perfection of God as he keeps a watchful eye on her running through the meadow of daisies he's designed just for her. She may be well now, the cancer no longer consuming her tiny body.

But for me, a far worse disease has just taken root.

PART III

Rebuilding Hope

Let all that I am wait quietly before
God, for my hope is in him.

—Psalm 62:5

18

Molly

May

I stood in front of the kitchen counter, spreading white icing all over a chocolate cake on the two-month anniversary of Elliot's death. With anger boiling under my skin, I meticulously iced the cake that I made each year for Elysa to celebrate Leah's birthday. It was a tradition she enjoyed immensely, and I knew Tanner appreciated it too—I had surprised him with the idea when Elysa was only two years old and running around calling me "mommy." I wanted Elysa to know of the sacrifice her mother had made for her; I wanted her to remember that before I loved her and called her my own, another had done the same for her.

It never bothered me before. I don't know why it bothered me now.

Perhaps it was because I didn't want to stop and remember Leah anymore. She had been a nice-enough girl, of course, but one that I hadn't really known that well. And she'd been the one to steal Tanner away from me during my wandering years as I'd only been trying to make sense of all the turmoil. If she hadn't stepped in, Tanner might have still been waiting for me when I finally did come back.

But then, we wouldn't have Elysa, so I couldn't dwell too long on the time that Tanner and Leah had been married. Ultimately Tanner and I had found each other again—it still caused me to shudder just a little bit thinking that the only reason we were together was because she had died.

Leah had died *six* years ago. Six. Surely enough time had passed by now that we could stop focusing on it so much, right? Elliot had only died *two months* ago, and I wanted to spend every minute of every day mourning that fact. And I wanted every single person in Green Lake to do the same thing. I wanted the days to stop passing as if nothing had happened. I wanted the sun to stop trying to burst into my windows and cheer me up when all I wanted was dark clouds to fill the sky and cold rain to fall.

But if I didn't set a beautifully iced cake onto the dinner table tonight, Tanner would look up at me with sad, confused eyes. Our house was filled with enough sadness and emptiness already, and I didn't need any more guilt washing over me.

Guilt from struggling to enjoy my once giggling, happy daughter. Guilt from rushing her along and not taking the time to just sit and drink her in. Guilt from sucking in my lower lip and tapping my foot when she just wouldn't move along in the grocery store aisles because she needed to look at *all* the different flavors of taffy filling the bins. Guilt from not being able to protect her from cancer. Guilt from not being able to make it go away or to ease her immense pain in the last weeks and days. Guilt from burying her and leaving her all alone in the cemetery across town and not spending every waking moment sitting by the small marker and filling her in on the details of the life she was missing out on.

The jangling of my cell phone on the kitchen counter jerked me out of my sad little world, and I wiped off the knife I was using before setting it down to pick up the phone. It was a number I didn't recognize, so I almost just let it ring to voice mail, but something prompted me to answer.

"Hello?"

"Molly?" a female voice I vaguely remembered asked.

"Yes. Who is this?"

"It's Justine. Your mom gave me your new number."

Justine was the other girl that had gotten raped by Jason in high school. She had only been fourteen at the time but had been far braver than I had been by having the courage to tell her parents what had happened and bringing Jason to justice. He went to prison for four years for what he did to Justine, since Jason had been nineteen at the time.

"Oh my gosh, how are you doing? It's been so long since I last talked to you!" Justine and I had always been so good at keeping in touch, but after Elliot was born, I had failed miserably on my end to keep communication flowing. Relationships die quickly when that happens.

"I'm good," she said. "I'm getting married in the fall." I could hear her happiness through the phone.

"Awe, that's awesome!" I gushed, truly happy for her. She had been dating Oliver for three years, and marriage had been in the picture for quite some time. I hoped that I would still get an invitation to the wedding even though I hadn't been the best friend to her lately.

"Thank you." Then she took a deep breath in. "I, uh, have something I need to make you aware of, Molly," she said, dramatically switching tones.

"Is everything okay?" I asked, automatically jumping to the worst conclusion ever. That seemed to come naturally to me these days.

"Everything is fine," she reassured. "I got a call from Jason the other day."

"What?" I exploded. "Why?"

"Hey, just calm down, okay? I was just as shocked and angry as you but just hear me out. He served his full four years and has been out for three years now. He went to Iowa State after he got out but had a really rough time, I guess. He lost his basketball scholarship after the trial, so I guess college was really tough for him—he was diagnosed with severe depression his second semester there. Ended up dropping out and working in a meat department in a grocery store somewhere and living out of his car for a while."

I rolled my eyes. Sounded like Jason had called just to elicit some pity from Justine—the nerve, after what he had done to both of us! He had no right to call and try and heap guilt on her for things he had brought upon himself. After all, if he hadn't raped Justine, he could have played basketball all four years, earned his degree, and moved on with his life. In my mind, it served him right.

"Am I supposed to feel sorry for him?" I asked.

"No. That's only part of the story. Let me finish."

I sighed. "Okay. Go ahead," I said, giving up on my cake for a moment and folding my legs up underneath me on a bar stool. I swiped a glob of icing off the cake and popped it into my mouth.

"As you can imagine, it was pretty hard for him to be living in his car. Just put aside your anger for a minute and just think about what it would be like to do that. He knew things weren't right and that he needed help treating his depression, so he moved in with his dad down in Colorado and started seeing a counselor. I guess he had a really awesome counselor or something because he finally realized that what he had done to us was wrong, and he called me to apologize."

I sat in silence for a while. "Molly?" she asked. "You still there?"

"Yeah. I'm here."

"He didn't say anything about calling you, but he sounded really genuine to me, and it wouldn't surprise me if he called you soon," she said.

I let out a sarcastic laugh. "Please, Justine. He was one of the most manipulative people I ever had the displeasure of knowing," I said, thinking back to all the charming things he had said for the short time we had dated. How he had convinced my entire family of what a nice, respectable young man he was. How easy it had been for him to get me to do anything he wanted me to do because I liked the way his smile made my stomach flop in delight.

Justine sighed. "I know how he was, Molly. But people change."

"Not everyone," I retorted, unwilling to believe that the young man who had attacked me and stolen my entire life and then turned around and did it again to another innocent girl could change and feel remorse. He was a monster. He'd always be a monster, and I didn't care that Justine seemed willing to forget about what he had done to her. She still did quite a few speaking events about sexual assault—her message was one of forgiveness, so of course it was easy for her to forgive him. What kind of inspirational speaker would she be if she couldn't forgive the person who harmed her? She'd be a hypocrite.

But not me. The only people who knew what had happened to me were family and close friends. Surely they wouldn't expect me to accept a call from Jason and tell him I had forgiven him—because I *hadn't*. I had moved on, yes. I was healing. I hardly thought about the attack anymore; I rarely had nightmares and even being back in Oak Ridge to visit my family wasn't too bad for me anymore. But if I really thought about it, I knew without a doubt that I hadn't forgiven Jason. And I wasn't about to, either.

"Well I'll leave that up for you to decide should he actually call you," Justine said softly. "I know you probably think I'm being silly for talking to him and letting him know I forgive him for what he did. I understand if you're not at that point and I'm not telling you to do anything. I just wanted to let you know so that you can be ready if he calls."

I regretted being snappy with Justine. She was just too sweet. "I'm sorry. I just..." I trailed off. Justine had no idea that I had just lost Elliot and that now really wasn't the best time to be confronted with something like this. "Things are a little overwhelming for me right now." I glossed over the details, not wanting to make her feel bad for calling with this news at such an awful time. "You're right—I'm not at the same point as you are. I don't know if I'll ever be. But thank you for the heads up. And happy wedding planning."

"Thanks," she said. "And if he does call and you're not sure what to do, Molly, you can call me. You still have my number, right?"

"I do. It's in my address book. I'll definitely keep that in mind. Thanks for the heads up."

"No problem. Talk to you soon."

I leaned forward and buried my head in my arms. I only had about an hour left before I needed to pick up Elysa from school, and I still needed to fold a load of laundry and finish up the cake. And I had no idea what I wanted to fix for supper either. The phone call had drained away the little amount of energy I had summoned up for the day, and I simply wanted to crawl into bed and fall into the wonderful dreamland that allowed me a glimpse of my sweet Elliot's face.

I couldn't do that, though. I had a cake that needed to be frosted, little pink socks that needed to be folded, and two hungry tummies that needed to be filled today. Time didn't care that I was sad, that I wanted to just sit and cry while someone else took care of my daily tasks. Time was a ruthless monster that I loathed with every fiber of my being.

That night after I placed a perfectly iced cake on the table after dinner—I had cheated and picked up a rotisserie chicken and some sides at the grocery store—I took a step back from the tender scene that I was really tired of seeing play out year after year on Leah's birthday. Tanner gently held Elysa on his lap and quietly retold the story of the day Elysa had been born and that her real mommy had died. Elysa never got tired of the story, and why should she? She was the star, the only reason Leah had chosen to refuse treating the cancer while pregnant. Tanner told her about a love all of us simply dreamed about: a love that was willing to sacrifice anything and everything. Selfless love.

I couldn't take it anymore. I felt my heartbeat quicken and my lungs close up. I was suddenly convinced that I couldn't take a breath in, and I knew I was on the verge of a panic attack. Not wanting to startle Elysa, I slipped out the front door and quietly shut it behind me, then sunk to my knees right on our front porch. It was the beginning of summer in our small town so the sidewalks were full of families out walking their dogs and joggers crisscrossing the roads, checking their watches to see if they were on pace. I didn't care that people could see me, though. Everyone knew of Elliot's passing and understood the turmoil I was in. Everywhere I went, I was met with looks of pity and uncertainty—people wanted to offer their condolences or to help us out with anything that we needed, but it was awkward. Most of the time, I rushed through the store or library or wherever it was just to avoid people's pitying eyes. I never thought I would be *that* mom.

I heard the door open behind me but was too busy forcing myself to breathe in that I didn't turn around to see Tanner's panicked eyes watching me. How many more traumatic experiences did he have to see me suffer through?

It was becoming a normal occurrence for Tanner to find me balled up somewhere, my knees pulled up to my chest and my head buried in my arms. As always, he sat down beside me, pulled me close to him, and tried his best to rock away the hurt.

"I don't think I can do it anymore, Tanner," I admitted.

"I know," he said. "Me either."

"No, not living without Elliot," I said, bringing my head up out of my arms to look at his confused face. "This—" I motioned inside. "This birthday thing."

He cocked his head in confusion. "What do you mean? The birthday cake and celebrating Leah's birthday was *your* idea, remember? And I think it's a good idea and something Elysa needs," he argued.

"Yeah, well, she's heard the story a thousand times by now. She knows what Leah did for her. Does she really need to be constantly reminded that her mom died when she was born?"

Tanner looked at me through pain-filled eyes. "It's not supposed to be a reminder that her mom died, Molly. It's a celebration that she *lived*. I want Elysa to remember her and appreciate what she gave up so that she could live." He paused. "You don't want her to forget Elliot, do you? How can she keep Elliot in the front of her mind if we don't talk about her and do things to celebrate her life?"

I swallowed hard. I hadn't thought of it that way.

Tanner sighed and raked his hands through his hair. "Look, I know these past few months have been really hard for you. They've been just as equally hard for me too. And I'm trying to be patient and understanding, I really am, but I'm still trying to come to grips with it myself. You can't ask me to stop telling Elysa about Leah and celebrating like this. That's not fair."

Hot tears trickled down my face. "I know," I whispered. I sniffed. "It's just...everything is coming at me all at once. Justine called me today and told me Jason contacted her, and—"

"Whoa, whoa, whoa. Slow down, you're talking a mile a minute and I can barely hear you. Justine? The...other girl?" he asked, not wanting to say "the other girl who got raped."

I nodded. "Yeah. He's been out of prison for a while, and I guess some counselor really got through to him and he felt the need to apologize to her. She wanted to give me warning in case he called me too."

"I see," Tanner whispered. "Well, I mean, that's good, right? He's getting his life figured out."

I glared at him. Tanner *hated* Jason—he always had. In elementary school, he used to pick on us all the time, sometimes to the point where I would cry, which only made him laugh in my face and try all the harder to get on my nerves. His taunting voice would sing, "Molly and Tanner sittin' in a tree, K-I-S-S-I-N-G," during every recess, and I remember for a short while, I'd refused to be seen with Tanner because it bothered me so much. That only lasted for about a week because even back then, I had needed Tanner in a way I had never needed anyone else, and soon we were back to playing tag with our friends and making up silly stories together on the playground, choosing to ignore Jason's teasing and just enjoy each other. When Jason moved away later, we had celebrated. It was terrible, but really, Jason had been cruel to us. Then he reentered our lives during our senior year when it seemed like things between Tanner and I might finally reach the next level, and Tanner's anger had been obvious. He came up with excuses as to why I shouldn't go out with Jason, why he was a bad guy, and that choosing to trust him was the stupidest move I could make. He ended up being right, fueling Tanner's hatred even more because after luring me away from him, he had hurt me in a way that made Tanner's blood boil even to this day.

"Don't, Tanner. Just don't," I seethed.

"What?"

"Don't play the holier-than-thou game you used to play with me back in high school. You hate him as much as I do, and you know that he doesn't deserve forgiveness."

"Well, I don't particularly like him. But if he's changed—"

I cut him off. "He's not changed. People like him don't change, Tanner. Period. They are monsters. Masters of manipulation. He probably realized when he got out of prison that he was alone and didn't have any sort of future ahead of him and panicked. Thought he could gallop back into our lives and woo one of us back to him so that he wouldn't have to live his pathetic life alone—he probably thinks Justine and I are still the gullible and naive little girls we were back then. He doesn't want to apologize, Tanner. And he doesn't deserve any of my time."

Tanner just stared at me. He was speechless. He finally said, "Okay. Well, if that's what you think, then if he calls, just tell him you don't want to talk to him. But in my opinion, it's not good for you to hold onto so much anger. That can't be healthy."

"You won't ever understand," I argued.

He stood up. "Right. Because I was just the one you abandoned so that you could drool over Jason. I was the one who watched you waltz around with him for weeks, like you had proven me wrong and wanted me to know what a jerk I was. I was the one who held you through the night it happened and never asked why in the world you were so sad that some jerk told you he wasn't ready for commitment. And I was the one who was there, Molly, when things got worse and you thought your world was ending. I was the one you seemed to have no problem leaving and not contacting for three whole years. So no. I guess I don't understand."

He walked inside and let the screen door slam behind him, causing me to wince. Why did I have to turn everything into a fight? Why couldn't I just let my husband comfort me and be there for me?

Because he was wrong, that's why. And he *didn't* really understand. He might have watched me go through all that, but he wasn't the one who actually *did* go through hell. And because of that, his opinion on forgiving Jason didn't really matter to me.

Jason was a monster. A monster who wasn't in a million years going to get my forgiveness.

19

Tanner

May

Molly stayed out on the porch all evening. I kept peeking out the window by the door to make sure she hadn't run off somewhere—I had never been worried about Molly running away again or going off somewhere to harm herself until after Elliot died. She was just so withdrawn lately, so quiet and unwilling to let me in on the turmoil she was feeling inside, and now I couldn't shake the pit in my stomach, the fear that one day I'd come home and she'd be gone. Again.

I didn't stick my head out and tell her to get a grip for Elysa's sake like I really wanted to do, though. When Elysa asked me why she was outside, I took her in my lap, nuzzled her cheeks, and said, "Mommy is sad, baby. Really sad."

She looked up at me with her deep-blue eyes. "Because she misses Elliot, right, Daddy?"

"Right," I answered. It dawned on me that neither Molly nor I had sat down with Elysa and *really* asked her how she was doing. We had of course explained to her what happened and that death was a permanent thing—that Elliot was safe in heaven now living without any cancer and that she wasn't ever coming back, just like her real mom wasn't either. We held her as she cried and could see that she missed her sister and was sad, but we hadn't truly asked her how she was or what she was feeling.

And so I asked my daughter, "Are you sad about Elliot, Elysa? Do you miss her?"

She nodded her little head seriously. "I miss her a lot. And I cry a lot at night because I am so sad."

My heart broke in two inside me. I had actually been watching my daughter in awe for the last two months because she seemed to be adjusting so well. I had no idea that she was crying herself to sleep at night. If I'd heard it, I would have been in her bedroom in an instant, holding her close and letting her know it was okay to be sad. Losing someone—especially someone as special as a sister—was not something I ever wished for my child. It was different than losing her mom, because she'd never known her and Molly had adopted her before she remembered not having a mom. With Elliot, though, she had a thousand sweet memories. A thousand reasons to be sad.

I drew her closer to me, and her little shoulders started shaking and I felt tears wetting my T-shirt. "It's okay, baby. Cry all you want. I bet that's what mommy is doing too—we're all so sad right now, and it's okay," I repeated over and over again.

As bedtime drew closer, I still didn't go out in search of Molly. She'd come in when she was good and ready. I sent Elysa to the shower, tucked her in and read her a bedtime story, and then kissed her forehead. For a while, I just stood outside her bedroom door, straining to hear her crying, but I didn't hear anything. So I moved on to the one room I'd been avoiding for weeks now.

Elliot's bedroom.

The door creaked open when I pushed on it, and I was hit by a wave of sadness as her purple bedroom walls came into view. Her white "big girl" bed was on the far wall with the covers pulled up perfectly and the pillows stacked neatly in place. All her toys were hidden in the white toy chest beside the bed, and dust was starting to collect on top of her dresser. Pictures of her little newborn face decorated the top of the dresser, and I picked one up and ran my thumb over her happy face. There had seldom been a time when she hadn't been smiling.

I sat down gingerly on her bed, not wanting to disturb a single thing. Her raggedy, beloved stuffed bunny that she had gotten in her Easter basket a few years ago was guarding the room, and I picked it up and brought it to my face, hoping her smell was still trapped in the bunny's velvety fur. It was, and I breathed it in deeply, wishing more than anything that I was holding my daughter in my arms and breathing in her freshly shampooed hair, not just her cherished bunny. Pink, as Elliot had dubbed her because of the silky pink lining in the ears, had gone nearly everywhere with Elliot and it showed. One ear was slightly crunchy because Elliot would suck on it, and the satin lining was wearing thin. She used to run her face against that silky lining, claiming that one side felt better on her cheek than the other one did. I pressed the more worn side to my cheek then tested the other, and sure enough, one side felt softer. I smiled. Even with Down syndrome, Elliot had been bursting with life and personality, something Molly and I wished the rest of the world would see when they looked at her and only saw her disability. Now the world would never have a chance to see what she was capable of.

The world was really missing out.

Later that night, when Molly finally did come back inside, we hardly spoke. We walked around each other in the kitchen tidying up, and eventually she wandered off to bed without me. Normally I would insist that we talk it out, but I was exhausted— both physically and emotionally. I didn't want to get into a fight tonight.

I crawled into bed later that night, kissed her on the cheek, and rolled over to my side of the bed without a word. And for a while, that's how we functioned—existing in the same house but not really *living* together—at least not in the way we'd done before Elliot's death. We slept in the same bed, ate dinner at the same table, and walked past each other in the hallway, but the joy— the hungry longing we'd had for each other when we first got married—well, that had evaporated quickly, just like the puddle of water that drips off you after climbing out of a swimming pool in the middle of July evaporates almost as quickly as it forms. And I didn't know what to do to fix it.

I couldn't just tell Molly to snap out of it and rejoin the world, to come to grips that Elliot was gone and never ever coming back, because *I* was still having trouble snapping out of it. I didn't feel like I had rejoined the world I'd left behind when Elliot died—a world of parents with healthy children. A world of parents who had never dealt with the reality of burying a child. We didn't belong in that world anymore, and we couldn't pretend that we did either. And I was having just as much trouble accepting that my sweet, blue-eyed little beauty would never come running toward me the minute she heard the door opening. That I would never again receive a sticky sweet kiss from her pink lips after she'd eaten a plate of waffles. That I would never again be called in to scare away the furry orange monster she was convinced lived inside her closet.

But the difference between the way Molly and I were dealing with the reality that Elliot was gone was that I was at least *trying* to make things normal for Elysa. Even though I didn't *want* to accept that reality, I knew that living life without Elliot was our new life and somehow, someway, we needed to figure out how to move forward. Molly had confessed to me that she wished the rest of the world would stop functioning as if nothing had happened. She wanted everything to stop and grieve for our loss, but that wasn't going to happen. The sun would keep rising. The days would keep passing, and the seasons would keep changing. I didn't want to blink and miss seeing Elysa grow up. She was hurting too, but if she saw her mom and dad stuck in a rut, obsessing over her deceased sister, she would most likely grow up to resent Elliot. I know she loved her sister and that she missed her deeply, but it must be hard to live in a world that was all about someone who wasn't even alive. She deserved our attention too, and I knew all too well that one day she would grow up and leave home. I wanted her to grow up in a home full of love and laughter, one that persevered through this difficult situation. One that demonstrated that she was loved and cherished and important.

I didn't want to forget about Elliot. But I needed to figure out where she fit into my world now, just as I'd had to do with Molly all those years ago. When Molly had run, she'd left no note and had cut all forms of communication with us, going so far as to dump her phone and buy a new car in an attempt to throw us off her trail. Because she had been eighteen and legally an adult, the police hadn't been willing to put out a search for her, especially since we had assured them that she had left on her own and hadn't been kidnapped. Molly's dad had laid out a plan of action to go looking for her, but Molly's mom and I had slowly shaken our heads no. Clearly, Molly hadn't wanted to be found. We figured that in a week, maybe two weeks tops, she would come back and we'd work through her issues with her. The weeks kept creeping by, however, and after a year of college, I knew I needed closure. I couldn't wait around for her forever. And so I did the hardest thing I'd ever done—I closed the Molly chapter of my life and moved on to the next one with Leah.

I never regretted doing that, as Leah and I had been very happy together, and ultimately I'd gotten Elysa. But I often wondered how things might have turned out if I *had* waited. What if Leah and I had never worked together on a school project and then started hanging out all the time? What if I'd ignored my common sense that was nudging me to move on without Molly and I'd never gotten married to Leah? Elysa wouldn't be here of course, but I had no doubt that if I had been single when Molly finally did return that we would have picked up right where we left off. We would have gotten married, and we might never have gotten pregnant with a child who had Down syndrome. A child that would develop cancer and die.

But of course, that's not how life had worked out. I *had* moved on, and I needed to do the same now. Moving on didn't mean forgetting. It just meant figuring out how to function in a foreign world and making that world feel somewhat normal. And happy. We could be happy again, right?

I was having a very hard time believing this after one particular incident. It was a rainy day toward the end of May and the three of us were cooped up inside the house—something we tried to avoid at all costs anymore. Molly and I would take turns entertaining Elysa in order to give the other an emotional break, but in reality, I was doing much more of this than she was. Since school was out for the summer, Molly had been taking Elysa over to Delilah's house so that she could play with Mandy while the two of them chatted. At night, I would run the rest of her energy off in our backyard, and on the weekends, I took her to the park for the majority of the afternoon. But since it was raining, the park and the backyard were out of the question, and we could feel the tension hanging thick in the air. I'd tried to lighten the mood by popping in an oldies CD, hoping to elicit even a small smile from my wife's lips as I waltzed through the kitchen putting away dishes. It had never failed to make her laugh before, but now she just shook her head at me sadly and unplugged the CD player. I sighed but didn't feel like arguing with her, so I let it go. After the dishwasher was unloaded, I plopped down on the couch beside Elysa and we snuggled in for a nap.

Molly's high-pitched scream was what woke me. I jolted up, realizing that Elysa must have wiggled out long ago because my side was cold. I quickly walked to the living room to see Elysa cowering on the floor in fear as Molly glared down at her, glass and water strewn all over the floor.

"What happened?" I asked gingerly.

"She broke one of our glasses," Molly snapped.

Elysa looked up at me with a single tear hanging at the corner of her eye. "I was just getting Mommy some water," she explained. Molly and I didn't particularly like the tap water in Green Lake, so we used a water purifier instead, which I could now see was lying empty on the floor beside Elysa.

"Yeah, well, she crawled up on the counter and got a glass down without asking, and then dropped the pitcher right on the glass and broke it," Molly huffed.

I knelt down beside my now silently crying daughter. "It's okay, sweetie. Accidents happen."

"It's not okay, Tanner. That was a *wedding* glass."

I squinted up at her and then looked back at Elysa, who now had a look of extreme panic and terror residing on her face. Molly had never treated her this way before. I helped her up and said, "Run off to your room and get changed. I'll come find you in a bit, okay? Me and Mommy need to talk for a bit, so stay in your room until I come get you." She nodded and headed for her room.

When I heard her door shut down the hall, I glared at Molly. "What in the world, Molly? You scared her half to death!"

"Yeah, well, she needs some more tough love. We go too easy on her," she mumbled as she began sweeping up the broken shards of glass.

"She's *six*, Molly. And her sister just died. I don't think a six-year-old who's trying to come to grips with something like that needs tough love. And that wasn't even tough love!" I shouted and then toned it down so I wouldn't freak Elysa out any more than she already was. "That was just mean. She was just trying to get you some water, because you know what?"

"What?" she snapped through clenched teeth.

"She's not stupid! She knows that you're refusing to deal with Elliot's death in a healthy way. She can sense that something's not right with you—that she can't act the way she normally would with you anymore because she's afraid you're gonna break down crying or snap at her again. She's trying to take care of you, Molly, because she's scared that her old mom is never coming back."

Molly didn't say anything. She just continued cleaning up the mess.

I snapped. I couldn't take it anymore—how was I supposed to help my wife if she refused to talk to me? I slammed my fist down on the counter, sending a bowl of apples scattering across the surface. Molly looked up, horrified.

"What am I supposed to do, Molly? How can I help you if you won't talk to me?"

A tear slipped down her cheek and splashed onto the floor. "It was a wedding glass," she finally said.

I just stared at her, dumbfounded. "Why does that matter?" I asked.

She set the broom against the counter and slid to the floor. I wanted to walk away, but I didn't. Just like I had always done in our relationship, I sacrificed my desire to be right and put on the Superman cape for her. I sat down next to her, drew her close to me, and kissed the top of her head. It was the most physical we'd been for weeks.

"Why does it matter that the glass she broke was a wedding present?" I asked again, gentler this time.

"Because," she blubbered, "it was something from our former life. And when she broke it...I don't know. I guess I finally realized that our past life is really gone, ya know?" She looked up at me through red-rimmed eyes. "We can't ever go back, and I don't know how to fit into this new life. I just feel like I can't breathe. Like I'm walking through some horrible nightmare that I can't wake up from, no matter how hard I try."

She'd perfectly explained what had just been on my mind. So instead of lecturing her on how wrong she'd been to yell at Elysa, I just continued to rock her and soothe her, and after a while, she melted into my arms. We stayed on the floor like that for half an hour until her breathing deepened, and I knew she was asleep. I scooped her up and carried her down the hall to our bedroom, and then tucked her into bed to sleep off the emotional breakdown she'd just been through.

After two hours, I got worried and went in to check on her. She was still sleeping, so I sat on the edge of the bed to watch her. What was she dreaming of? For the first time since the cancer diagnosis, I was seeing a look of complete peace on her face—something I missed deeply. I stretched my hand out and brushed a piece of her wavy brown hair out of her face, and then let my hand rest on her soft cheek. A cheek I longed to kiss and to nuzzle again. She stirred beneath me, and when her eyes fluttered open, my heart about stopped at what happened next.

She smiled at me. A real, genuine smile.

It was gone in a flash, but it had been there. I smiled back at her, and she sat up, rubbing her eyes. She let out a big sigh and then groaned.

"I messed up," she said simply.

I didn't say anything.

"I feel awful." She hid her face in her hands. She peeked at me through her fingers and whispered, "I'm sorry. Can you forgive me?"

I pulled her into a hug. "Of course I can," I assured her.

It's funny how sometimes a complete emotional breakdown is what's needed for us to realize we need to make a change. After snapping at Elysa over something as silly as breaking a cheap glass, Molly realized that. And after watching her carry around such volatile anger against her rapist and refusing to even consider the idea of forgiving him for the last few weeks, I realized that Molly had never gotten the appropriate help after the rape. For years, this simple fact had been buried, because honestly, before Elliot's death, Molly had been doing just fine. She had surrounded herself with good friends to help her cope, but those friends could only relate so much. After masking her deep anger and unwillingness to forgive for ten long years, the truth was finally coming out. She needed help—help that I could not give to her.

After a few years of marriage and even more years of close friendship with Molly, I knew better than to approach her with the idea of pursuing professional counseling right away. She needed to get a better handle on her grief and make things right with Elysa first, which she began working on right away. She climbed out of bed after her long nap and went to find Elysa, who was sitting at the kitchen table coloring a picture of a cat. Molly sat down next to her, picked out a coloring page, and for a while, the two of them just sat in silence and colored together. I decided to make a run to the grocery store in the hopes that while I was gone Molly would apologize to Elysa.

When I came back forty-five minutes later with grocery bags strung up my arms, the kitchen was empty and quiet. I unloaded the groceries and then wandered down the hall in search of them. I found them snuggled up in the glider we'd bought when Molly had been pregnant with Elliot—we'd moved the glider out of Elliot's room and into Elysa's after she died because Elysa had asked us to. She told us that when she rocked in it, she thought of all the times the two of them had sat together and read books. Molly held Elysa in her lap as the two of them poured over a scrapbook of Elliot's first years of life, being real with their emotions together for the first time.

I smiled. I knew it would still be a very long time until we felt something close to normal. But this was a good first step. Just like I'd had to convince myself of God's goodness in the midst of extreme trials in the early days after Leah had died, I was beating myself over the head with the same message now. God's goodness remains in the sunshine and in the pouring rain, and for the first time in a long time, I could see the end of the darkest days. Slowly but surely, he was leading my little family out of the darkness and into the dawn of a new day.

20

Molly

June

I swallowed and shifted uncomfortably as the counselor peered over her glasses at me. I shouldn't be here—I should be playing with my daughter at the park or baking some cookies with her to surprise Tanner with when he came home from work. Instead, I was sitting in a freezing cold office—the air-conditioning was on full blast, causing goose bumps to rush up my arms—addressing issues I'd worked through long ago. It was a waste of my time and of our money.

Tanner disagreed. After my outburst with Elysa last month, he seemed to think that unresolved issues from the rape were surfacing, and because of the stress and sadness over losing Elliot, I was spiraling out of control. That wasn't the case, though. The rape wasn't the issue. I was simply overwhelmed from losing Elliot so quickly, but I didn't feel like arguing with Tanner over it. Because both of us were the oldest siblings in our family, we were naturally stubborn and both thought we were right—I was convinced that I would be fine and that with time things would get better; Tanner was convinced that I *wasn't* fine and that I needed a professional to help me see this. So when he suggested counseling, I agreed, because once I faked my way through a few sessions, I could reassure Tanner that I would be fine and put the rape behind me once and for all. And we could finally move on after the last horrible year.

But my plan wasn't working out exactly as I hoped. I could talk about the rape with Delilah and Mary Beth for hours and not shed a single tear, but the first question Wendy asked me caused heat to rush to my face and tears to spring into my eyes. Suddenly I felt eighteen again, scared and angry and no idea which way to turn.

"Molly?" my counselor Wendy prodded gently.

I looked up at her, realizing that I'd dropped my head and had been staring at the floor in silence for who knows how long. "Hmm?" I asked.

She gave me a small smile. "I'd like to know why you think you're here today. You told me a minute ago that your husband Tanner thinks you need some help. But what are your thoughts on the situation?"

I crossed my legs and sat up straighter in the chair. "Well," I said properly, choosing my words carefully. I did not want to get too personal with this woman that I hardly knew and who had no business knowing too many details about my personal life. I would later find this visit very ironic, because I held a degree in psychology with an emphasis in counseling and had I been in her shoes, I would have been extremely frustrated at how closed off I was being. In the moment, however, I didn't care. "Tanner seems to think that I'm not handling my anger very well."

She nodded and smiled, encouraging me to keep explaining. I kept quiet, though. She was going to have to keep things flowing between us because I was certainly not going to be volunteering any information. She caught on to this right away and played along. "Okay. So Tanner thinks you're angry. About what exactly?"

I stared at her—we had spent the first twenty minutes of the session collecting my basic life information, including the fact that I had just lost a daughter to cancer and that at eighteen years old, I had been sexually assaulted. So I said as bluntly as I could, "About my daughter getting diagnosed with cancer and dying in less than a year."

Wendy gave me another soft smile. "I think you have a right to be angry, Molly. As a parent myself, I can't imagine losing any one of my children. This must have been a terrible year for you."

I allowed myself to melt into the back of the chair. Wendy had done what no one else in my life had done yet—she had affirmed my right to be angry. I knew that the well-meaning people in my life were giving me good, godly advice—that I needed to trust in God's plan and that in the end, he was working all things out for his glory. That it wasn't healthy to drag around so much anger against Jason and that God calls us to forgive and love our enemies. My brain knew that those words were true. But my heart wasn't there yet.

I often wondered where my emotions fit in with my relationship with Christ. I knew that I couldn't trust my heart and my feelings to lead me. After all, it said in Jeremiah 17:9 that, "The human heart is the most deceitful of all things and desperately wicked. Who really knows how bad it is?"

The people who gave the advice to "follow your heart" had surely never read this passage of scripture. But when you find yourself in the midst of darkness, this verse suddenly becomes much harder to swallow. The battle between what my heart was telling me to do, to hold onto my anger and let it drive me, and what my head was telling me to do, to let go of that anger and forgive, was real, and things were heating up. In the swirling midst of confusion, I found myself desperately lost. Was I justified in being angry? Could a God that created emotions in humans expect us to keep those emotions bottled up?

My mind flew to the passage in Matthew where Jesus is hanging on the cross with only a few minutes left in his life. A darkness had fallen over the entire land, and when things looked their bleakest, Jesus cries out, "Eli, Eli, lema sabachthani?" which means, "My God, my God, why have you forsaken me?" This verse had always perplexed me, and I wondered what Jesus meant when he cried these words. The sins of the world had been put on his shoulders; he was cut off from God's favor and enduring his wrath for those sins. Knowing that in that moment, he lost contact with his Father, was Jesus angry? One would think he had a right to be! As the sinless lamb of God, he had willingly nailed himself to a cross and taken the place of dirty sinners. He was being punished for things he had not done. But I'd heard Pastor Dennis preach about this passage, and he pointed out that Jesus's cry came straight out of Psalm 22, and that Jesus probably had in mind the rest of the passage that he was quoting, which moves on to a cry of victory. His loud cry wasn't just out of bewilderment of his plight, but a witness to the people standing around him that he was experiencing God-forsakenness not for anything in himself but for the salvation of sinners.

Still, the battle was clear. As Jesus hung in agony on the cross and thought about separation from the Father, it must have caused him great suffering. Perhaps he was angry. But he still knew that God had a plan, and that in the end, he would be victorious.

I gave Wendy an exasperated laugh. "To say it was a terrible year would be an understatement," I said. Suddenly I found myself opening up to her, despite my plan to keep our visits short, sweet, and void of any true emotion. "I spent the last four years figuring out how to parent a child with Down syndrome. I spent those four years tearing down the preconceived notions that I'd unknowingly been building against those with Down syndrome for my entire life. And just when I was finally seeing her potential…when I was allowing myself to plan a happy future for her and learning how to *truly* enjoy her differences, she was taken away from me," I choked through tears. "And now I don't know what to do. I feel like my purpose has been taken away."

Wendy jotted something down on the notepad sitting in her lap. "You've just described a basic component of what is known as family systems theory, Molly. Are you familiar with that term?" Wendy knew I held a degree in psychology. I nodded. "So you know that according to this theory, families function as one system and everyone has a role in that system?" I nodded again. "Good. So when something happens to throw off the balance of the family system—such as a death—it can be difficult to recover from it. The whole system is thrown off, and sometimes roles can change. In your case, your role as mother of a child with Down syndrome has been completely stripped away. It sounds to me like you placed quite a bit of value in that role and now that it's gone… well, you don't quite know what to do. Am I correct in saying this?"

Once again I nodded, unable to speak as tears were now streaming down my face. She reached over to her desk, grabbed a tissue, and handed it to me. "It's important to remember, Molly, that we can hold more than one role in our family. One of your roles has changed. But you have other roles that your family needs you to keep performing. If you're okay with it, I think we should spend some time discussing what you think your other roles are and what changes we can make so things at home are easier for everyone."

I stepped out into the sunshine after my session with Wendy was over with an unfamiliar feeling bursting in my chest. Hope. With her help, I had been able to see that I was lacking one important piece in my life: a purpose. For four years, my purpose had been to care for and protect Elliot. Now that she was gone, I felt like I didn't matter anymore. That any other purpose I may find wouldn't compare to the honor it had been to be Elliot's mother. But living life without a purpose sounded pretty bleak to me, and after the session today, I truly felt that things would start to improve.

But then the inevitable happened. For weeks whenever the phone rang, I would screen the calls, ignoring unfamiliar numbers—keeping a close eye out for numbers with a Colorado 303 area code—in the off chance that Jason did decide to call me and beg for my forgiveness. On a particularly busy day, however, when my guard was down and I was rushing around trying to get Elysa ready for an afternoon at the swimming pool, it happened. The phone rang, Elysa was running around with one flip-flop slapping the linoleum floor, one arm greased up with sunscreen, and Delilah was waiting out front with Luke, Mandy, and Jude. As I shoved two beach towels and a water bottle into our swimming bag, I grabbed the phone just as it was on its last ring.

"Hello?" I practically shouted.

"Oh, um, hello? Is this Molly?" a male voice asked.

The hair on the back of my neck immediately stood up on end, and I dropped the bag, the water bottle clanking against the floor and rolling across the kitchen. Elysa stopped running and came to see if I was okay. I waved her away and mouthed, "Go find your other shoe."

It had been weeks since Justine had called to warn me about the possibility of Jason contacting me, and with each passing day, I breathed a sigh of relief, believing that if he hadn't called by now, he never would. *It's probably not him,* I reassured myself. With this self-reassurance swirling around in my head, I resisted the urge to slam the phone back into the receiver and said, "Yes, this is Molly. Who is this?"

There was a long pause, and I strained to hear the voice on the other end, even checking to see if the man had hung up on me. The timer on the call was still ticking away, though, so I asked, "Hello? Are you still there?"

"Yeah, sorry," the voice said. "Molly, it's me. Jason. From high school."

Jason from high school? I thought. *What about Jason the boy who raped you?* That was a better, more appropriate title.

In that moment, all the work I had done with Wendy and all the praying I'd done for God to take away my anger seemed to fall away in one big rush. Seething anger boiled beneath me, and before I let Jason say another word, I hissed, "Go to hell," and hung up the phone.

I could still hear Elysa scampering around to find her lost flip-flop, so for a few moments, I worked through the panic attack I felt coming on. I took deep, cleansing breaths, closed my eyes, and whispered, "You're all right. It's okay," to myself over and over again. I didn't want Elysa to see me in my state of panic, so I pulled myself together, jogged down the hall to her room to help her find her shoe, and together we met Delilah and her kids out front. As I climbed into the front seat of Delilah's suburban, I checked the mirror to see if I looked like my normal self and was pleased to see how good I was getting at hiding my pain. Delilah didn't suspect a thing, and after a day of splashing with the kids at the pool, I cooled off some. I didn't feel like arguing with Tanner about how I had handled the situation, though, so the first time I ever discussed the incident was with Wendy two weeks later.

"Well, that's one way to handle the situation," she said with a sparkle in her eye. For a minute, I wanted to be angry at her for finding amusement at my pain, but sitting back and thinking about what I had done, I realized it *was* a little bit funny. And not at all like me—I had never ever told anyone to go to hell before, and from the little bit of information that Wendy knew about me, she probably never expected me to react that way.

I sighed. "I wasn't planning on doing that. I hadn't really thought through what I was going to say if he ever called me and when he caught me off guard like that…I don't know what happened."

Wendy leaned forward. "You told me a few weeks ago that when you went back to school, you wanted to get a degree in counseling so that you could help other girls who had been sexually assaulted like you had, right?"

I nodded.

"Okay. So what if you were in my place right now? Normally I work with women who are working through the initial pain of a sexual assault. We work on realizing the rape wasn't their fault, learning to trust people again, regaining the control that they felt they lost after the rape. With you, though, you've already worked through those things and are in a pretty good place. You've chosen not to forgive your rapist—and I'm not going to tell you that you should—but if our roles were reversed, what would you tell me?" she asked.

"Well, I...I would..." I stammered, realizing that she had stumped me.

"You don't have to answer that, Molly," she said softly. "But I want you to think about it. As a counselor, I'm not going to tell you what to do—I can give you advice, but the real work is up to you. As a Christian, though, I'm going to tell you what I think you already know and don't want to do. I think for you to truly have peace you need to forgive him, Molly. The choice is yours."

I walked out of Wendy's office with a much-different feeling pooling in my middle than last time. I couldn't quite put my finger on the feeling—uncertainty, maybe? Fear? Nervousness? Definitely not the hope that had been bursting from my body from our first meeting, because this time, Wendy hadn't told me what I'd wanted to hear. She'd challenged me, and I wasn't okay with it. I hadn't asked for it. And I didn't want it.

I wasn't quite ready to head home with all the conflicting emotions duking it out in my head. So instead, I drove down to the park. The park I hadn't visited since that cold January afternoon where I'd sat and fought with God right at the beginning of our journey of cancer with Elliot.

I hadn't been able to come back to the park after Elliot died. Elysa and I visited a different one across town now, but right now, that park was where I needed to be. Because it was the middle of June, the park was full of people, but I didn't care. I headed straight for the bench that I'd sat on back in January and watched the children running and playing without a care.

It dawned on me that the reason I was so angry at Jason and so unwilling to forgive him was because once upon a time, I'd been like these children. I'd been a carefree teenager during my senior year at Oak Ridge Christian High School, planning out my future at Iowa State University with Tanner and dreaming about all the adventures we'd have on campus together. I'd sat at the dinner table with my family and laughed with my brother Josh and my sister Savannah. I'd walked through the doors of the school every single day without a care in the world. And then one day, I'd met Jason and everything had changed.

I'd known for a long time that it wasn't fair to pin the whole thing on Jason. After all, I was the one who had drooled over him and his chiseled six-pack abs as Tanner and Kristina warned me to turn around and never look back. I always wondered how I hadn't seen the side of Jason that they did, and looking back, I desperately wished I had. The little girl inside me who was in love with the idea of being in love had clouded my judgment, however, and I had let him in.

I also knew that I couldn't blame myself for what had happened—that was the first thing counselors told girls who had been raped. Even though warning signs had been there, no one had expected Jason to rape me. There was no way I could have known that going inside Jason's house on that blustery fall day would send me spiraling out of control.

If I *really* looked at the situation, though, Jason seemed to be more at fault for what had happened. He was the one who had raped me after all! Sure, I had allowed him into my life. But I hadn't told him to rape me.

I squeezed my eyes shut. This argument was driving me crazy! Who was at fault? Who was I supposed to blame? To hate? The one thing that people had been beating into me for the last ten years was that the rape hadn't been my fault and that I couldn't hate myself for the way things had turned out. So if I couldn't blame or hate myself, who *was* I supposed to blame and hate?

Oh, dear daughter. Why have you let these thoughts take control?

I shot straight up. What was it about this park? Why did God's voice seem so loud here?

You have heard the law that says, "Love your neighbor and hate your enemy." But I say, love your enemies! Pray for those who persecute you! In that way, you will be acting as true children of your Father in heaven. For he gives his sunlight to both the evil and the good, and he sends rain on the just and the unjust alike. If you love only those who love you, what reward is there for that? Even corrupt tax collectors do that much. If you are kind only to your friends, how are you different from anyone else? Even pagans do that. But you are to be perfect, as your Father in heaven is perfect.

That passage of scripture, found in Matthew 5, had seemed a whole lot easier to swallow back in Sunday school when the only enemy I'd had was the boy who wouldn't stop kicking me underneath the table during lunchtime. Before Jason, I had never truly considered anyone to be my enemy, and since him, I had skimmed over this passage, reluctant to obey the Lord's command to love and pray for our enemies. Shame sliced through my heart as I rolled one line of that passage in my mind over and over again: *For he gives his sunlight to both the evil and the good, and he sends rain on the just and the unjust alike.*

In stubborn anger, I had made a distinction in my mind that God doesn't. I had made the decision that Jason wasn't worthy of my love and he had no room in my prayers. But in God's eyes, Jason was a precious child, a child that he had suffered and died for. In Colossians 1, it said that,

> For God in all his fullness was pleased to live in Christ, and through him God reconciled everything to himself. He made peace with everything in heaven and on earth by means of Christ's blood on the cross. This includes you who were once far away from God. You were his enemies,

separated from him by your evil thoughts and actions. Yet now he has reconciled you to himself through the death of Christ in his physical body. As a result, he has brought you into his own presence, and you are holy and blameless as you stand before him without a single fault.

Of course, Jason wouldn't be considered a reconciled child, holy and blameless, unless he had trusted in Jesus as his Lord and Savior, but that wasn't really the point—the point was, God didn't look at Jason and simply see a dirty, horrible man like I did, a man that deserved to be hated and turned away. He looked at him through compassionate eyes—eyes that saw what he *could* be if his life belonged to Christ. God doesn't filter people out like we do. We see people and think, "They aren't worthy." God looks at all of us the same and wants the same thing for us: to come to him. He offers undeserved forgiveness to *all* of us.

I thought back to a message my youth pastor had presented many years ago, one that had always stuck with me. He had opened his Bible up to the book of Jeremiah and read verse 6: "We are all infected and impure with sin. When we display our righteous deeds, they are nothing but filthy rags." No matter how good we think we are and how righteous we perceive ourselves to be, our good deeds are nothing but filthy rags to God. We might filter people into two groups—deserving and undeserving—but if you looked at the world from this prospective, we all fit into one group. Undeserving. All of us. The Goody Two-shoes who go to church our whole lives, the little old men who had served the Lord faithfully for years and years, the rapists, the murders, the outcasts. All of us.

But the power of Christ's death and resurrection overcomes this grim outlook! The passage in Matthew 5 came rushing back at me.

> You were his enemies, separated from him by your evil thoughts and actions. Yet now he has reconciled you to

himself through the death of Christ in his physical body. As a result, he has brought you into his own presence, and you are holy and blameless as you stand before him without a single fault.

If God in all his holiness could look upon me—in all my sin and darkness, offering up to him my filthy rags and still willingly send his son to die for me—to reconcile me and declare me to be holy and blameless, then surely I could forgive Jason. I certainly didn't deserve God's forgiveness, and I didn't think that Jason deserved mine. But God had given it to me anyway, and it was time I did the same.

I found it incredible that the one voice—Jason's voice—that had haunted me mercilessly for ten long years and had kept me locked in a prison of anger and unforgiveness was the very same voice that was about to set me free.

21

Molly

June

My hands shook as I sat at the kitchen counter holding our home phone. After my session with Wendy and my encounter with God at the park, I finally spilled to Tanner my brief phone call with Jason. To my surprise, he choked on a laugh when I told him what I'd said to Jason, and I shook my head.

"Not really like me, is it?" I asked.

He pulled me into a hug. "No. But it's understandable." He kissed my nose. "So what are you gonna do?"

"I'm gonna call him back," I answered, watching his eyes widen in shock.

"Really?"

"I think I need to," I said with a sigh. "Wendy made a good point—I'm not her normal client. Usually she helps women who have *recently* been assaulted and are working through the initial fear and confusion. It's been years since my own attack, though, and I know I'm in a pretty good place. The one thing that keeps me from feeling complete peace is this anger. I don't wanna seem selfish, like I'm just forgiving him so I can feel better. I'm trying to look at it through God's eyes, ya know? None of us truly deserve forgiveness, but he gives it to us anyway."

Tanner was thrilled. "Want me to take Elysa to the park to play so you have the house to yourself?"

I shook my head. "No. Maybe just out back…I don't know how the phone call is going to go. If I start going into a panic attack like last time, I don't want to be here alone."

"Good idea," he said, dropping another kiss on my nose. "Good luck."

That conversation had been a half hour ago, and yet here I still sat with trembling hands. I almost didn't do it. Suddenly, though, my fingers were scrolling through the recent phone calls section and pressing Send when it landed on Jason's phone number. I could barely hear the ringing over the pounding of my heart, and for a minute, I thought the phone call would go to his voice mail. But, much like I had done when Jason called me, he finally picked up, breathless and sounding a bit flustered.

"This is Jay," he said.

"Um, hi. Is this Jason Moore?" I asked, confused by the new version of his name he had given.

"Yes. Who is this?"

"Molly, Jason. It's Molly." I didn't know how else to describe myself to him; I hoped he remembered what my voice sounded like from our last call.

"Molly Taylor?" he asked in complete shock.

I smiled. "It's Molly Walters now," I told him.

"For real? You and Tanner got married?"

"We did. Been married for five years now."

"Wow. Well that's really great, Molly. I'm happy for you."

Conversation stalled after that. I hadn't expected the call to begin with awkward small talk and didn't know what to say—I figured since he had contacted me first, I should let him take the lead, so I waited.

I heard him take a deep breath in. "Listen, Molly. The reason I called the other week was because…well…because I want to apologize for what I did to you in high school."

I felt my throat closing up and tears burning behind my eyes, threatening to spill over my cheeks at any second. I thought I was stronger than this! More in control. Why did the very mention of the attack still make me react like this?

"Molly? Are you still there?" he asked.

"Yes," I managed to choke out. "I'm here."

"Okay," he said. "Well. I don't expect your forgiveness. What I did to you…It was just awful. I want to blame my stupid adolescent brain for what happened but I can't. Attacking you like that wasn't just an impulsive thing I did. I'm not trying to blame my cruddy childhood either, but you remember all those things I told you about my family?"

"I remember," I said, wiping my cheeks dry.

"It wasn't good for me growing up—my family wasn't there for me, and I grew up angry. I felt like I had no control over what happened to my family, so I looked for it in other places—the easiest place to find it was with girls," he said, the shame ringing out of his voice as clear as day. "I got some sick thrill out of roping girls in. Making myself feel powerful and in control."

"I guess I was a pretty easy target," I admitted sheepishly.

"No, no," he objected. "Don't think that being trusting and nice was what caused it. I take full responsibility for what happened, Molly. I was really messed up. Like, really messed up. The things I told you about my family…that was just the tip of the iceberg. I was obsessed with targeting girls—and it didn't matter who, really. At that point in my life, I was pretty confident that I could land any girl I wanted. And yeah…I admit that I looked for super trusting girls. But you weren't at all like I thought you would be— you didn't fit my stereotypical view of a naive, trusting girl. It was much harder for me to get what I wanted with you because…well because I really *did* like you, Molly."

"Really?" I asked, completely shocked. Here I had walked around for ten years thinking I had been the easiest of prey for Jason and that the time we had spent together was just a small part in his bigger plan to get me to jump into bed with him—that it had meant nothing to him, which was why it had been so seemingly easy for him to attack me when I *wouldn't* jump into bed with him.

"Yeah. I felt like a part of a real family when I was with you. I'd never spent so much time with a girl's family before you," he admitted. "It was nice."

"So I wasn't just some pawn in a game you played? I *did* mean something to you? Even just a little bit?" I asked, not sure I really wanted to hear the answer to that question.

"Of course," he assured, but my guard was still up. How many times had Jason lied to me before in order to get what he wanted from me?

I sniffed, commanding myself not to cry while on the phone with him. "Then why?" I pleaded.

He remained silent for a few moments. "I don't have an answer to that. I'm so sorry for what I did to you. If I could go back in time and make it right, I would. But I can't, so I'm trying to make it up to you in a small way by telling you how truly sorry I am. And I know that…that…well…that you. Ya know… that you got…pregnant," he finally managed to stammer out. He paused, and when he found his voice again, I could hear that it was thick with emotion. "I treated you terribly, and for ten years, I've wondered what happened to you and the baby. That's part of why I'm calling today. I know I told you I wanted you to get rid of it so I didn't have to pay child support, but I've changed, Molly. I understand if you don't want me to meet the kid, but at least let me start paying child support. It's the least I could do."

That's when I really broke down and the tears once again spilled onto my cheeks. I shook my head in agony—if only his change of heart had happened ten years ago! "I got an abortion, Jason."

"Oh," he replied in shock. Clearly he had not expected this from me at all—the only Molly he had ever known was the committed Christian Molly, a girl who would never get an abortion and probably wouldn't give her baby up for adoption either. He thought I had kept and raised our baby, and now he had no idea how to respond. "I…uh. Okay." He was speechless. I could tell that he was struggling with an appropriate response, probably not wanting to offend me by apologizing if I didn't regret it, but not wanting to seem relieved if I *did* regret it either.

"I'm sure you never thought that I would go through with it, but when you cornered me in that closet and threatened me with all that had already happened…I wasn't in my right mind," I explained. "I was already terrified of you and took your threat completely seriously. And then when I ran away…I don't know what happened. My original plan didn't include getting the abortion, but when I got to Minneapolis—that's where I ran away to—I panicked, I guess. I didn't have much money, no connections to friends or family or an agency that would help me, and I was still convinced that if I came back, you'd be waiting for me with a new threat. I got scared. I regret it every day of my life."

He groaned. "Oh, Molly. I am so sorry. You must think I am the worst person on the face of the earth. And you'd be right."

"For a long time, I thought you were," I admitted, half-jokingly. "It's been a long journey of recovery for me." Suddenly I realized that I had an opportunity to share the gospel with Jason, and even though I had spent the last ten years hating him, I jumped at the chance. After all, I had just finally realized that God turns no one away and that Jason—even though he had done terrible, terrible things—was just as much a child of God in need of a savior as I had been.

I took a deep breath in, silently sending a prayer up for guidance. "The biggest part of that journey has been finding forgiveness in Christ. I went into the abortion clinic knowing that abortion was wrong, but I chose to ignore the deep conviction in my heart. For a long time, I tried to ignore it and bury my guilt, but it wouldn't go away. I tried *everything* to make it go away. But nothing worked."

"I can relate to you on that one," he said sadly. "I didn't even think I had done anything wrong to you until my life started spiraling out of control." He took a deep breath in. "You weren't the only one I attacked, Molly." I decided against telling him that I already knew about the other attack and that Justine and I had found a great deal of healing out of talking with each other. "She pressed charges and I went to prison for a while. When I got out…my life was just out of control. It wasn't until I was homeless with absolutely no hope for a future that I finally realized that what I had done to the two of you was even wrong! For a while, I actually blamed the other girl for ruining my life, wondering why she couldn't have just disappeared like you had done." He choked on his shame. "I had a plan for a while to come back to Iowa and find you two—make you pay for ruining my life. When I started seeing a counselor, though, I was able to look at what happened and claim responsibility—I finally understood that *I* had been the one to ruin your lives. I kept seeing the counselor, found a way to forgive myself, and took some good steps forward."

I could see now why Justine had called me and warned me about Jason. He sounded one hundred percent sincere, and I truly did believe him. It was remarkable how much the two of us had changed—two messed-up, broken sinners coming to terms with our actions and doing our best to move on and make a good life for ourselves.

"I appreciate your call, Jason," I said softly. "I never thought I would be able to say this, but I'm glad you've seemed to find peace after all that happened. But just so you know, you can have *ultimate* peace and healing in Jesus too."

He let out a small laugh. "You always were a goody-goody," he teased gently. I remembered all the times that I'd tried to get Jason to come to church with me, but he had always shut down any conversation about faith. To my surprise, my heart ached at the thought of Jason still being an unbeliever. God intended that no one, regardless of what they had done or what the world thought they deserved, to be separated from him. Our free will allowed for us to reject his gift of forgiveness though, and even after what Jason had done to me, I wanted nothing more than for him to find the same freedom in Jesus that I had found.

"I've found so much peace in Jesus," I told him. "He offers forgiveness to anyone who asks for it, Jason. He doesn't turn anyone away."

"You don't know all the terrible things I've done, Molly," he argued, a hint of anger creeping into his voice. "And if rape is already on the list—twice, even, then you don't *want* to know. God doesn't want people like that in heaven. He looks for goody-goodies, and I'm the farthest thing from one."

"No one is a goody-goody," I argued back. "All of us are full of sin—and God doesn't compare sins the way we do. None of us is good enough for him, but through his great love, he offers forgiveness and salvation anyway. It's yours for the taking, Jason."

He cleared his throat. "I appreciate that, Molly. I really do. I don't see it that way, but it's something for me to keep in mind."

I couldn't believe the next words that came tumbling out of my mouth. "Know that I'm praying for you. I hope that one day you can see it differently."

Suddenly his cries were filling my ear, and I sat back, shocked. "Thank you, Molly. I never imagined this phone call to go this way. I still feel so awful, and I know that I don't deserve your prayers. But thank you anyway," he cried.

The heart that had been so hardened and stubborn for ten long years softened inside me. There was no longer a doubt in my mind that Jason was truly a changed man, and that even though he was still resisting God, that God was surely doing a great work in Jason's life anyway. This drastic of a change couldn't have come from anywhere else! And perhaps, just like he'd done with me, God was leading Jason down a rocky, tumultuous path that would eventually lead to forgiveness and redemption. It had taken me years to get there, so I held out hope that one day Jason would get there as well.

I glanced up at the clock, and I figured that Tanner was probably struggling to keep Elysa occupied outside for much longer. "I need to get going, Jason. Thanks for taking my call."

"No, thank *you* for calling. When you hung up on me the other day, I wasn't surprised at all, and I never in a million years expected you to call back and let me make things right with you." It sounded like his tears had returned. "Out of all the people that I messed with, I'm truly sorry you had to be one of them—you are a great person and you don't deserve what happened. I hope you can forgive me."

I let out a sad laugh. "I honestly never thought I would say this to you, but I forgive you."

And just like that, the final rusty chain that had been weighing my heart down for much too long unhooked and fell to the ground, clanking with a satisfying thud. I was free. I was finally free.

22

Molly

July

Before forgiving Jason and getting the closure I never knew I had so desperately needed, I didn't realize that dragging around such deep-seeded anger could have real physical effects on a person. Saying the words "I forgive you" had caused unknown anxiety to come sliding off my shoulders, and I was getting the best sleep I'd gotten in years. Even little Elysa noticed a change. On a beautiful sunny afternoon out at the park, she came running up to me and said, "Ya know, Mommy, you haven't been looking over your shoulder like you always used to do. What were you looking for anyway?"

I laughed and pushed a sweaty strand of hair out of her face. "I was looking for a bad man who hurt me a long time ago, I think," I explained to her as her face scrunched up in concern. "Don't worry, though. He's not a bad man anymore. And he isn't going to come hurt me."

For a few weeks, I allowed myself to float around on a cloud of happiness. The peace and joy from letting myself out of the prison of hatred was giving my life new meaning, but after a while, the newness wore off, and I found myself wrestling with a newfound emptiness. I compared it to the "camp high" that I had experienced many times before at summer Bible camps and retreats. I would spend a week immersed in God's Word and listening to amazing, life-changing speakers and then return home with a renewed sense of purpose and fire for the Lord. It would last a week, maybe two weeks tops, and then I would fall back into my safe routine. The excitement and passion would dwindle as I returned to school and daily life, and soon I would grow frustrated by the rut that I inevitably fell into—a rut of yearning for the long lost passion, of confusion and disillusionment.

My heart ached as I realized that yet again I was walking along the same sort of rut. I found myself praying for a passion, pleading with God to give me a purpose now that Elliot was gone and I couldn't be her champion anymore. It had been two years since I graduated and my psychology degree was going unused—taking care of my family had been my main concern after graduation, and Tanner and I hadn't made the time to sit down and make a plan for my career. Juggling crying daughters, folding pink frilly dresses, and cooking casseroles after a long day of chasing my princesses around had always come first—we always said that one day I would get a job in my field, after the girls were in school and things calmed down a bit. But for now, the degree hanging on our office wall was simply a signed piece of paper collecting dust, causing my heart a prick of sadness with each glance.

Maybe it was time for me to go out and finally get a job. Or to go back for more advanced schooling. *Something. Anything.* The year in between returning home to seek forgiveness and closure with my family and marrying Tanner had taught me that sitting around feeling sorry for myself wasn't an option. I full heartedly believe that God doesn't call us to sit on our couches waiting for some divine sign from him in regards to where he wants us to go or what he wants us to do. Sometimes we just need to stand up and *do something*. If we stumble down the wrong road or make a bad call—as I was known to do—he leads us back onto the right track if our hearts are open and receptive to his leading.

As I lay wrapped in Tanner's arms, listening to a thunderstorm rolling around outside our bedroom window on a sticky July evening, I admitted that I was feeling a bit lost. He lifted my chin up so that I was looking into his eyes and said, "I know. I can see it."

I smiled. "How do you know me so well?" I asked, settling back against his broad chest.

"Because I've loved you for twenty-three years." I looked up at him again with questioning eyes. "I loved you from day one—from the first time I laid eyes on you twenty-three years ago trapped under your pink bike," he said with a grin. Tanner and I had met my first day in Oak Ridge, where a group of boys had targeted me and pushed me off my little bike as they road past me on their two-wheelers. Tanner had been the only one to feel bad about my plight, and from that first day, we had been the best of friends. "It just took me a while to realize it, but I'm glad I did." He kissed my forehead.

I sighed. "I don't know what to do with myself anymore. It's not like my life doesn't have meaning without Elliot in it anymore...but I guess I just don't know where to find a sense of purpose," I explained. "I know I'm a wife. A mom. A daughter. A sister. But what else?"

"You're a follower of Christ," Tanner offered. "One who listens to his voice and takes notice when he puts desires into our lives. Not everyone notices that, Molly. Or they notice it and let fear get in the way of going out and doing something good. I think this is from him, love. And I love that you're recognizing it."

I was able to fall asleep with ease that night after Tanner prayed a prayer of direction over me, pleading with God to more fully reveal to me what it was that he wanted me to do. Everyone needed a Tanner in their life to help make the chaos more manageable. I drifted off to dreamland with a smile playing on my lips, so incredibly grateful that Tanner and I had found a way to each other again all those years ago. God had worked in mysterious ways in the past—I looked forward to what he had in store for me next.

I awoke with a start somewhere around three o'clock in the morning, startled out of a bizarre dream. In the first moments after waking up, I could remember hearing the cries of hundreds of babies, of seeing all their bald little heads bobbling in the arms of their young mothers. Extremely young mothers actually. Had all the moms in my dream been teenagers? I couldn't be sure. When I awoke out of the same dream multiple times over the course of the next few weeks, I was positive that the mothers were all teenagers. Why I couldn't get the faces of all those young mothers out of my brain? What was God trying to tell me?

An afternoon with Delilah, watching our little ones splashing around in a wading pool in her backyard caused the pieces to all fall together. Few things had ever made me feel more alive than ministering to young single mothers, like Delilah had been when I met her. I had found a great deal of joy out of being Delilah's confidant and pillar of strength when she had been a single mom to a tiny little Luke, and my heart had soared watching Chelsea choose to give her baby a good life through adoption. I realized, for the first time, that Delilah, Chelsea, and I covered the full spectrum of young motherhood—Delilah had chosen to keep and raise her baby, Chelsea had given her baby up for adoption, and I...well, I had made the unfortunate decision to abort my child. Together, the three of us held a wealth of knowledge and experience on what it means to be a teen mom and how each of the three choices—raising the child, adoption, and abortion— could affect a young and scared mommy to be.

As we sat sipping strawberry lemonade and laughing at our children's antics, I presented my sudden idea to Delilah. "What do you think about starting a pregnancy house with me?"

She looked over at me and squinted. "Where did that come from?"

I laughed. "It sounds crazy, I know. After I called Jason..." I trailed off. "I don't know. Something changed. I've been feeling lost ever since Elliot died, but it intensified after our conversation. And I've been having the weirdest dream for *weeks* now. I never really know what's going on in the dream—just that there are hundreds of babies. Being held by what I am convinced are all teenage mothers."

"Interesting," Delilah commented, still squinting. I couldn't decipher what her vague "interesting" meant. Jude was still just a baby, Mandy was nine and fairly self-sufficient, and Luke was thirteen now. She was at a point in her life now that would allow her to devote some time to starting a ministry with me now that two of her kids were older, but perhaps Delilah was worried about dividing her time between her children and a pregnancy house. Or maybe she doubted her ability to counsel and advise young women in the same position she herself had been in fourteen years ago. It was likely that she worried that the shame would come welling back up again if she worked with teenage mothers. Fear has a funny way of stepping in front of us and blocking out our view of the good things God has planned. No matter how many years passed for Delilah, that awful fear and shame would always be an obstacle that she had to maneuver around.

"Interesting *good* or interesting *bad?*" I prodded.

She sighed. "Both, I guess," she admitted, taking a big swig of her lemonade. "I like the idea—you're thinking of opening a home for pregnant young women with nowhere else to go, right?"

"Exactly," I confirmed. "Girls living in foster care that no one really wants anymore. Girls living in poverty who have no means to provide for a baby and whose families are putting lots of pressure on them to get rid of their babies. Or just any girl who needs a place to go."

She nodded. "That sounds great. It really does. But it also freaks me out a little bit," she admitted, going on to confirm my suspicion. "I still—after fourteen years have passed—feel like a failure to have gotten pregnant in high school. I love my son with all my heart and don't regret him in the slightest. But there are *still* people who will cast a judging glance my way in the auditorium at concerts and plays. Women who can only see the mistake I made and can't see how I learned from it and grew stronger in the Lord. And it hurts." She gave a little sniff.

I took her hand and gave it a squeeze. "If it will make you uncomfortable, don't do it. I won't ask that of you."

She laughed and waved a hand at me. "I think it would be good to push myself. Step out of my comfort zone. It just freaks me out, is all."

I understood completely. I would never push Delilah to do something that caused her pain, but I could pray that God would! I could do it without her; I could find more qualified people to help me get my project up and running. But there was no one else in the world I would rather do it with than her.

I called Chelsea that next day and proposed the same idea to her. I explained what I wanted to accomplish and that I felt that her experience giving up Jude for adoption would be extremely beneficial to the pregnancy house. She reacted much more positively, to my great surprise.

"I would be honored to be a part of your ministry, Molly!" she gushed with delight. "It's getting kind of lonely down here in Kansas City. I love what I do, don't get me wrong. But a change of pace might be kind of nice."

I promised that I would keep her posted on my progress and then turned to finding a place to house up to ten girls and figuring out how I would fund the ministry. I had made quite a few good connections to counselors, social workers, and therapists during my college years and got to work collecting phone numbers in order to start making calls to anyone willing to help me get my project up and running.

As I was working out those basic details, I knew I had to drum up local support, and once Delilah jumped on board a few weeks later after a battle with the Lord, we got to work, promoting the idea around Green Lake and the surrounding towns. We started planning a benefit dinner and silent auction to both raise money for our new ministry and to provide anyone who was interested in what we were doing with all the details of the pregnancy house. A number of men and women from our church asked to be involved, and we gladly welcomed anyone who was willing to lend a hand. After a few weeks of organizing, printing and hanging up fliers, gathering items for the silent auction, and decorating the fellowship hall of our church, Delilah and I grew giddy with excitement. So far everything had come together so smoothly, and we couldn't wait to see how God would bless us at the benefit dinner.

The last person I expected to see at the dinner was Cassidy Wilson. Things had been strained between us ever since Elliot died. I could see both pity and remorse mingling in her eyes—it was clear that she felt sorry for me, but I could also see the raw guilt she was trying so hard to hide from me. Maybe she finally realized—too little too late—how awful she had been to Elliot and that she had missed out on fostering a relationship with such a special little girl. If she truly *was* guilty, though, she hadn't yet acted on it. No apology, other than a brief hug and a "Sorry for your loss" at her funeral. Since that day, she tried to avoid me at all costs. I prayed that maybe God would restore one more broken relationship for me.

My heart beat with nervousness as I stood behind the podium, looking out into the buzzing fellowship hall at the church. My eyes found Chelsea's in the audience—she had driven up the day before to be here—and she gave me an encouraging thumbs up. I swallowed hard and then called out, "Attention, everyone." The room slowly quieted, and I commanded myself to calm down. "Good evening. Thank you for joining us tonight. We are so excited to foster relationships with individuals and businesses in Green Lake and the surrounding towns. We hope that you find this night informative and encouraging. To get started, we will be playing a short video about what unplanned teenage pregnancy looks like in America."

I stepped off to the side as the video began playing, watching to see how the audience would respond. Most of the people were nodding their heads and whispering comments to each other, and I breathed a sigh of relief that the reaction seemed pretty positive. It came as no surprise to me that the only person who was sitting back rigidly in her chair with her arms crossed tightly and her brows furrowed was Cassidy Wilson. Could it even be possible for one person to be so passionately against everything another person did? It seemed that no matter what I did, I offended her in some way. *Please, God, let her keep her mouth shut. Just for once. Please.*

God must have decided to test my patience that night, however, because during the question and answer session, Cassidy took the microphone and said, "I don't see how anyone who calls themselves a Christian could support something like this."

Delilah was at the podium directing this portion of the night, and I watched her eyes widen in shock. I twisted in my seat to look at Chelsea and she sent me a "What the heck?" look that I had to giggle at. This was typical Cassidy behavior that didn't surprise me in the least. I figured it was best to hear her out and make a combat strategy after. It had been foolish to think we could pull this off without a single problem anyway.

"Can you explain a bit more of what you mean?" Delilah asked.

"Certainly," Cassidy responded with a smug grim on her face. "We all know that teen pregnancy is a growing epidemic in our country. No one wants to see their teenagers getting pregnant, so we teach them to keep themselves pure and focus on school and sports instead. We don't want kids to start seeing pregnancy as a reward, which is what this pregnancy house would be. Think about it. If your daughter gets pregnant, you'd want her to feel bad about it, wouldn't you? You'd want her to understand that what she did was wrong, and that getting pregnant is a consequence that she has to deal with. Getting pregnant young means you'll struggle, that you'll have to make sacrifices and miss out. Why should we reward our kids with a plan B that they shouldn't be allowed to have after what they did?"

I wanted to clean out my ears and ask the audience if they too were hearing the same load of baloney that I was hearing. To my surprise, though, the audience started murmuring in concern. They could not all be thinking the same things, could they? It didn't make sense that having a safe, loving place for a teenage mother in need would cause the number of teen pregnancies to rise! Honestly, if I thought back on my own situation, I wouldn't have wanted to go to a pregnancy house while still living in Oak Ridge. Why would I if I'd had loving, supportive parents helping me? In Minneapolis, though, it might have saved my baby! If I'd had even one supportive, encouraging person in my life, I might not have aborted. I highly doubted, though, that growing up in a town that had a crisis pregnancy house to turn to if I needed it would have increased my chances of sleeping around and getting pregnant. My situation had been unique, however. I'd only gotten pregnant because of the rape.

I felt a sudden powerful urge to share my unique situation with this group, which I resisted with a vengeance. Only a handful of people in this town were aware of what I had done, and the possibility of being harshly judged kept me glued in my seat. As Delilah tried to stammer out an argument, however, I felt myself standing and moving to the front. My heart was now pounding out of the blue dress I was wearing, but somehow I kept walking. I took the microphone from a flustered Delilah and once again looked out to the buzzing audience.

"I understand your concerns, but I would like to take a few moments to address those concerns. I could stand up here and try to convince you in the same way that those who are against teaching strictly abstinence in sex education do—that kids are going to have sex no matter how much you push abstinence on them and that we need to protect them from the consequences of doing so. That's a battle I don't really feel like waging with you all, though." I then smiled, and the crowd laughed softly. "It is my firm belief, though, that kids *are* going to have sex. And they might get pregnant from it. I think this will continue to happen with or without a safe place for them to turn to if it happens to them, which is what the pregnancy house will be. It will *not* be a reward—think about it," I challenged in the same fashion that Cassidy had. "Think about what being a teenager was like. The pressure to fit in and belong was enormous. Why would any teenager willingly separate themselves by turning to the pregnancy house? This house would be a last resort for young moms—kids whose parents refuse to support them and forgive them for making a mistake. Kids in foster care who have no other place to go besides a group home when the foster family says, 'I've had enough.' Kids living in poverty who are being pressured to abort simply because the parents know they cannot afford to diaper and feed even one more tiny mouth."

The group fell silent, and Cassidy was now staring down at the melting bowl of ice cream that we'd served for dessert. "Kids who maybe weren't sleeping around. Kids who have been raped," I said, letting the harsh word fall over the audience. "Kids like me."

I could hear the majority of the people take startled deep breaths in, shocked. "That's right," I announced, now trembling.

"When I was eighteen, I was raped by my boyfriend. He had been pressuring me for a long time to sleep with him, but as a Christian, I didn't want to do it. When he realized that he was fighting a losing battle with me, he raped me," I managed to choke out through my ever-tightening throat. "To my utter dismay, I found out that I had gotten pregnant from the attack. As if being raped wasn't enough, I was then faced with the reality that I was pregnant, living in a small Christian town that would cluck their tongues at me in judgment, wondering why in the world their message of abstinence hadn't worked when they didn't have a *clue* what had really happened."

I let the audience shift uncomfortably in their seats for a few moments, begging God to let them see how good a pregnancy house could be for our area. "Most of you remember when I moved to Green Lake, I didn't have a baby with me, of course, so I will let you draw your own conclusions about how well I handled my situation. Had someone brought me to a crisis pregnancy house, like the one we're planning right now, I might still have my child with me here today to share his or her own thoughts about the ministry."

With that, I stepped down from the stage and sat back in my seat. Silence bounced off the walls for what seemed like an eternity, and my heart sank. Perhaps sharing such a heavy story had been the wrong call. But then, a single man stood up and began clapping. One by one, each person in the audience stood and clapped. Tears ran down my face as the people I had come to love and respect throughout my years in Green Lake surrounded me, laying their hands on me and encouraging me.

Delilah stood back up behind the podium and cleared her throat. "Are there any other questions?"

―⊸⊸⊸―

The rest of the night was a huge success—each item in the silent auction went for so much more money than we ever thought possible, and we secured donations and pledges that would help fund us during our first year of operation. Combined with an unexpected grant from the state, it looked like all the pieces were falling into place. We even had a potential operating site! An elderly woman who was preparing to move into a nursing home in the near future offered to sell her property at a steeply reduced price, and Delilah, Chelsea, and I listened with grateful hearts as Gretchen told us, "I know I'm nearing the end of my life. I raised five wonderful kids in that house, and now I want to bless even more wonderful kids. I want to be able to stand in front of my Maker one day and tell him I did something worthwhile for him."

Gretchen's farmhouse stood right on the edge of town. The place was massive—five bedrooms would easily house up to ten girls, and three full bathrooms would greatly help too! The kitchen was large and airy, the living room came complete with a cozy wood-burning fireplace, and a den provided a space for girls to draw away for some much-needed alone time. The backyard housed a spacious deck and an adorable gazebo—the perfect escape for a stressed-out teenage mother. There was also a large well-tended garden plot that Delilah and I planned to get the girls who could still help involved in. We even considered the possibility of putting in a chicken coop—it would be a great way for the girls to learn responsibility, and we could sell the eggs in the farmers market as a way to keep funds rolling in. With each meeting, Delilah, Chelsea, the growing group of volunteers, and I held, we got more and more excited.

At the end of the summer, with plans for the pregnancy house to open mid-winter, I was given a stark reminder of just how quickly life changes. For the first time since Elliot passed away, I was excited and passionate about something, and life seemed to be moving by seamlessly and effortlessly. Yes, it was stressful trying to get everything in order, but I was thrilled to find such satisfaction in the project. And then God sent me a curveball to remind me just how much I would always need him.

I got pregnant.

As I held my third positive pregnancy test in my hands, I wondered how it could be possible to be so shocked and scared at the possibility of being pregnant each and every time it happened to me. I had been scared silly the first time because of the rape and my fears of Jason, and with Elliot, I had simply been blown away by how fast it had happened and struggling with feeling unprepared and unworthy. Now, though, I was just plain angry.

How *dare* this baby waltz into my life when I was still so tender from losing my sweet firstborn? The *audacity* of this baby coming in during such a chaotic period. I didn't have time to have a baby. And I didn't think I was ready yet either.

After stewing for a few days, wallowing around in a pool of self-pity, I realized how ridiculous it was for me to be feeling this way! I was preparing to open up a house for confused and angry teenage mothers, where I would counsel and encourage them that they *could* be good mothers. That they *could* do it and come out stronger on the other side. I was planning on telling the girls who filled our rooms that their babies didn't have to be a burden, but that they could be a blessing—either to themselves if they chose to keep the baby or to someone else if they put the baby up for adoption. What kind of counselor would I be if I couldn't even take my own advice?

After wrestling with the extreme fear, confusion, and anger for a few days, I finally let Tanner in on my little secret, and he swept me up in his arms in delight. While tucked into his loving embrace, I was overcome with gratitude. Tanner had been here for each and every one of my pregnancy announcements, ready to stand by my side and love each baby. Even a baby that hadn't even been his. Even though I was scared and even though I was overwhelmed and still raw from losing my precious Elliot, I knew I could get through it.

It was during our second ultrasound appointment that we both knew without a doubt that this pregnancy was special. A downright gift from the Lord. The technician kept waving the wand over one spot, squinting hard at what she saw.

"What?" Tanner asked in a panic. What's wrong?"

"Nothing's wrong," she soothed. "You guys ready for some shocking news?"

I nodded, still a bit nervous at whatever news was about to be delivered. Tanner held tightly onto my hand and gave it a light squeeze.

"You're having twins! Twin girls, if I'm seeing it correctly. Congratulations!"

I let my head fall back in awe, and Tanner stood in shocked silence, that silly grin he only let come out and play when he was truly excited about something stretched across his face. Twin girls. Two special gifts from God that we knew were not replacements of the two daughters we had lost to abortion and premature death, but reminders that his mercies were truly new every morning and that he blessed those who faithfully followed and served him.

Later that night, we stepped through the still empty farmhouse that we'd bought from Gretchen. A few pieces of donated furniture graced the future pregnancy home, and plans were being made to fully furnish the remaining space so that we could reach our goal of opening the doors by March. "I have a surprise for you," Tanner said with excitement gleaming from his eyes.

"You do?" I asked with a smile.

"Stashed it in this closet," he answered, moving across the dining room to rummage through the closet. He pulled out a long painted board, trying unsuccessfully to hide the giant gift behind his back. I cocked my head in curiosity as he stood there holding it, and I took a deep breath in when he finally revealed his gift to me. Across the board, he had painted, "Eden and Elliot's House of Hope." The name the girls and I had unanimously chosen to call our new ministry.

"It's beautiful, Tanner," I choked out through tears. "I love it."

He hung it up proudly above the door, and we stood outside admiring it in the cool September air. Elysa was waiting for us to come pick her up from Greg and Delilah's, and Tanner and I eagerly looked forward to sharing the news about the twin baby girls with her that night. But for now, this moment was all ours. I stood beside my husband and best friend, my hands protectively cradling my growing baby girls. The pain of losing my first two daughters would never go away. But that didn't mean that I couldn't enjoy all that God was blessing me with now.

Because of how he had always provided for me in the past, I knew I could confidently step out into my new future without fear. There would always be twists and turns in my path. Moments when I felt like I couldn't go on anymore, take one more step forward. A verse that I had recently committed to memory rolled around in my mind, filling me with peace—"The Lord is my strength and my shield; my heart trusts in him, and he helps me. My heart leaps for joy, and with my song I praise him."

And that was the plan. A simple one, really, but one I knew was solid and sure. I would trust the Lord, remind myself over and over again that he was my help in times of trouble, and praise him through every valley and every mountaintop experience.

It had been the hardest year of my life. One that I would never wish on even my worst enemy. No hurt could compare to watching your child suffer and slip away from you. And no matter how much I wanted to simply give up and stop fighting, no matter how badly I wanted the world so stop carrying on as if nothing had happened at all, I knew that wasn't possible. And I knew it wouldn't be the last time I felt such an extreme sense of loss. The sun will always keep rising, though. And the sun that peeks its golden head over the horizon didn't have to be a source of frustration anymore. No, it was a source of comfort, a reminder of God's unfailing faithfulness and undeserved mercy.

Tomorrow, a new day dawned brightly. And I couldn't wait to step into it.

Epilogue

I swallowed nervously and looked hard at the phone in my hand. The slip of notebook paper that my counselor had given me earlier that day, with the number to a new crisis pregnancy house written neatly across the blue lines, had grown limp from my anxious sweating. Twice I had thrown it away and pushed it down into the trash, convinced that Eden and Elliot's House of Hope couldn't possibly be the right direction for me to move in.

Twice I had dug the piece of paper out from the trash, smoothing it out and agonizing over it. How could one little string of numbers cause this much confusion? My situation wasn't good and I knew it. But would running away to Green Lake—a town almost a half an hour away from everything near and dear to me—really solve anything?

I was only fourteen years old. Still a kid, really. I had been dating a much-older boy for only two months before I got pregnant. Dillon was twenty-two; we'd met at a college party that me and my friends had snuck into on a hot and sticky August night. Our meeting was something out of a movie—when he saw me, he did a double take, rubbing his eyes to see if he had seen correctly in an effort to make me laugh. It had worked, of course.

As a fourteen-year-old on the brink of starting high school in just a few weeks, I wanted nothing more than to shed my sheltered, geeky middle school skin and be popular. Dating a college kid would surely rocket me straight into the popular crowd at my school, so I let myself fall for him.

While he made his way over to me, some drunk girl spilled her warm beer all over my skimpy outfit. Dillon then rushed over to me and said, "Let me help you. It's a shame that such a pretty outfit get spilled on. What's your name?" Then he flashed his blinding white smile at me.

I fumbled out, "Elizabeth. My name's Elizabeth."

I then lied, "My friends call me Liz, though," in an effort to sound cooler, more mature. Liz sounded older, right? I saw my friends hide behind giggles, giving me thumbs up and encouraging me to go for it with Dillon.

Dillon took me upstairs to a bedroom and shut the door. "I know the girl who lives here, and I don't think she'd mind if I loaned you some clothes." I stood in the middle of the strange room shivering, the beer making my already-tight shirt stick even more closely to my skin. As Dillon rummaged through the girl's dresser drawers, he asked, "Has anyone ever told you how pretty you are?"

I blushed and stammered, "No." It was true too. My mom abandoned me and my older brother Seth when I was just four years old, and my dad had been too heartbroken and stressed out over raising two kids alone to pay much attention to my emotional well-being. He worked two dead-end jobs to pay the rent and put food on the table, but he never took the time to be a good father to either Seth or I. He never took Seth on any father-son fishing trips, and he never took me out for ice cream sundaes and let me order extra whipped topping and cherries, like I imagined other fathers did with their sons and daughters. He was distant and angry, and I spent most of my childhood avoiding him altogether. I never realized until that night just how much I craved male attention and affection. Dillon had me hooked right then and there.

"Well, that's too bad," he continued, turning around with a purple belly shirt and an even shorter pair of shorts than I was currently wearing in his hands. "Because you are gorgeous, Liz."

I blushed again and looked down. He walked over to me and lifted my chin with his hands, sending a zing of excitement down my back. "You gonna need some help getting into these new clothes?"

I squeezed my eyes shut, trying to block out the memory of Dillon peeling off my clothes and lifting me off the floor, kissing me hungrily. I didn't resist as he guided me through the ropes of having sex, offering up my virginity to him like it was no big deal. The first time had been protected, but the many other times over the next two months hadn't been, and well. Here I was now—fourteen years old, pregnant, and all alone.

The alone part was my fault, really. When I found out I was pregnant, I broke up with Dillon right away, and my heart broke when he shrugged and said simply, "Okay." It made it easier for me, not having to fight to convince him to break things off. But it hurt like nothing else had ever hurt knowing that I meant so little to him that he wasn't willing to fight for me.

My father's reaction had been much scarier. I barely knew my father, since he was never around, so I honestly had no idea that he would get so mad. He had never laid a finger on me before, so when he lunged at me and held my neck in his hand against the wall of our apartment, I crumpled in fear. The slap came next, blinding me with shock. Seth was out for the night so there was no one to fight for me. I screamed as the slaps kept coming, and a knock on the door sometime later snapped my dad out of it. He opened the door to find two police men saying a neighbor had reported screams, and they stepped past my father to see my bruised body huddled in the corner of our kitchen. My dad was arrested that night, and after an investigation by CPS, Seth and I were removed from his care.

My grades plummeted during my first weeks in foster care, and even though the family I was placed with was aware of my pregnancy and were willing to still house me, they didn't want to care for the baby when he or she was born. So my home was very temporary, and I felt more and more trapped with each passing day, like the walls were slowly closing in on me. I needed a new plan, and the school counselor had provided a new one with the number to Eden and Elliot's House of Hope.

Where else could I go, really? How many foster parents would take in a teenage mother with a newborn baby? How could I possibly finish school with the limited number of resources available to me here? The only other program that took in teenage mothers was in Kansas City, and that was even farther away than Green Lake. In my mind, my only option lay in a crisis pregnancy house in Green Lake.

Before I could talk myself out of it again, my fingers breezed over the keys and dialed the number. After a few rings, a cheerful voice rang out, "Eden and Elliot's House of Hope, this is Molly. How can I help you?"

I spilled my entire story to this stranger, and her warm answer caused a ray of sunshine to spread throughout my body. "You're exactly the kind of girl we wanted to help when we opened up our doors earlier this year, Liz. We have a spot for you, if you'd like it. We offer a full array of support for both you and your baby, and I think you'll find the environment to be safe and healing. You're welcome here, Liz. And you're wanted. Let me know how I can best help you."

I wiped the hot tears away that had begun sliding down my face. Maybe there was hope for me after all.